Shaken to the Bone

Books by Eleanor Fitzgerald:

The Ministry of Supernatural Affairs

Night People

The Black Carnation

Children of the Rat

The Midnight Aviary

Our Forbidden Future

Shaken to the Bone

Other Works

Oxford Junction

The Forest

Hymns for the Gallows, Volume One: The Trial

Hymns for the Gallows, Volume Two: The Last Meal

Hymns for the Gallows, Volume Three: The Hanging

Anima, Volume One: The Signal

This is a work of fiction. Names, characters, places, and incidents either are the product of the author's imagination or are used fictitiously. Any resemblance to actual persons, living or dead, events, or locales is entirely coincidental.

Copyright © Eleanor Fitzgerald, 2024

The moral right of Eleanor Fitzgerald to be identified as the author of this work has been asserted in accordance with the Copyright, Designs, and Patents Act of 1988.

All rights reserved. No part of this book may be reproduced in any form on by an electronic or mechanical means, including information storage and retrieval systems, without permission in writing from the publisher, except by a reviewer who may quote brief passages in a review.

Cover Art Copyright © Eleanor Fitzgerald, 2024

First paperback edition November 2024

ISBN: 9798865344520

Published Independently

Contents

Author's Note: Content Warnings..............................ix

Part One: Kith and Kin...1

Chapter One – Rain, Rain, Go Away...........................3
Chapter Two – Part of the Family..............................11
Chapter Three – Uncomfortable Reunions................21
Chapter Four – One Last Dance.................................29
Chapter Five – Yet More Secrets...............................39
Chapter Six – The Last Haunting...............................49
Chapter Seven – Uncharted Waters...........................61
Chapter Eight – Somebody Super Like You.............69
Chapter Nine – In Her Father's Footsteps..................77
Chapter Ten – Beat the Street....................................85
Chapter Eleven – Old Time Legends.........................95
Chapter Twelve – All for Freedom and for Pleasure
....105
Chapter Thirteen – Victimless Crimes.....................115
Chapter Fourteen – Blood from a Stone..................125
Chapter Fifteen – Not Welcome Here......................135

Interlude One – Death on Two Legs........................145

Part Two: Hunter, Hunted..151

Chapter Sixteen – Strange Coincidences.................153
Chapter Seventeen – The Morning After.................163
Chapter Eighteen – Red String Special....................171
Chapter Nineteen – When the Bough Breaks..........181
Chapter Twenty – Three's Company........................189
Chapter Twenty One – I Know the Drill.................197
Chapter Twenty Two – Lover, Mother, Drinker,

Failure……………………………………………207
Chapter Twenty Three – Can I Get a Witness?……..215
Chapter Twenty Four – Black Dogs of Legend……..223
Chapter Twenty Five – Your Love is a Life Taker…231
Chapter Twenty Six – Walk the Night……………….241
Chapter Twenty Seven – For Whom the Dog Howls 249

Interlude Two – Playing in the Dark………………..259

Part Three: The Wolf at the Door……………………265

Chapter Twenty Eight – A Brighter Side to Life……267
Chapter Twenty Nine – Grim Little Conversations. 277
Chapter Thirty – A Darker Shade of Black…………..285
Chapter Thirty One – Jenny O' the Fen………………293
Chapter Thirty Two – All For One…………………..301
Chapter Thirty Three – Touched by the Grave……..309
Chapter Thirty Four – It Comes At Night……………319
Chapter Thirty Five – Running the Gauntlet………..327
Chapter Thirty Six – The Night People………………335

Epilogue – We Only See Each Other at Funerals….345

Acknowledgments…………………………………..355

About the Author……………………………………358

Author's Note: Content Warnings

I have drawn from my own experiences and knowledge to create this novel as well as some fairly extensive research. This is a horror novel, above all else, and it is a tense, frightening narrative. As such, there are some content warnings that I would like to point out in advance, although I will not be too specific; I do not wish to spoil the plot, after all! This will be the last mention of these warnings so that the story may unfold uninterrupted. This list is not exhaustive, however.

- **Body Horror**
- **Medical Horror/Surgery**
- **Torture**
- **Graphic Violence/Bloodshed**
- **Institutional Violence**
- **Mind Control**
- **Kidnapping**
- **Suicide/Self Harm**
- **Child Abuse**
- **Funerals**
- **Chemical Weapons**

Thank you for choosing this novel, dear Reader. I hope you enjoy reading it as much as I enjoyed writing it.

THE MINISTRY OF SUPERNATURAL AFFAIRS

Pugnamus In Obumbratio

It is only as we fall into the yawning abyss of death that we truly understand who we are.

I was fortunate enough to rise out of it once again; to all that stood by me as it happened, thank you.

This book is for you.

Part One: Kith and Kin

Chapter One – Rain, Rain, Go Away

Charity

The rain drummed steadily on the window of the first class train carriage as it departed Liverpool Street Station. Charity Walpole sighed heavily and leant back in her seat, steepling her fingers.

"Wet break," she muttered, "again. I fucking hate the rain."

She focussed her gaze squarely on the heavy droplets that pounded on the glass, desperate to ignore the other passengers that were certain to be staring at her; not without good cause, either. With her bleached skin, gaunt post-cancer face, and scraggy crop of white hair, Charity Walpole was definitely out of place amongst the usual suspects that filled the carriage.

"Why is she wearing sunglasses inside, *in the rain?*" she heard one woman ask, and it was all she could do to bite her tongue. *I wish we could've rented a car and driven,* she thought, but with Edgar missing in action and Teaser Malarkey busy with Mallory's recovery from his Dryadic state, there was no-one in the Oxford Office who held a license.

"That's not strictly true, you know," Ivy said softly, tapping her pen gently on her book of crosswords. "Shy has a van, and I'm sure he would've driven us if we'd asked him."

"Reading my mind again?" Charity asked playfully, knowing all too well what the response would be.

"No, you're just-" Ivy began.

"Thinking loudly?" Charity finished, and her girlfriend nodded. "I guess I'm just nervous about seeing my family again, and showing up in that monstrosity of a panel van would not set the best tone for the next week.

"It's going to be hard enough as it is."

She rubbed her bleached eyes beneath her shades, wiping away the first tears that had gathered there.

"Your father died, sweetheart," Ivy said quietly, putting down her pen and taking Charity's hands in her own. "You're allowed to be upset."

"No, I'm not," she replied, more sharply than she intended to. "Everyone says that, but then you go to a funeral and you're supposed to be calm and composed, and you have to fucking greet everyone afterwards and thank them for coming, then you trundle on home to host the fucking wake and... and..."

She snatched her hands away, nervously running them through her uneven hair.

"I just fucking hate the rain, okay? It makes me feel trapped; hemmed in, even." Charity said, before taking a deep breath to try and calm down.

Across the aisle, the woman who'd commented on her sunglasses muttered something contemptuously under her breath. Without missing so much as a beat, Ivy reached across the aisle and tapped her cane lightly on the table in front of the woman to get her attention.

"Excuse me, ma'am?" Ivy said with all the sweetness of a coiled viper. "Would you be so kind as to not pass comment on my partner's appearance and demeanour, please? It really is most rude of you, and I would recommend that you *do not* do it again."

It's a shame that Michaela's no longer around, Charity thought. *She certainly would have put her foot down and whammied that judgmental bitch.*

Ivy smiled at Charity's thought and winked at her. The Séance waited for a few seconds longer than necessary before removing her cane. The woman unfolded her newspaper angrily, shaking the pages as if in response.

I can't fucking stand games like this, Charity thought, and got to her feet. Ivy opened her mouth to say something, but Charity shook her head and her partner settled back in her seat. The woman with the newspaper looked up in surprise when the Ghost sat down in the seat opposite her.

"Hi," Charity said.

"Uh... h-hello," replied the startled woman. Charity gestured for her to put down the newspaper and looked at her, smiling, as she did so. "Can I help you?"

"You can, actually," Charity said in her nicest, most diplomatic voice. "If you could stop fucking staring at me for the rest of the journey, that would be really decent of you."

The woman opened her mouth to protest, but Charity went on.

"Now, I know that I look pretty fucked up, and it's understandable for you to be curious. The sunglasses are for a light sensitivity I have, if you were wondering, and the scraggy hair and pale skin are from the extremely aggressive chemo that I recently finished. It was not a fun time, and it has somewhat lessened my patience of late.

"I'm also on my way to see my estranged family to bury my father, who died rather unexpectedly partway through my treatment." Charity leant forwards, interlacing her fingers as she stared at the woman through the darkened lenses. "As such, I'm a touch emotionally volatile at the moment, and not in the mood to deal with nosy-*fucking*-parkers, such as you.

"So, if you would be so kind as to mind your own business, at least until we get off this train, I would appreciate it." She gave the stunned woman a final grin. "Thanks in advance."

Charity returned to her seat, catching Ivy's eye as she did so and giving her an exaggerated wink. Ivy chuckled softly and returned to her crossword as Charity slumped down into her seat. She fidgeted for a few minutes, but could not find a comfortable position.

"Are you alright there?" Ivy asked after Charity's third string of muttered obscenities.

"I just can't seem to get comfortable," she said with a huff, swinging one leg over the armrest of her seat so that it dangled in the aisle. "I thought splurging extra for first class would give us a private cabin or something, but apparently standards have slipped recently."

"I think your expectations are more in line with the Orient Express than what Greater Anglia can provide, darling." Ivy blinked for a moment, then smiled and filled in another answer in her crossword. "Belmond, of course!"

"Why do you like those things?" Charity asked, crossing her arms huffily. "Don't they just feel like homework to you?"

"I like puzzles; I'm good at them." Ivy said softly. She looked at Charity's posture and cocked her head to the side, a curious expression on her face.
"Homework, wet break, and your whole demeanour; Freud would certainly have something to say about all that, especially in conjunction with seeing your

family."

"Don't psychoanalyse me!" Charity snapped, but there was no anger in her words. Deep down she knew that Ivy was right. Seeing her family, especially her mother, always made her feel like a small child again; unwanted, accidental, and always in the way.

Superfluous, she thought, *and better off invisible.*

She glanced at Ivy, but if her girlfriend had heard the words in her head and heart, she was doing a good job of hiding it. Regardless, Charity settled into a more conventional position in her seat and resumed staring through the rain-streaked window.

"It's just a week," she muttered softly. "What could possibly go wrong?"

"Will we be able to see the Broads?" Ivy asked as the train began to pick up speed as it left Ipswich Station.

"No. We won't get that close, I'm afraid." Charity looked at her lover for a moment, pondering one of her more peculiar behaviours. "Do you miss the water, Ivy?"

"I like the sea, if that's what you're asking," Ivy replied cautiously. "Is that what you were asking?"

"You go down to the river almost every day, no matter the weather," Charity commented, "or the canal at the very least. I've also heard you listening to seabirds on your computer when you're meditating, so I guess what I'm actually asking is this; were you from somewhere coastal originally?"

"I honestly don't know," Ivy said sadly, putting her completed crossword back in her bag. "My room on Betony Island overlooked the water, and listening to the birds always made me feel tremendously free.

"The same with the water, I guess; across that shimmering expanse could've been anything, but I was sure that it was the only way to something better." She smiled at the memory. "I loved watching the birds, especially the migrating ones; it never gets old, even if it's the fifth or sixth time seeing them arrive.

"I always felt sad when they left, though; I often wished they would take me with them."

You should've only seen them four times at the absolute most, Charity thought, taking care to guard her thoughts this time. *I remember hearing rumours about children that were born on the island, but I always thought that was just a myth...*

"If you want to go to the coast while we're in Norfolk," Charity said, trying to cheer Ivy up, "we can go to Great Yarmouth. They have a pleasure beach with a rollercoaster and everything!"

"That would be nice," Ivy said. "A nice romantic day at the beach, just the two of us, would be just the thing."

"Ah," Charity said, blushing a little with awkwardness. "Yeah, there's something I need to talk to you about before we get there."

"Oh?"

"So, um, it might be a bit hard to get some proper alone time when we're at the Big House."

"That's the Walpole Manor, right?" Ivy asked, and Charity nodded. "Yeah, you've already said that it's going to be crowded, but if we can find some time to slip away, that won't be a problem."

"Its the slipping away part that we're going to struggle with," Charity said sheepishly. "My two cousins, Caitlin and Catarina, are... well, they're a *lot*, and they've always stuck to me like glue whenever

I've popped in for a visit. They're about five years younger than us, but because Aunt Connie tends to indulge them, they're more like overgrown teenagers and they can sometimes struggle to take a hint."

"Autism is an inherited trait," Ivy muttered, but Charity did not hear her.

"They're both Ghosts, but they don't really rely on that skill much." She sighed heavily before she went on, already feeling her frustration with the twins building in anticipation. "Their father was a Tumbler, however, and they are both freakishly nimble, which makes getting away from them an absolute nightmare."

"I didn't know your Uncle Geoff was a Cep," Ivy said with surprise. Charity couldn't help but chuckle at her words.

"Oh, no! Geoff is just a plain old ordinary guy who married into an absolute madhouse of Ceps." She smiled. "I like Geoff; he's reassuringly ordinary, like baked beans. The twins' father, Alphonse, however, was an absolute hell-raiser. He died when they were small, and they see Geoff as more of a father than Alphonse ever was.

"I think his presence has done everyone in that house the world of good, truth be told." Charity settled back in her chair. "It was sweet of him to offer to pick us up from Diss, instead of us having to go all the way to Norwich only to catch a bus back to the Big House.

"He actually offered to come and get us from Oxford, but I didn't want to put him out like that." She thought for a moment, staring into the middle distance. "Although, if he offers to drive us all the way home, I might take him up on that, depending on just how badly things will go."

"Don't you think you're being a bit fatalistic, Charity?" Ivy asked gently. "Do you really think that your family will be that off around you?"

Here we go, Charity thought, and she mentally prepared herself for the final piece of information she had to share with Ivy.

"There's been a divide in the Walpole family for some time, Ivy, and right now my Aunt Connie is in the dead centre of that absolute shitstorm. The Ministry side of the family do not get on with her at all, and for good reason."

"Why is that?" Ivy asked, clearly growing more nervous as the conversation went on.

"My aunt, Constance Walpole, is the head of the Amberlight Private Detective Agency," Charity said softly, "although they're more like a private military corporation these days."

"They were the ones that attacked the Bureau's Forward Command Post," Ivy said, and Charity nodded.

"Yes. They're in open conflict with the Bureau, but their relationship with the Ministry is more of a cold war." She sighed heavily. "The whole thing is a fucking powder keg waiting to blow, however, and this could be the event that kicks the simmering distrust into all-out war."

The two sat in silence for a while as Ivy looked at her in complete shock.

"Well," the Séance said after she regained her composure, "at least things are never boring with you, Charity."

"This is true," Charity said, as the gentle rain began to worsen into a downpour, "but sometimes I think it would be nice to have just one easy day."

Chapter Two – Part of the Family

Ivy

Ivy and Charity stood outside Diss Railway Station, huddled beneath the former's large umbrella as the rain thundered down around them. Ivy wore her usual winter gear, including her stylish North Face parka, and was happily wrapped up against the chill.

Charity, however, had sheepishly revealed that she did not actually own a waterproof coat, so Ivy had insisted that she borrow one of Teaser Malarkey's wet weather oilskin slickers. The Ghost shuffled her feet awkwardly and adjusted the oversized garment to sit more comfortably on her spare frame.

The shuffling caused the hood to fall down once again, and Charity angrily wiped the condensation from the insides of her sunglasses. She stamped her foot, almost in a tantrum, splashing water over Ivy's suitcase.

"I hate this fucking thing," she said sulkily.

"I'm sorry we didn't have time to buy you something of your own," Ivy said, giving her arm an affectionate squeeze. "You did only tell me about it this morning, though."

"I'd rather be wet."

"Charity..." Ivy said, already tired of her girlfriend's rain-induced conniption.

"No! I look," Charity wrinkled her nose at the pervasive scent of liquorice that clung to the coat, "and smell like a fucking nonce, Ivy! It's humiliating. What was wrong with my usual leather jacket and jumpsuit?"

"Your jacket has more knife and bullet holes in it than actual material, and you can't wear a jumpsuit covered in knives to your father's funeral." Ivy tapped her nails on the handle of the umbrella idly, trying to keep her frustration to a minimum. "You specifically asked for outfit advice for this trip, so I gave it to you."

"I know," Charity said quietly, wrapping her arms tight around her chest. "I feel so self-conscious out in the open like this. I'm just used to being invisible, especially when things are at their most stressful."

"You can disappear if you want," Ivy replied. "This is a difficult time for you, and there's no shame in self-soothing."

"There's no point; I can't hide from my family."

Ivy blinked a few times as a thought suddenly occurred to her; something that had completely passed her by until now.

"Charity," she asked, "can Ghosts see each other when they're invisible?"

"Kind of, but it's more a pale, semi-transparent form than what you'd typically class as 'seeing someone'."

"So, like a-"

"Yeah, like a Ghost," Charity said with a chuckle. "It's where the name comes from, you know. It's the oldest gift out there, too, and no other species can boast true invisibility; that's reserved for humans alone."

"Can it manifest as a secondary ability?" Ivy asked, both genuinely interested and also pleased that Charity seemed to be relaxing a little. "You know, in the way that some people sometimes have shades of their parents' gifts in them?"

"No. If invisibility is going to be a gift at all, it'll be

a Cep's main one." She smiled at Ivy. "Ours is a blood that runs stronger, a tree whose roots grow deeper, and our blessing is older than the Old Gods themselves."

"It sounds like you're quoting someone," Ivy said, deliberately avoiding probing her girlfriend's mind. In her experience, some questions were better left unanswered. "You don't have to tell me who."

"I honestly don't know," Charity said. "It's an old Ghost adage. We've got more customs and social rules than you would ever believe; it's a shame I can't tell you about them, though."

Ivy wasn't sure how to respond to such enigmatic words, but luckily she was spared the awkward silence as Charity suddenly strode into the rain, waving excitedly at a bearded man in an old Barbour coat and a flat cap.

"Uncle Geoff!" Charity yelled, and Ivy smiled in surprise when she saw her girlfriend hug him, completely unprompted.

Now that is not a bet I would've taken, she thought. Geoff hugged the Ghost in return before Charity waved Ivy over.

"So," she said as Ivy approached, awkwardly carrying both of their suitcases along with the umbrella and her cane, "this is my girlfriend, Ivy Livingston."

"A pleasure," he said warmly, immediately taking both the cases from her. "Let me put those in the car for you; don't worry, I've got the heater running, so you'll be warm and dry in no time."

He led them both over to an ageing Volvo estate, and loaded their luggage inside. Charity instinctively went to get in the front passenger seat, but a look from Geoff stopped her in her tracks.

"You know better than that, missy," he said, not unkindly. "New guests get the front seat, and I'm sure Ivy would like to stretch out her legs a little."

"Thank you," Ivy said gratefully as she settled into the front seat and began to rub her cold, cramped calves. *It feels like this gets worse every single time I use my gift,* she thought, but decided that she would worry about the seemingly negative progression of her powers at another time. "My body isn't quite what it used to be, especially when it gets cold."

"I know that feeling," Geoff said with a warm smile. "Is everyone belted in?"

Charity and Ivy both nodded, and he started the car, pulling away from the station with barely a glance. *I wonder if he makes this run a lot?*

"So, Ivy, Charity tells me that you work with her in Oxford, with the monsters and all that."

"Yes, I do. That's actually how we met." Ivy smiled at Charity in the mirror, who beamed back at her. *I've never seen her so comfortable.* She gently reached out for her girlfriend's mind, but quickly withdrew when she realised that her calm was only skin deep. *She's waiting for the hammer to fall any minute,* she thought. *I'll let her have this moment of peace, then.*

"We met when we were fighting the Nightwalkers," Charity said excitedly. "Ivy's a mind reader, of sorts."

"Fancy that," Geoff said, as if Charity had merely made a passing remark about the weather or a local sports team. "Are you a professional, uh, whatever?"

"I'm a therapist by training," Ivy replied, smiling at his utter inability to articulate what Charity actually did for a living. "Although I work for the Ministry nowadays."

"Hmm." Geoff tapped the steering wheel as they left

Diss and headed into the Norfolk countryside. "We've a bit of a houseful back home, I'm afraid, what with all Dennis's old pals being in town for the funeral; we've put the two of you in Connie's study on the futon. I hope it's acceptable."

"That sounds lovely," Ivy said warmly. "Thank you for putting us up this week."

"Not a problem; family's family, especially at a time like this." He looked in the rear mirror at Charity. "Cat and Cait are buzzing with excitement to see you again, Charity. They even offered to have you in their room, but I thought the two of you would prefer a little bit of privacy."

"Thank you, Uncle Geoff," Charity said, clearly relieved. "Who else is staying at the Big House?"

"Your mother arrived this morning," he said, "and Prudence will be along later today."

Ivy shivered as if someone had just walked over her grave. She didn't need to look behind her to know that Charity's face would be set in a tight scowl, and all the heat seemed to vanish from the car.

"Are you alright, Charity?" Geoff asked.

"I'm fine," Charity replied. "Just peachy."

Happy fucking families indeed, Ivy thought sullenly. *This is going to be a long week.*

"Holy shit," Ivy muttered as Geoff pulled the car into the driveway of a Georgian mansion nestled in the Norfolk countryside. She turned to look at Charity. "Is this where you grew up?"

"No," she said quietly. "When I was little, Dad and Connie weren't on speaking terms. By the time they'd made up, I was enrolled in the Ministry Youth Academy; I only used to visit during the summer, and that was only after I was fifteen.

"I grew up in the field," Charity said, almost bitterly, "not playing house in a mansion, like the twins did."

"We would've welcomed you with open arms, Charity," Geoff said tenderly. "We always made sure that your parents knew that."

"I know you did, Uncle Geoff," Charity replied, her expression impossible to read. "I had made my decision by then, though; I knew where my path began, and it wasn't here."

"Never too late to change the road you're on," he said as he switched the engine off. "Do you still remember your way around?"

"I do. We'll take our bags to the room and freshen up before we come and say hello."

"Take as long as you need." He handed the car key to Ivy as he climbed out into the rain. "Just pop it on the little table by the door when you're done here, please."

"Will do."

"I'll put the kettle on then," Geoff said, and he shut the door behind him, trotting quickly towards the house to avoid getting drenched.

"Before we go in," Charity said, placing a hand on Ivy's arm, "we should make a plan of attack."

"Is that really necessary?" Ivy asked, and Charity nodded. *She looks like she's about to scream,* Ivy realised, and immediately decided to back down. "Okay, sweetheart; I'll follow your lead. What do we do?"

"Avoid talking to Lin as much as possible, and remember that even attempting to lie to her can cause a migraine or even a stroke. If you do end up cornered by her, just stick to neutral topics as much as possible, okay?"

"You don't want to introduce me to your mother?" Ivy asked, unable to hide how hurt she felt. "Your family do know about *us*, don't they?"

An awkward silence hung in the air between them, and Ivy sighed heavily. *Perfect. Just fucking perfect.*

"Connie knows about us, as does Geoff," Charity said sheepishly after an uncomfortably long time, "so we can assume that the twins know, too. As for the rest of them, I doubt they care-"

"I care!" Ivy snapped, and Charity sat back in her seat, shocked. "I won't be some dirty secret that you hide from your family, especially not in a situation where you expect me to support you. I can either be here as your girlfriend and stay by your side through thick and thin, or I can be just a pal that's here as a shoulder to cry on; I can't do both, Charity, so pick one."

"You're my girlfriend," Charity said without hesitation. "I'm not hiding you, Ivy; not in the slightest. All I ever talk to Lin about is work, so it just hasn't come up, and Pru... well, you know that Prudence isn't exactly in her right mind. You aren't a secret; you will never be a secret, because I'm proud to be with you."

"Thank you," Ivy said, much reassured.

"Once we're unpacked and have a cup of tea in hand," Charity said shakily, "I'll introduce you to Lin. I can't promise she'll be good conversation, but it's clearly important to you, so we'll make an appearance, together."

"You're a keeper, Charity Walpole," Ivy said with a grateful smile.

"Likewise, beloved." She leant forward and gave Ivy

a quick kiss. "We better get inside before Geoff thinks we've decided to sleep in the car; it sounds like real estate is at a premium and I don't want to have to bed down in the laundry room."

They exited the car into the pounding rain, with Ivy taking the keys and umbrella as Charity carried their bags inside. As she reached the door, Ivy clicked the little button that locked the Volvo before stepping into the warm and dry house.

She turned to place the keys in the bowl as instructed, but as she did so, she dislodged a stack of post that was piled up on the little table with her cane, sending a small avalanche of paper on to the wet floor.

"Oh, bugger!" Ivy swore, and immediately bent down to pick up the post before it got soaked through. What she saw, however, stopped her in her tracks.

Those are all missing posters, she realised with a growing sense of dread, *and every single one from the past two months.*

Ivy felt her blood run cold as the cascade of faces stared up at her, their eyes seemingly blank and full of impossible desperation at the same time. Her skin prickled into goose flesh as she placed the post back on the table with trembling hands, and something fearful stirred within her.

It was an all too familiar sense of being hunted; one that she hadn't felt since the previous summer and their fateful run in with the Master and his Nightwalkers. She realised that Charity was staring at her, and she quickly turned the paper over, hiding the information from her partner; no sense in troubling her with this now, after all.

Still, as Charity led her through Walpole Manor to their makeshift bedroom, her sense of fretful unease only worsened. She jumped at the chiming of a clock and startled at the sound of someone trotting down the stairs.

Something is very wrong, she thought, *and I have no idea what to do.*

She sighed heavily, and blinked back a mournful tear.

I wish Michaela were here.

Chapter Three – Uncomfortable Reunions

Charity

Charity's heart was in her throat as she walked hand in hand with Ivy into the kitchen of Walpole Manor. Their entrance took far longer than necessary; for Charity, every step was a hesitation. *This is going to be bad.*

She almost reflexively turned invisible when she saw her mother, Lin, sitting at the kitchen table with Helen Mickelson, her doctor and oncologist. With them was a third woman that Charity did not immediately recognise; she had striking features and cold, clinical eyes. *Something is familiar about her.*

"Helen?" Charity said, haltingly. "What are you doing here?"

"They were friends both with your father," Lin said sharply, gesturing to the two women she sat with. "*Dr Mickelson* was our superior when we were working in Hong Kong, so make sure that you show her the proper respect she deserves."

"I didn't know you worked with my parents," Charity said softly. "All these years, and you never said anything..."

"I, uh, didn't want to complicate our doctor-patient relationship with any prior connections or associations we might've had." Helen tapped her teacup anxiously. "I'm so sorry for your loss, Charity; Dennis was a wonderful man and a gentle soul."

"You should've told me," Charity muttered once again, almost completely thrown by the unexpected presence of her doctor at her family's home. "You were my doctor; aren't you supposed to disclose such things?"

"Charity!" Lin snapped, slamming her hand sharply on the table. "You will apologise to Dr Mickelson and cease this pointless insubordination at once!"

"I... I'm..." Charity began, but she felt Ivy's grip on her hand tighten and the Séance's anger flowed into her like a raging torrent. "I will not apologise for being blind-sided like this!"

"Charity," Lin began, getting to her feet, but Helen cut her off, desperate to defuse the situation.

"Please, Lin; there's no need for her to apologise. Come now, let's not fight," Helen said, and the mystery woman sat back in her chair and scoffed derisively.

"And who the fuck are you?" Charity demanded, turning her ire towards the stranger.

"You always were such a *firecracker*, Hillgreen," the woman replied with a smirk. "It was amusing when you were a child, but it's unbecoming on such a solemn occasion. Have you no sense of decorum?

"A little gratitude would not go amiss, either, considering all I've done for you."

Charity's eyes widened in recognition and she spoke her accusations through gritted teeth.

"You're Harper Cherry, aren't you?"

"That's-" Lin began, but Charity cut her off, barely able to keep her words from turning into a vengeful snarl.

"Harper Cherry, Inspired of the Third Eye, Deputy Director of the Ministry of Supernatural Affairs, and chief architect of Project Lamplight; did I miss anything?"

"You got them all, and here I am; in the flesh, no

less," Harper replied with a broad smile before looking pointedly at Ivy. "Now, aren't you going to introduce us to your little safety blanket?"

Charity immediately took an aggressive step forwards, but Ivy's grip held her back. *Just breathe,* Charity thought, and took a moment to collect herself before answering.

"This is Dr Ivy Livingston," she said, as calmly as she could. "She is one of the Agents in my Oxford Office and, more importantly, my girlfriend. We've been together a few months now."

"Oh," Lin said, genuinely surprised. "I had no idea that you ran the Oxford Office; I just assumed that someone else was in charge. I suppose some small measure of congratulations is in order."

"Mother, I have a girlfriend," Charity said softly, as Harper rose from her seat to rifle through the cupboards of her Aunt's kitchen. "I've finally met someone."

"You know, I actually thought that they would put Agent Malarkey in charge," Lin said to Harper as she triumphantly pulled a bottle of sparkling wine from the fridge. "She did pass the Ravenblade exam, after all."

"This is true, Lin," Harper said as she popped the cork on the wine, "but turning down such a prestigious position is not a politically savvy move. I'd have pegged Marsh for the role, personally, even if he is a half-breed."

Harper began pouring glasses of sparkling wine, placing the first of them in front of Lin, who thanked her politely, and then Helen next. Instead of picking up the wine, the Blight shoved it angrily back towards Harper with a scowl.

"Oh, Helen, don't be such a fucking spoilsport," Harper said, her gaze almost venomous. "What's a glass of wine amongst friends, especially in celebration?"

"I met someone," Charity muttered quietly, and when Harper pushed a drink into her hands, she burst into tears. Harper shook her head in pity, immediately resuming her pouring as she turned to Ivy.

"Say, Livingston, at least tell me that you're not a sourpuss like Helen," Harper said with a sneer as she handed the final glass to Ivy; the wine glittered menacingly in the pale green vessel. The older woman looked over her shoulder at the Blight, and chuckled nastily. "The younger generation should always know when to have a little fun, don't you-"

Harper's words were cut short as she turned back around and Ivy smashed the antique glass full of cheap sparkling wine into the smirking woman's face. The thin glass smashed, leaving deep cuts in Harper's cheek and splattering blood over Ivy's hand.

"That's for everyone that died on Betony Island," Ivy said coldly, before delivering a swift backhand to Harper's unbloodied cheek. "And *that* was for upsetting Charity. She's here to bury her father, you fucking ghoul."

Harper blinked rapidly, as if regaining her senses, and then a quiet, albeit slightly shocked, smile crept on to her lips. She reached up and touched the cuts on her face with her fingertips, looking at them afterwards as if she'd never seen her own blood before.

"Interesting," she said softly, looking at Ivy with her wild grey eyes. "Very interesting indeed."

They look so similar, Charity realised, and

desperately tried to keep the thought to herself. *The same eyes, the same curl of the mouth; Harper even smiles like Michaela did.*

"How about we all just calm down?" said a voice from the kitchen doorway. Everyone turned to look at Constance Walpole as she leant against the door frame with casual grace. "Harper, you should be able to patch yourself up in the downstairs bathroom. Lin, Helen, would you please clean up the blood and glass from the floor of my kitchen?"

"I think that Charity should-" Lin began, but Connie held up a hand to silence her.

"I would like for Charity to introduce me to her girlfriend," Connie said firmly. She smiled at Charity, who immediately started to feel a little better. "Why don't the two of you come for some tea in the orangery with me?"

She started walking before either of the two women could answer, so Ivy and Charity simply followed her through the sprawling house. Soon they were in a beautiful wrought iron orangery that was brimming with plants; whilst there were no flowers in the bleak midwinter, it was still comfortingly green.

"I love it in here," Connie said as she settled on a comfortable rattan chair. "Geoff finds it a bit too spare at this time of year, but in a couple of months when all the flowers are blooming it will be almost impossible to get him out of here.

"But that's not a problem for me; life is so much sweeter with someone to share it with." Connie reached out and gave Charity's hand a squeeze. "It's so wonderful to see you, darling, even if it is under such solemn circumstances."

"It's lovely to see you too, Aunt Connie," Charity

said, taking a seat next to Ivy on the little wicker sofa. "This is my girlfriend, Ivy."

"I'm sorry that I caused such a ruckus in your kitchen," Ivy said sheepishly. "I'll replace the broken glass and-"

"No need," Connie replied warmly, with an idle wave of her hand. "Nor do you need to apologise to me; I find Harper a most detestable woman, but the powers that be insisted that it would either be her or Kimberly Daniels here on behalf of the Ministry, so I chose the lesser evil.

"That, however, is unimportant right now," Connie said, pouring a cup of tea for each of them. "What I would like to know, however, is how the two of you met."

Ivy and Charity smiled at each other, and then Ivy launched into the tale of their battle with the Master and his Nightwalkers.

Sometimes, Charity thought as she watched Connie smile and nod enthusiastically at Ivy's story, *I wish you were my mother instead of Lin.*

"Your aunt is really lovely," Ivy said as she lay on the bed with Charity, gently tracing a finger up and down her naked thigh. "I must admit that she isn't what I expected, though."

"I know what you mean," Charity said, wishing that Ivy would stop teasing her and let her fingers wander a little higher up. "You wouldn't think she was a Ghost, would you?"

"A part of me still can't quite believe it," Ivy said with a chuckle, and Charity couldn't blame her.

Constance Walpole, despite being almost seventy five years old, was a vital, youthful, and bubbly person. She did not use her gift anywhere near as much as Charity did, so her complexion, whilst pale, still had a rosy, healthy glow to it. Connie had also not been ravaged by cancer, as most Ministry Ghosts were, and was comfortably plump whilst also being as strong and dextrous as Charity was.

She's what I could've been, Charity thought a little sadly. *I guess when I agreed to lay down my life in the service of the Ministry, I didn't expect them to take it piece by agonising piece.*

"Penny for your thoughts?" Ivy asked, and Charity raised a surprised eyebrow.

"You aren't listening in?" she asked, and Ivy shook her head.

"I'm trying to practice only listening in when I really need to," Ivy said proudly. "It's hard work, but the benefits are plentiful; as well as giving people their privacy, it makes things a lot easier for me.

"Sometimes I wish that I had a more simple gift, like yours."

"Being a Ghost isn't as cut and dried as it first seems," Charity said enigmatically. "We have rules and secrets and-"

There was a sharp knock on the study door and Ivy drew the covers over their nude bodies mere seconds before two women burst excitedly into the room. Ivy shot Charity a look, and she nodded in reply.

Yes, she thought as loudly as she could, *these are the twins.*

"Charity!" Cat yelled as she jumped on to the bed. "We're so pleased to see you! It's been so long!"

"Is this your girlfriend?" Cait asked, peering at Ivy. "She's not what I expected, but then I didn't really expect you to date anyone, not that being in a relationship doesn't suit you, though!"

Even listening to them makes me feel exhausted. Charity gave them a tired smile, and gestured for them to sit down. Even though the two women were in their thirties, their enthusiasm and eagerness always made Charity feel like they were still boisterous teens.

"Geoff said that you came on the train," Cat said to Ivy. "Did you come through London?"

"Yes. We got the coach from Oxford, and then caught the train from Liverpool Street-"

"Did you travel first class?" Cait interrupted and Ivy nodded, a bemused smile on her face.

"Hey, Ivy," Cat asked, and leant in close. "Geoff said you were a mind reader; do you know what I'm thinking?"

"It doesn't quite work like that," Ivy said and Charity laughed. "You know, Charity and I are quite tired after our trip, and tomorrow is going to be an exhausting day too; do you mind if we get some rest, please?"

"Oh, of course!" Cat said, getting to her feet with freakish speed. "We'll let you two get some sleep. Just let us know if you need anything, okay?"

"We will," Charity said, giving the twins a wink. "You get some sleep too, okay?"

"Definitely," Cait said as she reached the door. She lingered for a moment, with a small giddy smile on her face. "We meant it when we said that it was good to see you; both of you. It's nice to have you here. Sleep well, and goodnight."

"It's nice to be here," Charity said as Cait closed the door, and blinked in surprise for a moment when she realised that she meant it.

Chapter Four – One Last Dance

Helen

"She's yours, isn't she?" Helen asked Harper as she carefully stitched the wounds on her face closed.

"Who?" Harper asked, and then winced as Helen poked the needle into her face harder than she expected. "Ouch! Could you be more careful?"

"I am being careful," Helen said sharply. "You just need to stay still, and in answer to your question, I'm talking about Ivy; I can see the shades of you in her."

Poor woman, Helen thought, but left that unsaid. Harper gestured idly with an empty hand in response to her question.

"Does it really matter if she is or not?" Harper said with a sigh. "We weren't exclusive, after all, and I've contributed my valuable genetic material to several Ministry ventures throughout the years, you know; I'd hardly call that cheating."

Helen pulled the final stitch closed and tied off the suture with an expert hand before slapping Harper across the face, hard. The other woman whirled around, snatching the scissors from the table and pushing them against the hollow of Helen's throat.

"Just like old times, then?" Helen said coldly, and Harper couldn't help but smile. "I don't care about the cheating, or lack thereof, Harper; I care that you abandoned that poor child after everything she went through! You could've given her a stable home, at the very least, or-"

"They wanted to execute every single child that made it off that island," Harper replied sharply, snatching the blades from the doctor's neck and slumping back down into her chair. "I stuck my neck out to keep them alive, Helen, and it's still on the fucking chopping block. After the whole affair with Lola Oriole, I was genuinely surprised that Desai didn't have my corpse thrown in the Thames.

"I know Lin put in a good word for me, and the fact that two other Lamplight Subjects brought Lola in did a lot of good for our continued existence." Harper sighed sadly. "Besides, I'm not exactly parent material; Silas proved that when he killed those Agents-"

"He didn't do it." Helen's words were firm and her stony gaze could've cut through rock. "The inquest found him innocent; hell, Lin cleared him herself!"

"He's a Swarm, Helen," Harper said, almost sadly, taking the doctor's trembling hands in her own. "His mind is too fragmented for her to pin down, and that's without Max's influence thrown into the mix. The boy is too much like us to be innocent, but it's a testament to how much you love him that you're still sticking by his side."

"I'm responsible for him," she said quietly, "just like you're responsible for Ivy."

"If you say so," Harper said with a sigh, and touched her damaged face. "She got my blood on her hands; if she is mine, we'll have the proof soon enough."

"And if I'm right?"

"Then I'll offer her something to make it right," Harper replied enigmatically. "Hopefully that will satisfy your pathological need to nitpick over the unforeseen outcomes of your own actions."

"What the fuck do you mean by that?" Helen asked, but the sinking feeling in her stomach gave the lie to her question.

"We both know that Dennis and Lin would never have bred if it wasn't for your influence," Harper said bluntly. "You weren't happy with one child, though, were you? Trust old Helen Mickelson to have a backup to her backup, and Desai wanted a Seer after all."

Helen said nothing.

"Silas was our son by mutual agreement, but you forced that pale freak on to Dennis and Lin. Needlessly, in fact, which makes it even worse; by all rights, that surplus child should never have been born." Harper picked up Lin's unfinished glass and drained it. "Tell me, honestly, how did you expect her to react to seeing you here?

"Did you expect her to fall into your arms and treat you like the mother that she never had?"

"Why are you always so cruel?" Helen asked softly.

"You kept Lin from me," Harper replied, getting to her feet. "I'll never forgive you for that."

"Where do you think you're going?" Helen asked as Harper walked towards the kitchen door. "You think that you can start something like this and then just walk away?"

"I'm going to get some sleep," Harper said. "Lin is burying her husband tomorrow, and I want to be rested enough to support her through that. You ought to get some sleep too, and make sure to act appropriately at the service tomorrow; stiff upper lip and all that."

"I loved him," Helen said angrily as she blinked back tears.

"Yes, darling," Harper said sadly, "but he wasn't *yours*, was he?"

With that, she went to bed and left Helen alone in

the kitchen, weeping.

The rain drummed on Helen's umbrella as she looked on numbly at Dennis's coffin. It was lowered smoothly into the freshly dug grave as the uncannily pale vicar droned out the usual platitudes. *This isn't right,* she thought tearfully. *He would've wanted more life than this; more colour, more exuberance.*

Whilst Dennis Walpole's visage had been as bleached as his daughter's, his zest for life had only grown as he'd aged. When not working, he had dressed in lurid Hawaiian shirts and surf shorts, regardless of the weather.

Today, however, he had been buried in black; the one colour that he'd shunned after a lifetime of Ministry issue trench coats. *You deserve better than this,* she thought sadly, but quickly turned her eyes to the ground when she caught Ivy staring at her. Her cheeks flushed with shame and she tried to focus on something other than the man in the grave before her; anything else, in fact.

Her eye was caught by something glittering and shimmering in the corner of her vision. A sideways glance confirmed that it was an unusual silver coin, idly rolled across the fingers of one of the funeral attendees. He, like Helen, was not watching the lowering of the coffin; instead, his eyes were firmly fixed upon Charity Walpole.

Is that Reggie!?

A closer look confirmed her suspicions; the hint of the horns beneath his broad brimmed black hat, along with the glimpse of a tail beneath his raincoat made her sure that the man was Reginald Kellogg. Helen shook her head in contempt.

What on earth is he doing here?

Her attention was drawn back to the grave, however, when Lin stepped up to toss the first handful of dirt on to Dennis's coffin. Ever stoic, her face was set in a grim, rain-streaked frown as the wet clods of earth clattered on the wooden surface.

Next was Prudence, assisted by one of the carers from her residential home; once again, the grave dirt was impassively dropped on to the coffin. Helen bit her lip and fought hard to control herself. Every fibre of her being wanted to stride forwards and decry the entire ceremony for being too sombre and dour, almost to the point of being an insult to Dennis's memory.

Her eyes met Ivy's, however, and the Séance shook her head, almost imperceptibly.

Harper was right, Helen thought sadly as Charity stepped up to the grave. *This isn't the place to voice my grief; today is for his family, not me.*

She stifled a sob as her last thought drove a stab of pain through her heart, and she brought up a handkerchief to hide her tears. Charity shot her a look, however, and although her dark glasses made her expression difficult to read, Helen was sure it was one of relief.

The younger Walpole hesitated at the graveside, her handful of dirt outstretched and trembling over the coffin. It seemed as if she was stuck, and Helen saw tears streaming down her face, only partly hidden by the rain.

"I'm here," Ivy said, taking Charity's empty hand in hers. "Take as long as you need."

"Goodbye, Daddy," Charity muttered, almost too quietly to hear, but still she remained frozen in place.

Helen almost took a step towards her, however the spell was broken before she could move.

The Ghost let out a long, mournful wail before finally releasing the soil, which pattered wetly on the coffin below. Lin tutted disdainfully and Prudence shook her head, but Constance Walpole was immediately at her niece's side, helping her back to where her family stood.

Charity swayed unsteadily on the wet grass, clinging to Ivy for dear life, as Constance placed her own handful of dirt into her brother's grave. She was followed closely by Geoff and her two daughters, who all joined her in supporting the grief-stricken Charity after they'd said their goodbyes.

The rain continued to hammer down around them as the vicar stepped forwards to say a few final words as the gravediggers began to fill in the hole with their shovels. Helen took a deep breath and stepped forwards, plucking the white rose from the lapel of her jacket and tossing it into the grave along with the dirt.

Charity stared at her in shock, but Constance nodded knowingly and gave Helen a sad smile.

She understands, Helen realised. *Dennis always said that he had no secrets from her.*

"For old times' sake," she said quietly to Charity, both as an explanation and an apology for intruding on her family's sorrow. Helen stepped back quickly, fearing an outburst like the previous night's, but instead Charity gave her a small nod; nothing more than that, but the acknowledgement was enough to allay her worry.

Goodbye, Dennis, she thought as the shovelfuls of wet earth quickly filled in the grave. *I wish we'd had more time.*

She looked tearfully at the Walpole family as they held each other, completely lost to their grief.

Nobody ever has enough time.

"I think Mum might've over catered," one of the Walpole girls said as Helen looked at the virtually untouched buffet that covered the eight person dining table.

Are you Catarina or Caitlin? Helen wondered. *I never could tell you apart.*

"I told her that nobody would be hungry after burying Uncle Dennis, but she said it was the done thing, so here we are." The young woman smiled at her, almost too cheerfully for the circumstances. "She also said that you and Uncle Den were especially close, and that you'd probably want to put some soil in the grave, but Aunty Lin forbade it. I think the flower was a beautiful gesture, though; very classy, and it got the point across without causing too much of a ruckus."

"Thank you, uh," Helen faltered as she tried to decide which twin it was, but the young woman came to her rescue.

"I'm Cat. Cait's in the kitchen with Harper; we've both decided to keep her away from you this afternoon." Before Helen could reply, Cat went on. "We saw your little upset in the kitchen last night and thought you'd appreciate it if that ghastly woman was at arm's length."

"You were spying on us?" Helen asked, surprised that Cat would be so open about it.

"It's my fucking house," Cat said firmly. "I'll go where I please, as will Cait. We told Mum what Harper said about Charity, but apparently it will cause a *diplomatic incident* if we call her out on it here and now.

"Don't worry, though; she'll get what's coming to her one of these days."

Helen stared at the blonde woman in open mouthed shock.

"I think I might have some little sausage rolls; do you want any?" Cat asked, and Helen wordlessly shook her head. "More for me then!"

She bounced over to the table and began to load up a plate with a selection of party food. Helen continued to stare into the middle distance until she heard a soft chuckle beside her; she looked to her left and saw Geoff leaning against the wall, no longer in his black mourning outfit.

"I hope I didn't startle you," he said quietly.

"Not at all," Helen replied, trying to hide how flustered she was by the whole situation. "I didn't expect you to move so quietly, though."

"If you live in a house full of invisible women for long enough, you pick up a few tricks," he said with a wry smile. "I hope Cat has given you sufficient space to mourn; she and Cait are sweet girls, but they both can overstep sometimes."

"She's been nothing but thoughtful," Helen said gratefully, and Geoff nodded approvingly before returning to his spot leaning against the wall. *They're a family of leaners,* Helen thought, and was about to make a joke out of it when the sound of smashing glass made her head towards the doorway to the hall.

"What is wrong with you!?" Lin yelled from the kitchen, which was answered with yet more smashing.

"What's wrong with me!?" Charity screamed in response as she strode out of the kitchen, into the entrance hall. "What's wrong with the rest of you? How can you just stand there, eating fucking cheese and pineapple like it's a fucking church fundraiser?

"Don't any of you fucking feel anything?"

"Charity-" Constance began, but Charity shook her head tearfully, and walked through the front door and out into the rain, knocking over a side table in the process. Both Lin and Ivy went to follow her, but Constance caught the former by the arm, and held on to her tight. Lin stared at Constance, seething, as Ivy headed out into the downpour. "Let her go, Lin."

"I can't believe that she would dare to act so selfishly, especially today of all days!" Lin said, looking at the open front door in a state of total horror. "When she gets back, I swear that I'm going to give her the dressing down of her fucking life!"

"She's grieving, Lin," Constance said softly, though she still maintained a rigid grip on the Inquisitor's arm. "We all are, you included, and some space will do her good. Come on, I'll make you a cup of tea."

Helen watched on as Constance steered Lin back into the kitchen. *This is certainly turning into an eventful day,* she thought, as she went to shut the front door. She stopped to right the little side table, and tried to gather up the drift of paper that had fallen from it.

"We all mourn in our own way," Geoff said as he came over to help. "Still, it's safe to say that Walpole blood runs hotter than most."

Helen did not reply, however; she was frozen in place, staring at the missing posters in her hand. Geoff sighed heavily before taking them from her, and she looked up at him as he tucked them neatly under one arm.

"Don't pay them any mind," he said quietly. "Dennis

brought them over a few days before he passed away, and I keep forgetting to get rid of them. I don't want them to upset the girls, you see; there have always been a lot of vanishings in this part of the world."

Oh my god, she thought. *He died on a fucking case!*

"Geoff," Helen said, her eyes wide as she got to her feet, "I need you to start at the beginning; when did these disappearances start?"

"How far back do you want to go?" he asked, raising a curious eyebrow as he shut the door. "We're talking centuries, here."

"As far back as you can," she said, as he led her towards his study. "I want you to tell me everything."

Chapter Five – Yet More Secrets

Ivy

"Charity!" Ivy yelled as she ran through the heavy rain after her girlfriend. "Charity, wait!"

The Ghost didn't respond, but she did slow her pace enough for Ivy to catch up with her. As Ivy placed a hand gently on Charity's shoulder, she burst into deep, shuddering sobs. Ivy moved closer, determined to hold her close, but the Ghost's knees gave out and she fell to the wet ground in a weeping heap.

I should've grabbed an umbrella on my way out here, Ivy thought as she knelt beside her lover. Charity took Ivy's hands in her own, squeezing them so tight that Ivy feared that her fingers would break in her girlfriend's white knuckle grip.

Ivy didn't try to speak, but she did look around frantically for any kind of shelter that she could find; even a flimsy gazebo would've been better than staying out in the near torrential rain. Her eyes widened slightly as she saw a collection of outhouses nestled amongst some low trees, and decided to try and coax Charity to her feet.

"Charity, sweetheart," she said softly as the rain cascaded down her face, "you're going to get sick if you stay out in this too long."

"I don't want to go back in there!" Charity wailed. "I can't!"

"I know, babe," Ivy said, leaning in close to speak softly in her ear. "How about we go into one of those little buildings over there? I'm sure that your aunt and uncle won't mind if we loiter inside, at least until the rain stops."

"Lin will come and find us," Charity said through her tears. "She'll come to scream at me, just like she always does."

"Connie stopped her from coming after you," Ivy said, and extracted one hand to stroke Charity's pale hair as soothingly as she could. "It's just us, darling; I promise."

Charity didn't so much reply as let out a strangled cry, but she did clumsily get to her feet, slipping slightly on the wet grass as she went. Ivy glanced over her shoulder and saw that the ground floor windows of Walpole Manor were full of people looking at them both. She shot the onlookers a filthy scowl and resumed helping her lover to her feet.

"That's it, Charity," she said quietly. "Just focus on what's in front of you, and you'll be in the dry soon enough."

I wish I had my fucking swords, Ivy thought angrily as she stared at the Big House once again. *Then I could make them look elsewhere.*

They crossed the waterlogged lawn and reached the nearest building in less than a minute, but Ivy was already trembling with cold nonetheless. The freezing January rain was almost edging into sleet, and both women were without coats; Charity in a black wool pullover and Ivy in a black cotton blouse.

If the door is locked, she thought as her teeth chattered, *I'll just break a fucking window.*

I'm sure Connie and Geoff will understand.

Thankfully, however, the door opened as soon as she turned the handle and they both stepped into the dark, albeit dry, space. The scent of polish and motor oil hung in the air, and even in the gloom Ivy saw a faint smile creep on to Charity's face.

"I'll find a light," Ivy said, but Charity shook her head.

"No, Liv," she said, with a sniffle. "Please, just let me spend a little while without my glasses on, okay?"

"Of course," Ivy said, still slightly worried about tripping over or accidentally damaging something. "What is this place?"

"This is Connie's workshop," Charity said quietly. "She likes vintage motorcycles, and she fixes them up herself."

Ivy nodded quietly in the darkness, and she heard the distinctive click of Charity folding her sunglasses up.

"I always forget just how beautiful you are, Liv," she murmured. "I spend too long with glass in front of my eyes; it's like I'm just watching television instead of actually living in the world."

Charity took a few steps forward and sighed heavily.

"I always wanted to learn to ride a motorcycle, you know. My dad kept saying that he'd teach me, but something always came up at the last minute and now, well, I guess he never will."

"I'm sure Connie would be glad to teach you," Ivy suggested.

"I'm certain she'd enjoy that, but it wouldn't be the same." Charity turned to face Ivy, her pale eyes almost luminous in the dim light filtering in from outside. "It's something you should learn from your dad, isn't it?"

Ivy placed a hand on Charity's shoulder, but remained silent; now was the time to listen, not speak.

"I didn't learn much from my dad, at least when it came to life skills; everything was related to work, to the Ministry. I was fucking raised by other Agents, after all, so why should his death bother me any more than the other colleagues I've lost?

"Hell, I wasn't this upset when I thought the Master had killed Joseph!" She chuckled tearfully. "Joseph was family, so why the fuck should my dad's death be any different?"

She leant forwards, staring at Ivy now; there was a wildness to her eyes, a madness that Ivy found deeply unsettling. *I wish I could tell you that I understand what you're going through,* Ivy thought, *but this is unlike anything I've ever experienced.*

I never had any parents to lose.

"You know, Liv, the way everyone looked at me when I cried at his grave made me feel like I'd lost my fucking mind." She shook her head angrily. "Why the fuck did they do that? It's my father's funeral, and *I'm* the crazy one for getting upset!?

"I'm so sick of this stiff upper lip bullshit, Liv," Charity said, her shoulders slumping. "I buried my dad today, and I'm supposed to laugh and chit-chat and eat cocktail sausages like I don't feel anything?

"It's not fair! Today is supposed to be about saying goodbye to him, but instead I've got to spend it keeping up appearances for them." She gestured in the direction of the Big House. "It's all a big fucking show, and I never agreed to be in it! You should've seen how Lin looked at me when I mentioned his death, just in passing!"

Charity ran her hands through her hair and cackled madly.

"She looked at me like I was a fucking slug, or some other equally disgusting thing, for so much as daring to mention death *at a fucking funeral*! I know I kill people for a living, Ivy, but surely the rest of them aren't as detached as that?" She looked at Ivy; her eyes were almost pleading with the Séance to confirm that everyone else was mad and that she alone was sane. "Is that really what society is like?"

"People are afraid of death, especially on days like today," Ivy said softly. "They don't want to be reminded that it'll be their turn eventually."

"But this is the only chance to say farewell that they'll ever get! Why are they wasting it playing stupid social games?" Charity's laughs rapidly dissolved into sobs once again. "Why am I the only one who seems to feel anything?

"Is there something wrong with me?"

"No, darling; this is a completely normal response." Ivy pulled Charity into a tight embrace. "I've often thought that funerals like this aren't for everyone, and they certainly place an undue burden on those closest to the deceased. It's not fair of them to judge you for how you reacted; in so many cultures around the world what you did would be a completely normal response to losing someone so close to you."

"God only knows what I'd do if I lost you," Charity mumbled, but her words only caused her to cry even harder. Ivy wrapped her arms tightly around her girlfriend and, for the first time since the beginning of her chemotherapy, realised just how thin and fragile she was.

If I lost you, Ivy thought, *I would never be able to keep my feelings to myself.*

The whole world would drown in my grief.

Instead of voicing this, however, Ivy just held Charity tightly as the rain drummed loudly on the roof. The two women cried together for what felt like forever, and the gloom deepened as the grey of the rainy day waned into the gathering dark of late afternoon.

"We can stay out here as long as you like, sweet-pea," Ivy said, running her fingertips over the back of Charity's pullover. "All night, if it comes to it."

"We'll go back in when most people have left," Charity said softly. "We'll go back soon."

"We don't have to-" Ivy began, but Charity shook her head.

"We do. I have something that I need to do, once the sun goes down," Charity said darkly. Ivy didn't like the tone of her voice, but she nodded all the same.

"Whatever you want, darling. Today is for you."

"Thank you, Ivy." Charity buried her face in Ivy's neck. "Thank you so much for understanding. I love you so much."

"I love you too," Ivy replied. "I'll always be here for you; that's a promise."

Most of the mourners had departed when the two bedraggled women finally made their way back to the main house. Connie met them halfway across the lawn, much to Ivy's surprise.

"Oh, there you are," she said, as if she didn't know where they'd been for the past couple of hours. "I was just coming to get you both; Charity has an engagement this evening, I'm afraid."

"She mentioned," Ivy said warily, and Constance looked at her askance.

"She did?"

"No details, though," Ivy quickly clarified. "She just said that she would be needed after sunset."

"Oh. Good." This seemed to satisfy Constance, but

the older woman's behaviour immediately put her on edge. *What are you both hiding?* "I'm afraid the house will be rather empty this evening, Ivy, but there's a television in my office and plenty of food left over from the buffet, so I'm sure that you'll find some way to keep yourself entertained.

"Failing that, Helen is spending the night, and Lin and Harper will be around a while longer, although you didn't seem that fond of their company yesterday," Constance said delicately. "Regardless, we'll all be out late, so you needn't wait up."

"I'm a Night Person," Ivy said, almost defiantly. She glanced at Charity. "I'll be awake when you get in, no matter how late it is."

"Thank you, Liv," Charity said, before giving her a gentle kiss. "I better go and have a quick shower. Connie, would you be kind enough to show Ivy where she can dry her clothes, please?"

"Of course, darling," Connie said, slipping an arm through Ivy's. "Now you run along; you don't want to be late!"

"I'll see you in a bit, Ivy," Charity said, before jogging the last few metres to the house and disappearing through the door. Ivy went to follow her but Constance held her back, checking her motion with a surprisingly strong arm.

"Now, Ivy," Connie said softly, "I know that you're a naturally inquisitive person, and that you want to do all that you can to support Charity; I love you for that, I really do. What happens tonight, however, is not for *anyone* to know about, and I'm going to ask you to not put Charity in a position where she has to lie to you.

"What happens tonight is Ghost business, and it's for us alone. Do you understand?"

"Yes, Connie," Ivy said softly. "I give you my word that I won't pry."

"Thank you. You're a good woman, Ivy Livingston."

"I will ask you to keep an eye on her, though, Connie," Ivy said, more firmly now. "She's had a difficult day and definitely feels things far more deeply than Lin or Prudence. Keep her safe for me, will you?"

"You have my word." Connie let go of her arm and began to walk towards the house. After a few steps, however, she turned back to ask Ivy one final question. "I'm going to guess that you've not spent much time in front of a mirror in the last twenty four hours, have you?"

"Not even to do my makeup for the funeral," Ivy said sheepishly. "Charity did it for me, in fact."

"Hmm... Maybe you should take some time this evening to ponder your own reflection."

"Why?" Ivy asked, but Connie was already walking away once again. She sighed deeply and headed in out of the rain, not bothering to look at her distorted image in the darkened windows as she passed them. "Why does everyone speak in fucking riddles around here?"

She strode into the downstairs bathroom, locking the door behind her. She fumbled for the light switch for a few seconds, and then the room was suddenly bathed in a golden glow. Ivy looked at her bedraggled reflection; wet clothes, hair, and streaked makeup all served to make her look like a drowned rat.

Not to mention the burn scars...

"Good god, I look like such a fucking mess," she muttered angrily. She held her own gaze for well over a minute before realising that Connie had played an unpleasant prank on her. *Is the secrecy not enough?* Ivy thought, and decided to go back to her room and dry out enough to send Charity off on her mystery errand with a tender hug.

Then, just as she was about to turn away, her reflection winked at her.

Chapter Six – The Last Haunting

Charity

"I always wondered if this moment would come," Charity said softly as she donned the outfit that she'd picked out for that evening's ceremony; a lurid tropical shirt, bubblegum pink tracksuit trousers, and a lime green pea coat that her father had given her for this exact occasion. "I just wished I felt more ready."

"We're with you, Charity," Connie said from the armchair in the corner of the room. "I know this is your first time leading the Haunting, but you've been before. You know what to do, and this is your night, sweet pea; we'll follow your lead, no matter what happens."

"Will they name a successor tonight?" Charity asked, fiddling nervously with the hem of her coat, and Connie nodded. "It's going to be you, right? I mean, who else could it possibly be?"

"We'll see," Connie said, her tone both soothing and non-committal. "Nothing is certain until it happens, lovely."

"This will be Cat and Cait's first Haunting, won't it?" Charity said, after taking one final look at her outfit in the mirror and nodding approvingly. *Sufficiently gaudy; loud enough to raise the dead, in fact.*

"It is, and they're quite nervous. They weren't old enough to come when your grandfather died, after all."

"I'm not sure I was, either," Charity said, letting out a nervous chuckle. "Sorry, I get a bit giggly when I'm stressed."

"Your father was much the same; you really are his daughter, you know." Connie rose from her seat and pulled her into a tight embrace. "He would be so proud of you, Charity, and so am I. I want you to know that, before it all starts tonight.

"Are you bringing an instrument with you? I've got a spare-"

"I'm singing," Charity said, almost stunning her aunt. "I know I wasn't very good when I was little, but Joseph was as good a teacher as he was a killer. Is it alright to sing? It won't upset people, will it?"

"It's your night, baby; you sing your fucking heart out." Connie gave her a tearful smile and a peck on the cheek. "I need to go and make sure the girls are ready, and then Geoff will take us up to the church. I'll see you in a little while, darling."

Constance Walpole went to leave the study-turned-bedroom, but a question from Charity stopped her at the door.

"Aunt Connie," Charity blurted out, "will you teach me to ride a motorcycle?"

"I thought you'd never ask," she replied with a warm smile. "We'll start tomorrow afternoon, if you're feeling up to it."

"Thank you," Charity said as her aunt slipped out of the room. She ran her hands through her hair and let out a long sigh, tittering anxiously once again. *I get to lead the Haunting,* she thought as the reality of her situation finally sunk in. *Tonight, I'll be the most that a Ghost can possibly be.*

Whilst the many different types of Ceps had their own rites and rituals, those of the Ghosts were closely guarded secrets; none more so than the Last Haunting.

When one of their own perished, whether by illness, accident, or the slow decay of time, those touched by the life of the deceased gathered on the site of the burial to celebrate them one last time.

As Ghosts most often led quiet, unseen lives, the Last Haunting was a chance for their presence to be felt in their community, albeit posthumously; the assembled Ghosts would vanish from sight and run through the local area, singing, screaming, and causing absolute mayhem in the name of the departed.

There were rules to be observed, of course, but as long as the property damage wasn't *too* severe and nobody was physically harmed, the mourners had an effective carte blanche on their activities. The Haunting was always led by the person closest to the deceased; usually either a child, spouse, or sibling, but sometimes a colleague or close friend.

The event was exclusively for Ghosts, and any participant that mentioned it to those outside their own kind would immediately be shunned for the rest of their life. Given the gravity of the ritual, leading a Haunting was the most serious role a Ghost would ever be called upon to fill, and most would never be granted the opportunity.

Charity Walpole had always assumed that Constance would lead the Haunting when Dennis died, especially as that evening's event would be unlike any other that Charity would be likely to attend.

"They'll pick Connie," Charity muttered to her reflection. "They have to, don't they?"

Her question remained unanswered, but deep within her heart she knew there was another option; one that both thrilled and terrified her.

They could pick me.

The lights of Geoff's car disappeared down the hill as Charity led her aunt and cousins into the graveyard of the Church of St Mary, in the small village of Tharston. *He lived here his whole life,* Charity thought, *except for when he was stationed in Hong Kong, and now he'll stay here forever more.* The Walpole family had lived and died in that part of Norfolk for over five hundred years, and their bones were all buried together in the in the graveyard.

Will Ivy bring me home if I die before her? Charity wondered, but then shook her head slightly to clear it; she had a job to do, and it required focus.

The graveyard was already brimming with people; far more than had attended the funeral, at least visibly. Each wore garish clothing and carried some kind of noise maker; she saw antique gas rattles, singing sticks, fiddles, and Celtic drums, as well as countless others.

She walked carefully forwards and took her place at the foot of her father's grave. The rain had lessened to a gentle drizzle, but she still shivered with the cold, along with the sheer number of eyes on her.

"You've got this, darling," Connie whispered before she joined five other Ghosts to stand behind Dennis's headstone. Charity looked at them through her dark glasses and nodded at each of them in turn; they were the Phantoms, the most influential and powerful Ghosts in Britain. Usually there were seven in total, but the Grand Phantom, the head of their small group, was in the ground before them.

Tonight, before the Haunting would begin, they would declare a new Grand Phantom, as well as select a new member to replenish their ranks. Charity took a deep breath and bowed to the Ghosts at the head of the grave, granting them permission to begin their announcement.

"My Unseen Kin," began the oldest of the Phantoms, Reverend Wallace Paul, who had conducted the funeral earlier that day, "we gather here today to celebrate the life and mourn the passing of our Grand Phantom, Dennis Walpole. He was an honourable man, a dutiful husband, a loving father, and a Ravenblade, but most importantly, he was one of us."

"One of us," the attendants echoed.

"We will be led in his Last Haunting by his daughter, Charity Walpole, as per his request," Wallace went on, and Charity felt her heart flutter a little. *I still can't believe he chose me.* "Before this, however, we must appoint a new Grand Phantom; to lead us, to guide us, and to protect us in times of strife. Does anyone here volunteer to shoulder this terrible burden?"

Nobody spoke up, much as Charity expected; to volunteer would be a tremendous faux pas, worthy of a shunning.

"Indeed; our leader will be chosen, for those who would choose to lead are not worthy."

"Not worthy," everyone echoed.

"Our brother, Dennis, was arguably one of the most skilled Ghosts ever to walk this earth. His career and personal life are filled with achievements that almost no-one else can rival; it was not lightly that I once declared him to be the greatest Ghost alive.

"His moment, however, has ended; the sun has set on his life for the last time, and a successor must be chosen."

"Chosen." Charity felt the words leave her lips

almost unbidden; there was something deeper at work here; something older than civilisation and far more primal.

"In the twilight of his life Dennis proposed his successor, and we have been monitoring and examining this individual for almost a decade." The Reverend smiled as he spoke. "I am pleased to announce that she has passed the test, and I will proudly stake my life on the claim that she is not Dennis Walpole's equal.

"She is better."

Gasps ran through the assembled mourners. Charity felt something strange stirring in her chest.

"Do you accept this burden?" Wallace asked, his voice solemn and ringing with importance. "Will you lead us as our Grand Phantom?"

There was a beat of silence, and Charity looked at Connie, waiting for her to accept the position. Instead of speaking, however, the older woman gently shook her head with a smile.

Oh my god, Charity realised. *They're looking at me.*

"I don't want to," she said reflexively, and the Phantoms nodded.

"It is always so," Wallace said, his voice kind but firm. "We know that you do not wish to lead, Charity Walpole, but will you?"

I can say no, she thought, even as she replied with the complete opposite.

"I will."

"Then you have our loyalty, now and forever; this we swear," Wallace said, and his last two words were echoed by all present. "Welcome, Grand Phantom. On a personal note, you should know that you were all your father ever talked about; you were his crowning achievement. You should walk with your head held high, Charity, for you have earned it."

"Thank you," she croaked. Charity blinked rapidly, trying to clear the sudden tears from her eyes. She removed her glasses, no longer caring about the dim light that illuminated the church.

"That concludes our business," Wallace said as the other Phantoms returned to the crowd. "Charity Walpole, daughter of Dennis; the night is yours."

What... Charity thought as she sobbed gently. *What do I do now?*

She looked through her tears at her father's grave as the loss filled her heart and the true anguish of his death consumed her. She let out a pained howl and fell to her knees, weeping into the damp sod at her feet as the other Ghosts watched on.

After a while her sobs began to die down, and she took a shuddering breath as she got to her feet. Charity dried her eyes, wiped her nose, and found her centre as she got her breathing under control.

This one's for you, old man, she thought fondly as she began to sing Dennis's favourite song.

"Another red letter day," she sang out, her voice clear and beautifully mournful. "So the pound has dropped and the children are creating..."

"The other half ran away," Constance added, joining in with the song.

By the time they reached the chorus, all the Ghosts were singing along. Tuneful fiddles and harsh percussion blended together with the chorus of voices to make a send-off unlike anything Charity had seen before. Tears streaked her cheeks, but a smile crept on to her lips as she felt the spirit of her father moving amongst them.

It's time, she thought, and vanished. Within a few seconds every person in the graveyard had disappeared, but they still played on. Charity swayed and danced, unseen, to the music; once again she was a little child laughing in her father's arms as they strutted around their living room, silly as could be.

Then the song came to an end, and she let out a piercing scream which carried through the wet night for miles in every direction. Taking their cue from their newly appointed Grand Phantom, the other Ghosts followed suit, and the night exploded into chaos.

"Your smile speaks books to me!" Charity sang as the mob of Ghosts tore through the village, hooting, hollering, and howling at the night sky. "I break up with each and every one of your looks at me!"

Tears streamed down her face as the emotional release that she'd craved so desperately at the earlier funeral hit her like a freight train, and the music flowed through her, leaving her singing like a woman possessed.

"Say his name!" Constance called out.

"DENNIS WALPOLE!" the Ghosts screamed in unison, stamping their feet and clapping their hands for emphasis. "DENNIS WALPOLE LIVES FOREVER!"

"I see you, Daddy!" Charity cried into the darkness as she passed the last house and vaulted into a nearby field. She began to run through the mud, prancing and whooping at the top of her lungs. "I miss you and I love you and I can't wait to see you again one day!"

"Where next?" Connie asked as her vague, hazy form kept pace with Charity.

"What's over there?" Charity asked gesturing towards the lights of a nearby town.

"Long Stratton," her aunt replied.

"TO LONG STRATTON!" Charity commanded, and her retinue of invisible revellers cheered. "WE GO UNTIL THE FIRST FINGERS OF DAWN!"

"Walpole, Walpole!" The Ghosts continued the chant as they stormed through the fields and up the little roads that led to the town. Even though the night was wet and cold, their energy did not wane. *We are powered by something ancient,* Charity thought, her mind in a feverish daze. *Something older than god, older than time, perhaps.*

"If I could only reach you, if I could make you smile!" Charity sang as the Haunting entered the streets of Long Stratton, and the musicians accompanied her. Those that did not wish to sing simply screamed and cheered and banged their hands on bus shelters or kicked bins in order to make the loudest noise they could.

Whilst the residents of Tharston knew all too well what would occur at sunset when a Walpole was buried, the locals and visitors of Long Stratton were entirely unprepared for the Haunting that descended upon their streets. People rushed to their windows, bolted their doors, and dozens of calls were placed to the local police.

Those caught out on the street found themselves spun around and buffeted by a tide of playful Ghosts, kept upright by dozens of invisible hands even as they wobbled and flailed against the onslaught.

Charity's tears had long been washed away and her mood was closer to one of euphoric relief as she was filled with the ecstasy of sated grief. She broke off from the main group and danced down a side street, moving as if guided by some unseen hand.

What she saw, however, immediately shattered the joy in her heart and rooted her to the ground, eyes wide and body frozen with abject horror.

A young woman was screaming and pleading as a colossal black dog with glowing red eyes dragged her into the darkness between two bins. Her fingers scrabbled at the wet asphalt, ripping out her fingernails and tearing through her flesh all the way down to the bone.

"Somebody, please!" the woman cried, and Charity finally darted forwards.

By the time she reached the shadows between the large red bins, however, both hound and woman were nowhere to be seen. She peered into the darkness, but there was nowhere they could have gone to; the space was nothing but a cramped dead end.

Charity blinked the rain from her eyes, and would've wondered if she was going mad if it wasn't for the fingernails that remained wedged in the cracked surface of the badly maintained road. She walked slowly towards them and carefully picked one up, almost surprised when it, too, didn't vanish before her eyes.

That was real, she thought, all traces of the Haunting driven from her mind. She looked at the space between the bins once again and shook her head in disbelief. A presence next to her drew her gaze, and Connie's soft voice reached her ears, only slightly muted by the rain.

"I heard screaming," she said quietly, obviously looking at the blood and fingernails on the ground. "What happened here?"

"I have no fucking idea," Charity replied, closing her hand into a determined fist around the bloodied nail, "but I intend to find out."

"It's your night," Connie said. "What do we do now?"

"The Haunting is over," Charity said firmly, striding in the direction of Walpole Manor. "I have work to do."

<u>Chapter Seven</u> – Uncharted Waters

Helen

"It's a strange old place, this part of the world," Geoff said quietly as he pottered around his sizeable study, gathering up papers and pulling the occasional book from the shelves. "I'm not originally from here, you know."

Please, just skip the chit chat, Helen thought, but she kept a lid on her frustration. *He'll get there; I just need to be patient.*

"So, where do you hail from originally?" she asked, trying to sound casual instead of interrogatory.

"Oh, here and there, but I was born on the Isle of Wight. I actually saw Jimi Hendrix play there when I was sixteen; oh what a day that was!" He chuckled at the memory and placed the stack of research on the table between them before moving to a little side cabinet. "I'm going to pour myself a little tipple, if that's alright with you? If you'd rather I didn't, then I can just make a pot of tea."

"Please, go ahead," Helen said, genuinely touched by his concern.

"Just a small one," he muttered as he added a small tot of straw coloured liquid into a glass, giving her a smile as he did so. "I've got to run an errand later, so I can't have too much. Do you mind if I nip out for a few ice cubes; I won't be but a moment?"

"Not at all," Helen said, leaning forwards to look through the papers. "May I?"

"You get stuck in, and I'll be back in two shakes." He stepped out of the study and quietly closed the door behind him. *I wonder who told him,* she wondered.

Helen's alcoholism was not common knowledge, especially amongst colleagues; in fact, the only people in the Ministry that knew were Lin, Harper, and Desai. *Also Dennis,* she thought, *but he wouldn't let such a secret slip.*

Geoff returned before she could even lift the cover of the first notebook, entering just as softly as he left. He gave her a wink and handed her a glass filled with ice and a dark purple sparkling liquid. She sniffed it suspiciously, and blinked in surprise at the fruity, albeit tangy scent.

"Blackberry oxymel in fizzy water," he said with conspiratorial glee. "I hear that it's very *in* nowadays, and the twins rave about it; you must tell me what you think."

"What's it made of?" Helen asked, swirling the drink.

"Honey, vinegar, and fruit, I think," Geoff replied. "Non-alcoholic, though. I'm too much of a fuddy-duddy to try it, so you can be my guinea pig if you like."

"Ooh," Helen said in delight after taking a sip. "I used to drink something like this back in Hong Kong; it's quite refreshing. Thank you, Geoff."

"You're most welcome." He held up his glass. "Cheers."

"The same to you," Helen replied, and took another sip. "So, what's your poison?"

"Crème d'Abricot," he said sheepishly. "Not exactly what one might expect, but I picked up a taste for it when I was at seminary school."

"You wanted to be a priest?" Helen asked, intrigued.

"I can't picture that."

"I *was* a priest," he corrected. "I was on sabbatical when I came to Tharston, researching historic church legends. I've been all over the place, you know."

"So what happened?" Helen said, settling back in her chair. *I can see why Dennis used to enjoy your company so much.*

"I was up at St Mary's, and I noticed that an entire area of the graveyard was dedicated to the Walpole family. I asked Reverend Paul about them, and he suggested that I do not look any further into the matter. I never was one for following the rules, though, and I eventually found myself standing at Connie's door." He gave her a wry smile. "When faced with such a beautiful woman, the promises of eternal paradise do rather pale in comparison, wouldn't you agree?"

"I would," Helen said with a sigh. "Did Dennis ever tell you about-"

"He did," Geoff said quietly. "He spoke of you often, and wished that you had the opportunity to visit more regularly. Still, perhaps tonight is not the best night for such discussions, given the other guests under this roof."

"Understood," Helen said, although the relief of merely mentioning her closeness with Dennis lifted her spirits immeasurably. "So you stepped away from your calling to be with Connie?"

"And to raise the girls," he said firmly, "but between you and me, I was already having doubts about the church life; they viewed some of my extracurricular activities with disdain.

"Fucking hypocrites, the lot of them."

"What activities in particular?" Helen asked, almost

hoping that he wouldn't answer.

"Oh, nothing *unpleasant*, if that's what you're thinking," he said quickly. "I wasn't one of *those* priests; heavens no! I just happen to find the occult fascinating and I always got on far too well with the local Druidic circles for their liking; we tend to share a common love of classic rock and the old Mary Jane."

He looked through the rain streaked window at the fading daylight and sighed heavily. He finished the last of his drink and popped the glass on his desk before pulling on a faded Barbour overcoat.

"I've got to run that little errand I mentioned earlier, but then I'm all yours for the rest of the evening," Geoff said. "Feel free to sit and read for as long as you like, and if you're still feeling sociable after we've done what we need to do, I can dig out some of my old records and I can offer you a sample of the local green.

"Den did mention that you enjoy a bit of Boston with your pot, and I must say that after a day like today that sounds like an excellent wind-down to me." He grinned at her. "Are you game?"

"You must've been a terrible fucking priest," Helen said with a chuckle, and then nodded. "That sounds like just the thing. Do you mind if I use your phone whilst you're out? I need to get in touch with the Ministry and I'd rather not go through Harper if I can help it."

"By all means." He popped a flat cap on his head, hesitated for a moment, and then leant down to give her a tight hug. "I'm sorry for your loss, Helen. I know how much he meant to you, and today can't have been easy on you. I'll be back soon, so don't work too hard, okay?"

"Thank you, Geoff. Drive safe." Helen replied, wiping away a solitary tear. He tipped his cap to her before heading out. She let out a long whistle before diving into the pile of research that Geoff had gathered up for her, sipping at her oxymel once again. "Right, let's see what we're dealing with."

Mohinder Desai answered his phone on the third ring.

"Director Desai," he said formally. "How can I help you, Ms Walpole?"

"Oh, no," Helen replied in surprise, shocked that Desai would know where she was calling from. "Mohinder, it's Helen Mickelson."

"Ah, Dr Mickelson," he said, his voice immediately taking on its usual warm, albeit threatening, character. "What an unexpected pleasure to hear from you! How was the funeral?"

"It was a bit dour for my liking, but I've always preferred more of a celebration of life to the usual mournful dirges." She took a second to gather her thoughts. "Director, I think I've stumbled into a case here."

"Have you spoken to the Deputy Director?" Desai asked, without missing a beat. "Assigning resources to unfolding events is her responsibility, after all."

"With all due respect, sir, I don't think Harper's decision making would be unbiased in this particular instance." Helen bit her lip nervously as she paced around the office. "I'm requesting permission to call in some of our more talented detectives to further look into what I've found."

"Have you raised this with Constance Walpole?" Desai asked softly.

"No, sir. I came to you directly with the information I was given."

"Given by whom?" Every syllable was as sharp as a knife, and Helen realised what a dangerous game she was playing.

"The initial information was gathered by Dennis Walpole, who I believe was working independently. Once I became aware of it, further information, including a regional historical background was provided by a local scholar."

"Constance Walpole's consort?" Desai asked, and she confirmed his suspicions. "Hmm. You are quite aware that this information might not be accurate, Dr Mickelson?"

"I am, but-"

"An Amberlight ploy to tie up Ministry resources and waste our valuable time, perhaps?"

"Yes, but-"

"And you are aware that such a ploy would implicate the late Agent Walpole, tarnishing both his reputation and that of his entire surviving family?" It was less of a question than an obvious threat, but still she persevered.

"I understand, Director, but I feel that the situation occurring here still merits attention. May I please go over the details with you, at least?" She tried to keep the pleading out of her words, but her voice still cracked slightly at the end. She took a quick sip of her drink, which was a mistake.

"Helen, have you been drinking?" Desai asked, clearly having heard the ice clink through the phone's microphone.

"It's oxymel, Mohinder," she replied testily. "It's a fruit, honey, and vinegar soft drink popular with the youth. Now, are you going to fucking listen to me or not?"

She could hear his breathing through the phone as he thought for a moment, but instead of instilling fear in her, she just grew more irritated.

"Well?" Helen asked brusquely.

"Fine," he said after entirely too long. "Give me a quick summary and I'll see what we can do."

"As it currently stands, nine people have gone missing in the surrounding area in the past two months," Helen said. "According to the missing posters, each of them suffered a severe deterioration in their mental health in the days leading up to their disappearance; hallucinations, paranoia, and eventually a total psychotic break."

"Any bodies?" Desai asked.

"No, but the same thing has been occurring in this area for hundreds of years; every few decades another batch of between twelve and twenty two people go missing, all in a short space of time. The other information I've been given suggests that this phenomenon moves around East Anglia, but it seems that it is centred in this location.

"I'm requesting assistance to investigate this event before it goes dormant for another thirty or so years; maybe we can put a stop to it before anyone else dies."

"But nobody has died, have they, Helen?" Desai asked, and her heart sank. "People go mad and run away from their lives all the time; in fact, it's a wonder that more people don't, in my opinion. Your request is denied, Dr Mickelson, and I will be informing Harper in case you try to take this through the proper channels in an attempt to undermine my decision. Do you understand?"

"Dennis died investigating this!" Helen blurted out. "You didn't even do a fucking autopsy, so how can you be certain that he wasn't murdered?"

"Goodnight, Dr Mickelson," Desai said, his voice hard as polished granite. "Do not pursue this line of enquiry any further, or you will face disciplinary action; that's an order."

There was a click as the line went dead, and she just stared at the phone for a few moments in shock before slamming back into its cradle. Her hands trembled at the injustice of it all, but instead of letting her rage consume her, she harnessed it, condensing it into a sense of white hot determination.

"Fuck it," she muttered defiantly as she heard Geoff's car pull up outside. "I'll deal with this myself, off the books."

Besides, she thought as he came back into the room, hanging up his damp hat as he did so, *it's not the first time I've gone rogue.*

This time, however, I can't afford to get caught.

Chapter Eight – Somebody Super Like You

Ivy

Ivy lay back on the bed throwing and catching the tennis ball that she'd packed back in Oxford; having something to fiddle with always helped her to think more clearly. The rain pattered softly against the windows and she hoped that Charity's mystery errand was indoors, comfortably out of the inclement weather.

Aside from the startling wink from her reflection, her mysterious mirror visitor had not deigned to make themselves known again, and Ivy was beginning to grow impatient. *Kiki was always much better at wrangling us,* Ivy thought sadly, *but she's not here any more, so it's down to me.*

"Look," she said, sitting up to address the mirror, "we can do this the hard way, or we can take the path of least resistance and give ourselves the best start possible."

She stared at her reflection for a moment, but nothing happened.

"Won't you at least tell me your name?" Ivy asked wearily.

The woman in the mirror matched her movements for a few more seconds, but then she cocked her head to one side, a curious expression on her face.

"Aren't you afraid?" she asked, and Ivy noticed that the newcomer's voice seemed to emanate from the mirror, rather than from inside as Edgar's would. *How strange.*

"No, I'm not," Ivy said, getting to her feet. "I'm already used to being accompanied in my head, so this is nothing new. What is unusual, however, is that you have *my* appearance; don't you have one of your own?"

"I'm afraid that's not how it works, darling," the newcomer said with a flamboyant sigh. "I'm doomed to be a mere reflection, at least where appearances are concerned. Trust me on this; I'm a damn sight older than I look."

"So what are you?" Ivy asked, tracing her fingers along the mirror's surface. "And, more importantly, what does that make me?"

"You can think of me as a curse, if you like; most do."

"Vagaries won't cut it with me," Ivy said firmly. "If you don't tell me, I'll just have to find out myself."

She reached into the recesses of her own mind and, aside from the distant presence of Edgar, realised she was alone. Ivy's lips turned upward in a quiet smile as she turned the gaze of her third eye outward and immediately found the stranger in the mirror.

So, you're not a part of me at all, she thought, *but something attached to me instead.*

She traced a delicate mental finger through the murky waters of the mirror-creature's mind, and was flooded with a wealth of experiences spanning hundreds, if not thousands, of years. The newcomer's eyes widened and she took a step back from the mirror, a horrified expression on her face.

"You... you're a telepath?" she asked, almost fearfully, and Ivy nodded.

"Among other things," she said enigmatically.

"What's the matter? Why are you frightened all of a sudden?"

"I'm not supposed to interact with telepaths," whispered the stranger. Ivy folded her arms and adopted the stance of a stern schoolmarm, which immediately terrified the creature in the mirror. "No, please! I'll be good! Please don't hurt me!"

Before Ivy could say or do anything in response to the sudden change in the stranger's demeanour, the mirror-creature collapsed into a sobbing, screaming heap. Ivy reached out with her mind again, more carefully this time, and allowed the stranger's pain to flow through her.

Images of psychic violence, unimaginable torture, and centuries of isolation rushed past her in a flood of trauma and memory. What would've once swept her away now broke over her, like water on a rock; Michaela's death had changed something deep inside her, and she now felt more powerful than before, as if some kind of block had been removed.

I am awake for the first time in decades, Ivy realised.

The creature had clearly been tormented to the point of madness at some stage in its inexplicably long life, and the only thing that Ivy could feel towards it was compassion.

Not it, she corrected, *but her. She is a woman, as much as I am.*

"There's no need to be afraid of me," she said softly, crouching down before the mirror. "I'm not going to hurt you; that's a promise. Will you tell me your name, please?"

"You can just reach into my thoughts and rip it out," the stranger said, now looking at Ivy with wary eyes.

"You don't need me to tell you."

"I'm not going to violate your autonomy like that," Ivy said. "I won't touch your mind again without your consent; that's another promise. I would like you to tell me your name, but you don't have to if you aren't ready. My name is Ivy Livingston, and the other person you can feel in my head is Edgar Wainwright. There used to be another, Michaela Inglewood, but she died not long ago.

"If you're going to be a part of our system, I want you to feel welcome." She placed a hand on the mirror. "I'm not fighting who I am any longer; not any part of me, regardless of where they're from. We're stronger together, after all."

"You're serious, aren't you?" The strange newcomer sat up and looked at Ivy with bewildered eyes. "You're unlike anyone I've ever met, you know."

"Hopefully I'll be a trendsetter," Ivy said with a smile. "We can go as fast or as slow as you need; we've got all night, and then the rest of our lives together after that."

"Where have you been all my life?" asked the stranger with a tearful chuckle.

"Preparing for this moment," Ivy said, smiling at her double, "and I am so glad that I get to meet you."

"Likewise, Ivy Livingston," the stranger replied, reaching towards the surface of the mirror. "You can call me Max."

Before Ivy could reply, Max reached through the mirror and shook her hand.

"I'm still not sure I follow," Ivy said as Max paced around the room after trying to explain her ability to physically manifest for the fifth time. "Why don't you skip the mathematics and the physics, and just give me the simple version?"

"I..." Max hesitated. "Don't you want the full version?"

"We'll have plenty of opportunity for that in the fullness of time," Ivy said, "so let's walk before we can run, okay?"

"Darling, you have the patience of a saint," Max said with a chuckle. "Most of my previous... let's say *hosts*... have been more eager to kill me than understand me. I'm used to antagonistic relationships, especially where the humans I'm bonded to are concerned!"

"So you aren't human?" Ivy asked, and Max paused to consider this.

"I guess I'm not," she said after a lengthy pause. "I was supposed to be an elevated form of human, at least at my inception, but I think things have changed considerably in the intervening years."

"So you were created deliberately?" *This is getting interesting,* Ivy thought. *Kiki would've gone wild for this.*

"Who is Kiki?" Max asked, and Ivy raised an eyebrow. "I'm not pushing into your head; it's almost as if your surface thoughts are more obvious than others, and she's in them almost constantly."

Ivy paused for a moment, went over what Max had said, and aligned her conclusions before speaking.

"Kiki was Michaela; the one who died recently." Ivy spoke slowly and deliberately, watching Max's reaction for any signs of distress. "I'm going to make an educated guess that you can emulate the powers of the humans that you are bonded to, given that you're already displaying an early form of telepathy. Am I correct?"

Max nodded. *Right, I think I'm getting a handle on this.*

"As for accidentally listening to my mind, around here we refer to that as *thinking loudly*; sometimes a person's thoughts are too obvious not to overhear. If it's going to distress you, I will make an effort to still my mind when you're around."

"That's okay, darling," Max said with a sad smile, "but it's sweet of you to consider my comfort."

"Your well-being is important to me."

"I've picked up a lot of gifts over the years," Max said quietly. "I could try and bring her, Kiki, back, if that's what you wanted."

"No," Ivy said firmly. "Her death had meaning, and it gave her some closure after a life of horror; the decent thing to do is let her rest."

"As you wish," Max said. "Most people would leap at the opportunity to revive someone they lost, you know."

"I'm not most people," Ivy said, before attempting to redirect the conversation back to their original topic. "So, we've established that you aren't human; is that part of what allows you to manifest like this?"

"I suppose it is. I'm a conscious being attached to you, and a couple of others, at all times; your physical location determines what I can perceive and where I can be at any given moment." Max sighed heavily. "That isn't exactly how it works, but it's good enough for now.

"One might be able to argue that I exist as a perpetual dream attached to the people I'm bonded to, with the potential to become real at any time, but the truth is that I'm closer to being a kind of biological machine that exists in your body, all linked up by some kind of psychic connection. For the most part, you're the only one who can perceive me, but I can either take control of the host organism or manifest myself physically."

"And how can you manage that?" Ivy asked, absolutely fascinated by this latest addition to her life.

"I can use the latent power that arises from your connection to the Tangle, among other things, and focus it into organising the molecules in the environment around you into a simulacrum that I can control." Max gave Ivy a playful wink. "I'm neither dead nor alive, you see, but a terrible third thing that I can't quite explain.

"But I guess you could call this," she said, gesturing to her body, "a kind of flesh golem that I'm piloting, instead of a true manifestation of a physical form. It's just a puppet that I can operate with my mind, truth be told."

"That's incredible!" Ivy said, getting to her feet. "Have you always been able to do that?"

"No," Max admitted. "It was only in the past few decades that I bonded with someone who's able to externalise parts of his mind, and after that it was simply a process of trial and error."

"One final question," Ivy said, still awed at Max's unbelievable talent. "When you're with the man who can split himself, are you also a man?"

"I guess so," Max said. "I look like him, at least. Does it matter?"

"Only if you want it to," Ivy said. "Of course, if you-"

Her words were cut off as Charity Walpole burst into the room, wild eyed and soaked to the bone. Ivy looked around, ready to explain Max's presence, but the other woman was already gone. She glanced at the mirror, and her reflection winked back at her.

"Thank you for the enlightening conversation, darling. We'll pick this up again another time," Max said, before blowing her a kiss. As soon as the gesture was completed, Ivy's reflection returned to its normal state.

What a strange night, she thought, slightly bemused.

"What are you looking at?" Charity asked, looking at the silvered surface. "Is everything alright?"

"I'm fine, Charity," Ivy said gently. "You're completely drenched, though; are you okay?"

"I... I saw the most awful thing, Ivy," Charity said, her voice growing almost impossibly quiet. She held out a trembling hand and opened it to reveal a collection of bloody fingernails. "I'm not sure if I saw someone get killed tonight, or if something far worse happened to them."

She stared into the middle distance, her uncovered eyes wide.

"Charity, sweet pea, what can I do for you?" Ivy asked, and it took Charity a moment to respond, as if she was waking from a deep dream.

"Just get some sleep. We start in the morning." She began to remove her wet clothes, heading in the direction of their bed.

"Darling what are you talking about?" Ivy asked, and Charity responded with a firmness in her tone that Ivy hadn't heard in months.

"I need you rested, Ivy," she said as she climbed underneath the duvet. "Come first light, we've got a case to solve."

Chapter Nine – In Her Father's Footsteps

Charity

"Charity, Ivy," Helen said as the two women entered the kitchen on the morning after the funeral, "I need to talk to you about something important."

"There was a killing last night, Helen," Charity said as she set about making herself a cup of strong, black coffee. "No offence, but that needs to take priority today, I'm afraid."

"A killing, or a vanishing?" Helen said, entirely too calmly for Charity's liking. She whirled around and stared at the elderly Blight.

"Tell me everything, Helen; leave nothing out," Charity said, and Helen gestured to a pile of books and papers on the kitchen table. "What are those?"

"Other vanishings, all from this area in the past three hundred years or so. These," she said, handing a sheaf of missing posters to Charity, "all occurred in the past sixty days. Geoff said that your father was looking into these events when he died."

"He did?" Charity asked, her eyes wide with shock behind her dark glasses. Helen nodded as Charity rifled through the posters, drinking in the details. *Look once, see everything.* "We need to contact the Ministry; they need to send us reinforcements."

"Charity-" Helen began, but Charity cut her off.

"Helen, I can't play politics right now; who or whatever is behind this might have killed my father!" She slammed the posters on the kitchen table. "Now go and get Desai on the phone, protocol be damned!"

"Charity," Helen said, clearly exhausted already, "I'm trying to tell you that I called him yesterday, and that there's no help coming. I've been told to drop the matter entirely, or risk disavowal. I'm assuming the same threat applies to the two of you."

"Then what do we do?" Ivy asked, sitting at the table with an unhappy look on her burned face.

"We keep investigating," Charity said without so much as a heartbeat's hesitation, "and we fly under the radar as we do it. They can't disavow us if we don't get caught."

"It sounds like you've already formulated a plan," Helen said, almost proudly. "Are you going to include Constance in it?"

"Not unless I absolutely have to," Charity replied. "This is a murky situation at the very best, and bringing in any Amberlight assistance, no matter how slight, could cause a rather serious incident that could shatter the fragile peace between them and the Ministry.

"I won't be held responsible for a war that tears this country in two." Her shoulders slumped slightly. "I wish we had more help, but the three of us will have to do this on our own."

"Where do you want me to start?" Ivy asked. "I can listen to the aether no matter where I go, so just send me wherever you need me the most."

Where I want you is by my side, always, Charity thought loudly enough for Ivy to hear, but the words she spoke were ones of practicality, not romantic sentiment.

"I need the two of you to pound the pavements and find out what the locals know; I need witness statements more than anything, especially the most recent disappearances. There's a pattern here, but I can't see what it is yet." She looked at Ivy and gave her a grim smile. "Let Helen do the talking; she's more experienced in this kind of fieldwork and knows what to look for."

"I will," Ivy said, "and that frees me up to catch any stray thoughts they might be trying to conceal from us."

"Brilliant." Charity then turned to Helen. "Are you willing to bluff your way into the morgue if any bodies turn up? I know you're not technically assigned to this case, but you are a medical doctor and the remains of any victims will yield vital clues."

"Of course, Charity. Ivy, are you a medical doctor?"

"I'm a psychiatrist, but I've got enough experience to assist on an autopsy if necessary." Ivy gave Helen a bright smile. "I did pioneer the surgical removal of the Nightwalker fungus, after all."

"That you did," Charity said, her stomach churning uneasily as she remembered pulling the mycelia from beneath Mallory's skin. "You are an absolute ghoul at times."

"What are you going to do?" Helen asked, but her expression made Charity wonder if she knew already.

"I'm going to my father's house," she said, her voice trembling a little at the thought of what she had to do. "When Ghosts hide things they tend to stay hidden, at least from anyone who doesn't think like us. These posters can't be the sum total of Dad's work; he was far too skilled a detective for that to be it.

"I'll find his research, and then I'll go from there." Ivy handed Charity a cup of coffee and she took it gratefully. "One final thing, and then we can go our separate ways; whatever this thing is, I saw it last night."

"You did?" Ivy asked, looking at Charity with horrified eyes. "Why didn't you tell me?"

"I just wanted to get some sleep," she said, trying to avoid her girlfriend's gaze. "Even in the light of day, I don't really want to think about it, but it's important for you to know what we're dealing with."

Charity took a deep breath, but try as she might, the words just wouldn't come.

"It's a black dog, isn't it?" Helen asked after a while. Charity looked at her askance, suddenly filled with suspicion. "A monstrous one, with glowing eyes; I'm right, aren't I?"

Charity nodded slowly.

"You, uh," Helen cleared her throat awkwardly, "you used to have a recurring nightmare as a child about being chased through the countryside by a giant black dog with red eyes. You'd wake up screaming almost every night, almost impossible to console, and then one day the nightmares just stopped."

Charity stared at Helen, who met her gaze, even through the Ghost's dark glasses.

"You used to look so tired back then, and I'll bet that if you took those shades off you'd look just as tired now, wouldn't you?" Helen asked. Charity looked down at the table for a moment, and Helen went on. "You've started having the dreams again, haven't you?"

"How could you possibly know that?" Charity demanded. "I only ever told my mother about the dog, and even then, only when she woke me up from those awful dreams.

"It was the only kind thing she ever did for me."

"Charity, darling," Helen said quietly, "it wasn't Lin who held you after you had those nightmares; it was me."

Charity was cramming her fifth slice of marmalade on toast into her mouth as she walked towards the front door. She shuddered with dread as she heard the thundering of the rain; last night's drizzle had strengthened into a downpour once again.

"You're not thinking of walking to Den's place in *this*, are you?" Geoff asked from behind her, bouncing the keys to his car in his hand. "Come on, Charity, I'll give you a lift."

"You can't," she mumbled around a mouthful of toast as she turned on her heel to face him. "The Amberlight-"

"Connie's organisation only takes people like you," Geoff said with a wry smile. "I'm just an ordinary guy; a civilian, if you will. Surely my giving you a lift can't cause that much brouhaha?"

"I guess not," Charity said, finally swallowing the last of her breakfast. "Thanks, Uncle Geoff."

"Not a problem," he said, and they both went out into the rain. The roads were a little flooded, so the drive to Dennis's small cottage in Tharston took a bit longer than usual, but before too long Geoff was unlocking the front door.

Charity entered first and she thought she heard movement in his study, but it was impossible to tell over the sound of the rain. She took five quick steps along the narrow corridor and closed the door; if anyone was in there, they'd have to open a window to get out.

She reached up into the wooden beams and felt

around for a moment; her search was quickly
rewarded when her fingers closed around a tight
leather bundle. She brought it down and unwrapped it
with a smile. She strapped her father's combat and
throwing knives to her waist, chest, and legs, relishing
the feel of the well-worn leather-wrapped bone
handles under her fingers.

I always loved these, she thought. *I guess they're mine now.*

"How did you know those were there?" Geoff asked, clearly impressed. "Did Den tell you about them?"

"No," Charity admitted, "but it's where I would put them."

"Birds of a feather, it seems."

"I wish we were," Charity said sadly as she drew one of the blades and spun it deftly in her hand. "If we'd have been closer, I'm sure he would've told me about what was happening here."

"You had cancer, sweetheart," Geoff said, putting a reassuring hand on her shoulder. "He knew that you had enough on your plate as it was."

"I can't help but think that if I'd been here, he would still be alive." Charity sighed heavily and Geoff went to reply but she immediately held a finger to her lips, silencing him. She crossed the distance to the study door in a few soundless steps and flung the door open, blade poised to strike.

The room was empty.

"Nothing," she said softly. She turned back to her uncle. "Would you be kind enough to pop the kettle on, please? I think we're going to be here a while."

He nodded, and shuffled through to the kitchen as Charity entered the study; the beating heart of Dennis Walpole's home. Her eyes scanned over his desk, cabinets, and bookcase, looking for anything out of place.

A book immediately caught her attention; it protruded slightly from the shelf, disturbing the neat row of spines that faced out into the room. *Dad was a stickler for order amongst his books,* she thought, *and the dust has been disturbed.*

That book has been moved recently; today, perhaps.

She turned her attention away from the bookcase and began to busy herself at the desk, deliberately blocking the view of her hands with her body. There was a gentle rustling noise from behind her, much like the soft disturbance of a book slowly being moved. Charity leant back to stretch, tilting her glasses so that she caught a glimpse of the suspicious book in the reflection.

Gotcha.

She span around and slammed one hand into the book, smashing it against the back of the bookcase. There was a moment of soft resistance followed by a shrill cry of pain. With her free hand she reached over the top of the book and snared something thin and fragile in her dextrous fingers.

Charity flung the book aside and extracted the diminutive intruder. It dangled in the air as she held it by a set of iridescent fairy wings and thrashed its tiny hands in her direction. Its form was humanoid with skin unusually blue in colour; strangely, it wore a tiny flat cap and miner's overalls, although the material was almost completely translucent. Charity blinked in shock, surprised to see such a rare creature in the flesh.

"A pixie!?" she asked aloud. "What are you doing in my dad's study?"

"Waiting for you, you daft bint!" The pixie's voice was tinged with a Yorkshire accent, and something stirred deep in Charity's memory. "You took your fucking time!"

"Who are you?" she demanded, angrily shaking the tiny creature by its fragile wings. Geoff peered through the door to see what was going on. "Keep back, Geoff; it turns out we're not as alone as we thought we were!"

"Geoffrey, will you please tell your niece to let me go?" the pixie asked wearily. "And put the kettle on, will you? I could murder a brew."

"It's okay, Charity," Geoff said calmly. "That's just Henbane; they're a pal of your dad's."

You're the famous Henbane!?

Charity stared at her uncle in shock for a few seconds before placing the pixie on the desk, rather more roughly than she intended. Henbane shook out their wings and brushed down their translucent overalls with a huff.

"Tea's nearly brewed already," Geoff said, turning his attention to the pixie. "Remind me how you take it again?"

"Strong, with just a drop of milk, please."

"Sugar?" Geoff asked as Charity looked on, entirely nonplussed.

"Most definitely not!" Henbane said angrily, stamping one tiny foot for emphasis. "I may be a pixie, but I'm not some ducky boy from Islington!"

This day is the strangest of my life, Charity thought, *and it's barely noon.*

Chapter Ten – Beat the Street

Helen

"I hope Charity is coping alright," Ivy said as she looked through the kitchen window at the falling rain. "It's just been one thing after another, she's not had a moment to breathe ever since we got off the fucking train."

"How about you, Ivy?" Helen asked cautiously. "How are you holding up?"

"I'm doing fine, thank you," Ivy replied, almost defensively. "I'm more resilient than you might think."

"I'm glad to hear it." Helen drummed her fingers on the stack of books and papers anxiously. "Tell me, Ivy, after your altercation with Harper the other night, do you feel changed at all? Any new ways of thinking, or any striking divisions of personality that seem out of the ordinary?

"I'm only asking as a doct-"

"If you're going to pry, then at least ask about her by name," Ivy said sharply, cutting Helen off mid flow. The Blight blinked in surprise, and Ivy gave her an expectant look. "Well? We don't have all day, you know."

"How did you-"

"Telepath," Ivy said, tapping her temple sarcastically. "Are you actually awake yet, Helen, or do you need another cup of coffee?"

"There's no need to be rude!" Helen snapped, and Ivy scoffed. "What's so fucking funny?"

"You're prying into my mental state, and *I'm* the one being rude? Surely you can see the absurdity in that!"

Ivy winked at her reflection in the rain-streaked window. *There you are,* Helen thought. *Just as I suspected.*

"It's safe to assume that you've been introduced to Max, then?" Helen said, gesturing for her to sit. Ivy placed a hand on the back of her chair, but chose to remain standing. "Stubborn, aren't you?"

"My gift causes me to lose my physical capabilities if I overexert myself," Ivy said flatly. "I can see that I'll be leaning heavily on my cane before all this craziness is over, so please just let me enjoy the use of my legs whilst I can."

"It's that bad?" Helen asked, and Ivy nodded. "Oh; I had no idea. I'm sorry, please, stand as much as you like."

"No harm, no foul." Ivy cocked her head to one side. "So, how do you know about Max?"

"I've known him for decades now," Helen said, "or is it her, now that he... she, is inside you?"

"Gender is fluid; ever shifting definition and changing, like a river," Ivy replied sagely. "Max doesn't mind which pronouns you use, so go for whichever is easiest for you to follow."

"You speak as if you know him already," Helen said, folding her arms defensively. "He's not to be trusted; his mind is slippery, alien, and entirely unknowable."

Ivy frowned and leant forwards, fixing Helen with a piercing stare. *Her eyes are unsettling,* Helen thought. *I wish she would blink more often.*

"I'm curious what you think she actually is, Helen." Ivy continued to stare at her, and Helen was certain that she could see something shifting in the darkness of the woman's pupils; a mocking face, perhaps. "Go on, do tell; I'd like to know."

"I'm sure that you know that every prominent Cep family harbours a familial curse and-"

"She isn't a curse!" Ivy slammed a hand on the table for emphasis. "She's a living being and she has been through centuries of unrelenting hell; every generation telling the next one not to trust her, that she deserves the torment that she suffers... It sickens me."

"You can't believe what he tells you!" Helen said, her anger rising. "He's an accomplished liar, not to mention a killer, too!"

"And you aren't?" Ivy said hotly. "You hid so much from Charity, and I doubt your hands are cleaner than mine."

"I wasn't born to be a monster," Helen snapped, gesturing to Ivy's Lamplight tattoo.

"No, you weren't," Ivy said, completely unmoved by Helen's jab. "You chose to be one of your own free will, which is so much worse."

Fuck.

Helen sat back in her chair as if she'd been slapped by Ivy's words; they rang with truth and cut her to her very core. *Maybe Max has already got to her,* she thought, but in her heart she knew that this wasn't the case. *I shouldn't have started this conversation in the first place.*

"You're right about that," Ivy said softly, and Helen glared at her.

"Stay out of my fucking head!"

"I am. It's not my fault that you've not learned how to think inside the confines of your own skull instead of screaming every little thought you have into the void." Ivy sighed heavily. "So, Harper is my mother and... Silas, is it? He's my brother?"

"Half-brother," Helen snapped. "Harper is the only

blood that you both share; what a shame that it's so tainted."

"Who's my other parent?" Ivy asked, and Helen shrugged. "Does that mean that you don't know, or won't tell me?"

"I honestly don't know, but judging from your performance in Lamplight, it wasn't anyone particularly talented." Helen regretted her words as soon as she'd said them, and glanced at the floor, shamefaced.

What is wrong with me today?

"Charity always spoke so highly of you," Ivy said sadly, finally taking a seat at the table. "I hope that you'll be more your usual self when she gets back, or else she's going to be heartbroken. She's had enough shocks for a lifetime, Helen, so please try to be the person she needs you to be, even if that's just a false version of you.

"Hate me all you want, but please try to be kind to her; that's all I ask for."

Helen was speechless.

"As for Max, we spent several hours yesterday talking honestly and openly, and clear boundaries have been set." Ivy sighed heavily. "She isn't what you think; she's been through a lot of awful things and has only had that behaviour reinforced over many, many years."

"Why do you think I hate you?" Helen asked quietly.

"I can feel the grief pouring out of you, but the loathing is just as strong. It was present before we started speaking about Max, so it must be directed at me." Ivy's words were matter-of-fact, said with almost no emotion. "I assume that you think I'm not good enough for her, and maybe you're right. The important thing, however, is that she needs us to work together right now, so that's what we're going to do."

Ivy extended a scarred hand across the table.

"Truce?"

"I don't hate you," Helen said, but took Ivy's hand in hers all the same. "Dennis's death has brought up a lot of old hurts, and some wounds that I thought were healed are apparently just as fresh as they were when I first got them.

"I mean it, Ivy; I don't hate you."

Ivy did not reply, but gave her hand a gentle squeeze nonetheless.

"So, Dr Mickelson, where on earth do we start with all this?" Ivy released her hand and began to sift through the missing posters. "Do we go to each person in chronological order, or the police, or a third route that I haven't thought of yet?"

"We need to get a feel for the supernatural baseline of this place, and seeing as we aren't allowed to go to Connie or the twins about this, we'll have to get creative. Tell me, Ivy," Helen said as she remembered her conversation with Geoff the previous night, "what do you know about Druids?"

"Absolutely nothing," Ivy said, "aside from what I picked up from some New Age folks I was at uni with, but I'm guessing you mean the real thing?"

"I am indeed. Go and get your boots on; we're going for a stroll."

"In the rain?" Ivy asked, and Helen laughed at the grimace that crossed the younger woman's face.

"I've got a brolly." Helen gave Ivy a broad grin. "I promise I'll make it worth your while."

"How?" Ivy asked warily.

"Experience," Helen said with a chuckle as she got

to her feet. "This is going to be a real education."

The rain hammered on the umbrella as the two women trudged down the wet lanes of Bustards Green. Helen was moving slightly slower than she would've liked; Ivy was already leaning heavily on her cane, even though they had only been underway a short while.

"Do you need to take a break?" Helen asked Ivy, who shook her head.

"No, thank you; I'd much sooner be out of this than standing around in it." Ivy panted slightly as she walked. "I'm sorry, I thought that my recovery was further along than it actually is."

"Recovery?" Helen asked, confused. "Have you been ill?"

"Oh, no," Ivy said sheepishly. "My last mission nearly killed me, though."

"Where were you?" Helen asked, and when Ivy balked at the question, she let out a small chuckle. "I've the highest level of clearance, dear; I'll read the report eventually. Go on, what was your case?"

"Galaxy, Oregon."

Ivy's words stopped Helen in her tracks.

"Jesus Christ," Helen said softly. "That means you've only been back in the country for what, a week?"

"Nine days," Ivy said quietly. "I was on life support in hospital a fortnight ago. It was a rough few days, running around the mountains in the dark; we only just made it out alive."

"Why aren't you on leave?" Helen asked, serious now.

"I am," Ivy replied. "This isn't an official case, and

the two of us were planning to rest up at Connie's place, maybe take a trip to the beach; you know, normal holiday stuff."

Helen went to speak, but Ivy quickly silenced her.

"Don't you even think about telling me to drop out of this investigation," she said, her voice forceful enough to shake the raindrops from the umbrella. "Marsh is just as ill as I am, and he'd be down here in a fucking heartbeat if he knew what was going on. The Oxford Office is more like a family than anything else, and we look after each other, no matter what it takes."

"That sounds like the Hong Kong Office, back in the day," Helen said with a smile. "Back when Lin and Harper were less... uptight than they are now. I guess age affects us all differently, and Lin has to deal with life without the smoothness that comes from the occasional white lie-"

"Druids," Ivy said, rather impatiently. "You were going to tell me about the Druids before we meet them."

"Yes, sorry," Helen said as the two women began walking once more. "Funerals always make me nostalgic, but I'll try and stay focussed."

"Much appreciated."

"So," Helen said, pleased to have something concrete to focus on, "the Ministry likes to believe that it has, and indeed is, the final word on the supernatural in this country. Unfortunately, this just isn't the case; organisations have been around for millennia, operating in the shadows and bumping back against the horrors of the night.

"The British Circle of Druids is one of these, as is the National Warlock Convocation."

"Warlocks?" Ivy asked, a puzzled look on her face. "I thought that regular humans couldn't perform supernatural feats without the conditions necessary for magic to occur?"

"Warlocks aren't ordinary humans; they come under the category of semi-humans. In order to be recognised as a Warlock, a person must have at least one non-human parent, such as a Rusałka or Strix, or at least a direct descent from one. With me so far?" Ivy nodded and Helen went on. "It is from this non-human connection that their powers arise, so a Warlock's talent is entirely based on what bloodlines they come from."

"That would mean that Mallory and Francis are Warlocks," Ivy said, and Helen shook her head.

"They meet the blood qualification," Helen said, "but there's a whole bunch of politicking and funny handshakes required before you can be an *Official* Warlock. Mallory and Francis would actually be ineligible because they work for the Ministry."

"I'm beginning to get a feeling that the Ministry would prefer to be the only game in town," Ivy said darkly, "and between you and me, I'm glad it isn't."

"I completely agree," Helen said. "A little healthy opposition does wonders to root out corruption. So, as I was saying, Warlocks are an insular bunch, and particularly haughty about who joins their ranks.

"This often puts them at loggerheads with the Druids, who are a much more relaxed group. They'll take just about anyone, Cep or otherwise, and their power lies in an extensive knowledge of both the natural and supernatural world, along with some extremely complex rites and rituals. Whether Druidic Magic is actual magic is an open debate, but they can call upon some incredibly old and powerful forces, so their skills are not to be sniffed at.

"They're ambivalent towards the Ministry," Helen said as they came to a stop at the gate of a tiny little farm shop tea room, "so we tend to leave them alone, at least until they cause an accident or we need information. I've always liked the Druids, and we tend to get on quite well."

"So their true power lies in hiding in plain sight?" Ivy asked, and Helen nodded. "Surely they'd still need somewhere to gather, right?"

"Absolutely," Helen said. "There are Circles within Circles, and the whole organisation is surprisingly complex."

"How do they keep everyone in line?" Ivy asked, shifting from foot to foot to avoid standing in a puddle.

"Ask them yourself," Helen said, gesturing to the little tea room. "We're here."

"But this is just a farm shop with a cafe attached!"

"It's also the meeting place for the Tharston Druidic Circle," Helen said with a grin. "Come on, let's get out of the rain."

"Anything I should know before we go in?" Ivy asked, clearly nervous.

"Make sure you give your boots a good scrape before going inside," Helen said playfully. "For nature lovers, they're surprisingly funny about mud."

Chapter Eleven – Old Time Legends

Charity

"Here you go," Geoff said as he handed a cup of steaming hot tea to Charity, followed by a thimble sized cup for Henbane. The glittery-eyed pixie nodded curtly at him, and took a long sip of tea before letting out a groan of pleasure.

"Brilliant stuff, thank you muchly."

"Thanks, Uncle Geoff," Charity said quietly, unable to take her eyes off Henbane. The tiny creature was barely five inches in height, wings included, but Charity knew that they could shrink and grow at will; disappearing to little more than a pinprick of light or standing up to two feet tall, as the situation required.

"Take a picture, it'll last longer," Henbane said roughly.

"I'm not a theosophist," Charity said, a cheeky little grin on her face. "I was just wondering why none of the stories I've heard about you mention the fact that you're a pixie."

"It probably wasn't relevant," Henbane said, taking another sip from the miniature cup. It, ironically enough, was decorated with a tiny, albeit highly detailed, fairy motif. "We were Ravenblades together; surely that's the more important detail?"

"I guess so," Charity said, leaning back with a sigh. "Why didn't you come out when you realised it was us?"

"I didn't want to end up with one of those deep in my guts," Henbane said, gesturing at the knives that Charity wore. "You Lamplight types are all a bit fucked in the head, so they say; prone to violence, that's what I heard."

"Not all of us," Charity said, bristling slightly as Geoff raised a curious eyebrow. "As for you, Uncle, I'll fill you in on Lamplight later; it's not really relevant right now."

"In your own time," Geoff said cheerfully. "I must say that it's quite exciting to be a part of a proper mystery! I feel like some kind of Scandi-noir detective."

"You read too many books," Henbane quipped. "Books don't do you any good, besides being a convenient place to hide; too full of words for my liking. Far too many of the squiggly things."

"Letters?" Charity offered, and Henbane nodded. "You don't like *letters*?"

"Don't trust 'em. If you must note something down, pictographs all the way. Letters; eurgh!" Henbane shuddered for dramatic effect.

I must've hit my head last night, Charity thought as she sipped her tea, *and this is a hallucination occurring as I bleed out on the pavement in Long Stratton.*

"Why didn't you come over to the Big House?" Geoff asked. "Surely that would've been the best place to wait for Charity?"

"I couldn't," Henbane said, pointing to the window. "It's raining, see?"

"Pixies can drown in the rain," Charity said, answering Geoff's impending question. "They're surprisingly robust for their size, but are comparatively fragile alongside other Ceps. I'm guessing the phone was too unwieldy for you?"

"Aye," Henbane said with a nod, "but now that

you're here, we can pick up where Dennis left off. I assume you've seen the missing posters?"

"I have," Charity said darkly, "and I saw someone get taken last night. The Ministry don't want to get involved, so this one is off the books, I'm afraid."

She squirmed uncomfortably in her seat as she prepared to ask the most important question of her investigation; one that had been burning in her brain for over a fortnight.

"Henbane, did you see my father die?" Charity's heart fell as the pixie shook their head. "You must've been in the house, though; do you have any information for me at all?"

"I was upstairs," Henbane said softly, taking off their cap in respect for the dead, "and I heard a bit of a kerfuffle down in the kitchen. By the time I got down here, Dennis was on the floor, dead. I hid when Lin turned up, and I heard the paramedics mention a heart attack, or a possible stroke.

"In all honesty, Charity, in the time it took me to get down here, an assailant could've easily slipped away without a trace." Henbane sighed sadly. "I wish I'd been able to do something."

"I think he was murdered," Charity said decisively. "In fact, I'm certain of it."

"Charity, darling," Geoff said, gently placing a hand on her shoulder, "we don't know that for sure. He was an old, unwell man and-"

"It's a bit fucking convenient, though, isn't it, Geoff?" Charity snapped, pushing his hand from her shoulder. "He's looking into all these vanishings, and then he just so happens to have a fatal heart attack right as the pieces start to fit together; that's rather improbable, isn't it?"

"Sometimes people just die, Charity," Geoff muttered. "There's no rhyme or reason to it."

"And sometimes they get murdered, especially if they're in this line of work!" Charity retorted, and Geoff fell silent. The sound of the pouring rain filled the room, sending a chill creeping down Charity's spine. She turned to Henbane, who had just finished their tea with a long, loud slurp. "Are you with me on this?"

"Until the bitter end," the pixie said, placing a tiny hand on their faintly glowing chest, "come what may."

"Then let's gather what information we can and head back to Walpole Manor," Charity said, the drumming of her fingers perfectly in time with the rhythm of the falling rain. "I'm sure that you'd appreciate a change of scene and a nice, warm orangery to lounge in?"

"Nothing better in the world," Henbane said with a grin, which faltered all too quickly. "Charity, I should warn you that your father and I didn't get very far with our research; we scoured every single inch of the surrounding area and came up with absolutely no evidence."

"I found these," Charity said, fishing the fingernails out of her coat and placing them on the table. "Besides, I saw the creature that took the poor girl these are from."

"You saw it!" exclaimed Henbane, almost falling down with shock. "Hell, girl, you've been here barely three days and you're already weeks ahead of where we were!"

"Just the right place at the right time," Charity said with a sheepish grin. "It happens to me a lot."

"Well of course it does," Geoff said with a warm smile, putting an arm around her shoulders. "Den always said that you were a natural born detective, and that you had a real knack for finding evidence and leads that no-one else could."

"I've been in this game my whole life," Charity said with a grateful smile. "I guess some of it must've sunk in at some point."

"I'm sure it has, along with so many other things that life has taught you." He gave her a quick hug and then looked at the pixie on the table. "Pass me your cup, Henbane, and I'll give these a quick scrub before we leave.

"Even though a man's no longer with us, there's still no excuse for leaving him a dirty kitchen."

The rain stopped as the trio passed through the wrought iron gates, arriving back at Walpole Manor. Charity let out a loud sigh of relief and was out of the car the moment Geoff stopped, laughing and dancing in the clear, chilly air.

"Charity, darling," Connie said, opening the door as if she'd been waiting for them, "you've a visitor. He's currently in the orangery, but I can send him away if you'd like."

Why do I never get to enjoy a single uncomplicated moment?

"Who is it?" Charity asked, letting her carefree joy slip away into the brisk January breeze.

"It's Reggie, love," Connie said, her tone apologetic. Charity's face set in a hard frown, and her aunt immediately tried to defuse the tension. "I'll get rid of him, darling; I'm sorry, I should've known there was no need to ask."

"Don't," Charity said sharply. "I'll see him; he can explain why he thought it was acceptable to turn up to

Dad's funeral, unannounced and uninvited."

She strode towards the front door as Geoff and Henbane exited the car, slipping off her wet boots as she reached the porch. Charity glanced at her aunt as she passed, who was looking at her fearfully.

"I won't spill any blood on your property, Aunt Connie," she said softly, "but there's a fair chance that I'm going to hit him. I need to make sure that he gets the message this time."

"I don't mind if you make a mess," Connie whispered, palming a small knife to Charity, "as long as you clean up after yourself."

"Thank you," Charity said gratefully before heading through the interior of Walpole Manor in the direction of the Orangery. *The fuck does he want from me?* Charity wondered, spinning the blade idly in her hand. *Regardless of what happens, this will be the last time he sees my face.*

I'll make sure of that.

"Charity!" Reggie said warmly as she walked into the plant-filled room. Unlike when she'd seen him at her father's funeral, his horns and tail were on full display; the latter twitched excitedly when he saw her, and she couldn't help her shudder of discomfort.

"Why are you here?" she said softly, tucking the blade up her sleeve and out of sight. *If he so much as tries to touch me, he's losing that fucking tail.*

"I thought you might want a friendly face around during your father's funeral, and maybe we could-" Reggie stepped forward and placed a hand on her shoulder. Charity immediately punched him in the stomach, hard, and brought the palmed knife up to his face, holding the blade mere millimetres from his eye.

"You *do not* touch me," she hissed. "You will *never*

touch me again, Reggie, and I will make sure that you die awfully if you try. Do you understand me?"

He looked at her, clearly upset and confused, and she let out a frustrated scream before shoving him away from her. He stumbled over his own tail and fell clumsily on the tiled floor. Charity twirled the blade in her hand absent-mindedly as she stalked back and forth, a prisoner to her own rage.

"Charity, I didn't mean to upset you," he said pleadingly, and reached out in her direction. She roared at the top of her lungs before stamping on the fingers of his outstretched hand. He quickly snatched it back from beneath her boot and cradled his hand against his chest. "Why do you hate me so much?"

"Why don't you just fucking kill yourself, already?" Charity demanded as she tossed the knife at his feet. "You're the last one left, Reggie, so why not follow all the others instead of hounding my steps like a kicked puppy?"

"Were you always this horrible?" he whispered, and she dropped down into a crouch, her sunglasses level with his eyeline.

"No, Reggie; I wasn't, and I'm still not." She sighed heavily. "I'm sorry that they did this to you, but you need to stop making it my problem."

"But it hurts so much when you're not near me!" Reggie protested, and Charity gestured to the blade once again.

"Just ask me, Reg, and I'll make it stop," she said quietly. "It would genuinely be a relief for both of us."

"I thought about bringing you some flowers," he muttered, but stopped when she flinched at his words. "Would that really be so terrible?"

"Reggie," Charity asked tearfully, "do you actually

remember what's wrong with you? I know you've always had trouble keeping what's real and what isn't straight in your head."

"I..." His nervous smile faltered. "I'm not sure any more."

"Do you want me to tell you?" Charity asked, and he nodded. "It's going to hurt, Reg; it hurts you every single time."

"Please, tell me." His voice was barely audible. "Help me to understand."

It won't stick, she thought sadly, *but it'll get rid of him for now.*

Start with the easy stuff.

"Your name is Reginald Kellogg, and you were my partner when Joseph was taking some time away from the Ministry. We met in the Youth Academy, when we were still children; we were friends.

"You are a creature called a Familiar," she said, mentally preparing herself for what was to come. "You were designed as part of a Ministry eugenics program that ran parallel to Lamplight; you are a hybrid of Dryads, Djinn, Pixies, and dozens of other species. You were bred to achieve a specific goal, Reggie.

"Do you remember what that was?"

"Parasympathetic Adaptation," he said and she nodded. "Whenever I form a close bond with someone, I gain a gift or ability that is complementary to theirs. These abilities are permanent, but they wax and wane depending on who I'm currently closest to."

"And?" Charity asked.

"I'm not sure," Reggie admitted. "I thought that was it."

"Your ability means that you form an obsessive bond

with anyone that you derive a gift from," she said, her shoulders sagging heavily as she spoke. "You can't ever have an equal relationship with anyone, Reggie, because you become biologically bonded so easily, even in parasocial relationships. You were specifically designed to be in constant physical distress if you are not near one of your bound, which is why the Familiar Project has encountered an almost one hundred percent suicide rate in the decades after it ended.

"You're the last one left, Reg."

"You don't miss me?" he asked sadly, and she shook her head. "Not at all?"

"You tried to attack me, Reggie, when we were out on a mission," Charity said, trembling slightly. "I know you can't help it, but it's why you were expelled from the Ministry and it's why you aren't allowed to see me. They gelded you the last time you tried, and I hoped that would be enough for you to come to your senses.

"I shouldn't have spoken up in your defence, Reggie; maybe then they would've given you peace instead of continuing your torment." Charity got to her feet, picking up the knife as she did so. "I'm sorry that I keep having to hurt you, Reg, but you don't leave me any choice."

She gestured in the direction of the front door.

"Get out of here, Reggie, and don't come back." He hesitated, but she tightened her grip on the blade. "Go!"

"I'm sorry," he mumbled as he rushed past her and out of Walpole Manor. Charity simply stood in the humidity of the Orangery, sweating and crying in equal measure.

I'll see you soon, Reggie, she thought despondently.

"Charity," called her aunt after a short while, "are you alright?"

"I'm unhurt," she replied, which was only half true. "I always feel so horrid whenever I see him. His presence just brings back so many awful memories. I have no idea what to do with my day, now; I'm far too fucking worked up to even think about looking into the disappearances.

"What do you do to keep yourself sane, Connie?"

"I ride," she said decisively. "I swing my leg over one of my bikes and I let the lanes just swallow me up until I feel better. It's good medicine."

"If you say so," Charity said, barely louder than a mumble.

"I know so," Connie said, taking the younger Ghost by the arm, "and I'm going to prove it to you. By the time I'm done with you, you'll feel right as rain."

"I hate the rain," Charity said with a strained smile, but as Connie led her towards the bike shed, she realised that she was starting to feel a little better already.

Unfortunately for her, the delicate sense of peace blossoming in her heart was not to last.

Chapter Twelve – All for Freedom and for Pleasure

Ivy

"This is a very strange place," Ivy said idly, delicately cutting into an exquisitely moist slice of Black Forest Gateaux with a silver cake fork as she did so, relishing the light, springy texture of the sponge. "Are these people really Druids?"

"What makes you doubt me?" Helen asked with a wry smile.

"It's a bit heavy on the pink china and paper doilies," Ivy said, letting out a quiet chuckle before putting the cake in her mouth. She chewed slowly, groaning in delight as she did so. "Helen, this is fucking amazing."

"Druids do tend to enjoy the simple pleasures," she said through a mouthful of her own confection, "and the Tharston lot are a special breed, or at least Dennis used to say so."

"Tell me about Lamplight," Ivy said, blind-siding Helen completely.

"Ivy, we're here to-"

"Tell me," she said forcefully, and she felt the part of her brain that had once held Michaela's share of their gift quiver. *Interesting.* "I deserve to know, especially as you have clearance."

"It's because I have clearance that I can't tell you," Helen replied, almost pleading.

"We're not here as Ministry Agents," Ivy reminded her, "so it will just be two friends having a pleasant, confidential chat."

"Ivy, you really don't want to know."

"I didn't want to be in it either," she retorted, stabbing her fork into her cake with unnecessary violence, "but that didn't stop them then, so don't let concern for my well-being hold you back now."

Helen went to protest, but after a moment's consideration her shoulders slumped in resignation and she shovelled more of her lemon drizzle cake into her mouth.

"Fuck it," she said sadly through the sticky dessert, "I was against it from the start, and there's nothing to be gained by keeping their secrets any longer. What do you want to know?"

"Let's start right at the beginning," Ivy said, glancing at Max as she was reflected in the handle of the fork. "How were we selected?"

"It varied. Some of you were bred for purpose, as part of a genetic experiment. Others were orphans with rare gifts, and some were straight up sold to the Project. Some, like Charity and Prudence, were from prestigious families who wished to curry favour with the Ministry."

"And which was Charity?" Ivy asked, leaning forwards.

"I already told you..." Helen's voice trailed off as Ivy reached into her mind, raising her eyebrows in accusation.

"Don't lie to me, Helen." Ivy withdrew her mind and asked again. "Which was Charity?"

"She was what we referred to as a *Legacy Candidate*, because of her parentage, but she was originally conceived as part of a genetic experiment to create more Seers." Helen sighed. "I oversaw that whilst in the Hong Kong Office.

"I'm not sure if Charity knows that part, though."

"Let's keep it that way," Ivy replied. "At least for now; she's had enough difficulty regarding family to last a lifetime."

"We really should be following up on our leads," Helen said anxiously, but Ivy just smiled at her.

"All in good time," Ivy replied, letting her mind run over the Druids in the little tea shop, lifting fragments of information from them as she went. "I'm guessing that I'm one of the pure genetic experiments?"

"You are." Helen's eyes flicked to her plate. "I'm sorry about what I said earlier, Ivy."

"Water under the bridge," Ivy replied. "What's done is done. Now, tell me about what they did to us."

"I'm not familiar with the training they gave you, I'm afraid." Helen shifted nervously. "Is that what you mean?"

Ivy frowned at her, her disappointment plain on her face.

"Fine," Helen said after a lengthy pause. "Do you want to know about the accelerant or the Mindlock Protocol?"

"Both," Ivy said, "and I'm assuming that they're linked, so we'll start with the accelerant."

"Did Max mention these to you?" Helen asked warily.

"No," Ivy said. "Harper was thinking about them just before I glassed her."

"You shouldn't have done that, Ivy," Helen chastised. "She's the Deputy Director-"

"Tell me about the accelerant."

"Fine. It was an experimental compound designed to stimulate the development or evolution of a Cep's gift, ideally over the course of several years. Every single

Lamplight subject was given the drug in the hopes that they would become the most powerful Ceps in the world." Helen shook her head. "It was a fucking stupid idea, and we don't even know if it worked; we didn't even know how it would manifest.

"Some things are better left to Mother Nature."

"And the Mindlock?" Ivy said, her suspicions growing with every passing second.

"They didn't want you developing too fast, so a mental block was installed in every subject; one so severe that only death could accidentally remove it. It was designed to blunt your gift during training in order to allow you to safely develop into the perfect weapons.

"Then, when you were cleared for fieldwork, the block was to be removed." Helen gave Ivy a sad smile. "Unfortunately, the block still remains in all of you; it was one of the concessions that Harper accepted when the Project self-destructed."

"It'll be in my head until I die?" Ivy asked carefully.

"I'm afraid so," Helen replied.

No wonder I've been feeling so different lately, Ivy thought. *Did Kiki's death remove the block? Am I on the cusp of changing once again?*

"One last question," Ivy said, "and then we'll get on with our investigation."

"Go ahead."

"What did Dennis Walpole look like?"

"Why would you need to know that?" Helen asked, and Ivy looked at the silent pale man, dressed in a lurid shirt and wearing dark sunglasses who had been silently watching the Blight ever since they sat down. His gaze had not left her for a moment, and there was one word that kept coming into Ivy's mind to describe

his appearance.
Bleached.
"Ivy?" Helen repeated.
The silent man said nothing, and Ivy looked back at the oblivious doctor.
"Humour me."

"How many dead people are there?" Michaela asked the woman who sat alongside her on the bed, gently stroking her hair. "In the whole world, I mean?"
"I'm not sure, Kätzchen," the woman said gently. "Why do you ask?"
"You said that one day I'll be able to see them all," Michaela said eagerly. "I want to know how many there will be, so they all get a turn to talk to me."
"Such a silly little thing," the woman said with a sweet laugh. "There are millions and millions, Kätzchen; it would take forever to speak to them all. Not to mention that not everyone lingers after they die."
"Where do they go?"
"No one knows," she replied, laying Michaela down in her bed. "There are theories and guesses, but nothing more certain than that. Do you think about dying a lot, Kätzchen?"
"No, but you do." Michaela looked up at the woman's youthful face and frowned. "Your mind feels a lot older than you look, Dr Prentiss."
"I'm an old soul, or so they say," Prentiss said softly. She tucked the covers up to Michaela's chin. "Remember, little one, you only have to call me Dr Prentiss when we're out of this room. In here, you can call me-"
"Mother!" Michaela said with an excited giggle, and

Prentiss nodded gently.

"Yes," she muttered as she stroked the little girl's hair affectionately. "My own flesh and blood, at last. I have wanted a child for so many years, Kätzchen, and you are my little miracle. I am so lucky to have you."

"I love you, Mother," Michaela said, and Prentiss kissed her softly in the centre of her forehead.

"And I, you, sweet child. Get some sleep, little one; tomorrow we continue your training in earnest."

"What will I be learning?" Michaela asked eagerly, too excited to sleep.

"I will show you how to find a mountaintop in your mind," Prentiss said kindly. "From there, my daughter, you will be able to do anything."

Anything.

"Ivy?" Helen asked, reaching across the table to take her hand in hers. "Are you alright?"

"I, uh, was just wool-gathering for a moment," she said sheepishly. "I must've zoned out for a few seconds!"

"It's been almost twenty minutes," Helen replied, looking very worried. "Have you been getting enough sleep recently?"

"The usual amount; a few hours or so," Ivy said with a forced laugh, but Helen did not appreciate her attempt at humour. "Relax, Helen; sometimes I get funny turns. It happens when one of the others takes over."

"It looked more like an absence seizure to me," the doctor said quietly, but she did not press the issue any further. "We should discuss the vanishings with the Druids, if you're still up for it?"

"Why don't we get a bit of fresh air," Ivy said, getting unsteadily to her feet. "Seeing as it's stopped raining and all."

"If you're sure," Helen replied, sounding entirely unconvinced. She handed Ivy her cane and followed the Séance outside after leaving enough cash on the table for both their bill and a generous tip. When they were back on the wet tarmac of the country road, she looked at Ivy, expecting an explanation.

"We won't get anything more out of them," Ivy said sadly. She began to make her way slowly back towards Walpole Manor. "Hopefully we'll have more luck with different avenues."

"We didn't even ask them anything!" Helen said angrily, and Ivy leant on her cane with a frustrated sigh.

"Telepath," she said slowly, tapping her cane to emphasise each syllable. "That place was swimming in terror, Helen, and there were protection spells and warding staves up everywhere around the building.

"Whatever is out here killing people, they are trying their hardest to keep it out." Ivy began to walk again, albeit more slowly than before; trawling the minds of several people at once had weakened her severely. "Their magic is broad and non-specific; whatever we're up against, they don't know what it is either. Our only advantage is that this black dog creature doesn't know we're looking for it, and I'd rather not play that ace until we really need it.

"I'm hoping that Max is able to translate the carvings around the doorway; she seemed to think it was Ogham, and it looked centuries old to me. Hopefully that will give us more information."

"I didn't even notice that," Helen admitted. "You've a sharp eye, Livingston."

"Lamplight taught me well," Ivy said darkly. "Look

once, see everything."

"Words to live by."

"Indeed." Ivy paused for a moment. "I'm sorry that you lost Dennis, Helen. I'm sure the two of you made a formidable team."

"It's that much of an open secret?" Helen asked, seemingly unsurprised.

"There are few secrets where I'm concerned," Ivy replied, "and you were clearly more upset than Lin when it came time to bury him."

"Lin grieves in her own way," Helen replied. "She's a good woman, if a bit brusque, and Dennis was lucky to have her."

If you say so, Ivy thought, but she did not voice this. Instead, her attention was caught by the growl and rumble of an approaching engine. She stepped to the edge of the road, pressed slightly into the hedge, and Helen did the same.

"If you had the choice," the Blight asked softly, "would you go through Lamplight again, knowing what you know now?"

"Yes," Ivy said without hesitation. "I passed through that nightmare alive and relatively unscathed, and my life is so much richer for it now. I'd rather not lose what I have by chasing possibilities that might amount to naught.

"I'm actually happy, and that is worth any amount of pain."

Helen nodded silently, and Ivy's keen ears picked out the fact that there were two vehicles, not one, and they were moving in unison. As if to confirm her deduction, two vintage motorcycles rounded the corner, one with a sidecar.

The unadorned bike slowed to halt near them, and

Ivy recognised the feel of Connie's thoughts; confident, easygoing, but tinged with a hint of worry. The other rider's face was obscured by a helmet, but Ivy's eyes lit up when she heard the rider's voice.

"Hey there, beautiful," Charity said gleefully, "are you going my way?"

"I could be persuaded," Ivy replied coyly, before gesturing to the sidecar. "It looks like you're expecting company though."

"Oh, I'm just cruising," Charity replied with a chuckle. "I just like to be prepared, you know?"

"Ah, the mechanical equivalent of a toothbrush in one's purse?" Ivy asked, also laughing, and Charity nodded. "Then I guess I could spare a little of my time, on one condition."

"Which is?" Charity asked as Ivy climbed awkwardly into the sidecar.

"Take me the scenic route," she said. "I want to spend as much time with you as I can."

"As you wish," Charity said, passing a helmet to Ivy. "After all, we've all the time in the world."

"Indeed we do," Ivy replied, although deep in her heart she had a niggling feeling that her love affair with Charity was about to be cut short, permanently.

I've been wrong before, Ivy thought as Charity revved the engine. *Sometimes things don't end up like I expect them to.*

"Really?" Max asked, reflected in the sidecar's little mirror.

Yes, Ivy thought grimly. *They're often far, far worse.*

Chapter Thirteen – Victimless Crimes

Helen

Helen held tight to Constance's waist as the motorcycle roared throatily along the road towards Walpole Manor, and for a moment she was transported to a different time.

The Walpole she held was Dennis, not his sister, and instead of the pastoral scenes of rural Norfolk, they hurtled through the streets of Hong Kong in pursuit of a shapeshifting serial killer. The ride was exhilarating, but it was nothing compared to finally having her arms around the man she loved, albeit only for a short while.

No journey will ever be as wonderful as that one, she thought sadly as she returned to the present. *Even though I nearly died in the conflict that followed, it was still the ride of my life.*

What had surprised Helen, however, was the fact that Connie had let Charity out of her sight with one of her precious motorcycles; she barely let the twins use them, and then only with her direct supervision.

I'm sure she has a good reason, Helen thought as they coasted to a stop outside the Big House, and she groaned slightly as she dismounted the bike. Connie let out a mirthful chuckle as she pulled off her own helmet and grinned at the aching Blight.

"Out of practice?" she asked, and Helen nodded. "That's a shame; a daily hard ride does one the world of good, and it definitely keeps you young!"

"You didn't take the bike out yesterday," Helen retorted, and Connie gave her a wicked smile.

"I didn't specify what kind of ride," she said with a naughty giggle. "Geoff's not just for making the tea, you know."

"Would that we were all so lucky," Helen said with a heavy sigh. "Unfortunately, the Ministry takes up far too much of my time to find someone that meets my exacting tastes."

"You can't hold a candle forever, Helen," Connie said, swinging a leg nimbly over the bike in order to wheel it over to the shed. "Women like us aren't cut out to be nuns, you know."

"I'll take your word for it," Helen said, her mood beginning to sour. "I think I'll head inside before the heavens open again."

"Geoff and Henbane are in the kitchen," Connie called. "Would you ask Geoff to be a dear and brew up, please?"

"Will do," Helen replied, swiftly walking through the large front doors and into the house. *Henbane's here,* she mused, a little smile creeping on to her lips, despite the ache in her legs. *It's beginning to feel a bit like the old days.*

Geoff was filling the kettle as she entered the kitchen, and Henbane tipped their translucent flat cap; their other hand was curled around their mouth, as if holding a cigarette. There was no smoke, however, as even though Henbane had adopted the mannerisms of smoking, they detested the smell. Helen took a seat at the table and stretched slightly.

"I heard Connie arrive home, so I thought I'd make a pot of tea," Geoff said as he set the kettle to boil. "Would you like a cup?"

"Please." Helen groaned slightly as she tried to rub the ache out of her thighs. "I fucking hate getting old."

"You're not old, Helen," Henbane said firmly, "you're just out of practice. Den was still riding up until the day he died."

"And now Connie has his daughter on one of those dangerous machines," she replied with mock sincerity. "Lin will have her guts for garters; you know what she always says about them."

"Even a simple trip can end in death!" Henbane said, aping Lin's tone and delivery perfectly. "I wonder how long it'll be before Charity takes a spill?"

"She won't," Geoff said, lingering by the kettle. "She's taken to riding like a duck to water, and it's not like she's going to come a cropper through an unforeseen hazard."

"What makes you say that?" Helen asked.

"Den said that she had an almost supernatural knack of being in the right place at the right time, not to mention her uncanny ability to find things that are otherwise extremely well hidden," Geoff said. "He also told me that she can walk through a hail of bullets without so much as a scratch."

"You talk like she's some kind of Seer..." Helen said, initially as a joke, but the more she thought about Charity's skills, the more it made sense. "It can't be the case, though... Can it?"

"I'm not one of you," Geoff said, "but the Twins have a decent amount of Alphonse's gift in them, and her veins are brimming with Seer blood, so it seems entirely possible to me."

"Downright probable, even," Henbane said gruffly as the kettle boiled. Geoff busied himself with filling the teapot as Helen mulled his words over; hadn't Charity herself once mentioned about being able to predict an opponent's moves with near perfect accuracy, especially in melee combat?

"Do you think she knows?" she asked quietly.

"No," Geoff replied, "and it isn't our place to tell her. Some things are best left unsaid, and this is definitely one of them."

"Are you sure?" Helen asked fretfully. "I'd want to know."

"She isn't you," Henbane said sharply, "and I agree with Geoff; nobody needs that kind of knowledge. Just let the girl run on instinct and she'll continue to do just fine."

"Fair enough," Helen said, although she had to hold back her urge to argue with the diminutive pixie. "Why don't we turn our attention to other matters?"

"Like your little investigation?" Connie said as she sauntered into the room. Helen shot Geoff a look, but the Ghost shook her head. "Geoff would never get me involved in something like this, Helen, and besides, I'm savvy enough to spot an off-the-books operation when I see one, especially taking place under my own roof."

"Listen, Connie, it's best for everyone if you don't get involved," Helen said, desperate to preserve the boundary between their investigation and the Amberlights. "Charity explicitly asked me to avoid getting you involved."

"I was with Charity when she saw that poor girl vanish," Connie said, taking a seat at the table. "Like it or not, I'm a witness to this and that makes me involved."

"But the Director-" Helen began, but Connie cut her off sharply.

"Fuck Mohinder Desai!" she snapped. "He didn't have the decency to come to my brother's funeral, and he certainly doesn't get to dictate what happens in my own home. I'm helping, damn it!"

"We're helping too!" said a voice from a seemingly empty corner of the kitchen, and Geoff shook his head with a weary chuckle. He shot Helen a look of resignation and she sighed heavily. "Cat and I can be useful, we promise."

"I'm sure you will," Connie said, trying unsuccessfully to hide a smirk. "So, Helen, why don't you bring us up to speed?"

"Fine," Helen said, running her hands through her hair in exasperation, "but I would like to make one thing perfectly clear before we start."

Connie gestured for her to continue.

"You Walpoles can be fucking maddening sometimes."

"That we can," Connie said, almost proudly. "Now, tell me about these vanishings."

"A real case!" said one of the twins excitedly. "This is going to be so much fun!"

Fucking hell, Helen thought as she pulled out her sheaf of notes, *this is going to be a long few days.*

"Are you sure?" Helen said down the phone, loud enough for the entire room to hear. It was getting late, long past sunset, and the twins and Henbane had retired for the evening, leaving just Helen, Geoff, and Connie alone in the kitchen.

Charity and Ivy were still nowhere to be seen.

"Yes, Dr Mickelson, I'm sure," came the brusque reply of Annika Eastly, Helen's go-to contact for all things post-mortem. "There have been no bodies matching any of those names, and we've had a surprising dearth of unidentified bodies in recent months."

"What about expanding the search to a national scope?" Helen asked anxiously, pacing as she did so.

"This *is* on a national scale, Helen," Annika snapped, "and a thank you wouldn't go amiss, either, you know."

"I... I'm sorry, Annika," Helen said, feeling suddenly deflated. "It's been a rough few days, and I'm not myself. Thank you for looking into this for me; I really appreciate it."

"You're welcome, Helen," Annika said, her tone softening. "I hope you're around people who can take care of you, and I'll put an alert on those names for you; if anything turns up, I'll give you a call right away."

"You're a star," Helen said, shaking her head at her friends at the table. "Take care, and we should catch up soon."

"Likewise, Helen." There was a click as the call disconnected and Helen hesitated for a moment before placing the phone back in its cradle. She took a deep breath, and then rejoined those gathered around the kitchen table.

"No joy?" Geoff asked.

"None of these people are dead," Helen said, almost angrily. "They're just... gone. No bodies, no crime scenes, no evidence whatsoever; this is a case unlike anything I've ever dealt with. What can snatch people and spirit them away without a trace?"

"You said that Charity saw a black dog?" Geoff asked and Connie nodded.

"She said it was monstrously big, and that it dragged that poor girl to her doom."

"I thought you said that *you* saw it?" Helen said, a

little too sharply.

"I saw the aftermath," Connie admitted, "but I've no reason to doubt Charity; if she says it was a dog, then she saw a dog."

"This might sound a little mad," Geoff said after a moment of quiet contemplation, and he gestured to the missing posters, "but are we completely certain that these people were alive to begin with?"

"Geoff," Helen said, pinching the bridge of her nose in frustration, "just tell us what you're thinking, please."

"Well, this part of the country is full to the brim of tales of Black Dogs, some of which have supposedly killed people. They're based on the age-old tradition of Church Grims; a dog buried in a graveyard that is supposed to shepherd the wayward souls of the deceased to the next life."

"Are these things common?" Helen asked, and Connie nodded.

"They're almost ubiquitous in this part of the world. Hell, even St Mary's has a dog buried under the gate to the churchyard! If the legends were true, Helen, we'd be swimming in Black Dogs." Connie sighed heavily. "It must be something else."

"Not to mention that Grims don't take the living," Geoff said, and Connie nodded. "Hopefully Ivy's translation of the Druid's spell will give us more of an idea as to what we're dealing with."

"Where are they, anyway?" Helen said angrily. "Here we are, doing all the work, and they're just... gallivanting through the lanes."

"They're young and free, Helen," Connie said. "Let them enjoy the break in the rain to blow off a little steam."

"Would that it were so easy for all of us," Helen said bitterly. Connie reached out and took her hand gently in her own. "I'll be alright, Connie; I just need to wrap my head around the fact that I'm on my own now."

"Even though he's gone, Helen," Connie said, gently tracing her fingertips over the back of Helen's hands, "you're not alone. There are plenty of people in this world that care for you, you know."

"Are you coming on to me, Connie?" Helen asked and Connie couldn't help but give her a little smile. Helen glanced at Geoff, her eyebrow raised. "You too?"

"I'm not a priest any longer," Geoff said with a chuckle. "I'm allowed to have all the fun I want, and Connie mentioned that the two of you have a history."

"Youthful shenanigans," Helen said, "albeit enjoyable ones, but we're not so young any more."

"We're also not dead yet," Connie said, "and life is for living, so how about it, Helen? Let's be young again, even if it's just for one night."

"Maybe another time," Helen said, withdrawing her hand from Connie's. "Things are still too fresh for me at the moment. Sorry."

"Nothing to apologise for in the slightest," Geoff said. "Maybe what we really need is some sleep."

"Indeed," Helen said, and she rose from the table. "Goodnight, both of you. Sweet dreams."

"Likewise," Connie said as Helen walked away, and headed back to her room. As she lay wide awake in the still January darkness, however, she began to feel doubt and fear creep in around the edges of her mind.

Did I make the right choice?

A finger of ice down her spine made her shudder and she sat bolt upright in her bed, trembling in her pyjamas. Another chill sent her scrabbling for the door and she took off along the dark corridor, desperate to find someone else awake. Without thinking, she burst into Connie and Geoff's bedroom, tears in her eyes.

They sat up, reading by the light of a dim lamp, but both were on their feet in moments, taking Helen in their arms. Connie made soothing noises as they led Helen to sit on the edge of their bed.

"What's the matter, darling?" Connie asked gently.

"I don't want to be alone," Helen blurted out, clutching at the covers like a drowning woman. "It was just so dark and cold, and I'm just feeling so old... please, don't leave me tonight."

"We won't," Geoff said softly. "The bed is big enough to sleep three comfortably, and you're welcome to stay in here with us."

"Can we leave the light on, please?" Helen said in a small voice, and Connie nodded. "Thank you."

"Would you like me to read to you?" Connie asked, and Helen hesitated for a moment before nodding nervously. "Well, get comfortable and then we'll get started."

Soon enough Constance Walpole was reading to Helen as she lay snuggled up between the two of them. Helen's fear began to subside and she fell asleep far quicker than she had ever managed alone, oblivious to the evil and violence that was occurring out in the moonless dark.

Chapter Fourteen – Blood from a Stone

Ivy

The motorcycle roared and rumbled through the lanes as Charity piloted it with uncanny ease, and Ivy couldn't help but marvel at her partner's seemingly endless well of skills. The chilly wind cut through the waterproof fabric of Ivy's raincoat and she wrapped her arms tightly around her chest.

If I'd known we were going on an open air ride, I would've worn a jumper.

"Charity," Ivy called out, "where are we going?"

"I need to you to look at something for me," the Ghost replied, and Ivy gave her a thumbs up. She revved the bike's engine once again and took a right turn that was signposted 'Long Stratton', and Ivy realised where they were headed.

She wants me to feel for echoes and vibes around the place where that woman disappeared.

Ivy could feel the joy radiating from Charity, but there was something darker underneath the Ghost's happy exterior; something both mournful and violent. Ivy shifted uncomfortably in her seat and tried to mentally guard herself from the inevitable emotional bleed from her girlfriend.

"Do you want me to help?" Max asked, lending her strength before she could even answer.

Thank you, she thought, and took another look at Charity, this time catching sight of the bone handled knives that she now wore. Ivy frowned when she saw them; Charity had expressly told her to leave her weapons at home, and here she was, flaunting her new blades in broad daylight.

The bike wavered slightly as Charity's grip on the handlebars suddenly tightened, and she shook her head as if to clear a lingering dream from it. Ivy caught her eye and she could feel their gazes meet, even through the dark glass of Charity's sunglasses.

Charity slowed the bike down, and brought it to a controlled stop in the entrance to a field.

"Are we here?" Ivy asked as Charity pulled her helmet off.

"No," Charity said. "I need to be able to focus on the road, but there's a hell of a cloud of anger surrounding you, so I thought we'd talk it out before we went on; we're no good to anyone if I wrap us around a tree.

"So, Liv, what's eating you?"

"I..." Ivy began, but she quickly realised that the knives were not the true source of her frustration. *No point in being dishonest,* she thought, *although this is going to hurt.*

Courage, Ivy.

"I saw your dad today, Charity."

"No you didn't," Charity said immediately, visibly shaken by Ivy's words. "Why would you say something like that?"

"I saw him, Charity; please, believe me!"

"You weren't here when he died and you didn't know him, so there's no way you could conjure him!" Charity said, her voice growing more panicked by the moment. "Besides, that's Edgar's skill and he's fucking AWOL, so what the fuck are you talking about?"

"Charity-"

"Are you trying to upset me?" Charity said, glaring at her. "Why would you say something like that to me!?"

"Charity, I saw him earlier today!" Ivy said, almost pleading. "He was staring at Helen whilst we were visiting the Druids and-"

"Helen!?" Charity roared, and Ivy instantly knew that she'd made a mistake. "Fucking *Helen*!?"

Ivy reached out a hand to comfort her, but Charity slapped it away and clambered off the bike.

"You must be wrong, Ivy. Why would he appear to her instead of me, huh?"

"I don't know, Charity, but I was the only one who saw him. Helen doesn't know."

"Then you didn't see him!" Her voice was more shrill than Ivy had ever heard it, and she was beginning to hyperventilate. "There's no way he would ignore his own daughter to spend time with that... *tart*!"

A memory flashed into Ivy's brain as it overflowed from Charity's mind; Joseph Evans screaming at her that the young man that she was certain had seen her, Thaddeus Thane, couldn't possibly have done so.

How strange, Ivy thought. *She never told me about that.*

"Are you poking around in my head?" Charity said softly, her voice full of anger.

"I'm just looking over the memories that you clearly want me to see," Ivy replied, using her cane to assist in her awkward exit from the sidecar. "Is it so out of the realms of possibility that I can see him, Charity?"

Charity did not respond. Instead, she tightly gripped the metal gate to the nearby field, the leather of her gloves creaking under the force of her anger.

"I promise that I saw him, Charity, or at least I thought I did," Ivy said softly. She placed a hand gently on the Ghost's shoulder. "I've been seeing some strange things since Kiki died, and Helen mentioned something about an accelerant used during Lamplight-"

"I believe you, Ivy," Charity said, her voice small and fragile. Tears ran down her cheeks from behind her sunglasses. "I've felt him, here and there, you know."

Ivy planted a small kiss on her cheek.

"I'm just so fucking angry," Charity said after a moment. "I've never been this angry in my life."

"I'm sorry, I-" Ivy began, but Charity shook her head.

"I'm angry at him, not at you," the Ghost finally admitted, and Ivy nodded solemnly as she went on. "I'm angry that he hid things from me; the disappearances, his relationship with Helen, and so many other things on top of that. But most of all..."

She let out a sob and Ivy wrapped her arms around her.

"Most of all, I'm so fucking angry at him for dying." She continued to weep. "He was my father; he should've kept me safe and happy, and he should've been the one to teach me to ride, instead of leaving me with his unfinished fucking business to deal with!"

She let out a scream and the gate creaked audibly as the steel buckled and gave out under the sheer force of her grip.

"He was my father," she whispered once the scream died down, "but not fucking once did he try to be my dad."

"I'm sorry, sweetheart," Ivy said. "That's awful, and you deserve so much better."

"This isn't the point where you tell me to be grateful that I had any parents at all?" Charity asked, and Ivy shook her head.

"That would be an awful thing to say at the best of times," Ivy said softly, "and it would be especially cruel now. Your anger is completely justified, Charity."

"Thank you, Ivy." Charity let go of the gate and pulled Ivy into a tight embrace. "I'm lucky to have you."

"Is there anything else that you want to talk about?" Ivy asked, and Charity let out a tearful sigh.

"I suppose I better warn you about Reggie." She ran a hand through her hair, and Ivy felt a stirring of longing in her heart. "He was my partner back in the day, and now he's... I guess he's my stalker, now."

"Oh," Ivy said softly. "Was he the fellow with the horns and tail at the funeral?"

"That was him," Charity replied. "The nature of his obsession with me isn't his fault, though, but it will take a bit of explaining. Truth be told, I'm not exactly sure where to start."

"You don't have to tell me now," Ivy said kindly. "If you'd rather wait until another, less stressful, time, we can talk about it then."

"Thank you, Liv," Charity said, and gave Ivy a small kiss. "You're a real catch."

"I do my best," Ivy replied, blushing slightly. "You know, I really like your aunt and uncle, Charity; they're good people, as are your cousins."

"Yeah, they're alright as family goes. They seem to like you, too." She grinned and turned back towards the motorbike. "Are you ready to get underway again? I'd like you to take a look at the site of the vanishing before it gets too much psychic contamination."

"Is that a thing?" Ivy asked, her eyes wide, and

Charity shrugged.

"Fuck knows," she said with a playful smile on her face, "but it sounds plausible, doesn't it?"

"We better step on it, then," Ivy said with a giggle, "just in case."

"Hold on tight," Charity said, revving the engine as Ivy got settled in the sidecar. "This time I'm really going to put her through her paces!"

"I'm not feeling anything," Ivy said as she strode back and forth along the row of large bins that Charity had pointed out to her. "To be honest, though, I never was much good at catching glimmers of the past; the remote viewing I did at Lamplight always had a human subject to focus on, rather than an area or a vibe.

"Can you describe the woman a little more?"

"Dark hair, shoulder length; mostly dry so she couldn't have been in the rain long. White, freckles, green eyes; about five and a half feet tall, maybe twenty five, thirty at the outside. Blue jumper with white knitted sheep, also mostly dry, and jogging bottoms. Not sure about boots, but I'd wager that she was barefoot or in slippers."

I always forget just how good at this she is, Ivy thought as her girlfriend rattled off the description of the woman she'd seen for barely any time at all. *It would be hot in different circumstances.*

"You think she was originally indoors?" Ivy asked and Charity nodded. "Then why not just stay there?"

"This thing seems to be able to teleport, or at least phase through physical objects." She shook her head with a sigh. "Of all the times not to have a fucking Tracer with us..."

"Maybe we could call Teaser?" Ivy suggested.

"Even she would struggle to pick up a trail after this much rain. I'm genuinely amazed that she performed as well as she did back in October." She reached into a pocket and pulled out a small plastic bag containing the bloody fingernails she'd collected from the scene of the crime. "Would these help you focus on our missing gal?"

"They might," Ivy said, hesitating a little before taking them from Charity. "Here goes nothing."

Ivy closed her eyes and allowed her mind to drift along the delicate threads of the Tangle, feeling for any hint of the monstrous dog or the missing woman. There was definitely something in that spot in space; some kind of damage or contortion that made the supernatural subspace nearly impossible to navigate.

"It's no good," Ivy said angrily, frustrated at her own limitations. "There's some damage to the Tangle here, though; I'm not sure what that means."

"It's a Knot," Charity said. "It's the psychic residue from a traumatic event; usually a violent death. Marsh uses them to paint his horrible little pictures."

"Huh. I'd always wondered what those felt like," Ivy said.

"And you couldn't feel that before?" Charity asked, peering at her over the top of her glasses, and Ivy shook her head. "Not even at the False Cardinal or when you were in Galaxy?"

"Nope. Nothing like this."

"Maybe there's something to the accelerant after all," Charity mused, shoving her hands in her pockets. "Give me a little while longer to just... I dunno, suss out the vibe, I guess?"

"Go ahead," Ivy said, and Charity began to pace

back and forth, occasionally pausing to touch the ground or squat down to look at the battered asphalt. Ivy had a bemused look on her face, which almost became outright laughter when Charity sniffed a handful of wet grit before tossing it back to the ground.

She's very hot, Ivy thought, *but sometimes downright bizarre.*

"Now that's weird," Charity said, standing up once again, wiping her hands on her leather coat as she did so. "Useful, but weird."

"The suspense is killing me," Ivy replied, "so just tell me, already."

"I'm allergic to dogs," Charity said. "Like, stupidly allergic, and yet there's nothing here that's setting me off. That's profoundly strange, but then again, it could just be the rain."

Charity did not sound convinced, however, and resumed looking over the crime scene once again, this time focussing on the spot where both woman and dog had disappeared. Ivy was about to say something when Charity finally spoke.

"Fuck it," she said after almost three solid minutes of staring at the spot between the bins. "We're not getting anything here. Why don't we go find some dinner, and then we can plan whilst we eat?"

"Are you hungry?" Ivy said, a smile forming on her face.

"Fucking starving," Charity said. "I was invisible for fucking hours last night, and I am famished."

"What are you feeling?" Ivy asked, knowing full well what the answer would be.

"Chips," Charity said hungrily. "Hot fresh chips, fucking smothered in salt. A cup of Teaser's coffee would go down a treat, too, but I know that's out of reach."

"Only a few more days on the coffee, darling," Ivy said, "but I think we can find you some chips without too much hassle."

"Oh, you do spoil me," Charity said with a chuckle as they walked back to the bike.

"You're worth spoiling! Not to mention-"

Ivy stopped short and turned on her heel, scanning the nearby houses for people.

"What's wrong?"

"It felt like we were being watched," Ivy said softly, "but just for a moment."

"Is it gone now?" Charity asked, tensed like a predator.

"I think so," Ivy said, "but it felt just like that morning when you followed me home from the JR."

"You think there's a Ghost around here?" Charity asked, her lips barely moving.

"I'm honestly not sure," Ivy whispered, "but let's get out of here all the same."

The two women mounted up and sped away from the bins, but Ivy could not shake the sense of being followed.

Whatever it is we're looking for, she realised, *is now aware that we're on its trail.*

Hopefully we'll find it before it finds us.

Chapter Fifteen – Not Welcome Here

Charity

"You know, these aren't bad," Charity mumbled around a mouthful of chips. She had stashed her bandolier of knives in the lockable compartment of the sidecar, but she still kept one small blade in her belt.

Better safe than sorry, she thought as she chewed loudly, *especially if Liv's got a bad feeling.* It took her a few more mouthfuls to notice that Ivy was staring at her from across the table, elbows resting on the slightly sticky plastic tabletop.

"Everything okay?" Charity asked before stuffing an entire handful of chicken bites into her mouth. She looked expectantly at her girlfriend as she chowed down on her dinner, cheeks bulging slightly.

"I always forget how... enthusiastic you can be, especially when the hunger really takes hold of you," Ivy said with a soft smile.

"I'm sorry," Charity said, covering her mouth so that Ivy wouldn't see the half-chewed chicken that coated her tongue and teeth. "I get so caught up in how ravenous I am that I forget that I can be a bit disgusting to look at. I'll try to slow down from now on."

"It wasn't a dig," Ivy said. "Eat however you want; I don't find you disgusting, and I never will."

"You should see Shy go to town on a bowl of rasmalai," she said with a chuckle. "That boy can almost out-eat me."

"Almost?" Ivy asked playfully.

"Almost," Charity confirmed, "but not quite. How

about you; ever seen anyone eat the way I do?"

"Just once," Ivy said, almost dreamily. "Although he was a Ghoul, so I'm not sure if it counts."

"When did you meet a Ghoul?" Charity asked, stopping what she was doing entirely; one hand was frozen halfway to her mouth as she stared at Ivy. "Knowingly, I mean?"

"It must've been in the late sixties, maybe the early seventies," Ivy said with a sigh. "He was an American GI that came over for the war and was declared KIA, so he just ended up staying here. He was a huge fella, but had a remarkable sense of humour for someone who had died more than once."

"And I'm talking to Ivy right now?" Charity asked carefully, and her partner nodded. "Ivy Livingston?"

"Yes," Ivy said, clearly confused. "Who else would I be?"

"I'm not sure, but you're describing something that happened before you were born," Charity said firmly. "Are you alright, Liv?"

"I... I'm not sure," she said with a slight shake of her head. "Something strange is happening to me, Charity, and I was planning on telling you today, but things have gotten away from us a bit. Can I tell you now?"

"Go ahead," Charity said, putting down her food to give Ivy her full attention.

"I think it all started the night before last, when I attacked Harper." Ivy hesitated for a moment, and then went on. "I got her blood on me, and I seem to have, uh, *contracted* some kind of psychic entity."

So it is true! Charity thought, wide eyed.

"I take it you already have a bit of knowledge about Maxine, then," Ivy said with a gentle smile.

"I've heard rumours," Charity said, "and I thought

that you and Harper looked a bit similar when you got into your disagreement."

"I'm assuming that the rumours about Max are that she is some kind of bloodthirsty serial killer?" Ivy asked, and Charity nodded. "That's not true. Yes, she has a certain capacity for violence and aggression, but so do we. What sets her apart, however, is that she's endured centuries of torment, so it's totally expected that she might act out from time to time.

"You and I are both products of Lamplight, Charity, so we can understand her far better than most." Ivy reached across the table and took Charity's hands in hers. "Please give her a chance, for me?"

"Do you trust her?" Charity asked, and Ivy nodded. "That's good enough for me."

"Thank you," Ivy said. "I'm afraid that there may be a little bit of memory bleed at the moment, but we're working on putting effective boundaries in place."

"Just let me know if you need my help with anything," Charity said, "and thank you for being honest with me. It would've been all too easy to hide her, after all; you could easily blame her on some kind of stress reaction to losing Michaela or..."

Aha.

Charity's eyes widened as she thought about the list of missing people and their almost ubiquitous mental decline beforehand.

"Ivy," Charity said, leaning in and lowering her voice as she did so, "when you were a shrink, were there warning signs if someone was about to go completely off their rocker?"

"That's not exactly how I would put it," Ivy said pointedly, "but there would be signs, yes. Are you thinking about the hallucinations and paranoia our victims were experiencing?"

"Yes, but I'm thinking about signs before that; less obvious ones that wouldn't be easily recognisable to the untrained eye. What would you expect to see?"

"Mood swings, increased isolation, poor sleep," Ivy said, clearly combing her brain for information, "an increase in risk taking behaviour-"

"That's the one!" Charity said, completely unsure of why it was so important. "What kind of behaviour are we talking about?"

"Drinking, gambling, drug use, casual sex," Ivy said, almost in a monotone. "It really depends on the person, Charity. Where are you going with this?"

"If I was going to off a bunch of people, or at least kidnap them," Charity said, thinking back to her Lamplight training, "I wouldn't just do it right away."

"Why not?"

"It would be too obvious," Charity said darkly. "You've got to cut them off from their support network, or else people will come looking if they vanish. It's especially important if you're going to fake a suicide; if a perfectly fine person kills themselves, friends and loved ones look into it, but nutters do it every single day."

"Sometimes you worry me, darling," Ivy said, but her tone was not one of concern; instead she was clearly intrigued by the Ghost's line of reasoning.

"I had a life before I met you," Charity said with a wicked smile. "But as I was saying, driving someone round the twist is easy if you're invisible, and soon enough they'll wind up isolated and vulnerable.

"That's when you move in for the kill."

"Are you saying that these vanishings aren't attacks of opportunity?" Ivy asked.

"Bingo. They have all the hallmarks of a sustained, deliberate campaign against selected targets," Charity said, almost gleefully. "There's a term amongst Ghosts for this method of isolation before a kill."

"Which is?"

"It's known as a Death Curse," Charity said, "and it isn't undertaken lightly. In fact, aside from major political assassinations, I've only ever known it to be used for one thing.

"Revenge."

"Do you think you can do it?" Charity asked as they strode along the main street of Long Stratton. Their ultimate destination was the town's largest and most popular pub, but Ivy was keeping her mind open in case something useful caught her attention.

"I think so," Ivy replied. Charity's plan was to trawl the town's watering holes, betting shops, and supermarkets looking for people acting strangely whilst Ivy listened out for thoughts of black dogs or recent grudges.

It's not the most elegant plan, Charity thought as they walked, *but if we can nip this in the bud and keep someone alive, then that's worth the clunkiness.*

"I wish I had my swords," Ivy muttered, "or at least my Jack; I'd feel a lot better about hunting this damn creature if I had a way of protecting myself."

"You don't think that I'd look after you?" Charity asked sweetly, grinning like a mad woman.

"I'm sure you'd enjoy the fighting more than I would, but you aren't always going to be there, you know." Ivy gave her a grin. "What if I'm attacked in the shower?"

"I'm not allowed to join you in the shower?" Charity

said, feigning offence. "You know, I remember there were a spate of deaths that resembled shark attacks in a Welsh mining village some years ago. They never found out what was behind it, but it seemed to resolve all on its own."

"You think this phenomenon is going to burn out?" Ivy asked, and Charity shook her head.

"No. This is deliberate and targeted; the gaps between the waves of vanishings are calculated to hide the true extent of what's happening." She frowned a little. "Something about this feels strangely familiar, but I can't quite put my finger on it."

"Helen mentioned that you used to have nightmares that were a lot like this," Ivy said, as if trying to remind her. "Could that be why?"

"They were just dreams, Ivy; small children have nightmares all the time." She looked across the street at the pub; two people were leaving in a hurry, clearly upset by something. She was about to mention it to Ivy, but the Séance's head immediately turned in that direction. With little more than a nod to acknowledge the other's skills, the two women marched towards the pub.

"You want me to lead?" Ivy asked as they reached the main door.

"Let me do the talking, if there is any," Charity said. "We'll start with finding them, then we'll get a table within eyeline; all you need to focus on is skimming thoughts from our target. Got it?"

Ivy gave her a thumbs-up, and they went inside, the Ghost palming her blade to the Séance, just in case. Charity had eyes on their victim in a matter of seconds; a young man with wild eyes, red rimmed from crying, was sitting in the corner with a pint in his trembling hand, talking to himself.

He's further along than I thought, Charity noticed, and Ivy carefully picked a seat across the room from the unstable man. Several of the locals shot the two women dirty looks, but Charity made a point of ignoring them as she walked to the bar.

"Evening, boss," she said, leaning on the polished wood as the bartender approached; he did not look pleased to see her. "One lime and soda, please, and a half of Doom Bar to go with it."

"You new in town?" he asked. "Not seen you in here before."

"I'm only in town for a few days," Charity said nonchalantly, keeping one eye on the mirror behind the bartender. "I buried my father yesterday, so I thought I'd pop in here with my partner and raise a glass to him."

Two of the locals had risen from their seats and were walking over to the bar. *Nice and easy, lads,* she thought, *let's not start something you can't finish.*

"I think I'll have a bag of pork scratchings to go with my drink," Charity said, but still the barman only glared at her. The two men joined her at the bar, one on her left and the other on her right. "What are you having, fellas? I'm buying."

"Your money's no good here, freak," said the man on her left. "I've lived around here long enough to know a Walpole when I see one. How about you and your dyke girlfriend do us all a favour and fuck off, alright?"

"He's right," the barman said. "Go on, before there's any trouble."

If anything kicks off, Charity thought loudly enough for Ivy to hear, *you stay on our man in the corner.* She saw Ivy nod in the mirror, and took a deep breath.

"Look, boys," Charity said, placing both her hands flat on the bar and bending her knees a little, "I really don't want to get into it today, so how about we all have our drinks and then we can go our separate ways."

"He said to fuck off," said the man at her right. "Don't make us hurt you."

"You aren't gonna serve me, are you?" The barman shook his head and she sighed heavily. *Why can't anything ever be easy, just for once?* She turned to look at the man on her left, pivoting her weight to her left foot. "Can I at least take my coat off before you try and smash my head in?"

The man on the right swung first, just as she expected, and she delivered three swift kicks as he moved; knee, groin, and then face as he fell to the ground. The man on her left reached for her arms, but she stepped out of the kick and back into him, smashing his nose with her head as she did so.

"You fucking bitch!" he roared. Behind her, the barman was already calling the police, and the terrified man bolted for the exit. Thankfully, Ivy was hot on his heels, but as Charity watched her go, the man with the broken nose cold-cocked her in the jaw, sending her staggering backwards.

"Ow!" Charity yelled, putting one hand gingerly on her face. The man swung again, but she caught his wrist in her hand and angrily snapped it with a mere twitch of her arm. He cried out as the bone audibly broke, and his friends were all getting to their feet as the first police officer burst into the pub.

Were they fucking camped outside? Charity wondered as she was roughly shoved to the ground and handcuffed. *I hope Ivy is able to stay on our target's tail.*

What a way to end such a fucking mad day.

"You a Walpole?" asked the officer at her back, and she couldn't help but laugh.

"No, I'm Frosty the fucking Snowman," she quipped, and was rewarded with a hard punch to her kidneys. She laughed again, but winced as she tasted blood in her mouth. The policeman hauled her to her feet and spun her around to look her in the eye. She winced as he removed her sunglasses and squinted her eyes against the glare of the electric light inside the pub.

"Where's your girlfriend, then?" The cop shoved her and asked again. "We know you weren't alone, so where is she?"

"Get a warrant, pig," Charity said with a bloody grin that remained on her face even as they dragged her outside and bundled her into the police car.

I've never been arrested before, Charity thought. *Well, this is certainly going to be interesting.*

Interlude One – Death on Two Legs

The night air was still chilly from the recent rain, but Peggy Wilbur was grateful for a clear night to walk her dog, especially after the seemingly endless inclement weather that had been plaguing Tharston in recent days.

Though the skies were full of clouds, there was still enough light to navigate by, even without her little wind-up torch. Her dog, Jasper, sniffed and snuffled along the edge of the lane, stopping every few seconds to investigate the scent of some rabbit or badger.

It's nice to be out of the house, she thought with a sigh. Her husband, Billy, had insisted that they'd stayed inside the night before; some age old village superstition, or something like that, at the very least. When the sounds of hooting, singing, and hollering had burst out through the darkness, she had idly assumed that there was a football match on, or some other sporting event.

Peggy didn't desperately care for sports and nor did she enjoy the quiet village life that she'd ended up with. She'd married Bill right out of university, back when he could've been someone, but he soon brought her back to Tharston when his parents perished in a gas leak, and here, it certainly seemed, is where she would now stay.

"Jasper, don't get too far ahead!" she called out, but the dog was a wilful creature and continued on in spite of her yells. "God damn it, Jasper, get back here!"

Instead of taking the left turn that would lead him home, Jasper headed right, up the small hill towards Tharston Church, and Peggy was left to trail after him, fruitlessly calling his name in the otherwise still night air.

"Fucking dog," she muttered breathlessly as she strode up the hill after him. "I'm getting too fucking old for this bullshit."

Peggy was only fifty four but the sedentary pace of village life had taken its toll on her; her mind, body, and spirit had all become soft, unused to any real hardship. Whilst many would've considered her life enviable, the truth was that she was going mad with the monotony and boredom of it all; white picket fence, a cottage in the village, and her only son living in the nearby town.

It was almost perfect, and that perfection stifled her to death.

Maybe I should head into Long Stratton and meet a young man at the pub, she thought dreamily, her mind wandering as she walked. *It wouldn't mean anything, of course, and Billy would forgive me, but it would at least mean some excitement for once!*

She was so lost in her own thoughts that she failed to notice that Jasper had vanished entirely from the lane and that a pale fog was slowly closing in around her, limiting visibility to barely a dozen yards. Anyone else would've noticed the strange stillness in the air, but Peggy was far too wrapped up in her extramarital daydream to see what was happening right in front of her eyes.

A muted sound reached her ears after she'd been wandering alone in the mist for a few more moments; a rhythmic clip clop that grew sharper with every passing second, slow and steady yet full of purpose.

Is that a horse? Peggy thought, and immediately snapped out of her reverie. She glanced around fearfully at the fog, suddenly aware of just how disoriented and alone she was. *Who would be riding a horse at this time of night?*

"Jasper!" she called, clapping her hands to get the mutt's attention. "Jasper, where the fuck are you!?"

The dog was nowhere to be seen, however, and Peggy felt a chill run down her spine as the horse came ever closer; step after unhurried step. She reached into her bag to find her wind-up torch, but all she managed to do was fill the night with swearing and the racket of jangling keys.

The fog continued to deepen, obscuring all but the closest landmarks. Even the trees that lined the lane vanished, plunging Peggy into a kind of timeless void as her skin prickled into goose-flesh and her blood became ice water in her veins.

Maybe the horse has just gotten out of a field, she thought, her fear driving her to near hysterics. *Yes, that's sure to be it!*

What else could it possibly be?

It was scarcely a hundred heartbeats later that a thin equine figure loomed up out of the fog, and Peggy let out a horrified scream when she saw the horse's bare, fleshless bones. She staggered backwards as the first sinews and tendons began to appear on the creature's body, followed quickly by the bloody muscle fibres as they knitted together, coating the bones in firm, powerful flesh.

By the time the horse passed her as she jabbered madly on the lane, it was fully formed and looked no different from an ordinary beast of burden, save for a malicious glint in its eyes. Its greyish black coat glistened with moisture from the mist as Peggy tried to back away from the looming monster.

"Don't mind Gunpowder, Mrs Wilbur," said a charming voice from behind her. "He won't do you any harm."

Peggy whirled around to see the last of the flesh wrap on to the leering skull mere inches from her own face. The skin that followed was impossibly pale whilst still being uncannily handsome, aside from an ugly scar that crossed the newly formed man's face.

"Good evening, Mrs Wilbur," he said, tipping his hat politely. His manner was one of familiarity, but Peggy couldn't place him. His eyes were sunken into deep dark sockets, and the rest of his clothes looked centuries out of place, whilst a brace of pistols were strapped across his chest.

"Wh-who-who are you?" Peggy stammered, barely able to get the words out.

"Just a fellow traveller, my dear," he replied jauntily. "I thought that it was a nice evening and that it might do me the world of good to take the air, but now I'm of a mind that a spot of sport might prove much more entertaining.

"Are you a sporting woman?"

Peggy shook her head wordlessly.

"I didn't think so," he replied sadly, placing a hand on the horse's glistening coat. "I'm not talking about rugby or cricket, though. When I talk of sport, I mean much older, much bloodier pursuits. Have you ever hunted?"

Another shake of her head made him sigh heavily.

"Let me tell you something, Mrs Wilbur," he said, taking Gunpowder's reins in hand. "A mad dash, followed by a vicious clash, is far more enjoyable than the old stand and deliver routine, even if that was a tidy little earner back in the day."

Who are you? Peggy thought, but she remained rooted to the spot.

"The thrill is all in the chase, you see, Mrs Wilbur," the man said as he mounted the huge horse and settled comfortably in the saddle. He reached down and drew a vicious looking sword, with a basket wreathed in gilt roses. He pointed the blade past her, down the lane. "If you can reach the Church, you will be safe.

"I'll even give you a head start," he said, laughing heartily. Peggy continued to stare at him and he frowned at her. "I'm not going to tell you again.

"Now run!"

He roared these last words and she took off in a state of terror, screaming as she went. The rider urged Gunpowder into a gentle canter, before breaking into a full gallop, and within a few short moments he was upon her.

His gilded floral blade flashed through the air, striking her down in a spray of blood that tinged the thick fog a ghastly pink colour. The rider laughed and cheered as he twirled the blade in his hand.

"What a night to be alive, boy," he cried out, urging the horse onwards as the scar on his face faded to nothing. "Oh, what a night to be alive!"

*Part Two: Hunter, Hunted*

Chapter Sixteen – Strange Coincidences

Helen

Helen woke to the shrill ringing of her work phone. A quick glance at the clock confirmed that it was barely seven in the morning, and she let out a pained groan. She staggered out of bed and down the corridor, finally answering the damnable device with a guttural grunt.

"Helen?" asked the voice on the other end of the line. "Helen, are you there?"

"Annika, is that you?" Helen rubbed her eyes as she groggily murmured her words.

"Yes. We've had a body come in, Helen, and... well, you should just get down here to look at it." The hint of fear in Annika's voice caught the Blight's attention, and she was suddenly wide awake. "To tell you the truth, Helen, I've not seen anything like it. Please hurry; I won't be able to keep the officials held back for too much longer."

"I'll be underway in a few minutes," Helen said, already pulling clothes out of the wardrobe. "Where do you have the body?"

"Norfolk and Norwich University Hospital. I'll meet you at the main entrance and will walk you down. It should be a thirty minute drive at this time of day, if you're still at the Walpole Place."

Helen blinked in surprise.

"Annika, are you *here*?"

"I came up last night," Annika admitted as Helen cradled the phone with one shoulder, letting her get dressed more quickly. "Everything you told me, it just put me on edge in a way that I can't explain, so I thought it would calm me down if I took a few days in Norfolk to reassure myself that you hadn't found anything."

"And?"

"Oh, you've definitely found something, Helen," Annika said. "I assumed you wouldn't have any knives with you, so I brought a spare set."

"You think of everything. Thank you," Helen said, juggling the phone from one hand to the other as she pulled on her scrub top. "Any way you can stall for more time? Maybe send the police out looking for our mystery black dog?"

"Helen, this wasn't an animal attack."

Oh fuck, Helen thought. *This has just got a lot more complicated.*

"Helen?"

"The victim doesn't match the criteria I gave you?" Helen's brow furrowed. "Annika, what the hell is going on here!?"

"Just get here and I'll show you, damn it!"

Annika hung up and Helen stared at the phone in disbelief. *Two cases at once? How can that be possible?* She turned and saw Connie looking at her from the bedroom doorway; she was already dressed, seemingly ready to go if Helen needed her.

"You've always had an uncanny sense of timing," Helen said with a smile. "There's been a death; walk me out?"

"Of course," Constance said, and fell into step beside her. "I hope that our *invitation* yesterday evening wasn't too forward; I'd hate to burn a friendship over something like that."

"It wasn't," Helen said, giving her a smile. "I just

need a little space to grieve, but if it still stands in a few months' time, I might swing by for a long weekend."

"You're always welcome." They reached the bottom of the stairs and Helen set about putting her boots on. "Something has got you worked up about this case; care to share what it is?"

Fuck it, Helen thought, *she's got almost as much experience as me and she knows the area well; maybe she'll have an insight on what the hell is going on here.*

"Tell me, Connie, given all your time with Amberlight, what would you say are the odds of two cases occurring simultaneously?" Helen looked at the Ghost who frowned. "Well?"

"Remote," Connie said after a few more seconds of contemplation, "but not unheard of; this is a particularly haunted part of the country."

"It's no Prague, though," Helen said as she searched for her keys.

"This is true, but this is blood-soaked ground nonetheless, especially around here." Helen nodded as Constance spoke, before swearing softly. "Misplaced your keys?"

"I swear I had them-" Helen began, but the jangle of the landline stopped her in her tracks. Constance strode over towards the phone as Geoff quickly trotted down the stairs, slipping a worn tweed jacket over his slightly crumpled blue shirt. "Geoff, you haven't seen my keys, have you?"

"Afraid not, but Connie asked me to give you a lift anyway."

"I have a car!" Helen said firmly as Connie spoke softly down the phone. "I just need to find my keys."

"Helen, darling," Connie replied as she replaced the receiver, "you drive a *vintage ambulance*. What happened to flying under the radar?"

"I..." Helen tried to find a defence, but came up empty handed. "Yeah, okay, that's a good point. Ready when you are, Geoff."

"Just putting my shoes on," Geoff replied, and Connie took her motorcycle jacket down from the rack. "Ooh, is it a group outing?"

"Unfortunately not," Connie said, clearly shaken. "That was Ivy; apparently she and Charity were following up a lead in Long Stratton last night when things went south."

"What happened?" Helen asked. "Are they alright?"

"Ivy's fine, but Charity got attacked in the pub and is currently locked up at the police station."

"They arrested her for *getting* attacked!?" Geoff said, outraged.

"The locals don't much care for our kind, I'm afraid," Connie said. "It's the main reason that I don't like the girls going into Long Stratton without me. You two better get going; the roads around Norwich will snarl up sooner rather than later, and it sounds like you don't have a lot of time."

"What are you going to do?" Helen asked as she headed for the door.

"I'm going to remind the cops which side their fucking bread is buttered on," Connie said angrily as she pulled on her riding boots. "They've gone far too long without a ringing in their ears. It's time to put a bit of stick about."

"You made good time," Annika said, greeting Helen outside the main entrance to the hospital.

"I got a lift with a friend," Helen replied. "He knows the area well, and he's going to stay nearby to pick me up when we're done here."

"Good." Annika Eastly gestured for Helen to follow her, and began to make her way through the hospital in the direction of the morgue.

She looks terrible, even for her, Helen thought. *Whatever this is, it's clearly upset her greatly.*

Annika was a Sleuth; a catch-all term for any Cep with a gift suited to investigation. Her particular talent allowed her to see through the eyes of the dead, granting her a glimpse of the last thing they saw before they died. It was a highly useful skill, but being exposed to such things had a detrimental effect on Annika's mental health, so she used it sparingly.

Not to mention the eventual outcome of her gift, Helen thought sadly. Once she had seen enough Death Snapshots, as Annika called them, she would be rendered completely blind, but not before seeing one final vision; that of her own demise. *What a terrible fate.*

Annika was almost forty years younger than Helen, but her hair was prematurely greying and her face lined with worry. She carried a collapsible white cane on her belt, just in case, and kept her hands covered by two pairs of gloves; physical contact with a corpse was necessary for her gift to work, and she had learned early in her career that even an accidental brush of the hand was enough to grant a vision.

"Did you, uh, take a look yet?" Helen asked as they walked.

"Yet!?" Annika replied with a look of outrage. "I'm already doing you a fucking favour, Helen. Asking me to use what little gift I have left would be a bridge too fucking far, don't you think?"

"I'm not asking you to," Helen said, "but I know that you do have a certain ghoulish curiosity to you..."

"Not about this," Annika said with a frown and a shudder. "I brought you a set of knives, but I don't think you're going to get much use out of them."

That's worrying.

"Where was the body found?" Helen asked as they went deeper into the bowels of the hospital.

"Near St Marys, in Tharston," Annika replied. "Not far from you, actually."

"There's no need to say it in such an accusatory tone," Helen snipped. "If you've got something to say, just fucking say it."

"That's not what I meant..." Annika sighed heavily as they reached the door to the morgue. A security guard sat at a desk outside, an electronic pass on his belt. "It's just that this death coming hot on the heels of your phone call... well, it's just all a bit fucking weird. I'm frit up, Helen, and I don't like this one bit.

"In fact, as soon as we're done here, I'm getting in my car and driving right back to Birmingham. Hell, if I still feel like this when I get behind the wheel, I'm not even gonna stop; I'd rather piss in my knickers than stay here one more minute than is absolutely necessary."

"Shall we?" Helen said, gesturing to the door before popping an extra strong mint in her mouth; an old corpse-cutter's trick to keep the smell of death at bay. Annika took a deep breath and nodded at the security guard at the desk, who opened the door for them.

"After you, Dr Mickelson," she said, her voice quaking a little, "and don't say I didn't warn you."

The body on the slab was separated into two distinct pieces; the killer had cut the victim from left hip to right shoulder, or vice versa. Telling which way it had been originally would be impossible, given the state of the corpse; centuries of withering and decay had rendered the body almost unidentifiable.

The shrivelled skin was pulled taught over the skull, and the few remaining wisps of hair were brittle as spun glass. Helen stared at the body in confusion; if the case had been something as simple as grave robbing, Annika wouldn't have called her.

"Where did you find this?" Helen asked, slipping on a pair of nitrile gloves as she prepared to examine the obviously exhumed body.

"They found her on the road leading to the church, in the early hours of the morning," Annika said, keeping her distance. "And before you ask; no, none of the graves have been disturbed."

"So we don't have an ID on the victim, then?" Helen asked, not expecting a reply. Annika's answer took her by surprise.

"Our vic's name is Peggy Wilbur," Annika said. "Born on the fifteenth of December, Nineteen Sixty Nine; that dessicated body before you is only fifty four years old."

"Fuck off," Helen said reflexively, looking at Annika with disbelief. "This body is at least two hundred years old, maybe even older; well preserved, yes, but certainly not from a woman who died recently!"

"She died last night," Annika said. "Her husband reported her missing at around ten o'clock when she didn't return after taking their dog, Jasper, for a walk."

"You must be mistaken," Helen said, peering in for a closer look.

"Check her teeth." Annika's tone was firm and Helen did as she was told. "Back left molar; there's a white filling. You'll also note a bonded retainer behind the top front teeth."

"My god," Helen said, her blood running cold as she saw exactly what Annika described. "This really is her, isn't it?"

"The dental records are a perfect match; her last check-up was just before Christmas, so the latest details are barely a month old. Besides, she was fully clothed when she was found, and her purse was untouched." Annika leant back against the wall. "The ageing isn't what scares me about this, though."

"Then what is?" Helen asked, now dreading the answer. Whilst Annika could be a touch histrionic when relaying the details of a case, this time she was being downright restrained. Annika gestured to the computer screen near the body, and Helen moved closer for a better look. What she saw were several photographs taken with a microscope-mounted camera. "What am I looking at here, Annie?"

"Photographs of the wound edge, taken under several different kinds of light; scroll down to look at the last ones." Annika waited as Helen looked at the pictures. "What do you think?"

"If I didn't know better, I'd say that some of these show signs of cryogenic burns," Helen said, "but localised only to a small area around the slicing wound."

"I thought the same thing. Go on; what else do you see?"

"It appears that the body was severed with a single blow," Helen said, moving between computer and corpse, "but something that hit with such force should've caused some fracturing of the bones. These have been cut as neatly as the flesh, which... well, it's impossible.

"You can't make a blade sharp enough to do that, and a laser or something similar would cause a different burn pattern. Even a blade made of ice would've left bone fragments around the wound." Helen shrugged her shoulders in anger. "I have no idea what could've done this, Annie."

Annika continued to stare at the body on the slab.

I might not know of anything, Helen realised, *but she does.*

"Annie?" Helen asked softly. "Annie, what do you think did this?"

"Windstahl," she said quietly. "I've only seen a weapon that old once, but it was definitely born of the Königsfeuer. That's the only thing that could do damage even comparable to this."

"Fucking hell," Helen said, her voice almost a whisper. "Dwarven Wind-Steel is so rare that I've never actually seen it, let alone its effects on the body. There must be, what, maybe a dozen of those weapons in Europe, twenty at the most?"

"There are five," Annie said, "and the Ministry has a record of them all."

"This is bad, Annie," Helen said, looking at the body. "Whoever is doing this has powers that I wouldn't have thought possible, and they're still out there."

Helen took a deep breath and looked at her friend sadly. *I hate to put you in such a position, but we can't have someone like this just running around unchecked.*

"Annie," Helen said, her voice trembling, "I'm sorry,

but I really do need-"

"I know you do," Annika replied, already taking her gloves off. "I knew it would have to happen the moment I saw the body."

"I'll be here with you, the whole time," Helen said as Annie approached the corpse, psyching herself up to do what had to be done. "Good luck."

Annie nodded and gently placed her bare hands on either side of the corpse's face. Her eyelids flickered for a moment and then she froze in place, staring into the middle distance. Helen waited for a little over a minute, but still Annika's condition didn't change.

"Annie, are you alri-"

The Sleuth's eyes snapped back into focus and she let out a blood-curdling scream.

Chapter Seventeen – The Morning After

Ivy

Heads are about to roll, Ivy thought as she saw Constance Walpole's motorcycle pull up outside the Long Stratton Police Station. It was only a small single-storey building, but to Ivy it seemed like an impenetrable fortress; she'd been trying for hours to speak to Charity, but the officers inside had done nothing, aside from repeatedly fobbing her off with excuse after excuse.

"Are you coming with me, or waiting out here?" Connie asked once she'd removed her helmet.

"Wild horses couldn't hold me back."

"Good. Roll your sleeves up a little; they don't know the specifics of Project Lamplight, but a glimpse of the tattoo should be enough to put the fear of god into them." Connie took several deep breaths in an attempt to calm down; Ivy could feel the anger radiating from her, like heat from a bonfire. "I don't want to boss you around, Ivy, but let me do the talking, okay?"

"I saw what happened..." Ivy began, but Connie shook her head.

"They don't care about that, I'm afraid. They're trying to send a message, so we need to send one back." Connie gave Ivy's shoulder a squeeze. "It's not that I don't trust you to do this, Ivy, but what's needed here is clout, not skill; both of which I have in spades. Do you understand?"

Ivy nodded, leaning heavily on her cane. It had been a long night, and she was dead on her feet.

"Thank you for trusting me; you're a great gal, and

Charity is lucky to have you. Let's go get her out of here." Connie took one final breath and squared her shoulders before striding purposefully into the police station, with Ivy hot on her heels.

At the sight of Connie, the officer manning the desk balked slightly and Ivy couldn't help but smirk at his dread. *This might actually be fun.*

"Where's your boss?" Connie asked, leaning on the man's desk and staring at him through her dark glasses. The constable began to stammer out a response, but Connie raised a finger to silence him. "I don't want excuses, boy; I want to speak to Inspector Patrick Yates, and I want to do so right now."

The constable swallowed slightly and managed to recover enough courage to speak.

"He's, uh, busy at the moment, ma'am." Ivy raised an eyebrow; the man's voice had barely broken, it seemed. "I'm afraid that you'll need to come back later, or make an appointment."

Connie stood up with an angry grunt, ready to scream the place down if necessary, but something stirred in Ivy who leant forward and uttered a command to the constable. She wasn't entirely sure what she had said, but her intent was clear.

Go and get him.

The constable's right eye twitched a little, as if he was fighting her nebulous words, but then he nodded shakily and got to his feet. After he had entered one of the little backrooms, Constance turned to face her.

"What the fuck did you do to him?" she asked, both horrified and impressed.

"Kiki used to refer to it as 'putting the whammy' on someone, but Charity calls it Brainjacking; to be honest the latter feels more accurate." Ivy glanced at the floor. "I wasn't sure I'd still be able to do it, so it's as much of a surprise to me as to you."

"Jesus," Connie said, letting out a dark chuckle. "You wanna come and work for me? I'll pay you triple whatever the Ministry gives you."

"That's a kind offer," Ivy said sheepishly, "but I think I'd rather stick with Charity, if that's okay. No offence meant, though."

"None taken; loyalty is a virtue, especially in this business." Constance glanced down the corridor. "This Brainjacking that you do; it doesn't hurt them, does it?"

"It didn't used to," Ivy said, trying not to think about Joseph Evans ramming the orbitoclast into his brain, "but now I'm not so sure. It's changed since then."

"Hmm. Maybe keep it in your back pocket for now, lest we get ourselves into hotter water than we're already in."

"Agreed," Ivy said as the constable returned to his desk, his face drooping slightly on one side. *Oh dear,* she thought nervously. *I think I hurt him quite badly.*

"Inspector Yates will be with you shortly," the man said, slurring his words significantly. He glared at Ivy, his eyes unfocussed. "You did something to me, didn't you?"

Ivy went to push him further with her denial, but Max spoke up first, reflected in the polished chrome of a desk lamp.

"Don't," she said firmly. "Constance was right; you'll kill him if you push him too hard."

"I don't know what you mean, sorry," Ivy said to the injured constable and let a little of her feigned confusion wash into him. Whilst it was not as powerful as an implanted thought, it was enough to halt the constable's questions.

"What do you want, Constance?" asked a swaggering man in a cheap suit as he walked towards the two women. "Can't you see that I'm busy?"

"Inspector Yates; always a pleasure to see you. Is there somewhere that we can talk?" she asked, smiling as warmly as her anger allowed.

"Like I said, I'm a very busy man and we're short on space today, so why don't we do this another time?" Yates looked past Connie at Ivy. "I thought I already told you to get lost; are you going to do as you're told, or do I have to book you too?"

"She's with me, Yates," Connie said folding her arms defiantly. "I'm here to ask you why you're holding my niece."

"She attacked two men in a pub," he replied with a smug grin on his face. "Unprovoked, too, according to the bartender; very nasty business all round, this."

"Can I see the CCTV footage, please?" Connie asked. "Seeing as it is clearly so cut and dried, that shouldn't be a problem."

"It wasn't working, unfortunately, but we've got all the witness statements we need, nonetheless." His grin widened. "It's time that you Walpoles learned your place."

"Look, Patrick," Connie said, almost casually, "why don't you just let her go? She apparently took a licking, so can't we call it even?"

"Even?" Yates scoffed. "You pale freaks think that you can do whatever you like-"

"Such as solving crimes for you?" Connie asked, cutting him off. "Catching killers? Generally doing your job for you, whilst you strut about like the fucking cock of the walk?"

"That's in the past," Yates said. "You want to settle that, then just invoice me for your services."

He began to chuckle, but his laughter was cut short when Constance produced a piece of paper with a flourish. He took it in shaky fingers before unfolding it and looking it over. His eyes widened as he did so.

"That's the standard Amberlight consulting rate," Connie said sweetly, "and I've spared you the late payment fees, but that's only because I'm such a generous soul."

"This... this is over three million pounds!" Yates tossed the invoice back at her. "You're mad if you think that we'll pay this."

"I don't expect you to pay it," Connie said, "but I do have a paper trail that justifies *each and every charge*, which I will send to your superiors, and then their superiors; all the way up if I have to. My calculations are correct, I assure you; I studied at the London School of Economics before getting a Master's in Financial Science from Osney College, Oxford.

"I will fucking bury you in debt, Yates, and the Amberlight Collections Agents will exsanguinate you." She grinned as the colour drained from his face. "Or, Inspector, you can let Charity go, and we'll call it quits."

"You can't do this," he muttered softly.

"You have no idea of what I'm capable of, especially where family is concerned," Connie said sharply. "And if you decide to hold her, then your witnesses can be cross-examined by Yun Lin; you remember her, don't you, Yates?"

The Inspector said nothing, but Ivy could feel terror take the very heart of him.

"Well, even if you don't, I'm sure your brother does,"

Connie said nastily, "if he has enough grey matter left to even have memories, that is."

"Just take her and fucking go," Yates muttered, staring into the middle distance. "I've had enough of your kind for a lifetime."

"A wise choice Patrick," she said with a smile. "You can keep the invoice, though; I have copies."

He stared at the ageing Ghost with pure hatred in his eyes.

"Now, Inspector," Connie said, folding her arms once again, "why don't you go and get my niece?"

"Ivy!" Charity said happily, throwing herself into her girlfriend's arms. Ivy noticed that they'd taken her glasses, and the Ghost was squinting to protect her eyes from the light. She glanced at Constance, who was signing for Charity's belongings.

"Where are her glasses?" the older Ghost asked sharply. "She has a medical condition and needs them to protect her eyes."

"She didn't have any when we brought her in," Yates said, but Constance took a step closer to him, causing him to throw his hands up in a demonstration of innocence. "I mean it! The lads at the pub must've taken them off her."

"The pig that nicked me has them," Charity said, "and I only had *one* black eye when I came in."

"You hit her?" Ivy asked, anger flaring in her like a supernova. "You fucking hit her?"

"I-" Yates began to say, but Ivy lashed out at him, much as she had done with the constable.

Tell me the truth.

"She... she spoke back to me," Yates said, drooling slightly. "She's a smart mouthed bitch..."

Ivy stepped forwards and shoved her hand in his pocket, fingers closing around Charity's glasses. As she was close to him, she risked using her gift one last time, letting a flood of words and whispers pour from her lips and into the Inspector's ears.

Patrick Yates, she instructed, *fuck all the way off.*

The Inspector stared at her before turning on his heel and walking slowly out of the police station. Where he was headed was anyone's guess, but a smile of grim satisfaction crossed Ivy's face as she handed the sunglasses back to Charity.

"Here you go, sweet pea," Ivy said, giving her a light kiss on her unbruised cheek.

"Thanks, Liv," Charity replied, and let out a tremendous sigh of relief as she donned her protective eyewear. "Oh, that's so much better."

"We should be off," Connie said, leading the two of them out of the building. Across the car park, Yates turned on to the road and kept going, oblivious to everything around him. Constance gave Ivy a look, but said nothing regarding the obviously brainjacked Inspector. "Are you alright, Charity?"

"I've had worse," Charity said and gave her a strained smile before wincing in pain. "I think that bastard in the pub cracked one of my teeth, though. Hopefully it'll heal up soon. Enough about me; Ivy did you get anything from our potential target last night?"

"Nothing useful, I'm afraid," she said sadly. "Just a lot of nervous walking around, but they definitely tried to be around people for as long as possible. They did seem to relax when the sun rose, however, so that might mean our black dog is limited to the hours of darkness."

"That's little comfort in January," Charity said

sullenly. "Well, at least we can start afresh today. If we're lucky, Helen will be awake enough to join in as soon as we get home."

"Helen's on the job already," Connie said, stopping both the younger women in their tracks. "She and Geoff headed over to Norwich first thing this morning; apparently there was a suspicious death last night."

"The dog?" Charity asked, and Connie shook her head.

"Something else; whatever it was shook her friend up so badly that she couldn't elaborate over the phone." Connie sighed heavily. "She asked me whether I thought we were dealing with separate cases, but without any details it's impossible to say."

"Well, we do know one thing," Charity said, pulling her jacket on as it began to rain once again. "Things are going from bad to worse.

"I hope she finds some kind of lead in Norwich, or else we're dead in the fucking water."

Chapter Eighteen – Red String Special

Helen

Helen watched Annie's car drive off into the distance as the first heavy, fat raindrops landed on Norfolk and Norwich University Hospital. She shivered slightly, and pulled her coat tight about her chest.

"I should've brought a fucking umbrella," she muttered, and contemplated texting Geoff so that he could come and pick her up, but something about the body still called to her.

I've missed something important, she thought anxiously. *I'm certain there's more to see; I should go and have another look.*

She turned on her heel and headed back into the comparative warmth of the hospital. Her mind raced as she walked and she drummed her fingers on her thighs; it had been easy enough to get into the morgue with Annie's connections paving the way, but she had no such methods currently available to her.

"Working off the books is a fucking nightmare," she grumbled.

Helen rounded the corner and saw a security guard sitting idly outside the entrance to the morgue. He had already seen her go in once, and was certain to ask questions if she returned unaccompanied. She flexed the fingers of her right hand as she mentally worked through her library of pathogens, searching for something that would achieve her goal without killing the poor man.

Norovirus it is, she thought, *and I just hope it doesn't trigger an outbreak in the hospital.*

She flexed her fingers once again, her eyes flashed a sickly hue of yellow, and the security guard bent over in pain, clutching his stomach. The growls of protest from his innards were audible even where she stood, and the colour drained from his face as his breath came in short, laboured pants.

"I'm sorry," she whispered.

The man at the desk groaned loudly as his bowels emptied into his trousers, just as vomit burst forth from his lips, spraying the computer in front of him with infectious material. He let out a sob mere seconds before the second wave of vomiting struck him, leaving him red faced and retching with tears in his eyes.

I might've overdone it a little.

He got unsteadily to his feet just as his bowels contracted once again, and Helen wrinkled her nose at the foul smell; even though she was immune to all the symptoms she caused, her gift did nothing to mitigate the shudder of visceral disgust that rocked her body. He staggered past her, and she lifted the electronic pass from his belt with practised ease.

She quickly slipped inside as soon as he was out of sight.

"More haste, less speed," she said softly as she located the body of Peggy Wilbur in the walk-in chiller. Her breath fogged in the air as she drew back the sheet, and she frowned as she was once again faced with the advanced rate of decomposition of the body. "Take your time and look carefully."

Examining the corpse was easier without Annika's fretful presence throwing Helen off her usual A-game, and she finally found what she was looking for on her third pass of the body. She bent down to examine the late Mrs Wilbur's hands, and noticed dirt beneath the fingernails.

"Easily overlooked if they assumed that you were hauled out of the ground, but you weren't," she said with a triumphant smile as she collected a small sample. "They found you on the asphalt, so I wonder where this came from?"

She leant forwards to take a final look at the dead woman's teeth, but a faint whiff of the corpse, now unblocked by the tang of mint, reached her nose and stopped her dead in her tracks. She brought her face close to the corpse and inhaled deeply.

A smell that suggested wetness, acidic with rotten plants, assaulted her nose and made her gag slightly. She broke with convention and removed her surgical gloves and gently touched the dead woman's skin; it was almost waxy to the touch, as if she had been preserved in some kind of clay. The smell, texture, and strange appearance of the body reminded her of something, but it remained just out of reach.

"Damn," she muttered angrily, pocketing the little vial of soil for later analysis. "I better go before the security bloke is done cleaning himself up in the bog-"

She stopped, frozen in place by her own words.

There it is, Helen thought as the final piece of the puzzle clicked into place in her head. A smile crept on to her lips as she covered the body and exited the morgue, depositing the guard's pass on the floor in a plausible location.

You taught me well, Den; in and out without so much as a whisker out of place.

Her smile persisted as she strolled through the hospital corridors, even with the rain now hammering on the window panes. She pulled out her phone to text

Geoff, but jumped as it rang in her hand.

"Hello?" she asked, still shaken by the uncanny timing.

"Helen?" It was a woman's voice, familiar, on the other end of the line.

"Speaking. Who is this?"

"It's Noor," the woman said, "Noor Turner."

Of course it is, she thought with a chuckle. *Who else, but a Seer, could call the moment I looked at my phone?*

"Hello, lovely," Helen said, her earlier smile returning. "How are you doing?"

"I'm alright, thank you," she replied. "I'm just looking after Silas's ferrets at the moment; they're demanding little monsters, aren't they?"

"They most certainly are, but so is he." Helen looked out of the window as two more hospital security guards walked past, hiding her face just in case. "Is this just a social call, Noor, or is there something you need?"

"I do actually need your help with something," she said softly, "but it will need to be off the record, if that's okay?"

"It seems to be the season for it," Helen muttered, and then answered more clearly. "Of course, Noor."

"I'm trying to find my friend, Dee; do you remember her?"

"Black girl, muscular, bleach blonde hair, rather talented with lightning?" Helen asked, and Noor confirmed. "I seem to recall that the two of you had a nasty falling out; is it wise to go looking for her?"

"I can't explain it, but if I don't find her something terrible is going to happen. I'm not sure when, but I can feel it. I know she doesn't want to see me, but I can't think of another way to avoid what's to come. Will you help me, Helen?" Noor's voice was almost tearful with anxiety.

"Of course; I'll put out some feelers and see what comes up. I assume you want the Ministry completely uninvolved?"

"She doesn't exactly respond well to authority figures," Noor said, "and I'd rather things didn't escalate any further between us."

"Understood. All information will come right to you."

"Thank you."

"Does she have any aliases?" Helen asked, pulling out a scrap of paper and a pen to awkwardly scribble down any pertinent details.

"Her stage name was Hacksaw, and she also went by Beef for a while. Her full name is Delilah Adaolisa Baxter, but she might be using her maiden name; Obie." Noor hesitated for a moment. "I'd also appreciate it if you could find out what happened to her parents, Chidy and Uchena, for me.

"They died during the fire in Dartford, and part of our falling out was... related to that, let's say."

"I'll do what I can. Do you want me to send any leads to your work email?"

"It's probably best to pass them along to Silas, who can let me know from there."

"Layers of separation; you're a smart girl, Noor Turner," Helen said with a smile. "You'll go far in this world, that's for sure. I'm afraid that I'm rather busy at the moment, so I'm going to have to cut our chat short. Take care, and say hello to the boys for me."

"I will do. Thank you again, Helen." Noor paused for a second, before blurting out her next words.

"Ring a Ring o' Roses, Golden as the Dawn."

"Noor, what are you talking about?" Helen asked, blinking in surprise.

"Death comes driving down the highway, in its Sunday best." There was another pause. "Sorry, Helen, I don't know what came over me there. Talk soon."

Noor ended the call abruptly, leaving Helen staring at her phone in utter confusion. After a few seconds of stunned inaction, she gathered her wits enough to text Geoff to come and meet her.

Seers, she thought as she made her way towards the main entrance, *they never make a blind lick of sense, until they suddenly do.*

By then, though, it's normally too late.

"Any joy?" asked Geoff as Helen climbed into the Volvo, shivering from the chilly rain.

"After a fashion," she replied. "Did Connie have any luck with Charity?"

"Yes, she did," Geoff said as he navigated away from the hospital and towards home. "Charity and Ivy are back at the house, although they're both absolutely exhausted and Charity is a little worse for wear.

"How did your autopsy go?"

"It was an experience," Helen said, giving Geoff a strained smile. "Annika was right to be spooked, though; we are dealing with something completely beyond the pale. I'm not sure how it fits in with Charity's Black Dog, but it'll come together eventually."

"They might be unrelated," Geoff said quietly. "Stranger things have happened."

"I guess, but that just doesn't feel right to me." Helen looked at the flat landscape through the rain-streaked window. "Have there ever been any bog bodies found in Norfolk?"

"Several, yes," Geoff said, "although they tend to turn up in strange places. I've got a book on it at home; you're welcome to take a look if you want."

"That would be helpful, thank you." Helen sighed heavily. "This is going to sound crazy, but I have an important question for you, concerning what I saw today, and I need you to answer honestly. Can you do that for me?"

"Ask away," Geoff said, calm as ever. "I'll answer as best I can."

"Have you ever seen any Dwarves in or around Tharston?"

"I'm assuming we aren't talking about humans, here?"

"No. The legends say that they would be of a similar height to a small man, but would have large hands and black bones..." She trailed off as she realised how useless her line of questioning was. "You know what, let's ignore that. New question; does Tharston have a history of ghosts?

"Not the kind that Connie is, but proper ghosts; spirits of the dead, etc. Any legends like that?"

"There have been rumours of poltergeist activity following funerals," he replied enigmatically, "but I get the feeling that you have something specific in mind."

"I do."

"Then just tell me what it is!" he replied with a good natured chuckle. "Good grief, you Ministry types spend so long talking around questions that it's a wonder that you ever get any answers!"

"Are there any stories about a ghost on horseback?"

Helen asked. "It wouldn't appear often, and it would leave death in its wake."

"Is this linked to the bog bodies?" Geoff asked, and Helen nodded. "In that case, yes, there is."

I knew it.

"Can you tell me about it?" Helen asked, and Geoff nodded happily.

"Gladly. It's an old story, dating back to the eighteenth, maybe seventeenth, century, and it centres on an unkillable highwayman, Smiling Jack, and his immortal steed. I'll tell it to you properly in a moment, but it all hinges on Jack's magic sword; it allowed him to steal away the vitality from his victims, which in turn gave him eternal life.

"It's a hell of a tale."

"There's always a kernel of truth to these things," Helen said.

"You're right about that, and I have it on good authority that this story is true."

"Finally, we're getting somewhere!" Helen said, grinning in triumph.

"I wouldn't get too excited," Geoff replied. "Smiling Jack isn't your killer, I'm afraid."

"How can you be sure?"

"Because one of Connie's ancestors put him to rest centuries ago." Helen's face fell at Geoff's words. "I'm sorry to disappoint you, but it might be something worth looking into, at least."

"I suppose so," Helen said, trying to sound optimistic, but failing. In her mind's eye, she kept seeing Annika's screaming face; her terror inspired by Mrs Wilbur's last vision, and a fleeting glimpse of her killer.

It had been an image of a ghostly highwayman on a

terrible, devilish horse, bringing down an ornate sword in a deadly swing; exactly what Geoff's words had brought to mind. She slumped in her seat, more confused than ever.

There's still something I'm missing, she thought angrily, *and if I don't figure it out soon, it's going to get people killed.*

I can't lose anyone else. Tears ran down her cheeks, mirroring the motion of the rain. *Not here, not like this.*

She stared at the rain-drenched countryside as they sped on their way back to Walpole Manor.

"I fucking hate this place," Helen muttered.

Unknown to and unseen by her, in the back seat of Geoff's car, the spirit of Dennis Walpole nodded in agreement.

Chapter Nineteen – When the Bough Breaks

Charity

"You really should get that tooth looked at, Charity," Cat said, kicking her legs idly as they dangled over the arm of the sofa.

"She's right," Cait chimed in from her spot on the living room floor. "You're wincing every time you try to chew something."

"I'd rather not have someone filling my mouth with metal and clattering about in there, but thank you for the advice all the same." The freshly showered Charity sighed heavily, wishing that she was anywhere but Norfolk in that moment.

Well, not anywhere, she thought as her mind drifted back to Betony Island. *I can't imagine the awful life that Lola must have now.*

As much as she would protest otherwise, sending one of her own back to Betony had given her nightmares that she could not seem to shake. She'd contemplated telling Ivy about them, but her grief over Kiki's death was still too fresh.

"Some things are best dealt with alone," she murmured, looking at her left wrist. The bruises from the handcuffs had made her white tattoo stand out more starkly than she was used to, and the ghosts of her past were playing on her mind. "You were a monster, Lo, but you deserve better than that place.

"I should've killed you."

The twins glanced up at her words, but did not

comment on what she had said. Charity caught Cat staring, and raised an inquisitive eyebrow.

"What's that?" Cat asked, gesturing at the tattoo.

"You don't know?" Charity asked, dumbfounded. *I thought everyone on earth knew about Lamplight by now.*

"I know that mum asked us not to ask you about it," Cait said softly, "but it's clearly making you sad; is there anything we can do to help?"

"It's like a scar," Charity said softly. "It's a reminder of bad times, but also proof that I survived them."

"Why don't you get it removed?" Cait asked.

"I can't." Charity chuckled darkly. "This isn't any ordinary tattoo. It's Accountant's Ink; indelible, adaptable, and permanent, whilst also being forever linked to the Cep that marked me."

"Who did it?" Cat asked, her tone betraying her building anger.

"A man named Marcel Dupont." She sighed sadly. "Ivy has one too; they started out the same, but each changed to reflect our personalities and skills. Like I said, an Accountant's Ink is adaptable, and even people who don't know what it means get a sense that it's... evil, I guess.

"Sometimes I wonder if it's alive, and what it would think of me if it was."

"Do you want us to help you deal with him?" Cait said, coming to sit on the side of Charity's armchair. Charity shook her head and laughed softly. "What's so funny?"

"I don't think your mother would approve of me getting you into such hobbies," Charity said, not unkindly, "especially seeing as your skills are more suited to the role of circus acrobats, rather than hardened killers. It's sweet of you to offer, all the same."

"We can fight," Cat said firmly, getting nimbly to her feet. "We said that we'd help you, so let us!"

"You don't want that, so stop fucking asking!" Charity said sharply, truly feeling the responsibility of age for the first time in her life. "Enjoy your life of luxury and stop trying to play with knives; you're not made for it."

Her tooth was giving her more trouble than she would care to admit, and all she wanted was some peace and quiet after a night of police brutality, so Charity rose from her seat with the intention of heading to bed.

Cat, however, had other ideas and took a swing at Charity, clearly trying to wind her. Charity caught the younger woman's wrist with ease and twisted her into a painful armlock, immediately snatching a letter opener from the nearby side table and pressing it against Cat's neck.

Cait went to lunge at her, but Charity swept one leg through her pathway, knocking her to the ground, and placed her bare foot on Cait's slender neck. She held both women in place for a moment, silently raging, before letting them go.

Cat took a step back and opened her mouth to speak, but Charity roared at her, stopping her words dead in her mouth.

"NO! FUCKING STOP IT!"

The twins stared at her, speechless. Charity took a deep breath, mindlessly twirling the letter opener in her hand as she tried to get control of her emotions.

"This is not a fucking game," she growled at the two women, who both flushed a deep shade of shameful red. "This is real life, and if you treat this like it's some kind of silly playtime, you will die.

"You will try and fight someone like me, and they will kill you without even trying. You will die, and you will be dead forever!" She ran her free hand idly through her hair, unsure of how to make the twins understand what they were asking her to do. "They made me learn how to kill when I was four years old, and look at me now!"

"You're a living legend," Cait said breathlessly, and Charity looked at her in horror.

"I'm a fucking monster! I am *not* someone you should aspire to be." She shook her head angrily. "You may be in your thirties, but you are still children; just play your little games, enjoy your lives, and let the rest of us do the heavy lifting."

"You are the Grand Phantom!" Cat replied, puffing her chest out arrogantly. "If you can't teach us, then maybe you don't deserve that title."

"Then fight her for it," came a voice from across the room. The two girls whirled around to look at Constance, but Charity had noticed the movement in the corner of her eye and was not startled by her aunt's appearance.

"I wasn't gonna hurt them, Aunt Connie," Charity said softly. "I just-"

"They struck first, and everything you said is correct, Charity; you're not in the wrong here." Constance turned to look at Catarina. "Either you apologise to her for what you said, or attack her; it's up to you.

"Either way, you need to show some fucking humility when you speak to her."

"But, Mum-"

"Would you speak to me like that?" Connie asked sharply. "I know you definitely wouldn't have spoken to Uncle Dennis in that tone, but for some reason you think that it's acceptable to treat your cousin like a punching bag!?"

I feel like a fucking punching bag, Charity thought, but Cat looked at her defiantly. Cait took a step back, though, suitably cowed by Charity's actions and her mother's anger. *You always were the smart one, Caitlin.*

"Fine, I'll fight her," Cat said, her stance moving from arrogance to full swagger. "I can take her."

"Charity," Connie said softly, "please don't kill her."

"I won't," Charity said, her shoulders slumping. "Come on, Cat; I just want to go to bed and get some re-"

Cat lunged at her as she spoke, and Charity sidestepped her clumsy blow, driving the letter opener into her cousin's eye as she went. She was careful to stop the decorative knife from entering the young Ghost's brain, and Cat fell to the floor, screaming, as Charity pulled the dull blade out, ruining any chance of saving the eye.

Cait helped Cat to her feet, and the twins left the room, with the latter dripping blood on the floor as she went. Charity sighed heavily, and handed the letter opener to her aunt, who placed it on the table.

"We'll deal with that later," Connie said, leading Charity towards the kitchen. "Come on, lovely; let's go and have a cup of tea."

"I did warn them," Charity said softly. "I just hope they don't hate me for this."

"They'll be angry for a while, especially Cat, but they'll understand that what you did was necessary; it will keep them safe in the long run." Connie gave Charity a sad smile. "One day I'll tell you about something similar your father and I pulled, back in the day."

Charity looked at her aunt for a few seconds, as if she truly saw her for the first time.

This entire family is completely mad, she realised. *We've all been living in the shadows our whole lives, and now that darkness has come home to roost.*

At least I'm not perpetuating the cycle, she thought, trying to ignore Cat's blood on her hands.

Charity was on her second cup of tea when Helen and Geoff returned from their trip to Norwich. Charity gave her an awkward wave, half-expecting Helen to fly off the handle at the sight of her bruises.

Helen barely reacted, however, but Geoff's response shocked her.

"What the fuck did they do to you!?" he said, trembling with anger. "What the fuck happened to being innocent until proven guilty? I should go down there and give that Inspector a piece of my bloody mind!"

"I already put the screws to him, dear," Connie said, handing him a cup of tea. "He won't be troubling us again."

"Not to mention that Ivy got into his head and scrambled things around a bit," Charity said, warming her hands on her cup. "He looked like he'd had several strokes by the time she was done with him."

"I didn't know she could do that," Helen said softly. "Mind control is an atypical gift at the best of times, but it's especially rare in a Séance."

"I thought it was quite common," Charity said. "I

thought they could all bend people to their will."

"Ghosts and spirits, yes," Helen said, "but the living are another kettle of fish entirely. How long has she been able to do that?"

"Since I met her, for sure, and maybe earlier than that." Charity looked her in the eye. "It's not Max's influence, if that's what you're thinking."

"Who's Max?" Geoff asked.

"That's for another time," Connie said gently. "Oh, and before you find out from one of them, the twins attacked Charity. Cait backed down before things got too heated, but Cat pushed her luck too far; they're both upstairs now, tending to Cat's wound."

"What did you do to her?" Geoff asked, his voice gruff but not angry.

"She put her in her place," Connie said forcefully. "It's long overdue."

"We'll talk about this later," Geoff muttered. He turned to Helen. "Would you be able to go and patch up Cat as best you can, please?"

"Of course." She glanced at Charity as she rose from the table. "I'll fill you in on what I found a bit later on; things are more complicated than they first seemed."

"Take your time," Charity said. Geoff was still staring at her, and she squirmed in her seat. "I think I might go and have a lie down."

"That sounds like it would be for the best," he replied evenly.

She wordlessly left the kitchen, hoping that she hadn't permanently ruined her relationship with her uncle. Charity knew that he loved her, but the twins were his world and now she had harmed one of them irreparably.

She was so lost in her thoughts as she entered the

study-turned-bedroom that it took her a few seconds to register that there was not one, but two versions of Ivy in the room. In fact, they were naked and in bed together.

Just one simple day, please, she thought numbly.

Charity looked at both women, blinking slowly in shock. There was a moment where one of them, although she had no idea which, looked almost ashamed by their actions, but the other simply gave Charity a sultry, knowing smile and beckoned for her to join them.

"Fuck it," Charity muttered as she began to pull off her clothes, "why not?"

"You deserve some fun, darling," the shy one of them said, almost purring.

"And you must be Max," Charity replied. "A pleasure to meet you."

"Not yet," Ivy said playfully, "but it soon will be."

Charity chuckled and fell backwards on to the bed, landing comfortably between the two women. Ivy immediately began to touch and kiss her, whilst Max was more reserved.

"Go ahead," Charity urged. "I won't bite, unless you ask me to."

"The first is with the eye, and all that," Max replied wryly.

"As you wish," Charity said, waving an idle hand. "Either way, I've had a rough few days, so I only really have one request for the two of you."

"Which is?" Ivy asked.

"Fuck me until I can't feel a damn thing any more," Charity said, closing her eyes. "Give me total and utter bliss."

__Chapter Twenty__ – Three's Company

Ivy

Ivy collapsed on to the bed with a groan as Charity went to have a shower. Her entire body ached after a night on the frigid streets of Long Stratton, and she awkwardly wriggled out of her clothes. Although she wanted to curl up and snuggle down with Charity, a part of her hoped that the Ghost would linger in the hot water so that she could have the whole bed to herself.

She turned her head to look at Max, who was similarly undressed in the mirror, but sitting chastely on the edge of the bed instead of untidily slumped on the crumpled covers.

"Behold, perfection!" Ivy said with a mad giggle and a sweep of her arm. She winced as she lowered her cramped limb, crying out when a jolt of pain shot through her shoulder. "Oh, fuck! Ugh, I must've pulled something or trapped a nerve."

"Want me to give you a back rub?" Max asked.

"That seems like a rather crass use of the ability to manifest in the physical world," Ivy said, "but I'd appreciate it all the same."

"As you wish," Max said, and less than a heartbeat later Ivy felt powerful fingers kneading her tense, aching flesh. "You know, you really should look after your body thoroughly, Ivy."

"Using my gift wears me out," she mumbled into the pillow, mingled with animalistic grunts of satisfaction. "It's not neglect, as much as it looks like it."

"Oh, I know," Max replied softly, using a firm elbow

now, "but it works the other way round, too; the more physically robust you are, the more powerful feats of channelling you'll be able to perform."

Max continued to massage Ivy as her mind wandered and she completely lost track of time.

"It was strange, but putting the whammy on those cops earlier didn't tire me out in the slightest," she said after a while. "There was a time where that would've fucking floored me, but today I scarcely felt a thing."

"Would you like me to explain that to you?" Max asked, leaning down to whisper in her ear, her tongue tickling the lobe just a little as she spoke.

Oh, that's nice.

"I aim to please," Max whispered, and planted a gentle kiss on Ivy's neck before straightening up once again. "So, let me tell you about your little mind-bending talent, but first of all, what was it you called it again?"

"Brainjacking," Ivy said sheepishly. "That's what Charity called it, at least."

"Ah," Max said knowingly, "that's where the difference lies, you see."

"Go on," Ivy replied, barely noticing that her battered body was feeling far better than it normally did.

"Brainjacking, if we're using the technical definition, is the placing of a single thought or precise command into the mind of another; it usually requires direct eye contact and it takes a severe toll on the user, because they have to force their will in." Ivy could hear a smile in Max's voice. "It's the most common form of mind control, and it can, with practise, be resisted.

"Preaching is another, but you already know how that works. There are countless others too; glamour,

Sirensong, and weaving, to name a few." Max paused her ministrations to focus on what she was saying to Ivy. "None of those are the tools of a true telepath, though."

"I'm a Séance," Ivy said softly. "Apparently I'm not supposed to be a true telepath."

"Yet, here you are," Max replied firmly. "What you, and other telepaths, do when you put thoughts in someone's mind, is known as Whispering. You push a broad suggestion or vibe out towards their mind, and your mouth produces a torrent of barely audible words that reinforce the idea.

"The target takes on the mental burden of sorting through the noise to find the words that best fit the suggestion in the manner they find most persuasive; humans are agreeable social animals by nature, and Whispering takes advantage of that."

Ivy thought of the surge of words that had escaped her lips in the Police Station, and how even she had been unsure of what she'd said. *I felt so powerful,* she thought darkly, *and it was so fucking easy.*

A part of her was revolted that she could wield such a power, but another, deeper, part was relieved to have her mind control skills back; after all, if she had been without them in the summer, Joseph Evans would've lobotomised her.

Kill or be killed, Ivy thought. *That was Michaela's philosophy, and it earned her an early fucking grave.*

"She died to save your life, Ivy," Max said quietly. "I don't mean to intrude, but Exceptions exist for a reason; it isn't just a quirk of luck or genetics. You were chosen to have this gift, Ivy Livingston, and I find that notion rather encouraging.

"It makes me feel as if someone is looking out for

us."

"Do you really believe that?"

"Given the horrors I've endured," Max said softly, "I have to hold on to the belief that it has all happened for a reason; otherwise, all the torture and torment were for nothing."

A beat of silence hung in the air between them.

Maybe Edgar is the Séance, she mused, *and I'm something else entirely.*

Is that even possible?

Rather than confront such an existential question, she decided to focus on a more practical one.

"Tell me more about this Whispering, Max; can it be resisted?" Ivy asked.

"Rarely, and even then only by-"

Max's words were cut off as the door handle rattled. The mirror woman rolled off of Ivy's back and gathered the covers to hide their shared nudity as Charity walked into the room.

Well, Ivy thought as a smile crept on to her face, *this could be a recipe for a lot of fun.*

Ivy ran her fingers gently over Charity's alabaster skin, marvelling at just how pale she truly was, especially in contrast to the dark bedclothes that she was sprawled on top of. She sighed heavily as she leant in to plant a kiss on the inside of her girlfriend's thigh, all while Maxine ran her fingers through Charity's hair.

"Talk to me, Liv," Charity said, her voice little more than a breathless whisper. "Tell me what's going on in that head of yours."

"I was just enjoying how impossibly pale you are," Ivy said lovingly. "It's like you're made of paper; some beautiful origami creation, almost translucent in its delicacy. Sometimes I'm surprised that you have a shadow at all, you know."

"What would you do if she didn't?" Max asked, making eye contact with Ivy.

"Then I would fade into the darkness," she replied, her breath stirring the small patch of white pubic hair between Charity's legs, "becoming your shadow, if that's what you wanted, lover."

"You'd move lockstep with me, all through our lives?" Charity asked, gasping as Max slipped her tongue into her belly button.

"For all time," Ivy said, and moved lower down, tracing her lips over Charity's vulva. The Ghost groaned in anticipation and closed her eyes as she waited for Ivy's ministrations to grow firmer and more frantic, as they always did.

"You eat my cunt like you need it to survive," Charity moaned as she sunk her fingers into the Séance's thick hair.

"I do," Ivy murmured, savouring her partner's exquisite taste and texture.

If you were my last meal, lover, she thought dreamily, *then I would walk to the gallows a satisfied woman.*

The strange mirror dweller sang softly while her touch danced over Charity's bruised flesh; neither Ivy or Charity noticed that the darkened patches of the Ghost's skin returned to their usual sun-bleached whiteness wherever Max's fingers lingered.

As miraculous as her touch was, the strange doppelganger's skills were second fiddle to Ivy's considerable talents. Charity squirmed and moaned as Ivy's tongue directed more and more attention to her increasingly sensitive clitoris, and Max leant back on an idle elbow to watch the two women fuck.

"Care for a taste?" Ivy asked as she came up for air. Max grinned and kissed her deeply, making sure to get plenty of Charity's juices on her face before she turned to kiss the Ghost.

"I am an absolute treat," Charity said with a shuddering giggle as Ivy brought her ever closer to the orgasmic oblivion she craved. She pushed Ivy's face back against her cunt, grinding her hips with the urgency of someone on the cusp of sweet release, and her girlfriend was only too happy to oblige her unspoken request.

Ivy faltered for a second as she heard, rather than saw, Max rise up from the bed. The strange mirror woman leant in close and whispered an apology to her host, along with a question.

"I'm afraid I'm needed elsewhere," she said in hushed tones in Ivy's ear, "and I would like to know if I could borrow a smattering of your power for a while? I need it to save your brother's life."

Take what you need, whenever you need it, Ivy thought. *Come and go as you please, too; my mind is not a prison.*

"Thank you," Max whispered. "Have enough fun for both of us."

I will do, Ivy thought, but Max was already gone. Instead of searching for her, she resumed her licking with renewed intensity.

Charity's orgasm began suddenly, almost without any warning. Ivy couldn't help but grin as she gripped her lover's thighs, holding on for dear life as she pushed the Ghost over the edge again and again and again, causing her to scream with pleasure as she scratched at the bedclothes like a woman possessed.

Soon she was left trembling and breathless, with a blissful smile on her face. Ivy looked up at her, making eye contact in the dim light as Charity's irises glowed and trembled, almost as if they were straining against the very confines of her eyes.

I've never seen them do that, she thought, but their curious behaviour soon passed and Ivy was left wondering if she imagined it. Charity caught her looking, and gave her an exhausted, but satisfied grin.

"Admiring your handiwork?" she asked, and Ivy nodded. Charity chuckled softly as she continued to speak. "I'm sure the whole house heard that, but I really don't care."

"Did I give you the bliss you wanted?" Ivy asked, moving up beside her, nestling her damp face into the warm hollow between Charity's neck and shoulder.

"That, and then some," Charity sighed. She looked around the dark room, confused. "Where did Maxine go?"

"She apparently had other business to attend to," Ivy said softly. She nuzzled her nose against Charity's cheek, but the Ghost yelped in pain. "What's the matter, Charity?"

"My fucking tooth," she grumbled. "That fucking bastard cracked it when he hit me. I was hoping that it would heal up on its own, but I think it's too far gone; some injuries are too grave, even for me.

"I don't even think I can go down on you tonight, Liv," she said grumpily. "You know how much I hate to be a Pillow Princess!"

"You are anything but, Charity," Ivy said with a chuckle. "Besides, I'm so tired that I think I'd rather just get a good night's sleep."

"If you say so," Charity said, sulking slightly.

"Hey," Ivy said, placing her finger underneath Charity's chin as carefully as she could, "you can see a dentist in the morning, and then fuck me senseless the moment you're patched up."

"If I can get an appointment before the summer," Charity muttered. "You know how bad it is nowadays."

"You're in Norfolk," Ivy said with a smile. "Just throw the Walpole name around a little; that's sure to open some doors for you."

"And if it doesn't?"

"Then I'll give them a talking to," Ivy said, grinning in the darkness. "It's amazing what a whisper can achieve."

Chapter Twenty One – I Know the Drill

Charity

Charity tried not to think about the growing pain in her mouth as Geoff drove her to the small town of Newton Flotman. She'd spent over an hour calling around every NHS dentist in the area and not a single one of them had any available appointments, even for a dental emergency like hers.

Constance had offered to get in touch with hers, but she was all the way down in London and Charity did not wish to travel such a distance, especially in the middle of a case. Besides, a short car journey with Geoff was proving to be uncomfortable enough.

"You, uh, don't have to come in with me," Charity said quietly in a desperate bid to break the awful silence.

"If you'd rather go in on your own, that's entirely your choice," he said, his voice barely audible over the rumble of the road.

"I'm not sure how long it's going to take, so I can just get a bus back to Long Str-"

"I'm not angry at you," Geoff said, cutting across her words. "I know that Cat attacked you first, and that you were just defending yourself."

He sighed heavily and drummed his fingers on the steering wheel. He shot her a glance and gave her a sad smile.

"I mean it, Charity; I'm not angry with you." He turned his eyes back to the road as his voice hardened. "I *am* angry at Connie, however; she was the fucking adult in the room, and she pushed the whole situation into violence when she should've defused it instead.

"I know that you're the Grand Phantom, and that you're supposed to have the loyalty of your Ghosts, but this archaic method of enforcement by violence is just barbaric." He frowned as he spoke. "I know that traditions are important and I know why you have some of them, especially the Last Haunting, but maybe it's time to change the way things are done.

"A more gentle approach would create a new generation of Ghosts that aren't destined to be killers and spies."

Charity stared at him in shock.

How does he know all this?

"Now I'm not saying that having a few members of your community trained in warfare and espionage isn't useful from time to time, but when you can't even come together to mourn your kin without risking a faction war, things have clearly gone too far." He reached out and took her hand in his. "You can be the first one to really make a difference, Charity; you can push them to do better, to *be* better."

She opened her mouth to reply, but he shushed her before she could speak.

"I know that you're not allowed to discuss any of this, which is why I'm talking *at* you." The first hint of a smile crept on to his lips. "I can probably guess at what you were about to say, so I'll answer as best I can.

"Regarding where I heard all this, there are written records aplenty on the topic and some are by the more loose-lipped Walpoles; not all members of your family were as devoted to the art of secrecy as the current generations are." He tapped his fingers on the steering wheel as he went. "The main source was a Walpole who fell out with the family so badly that he was buried in an unmarked grave and his name was scrubbed from every family tree and record; or so they thought, at least."

Geoff whistled softly through his teeth for emphasis.

"No-one does feuds quite like us," Charity said with a soft chuckle. "I'm not surprised that we punished him so severely; to betray us like that is... well, it's just unthinkable, Uncle Geoff."

"Still, I'm glad he did," Geoff said softly. "His choice to speak out about the mysteries of the Ghosts has given me the information to respond to yesterday's actions and apportion blame where it is deserved.

"Believe me, Charity, after what happened to Cat yesterday, Connie is officially *on notice*." Geoff sighed sadly. "We'll get back to normal soon enough, but a few weeks of an uneasily shared bed is worth it to protect the girls, and to protect you.

"The rogue Ghost's name was Garland, in case you were wondering." He sighed heavily. "I don't think anyone should be removed so completely from the world; we all make mistakes in the moment, be that spilling secrets, taking eyes, or egging on fights."

There were a few minutes of silence before the Ghost replied.

"Thank you, Uncle Geoff," Charity said softly.

"What for?"

"For understanding." She stared through the rain streaked window, blinking back tears. "I hope Cat and Cait will forgive me, eventually."

"They will. They love you more than anything, Charity; whenever they see you, you're all they talk about for weeks afterwards." He gave her a quick smile. "They're odd girls, but they're good at heart.

"I'll make sure that they know that Connie forced your hand."

"I'm so tired, Uncle Geoff," Charity said, suddenly exhausted and furious at the same time. "I'm so sick of having my hand forced; of being treated like a weapon or the instrument of someone else's will.

"I'm seeing a Ministry therapist, but it seems that all she's focussed on is getting me back on my feet and into the field. It was the same with my cancer treatment over the years; just enough to keep me working, to keep me killing for them."

"Do you not want to do it any more?"

"It's all I've ever known," Charity said quietly. "I wasn't even allowed to be a child. I've always been a weapon to them; even my parents thought the same."

"You know, if I may call on some training from an earlier life," Geoff said softly, "sometimes stepping off the path you were planning on taking is what you were meant to do all along. Can I ask why you're feeling like this now, instead of earlier?"

"My team..." Charity said quietly. "My team are people, Uncle Geoff; real people, and they treat me like a person, too. Hell, one of them was even real enough for me to fall in love with, without either of us even knowing it was happening!"

"That sounds like a good thing," he replied. "It sounds like you found your compassion."

"You don't understand what that means," Charity said, sobbing now. "All the people I've hurt, the ones I've killed... suddenly, they're real people too. If you're right, and this is my humanity finally surfacing, then it's tearing me apart.

"My compassion is killing me, Uncle Geoff." She put her head in her hands. "I'm drowning in guilt."

Geoff stared at the rain-soaked road for a moment before speaking, and when he did, Charity broke down into hysterical sobs.

"I forgive you for what you've done, Charity," Geoff said, "and what you're feeling now; the humanity that you're allowing yourself to experience, in the face of all your training, that is why I think you can lead the Ghosts to a better path, sweetheart.

"I'm so proud of you, Charity."

"Thank you for seeing me at such short notice," Charity said as she sat awkwardly in the dental examination chair. "I, um, I've not been to the dentist for a long time, so I'm sure that my teeth are pretty grim.

"Sorry, in advance."

"No need to apologise," the dentist said, giving her a warm, perfect smile. "You know, I actually didn't have any available appointments for a while, but then you said that you were a Walpole and... well, I must confess that my curiosity got the better of me and I decided to cancel my lunch break to see you."

"Why?" Charity asked, suddenly wary.

"I've lived in and around this area for a while, and the Walpole family is legendary," he said with a chuckle, "or infamous, depending on who you ask. I'm sure my salmon sandwiches will understand that I wanted to spend my lunchtime with someone with a little more celebrity than them.

"I'm not sure I gave you my name over the phone," he said, snapping on his examination gloves. Charity noticed the woven bracelet that he wore; bright blue with a stylised lizard. "I'm Nicholas Gardener, but you can call me Nicky."

"Nice bracelet, Nicky," she said, unsure of what else to say. *Why can't he just get on with it?*

"Oh, thank you," he said with a laugh. "I got it in Lanzarote; a pretty lady gave it to me under the light of a full moon."

"Sounds like a lucky charm to me," Charity said, still on edge. "Can we, uh, get on with this, please? I'm a bit funny about doctors and dentists; no offence meant."

"Of course, and I understand entirely! Please, settle back in the chair." As she sat back, he leant in and gave her a conspiratorial whisper. "Between you and me, graveyards are my personal phobia."

He quickly got her all set up, and then deftly checked around her mouth with assorted dental tools; Charity did now know what they were technically called, and she did not care to find out, either.

I've not been in a dentist's chair since Lamplight, she thought anxiously. *And once today is done, hopefully I'll die before I get back in another.*

Nicky was humming softly as he was clattering around in her mouth, and Charity winced suddenly as he sharply tapped her damaged tooth.

"I take it that's the one that's giving you trouble?" he asked, and Charity replied as best she could. "Well, it's got quite a bit of damage to it, so I can either repair it for you or pull it out. I try to save as many teeth as possible, however, and the repair won't be complicated, but it's ultimately up to you."

"Will I have to come back for a repair?"

"I can do it for you today," he said. "I've got a special kind of resin that mimics the natural material of the tooth, so your body won't even know the difference; it's quite spectacular stuff, if I say so myself!"

"Then we'll go for the repair," Charity said, closing her eyes. He reached for a clipboard with some forms on, but she waved her hand at him. "I'll sign all that later; let's just get this done."

"Alright then!" Nicky said, almost gleefully. "I do enjoy your enthusiasm, Ms Walpole. Your teeth are beautiful and completely stainless, too; do you get them whitened?"

"After a fashion," Charity replied enigmatically. "Are you going to need to give me an injection?"

"Yes; there's a touch of drilling involved, and I don't want you to feel any pain."

"I'd prefer to skip it, if that's possible, please."

"Are you certain?" he asked, and she nodded. *It won't work on me,* she thought, *and let's just skip the conversation that realisation will start.* "As you wish; you're a brave girl!"

Charity closed her eyes and tried to lose herself in the meditation techniques that she'd learned during her time at Lamplight, but the shrill whine of the drill and the sensation of it skittering on her teeth made her clutch the armrests for dear life. Soon pain was shooting through her mouth and the scent of burning bone filled her nostrils, threatening to plunge her back to the day that Betony Island was engulfed in flames; the catastrophic end to Project Lamplight.

I should've brought Ivy with me, she thought, her eyes screwed up against the pain, but then the drilling was done as quickly as it started. *Is that it!?*

"I've just got to apply the resin," Nicky said, "and then it's just a quick blip of UV light to set and seal it, then we'll be all done."

Charity exhaled heavily as he mixed up the plasticky

substance, but was genuinely surprised at the skill of the eccentric dentist. *I thought they were supposed to have assistants,* she mused, *but I guess this is the private sector; maybe the rules are different here.*

"You know," Nicky said as he applied the resin, "when you first walked in, I thought that you would have a lovely smile hidden underneath that pained frown, and when we're done, I'm certain that you'll prove me right."

Weirdo.

"I'm just going to give the resin a quick blast of UV light, so just shut your eyes for me, lovely," he said, and she did as he asked. The uncomfortable, yet familiar, feeling of ultraviolet rays on her skin made her tremble slightly, but he did not seem to notice. It was over after less than thirty seconds, and Charity opened her eyes wide in shock.

"That's it?" she asked.

"Almost," Nicky replied with a chuckle. "I just need to give it a quick polish, and then we'll check how comfortable you're feeling."

A different drill buzzed in her mouth this time, polishing the surface of the repaired tooth. It only took a minute or so, and then he invited her to give her mouth a quick rinse. She bit down gingerly, but found that not only was the pain completely gone, the tooth also fit better than it ever had before.

"Feeling good?" he asked, already knowing her response, and she nodded.

"Damn, Nicky, you're pretty good!" Charity said as a nervous giggle escaped her lips. She smiled sheepishly at her own jitters.

"There's that smile that I knew was hiding away there!" Nicky beamed at her, and Charity felt her flesh creep a little. *Steady on, mate; no need to get too excited.*

"Can I get up now?" she asked.

"Yep," he said, as she got to her feet. "That's it; you're all good to go."

"How much do I owe you?" she asked, reaching for the tattered wallet in her leather coat.

"You know what, don't worry about it," he said with a kind smile.

"Are you sure?" she replied, freezing in place. "I can afford it."

"I got to meet one of the elusive Walpoles, which I will dine out on for the rest of my life; that's payment enough." He chuckled at her. "Go on, Charity; you get on home now, before I change my mind."

"Well, thank you, Nicky," she said, giving him an uncomfortable smile. "Take care."

"And you," he said cheerfully, and then called after her as she headed through the door and back out into the busy waiting room. "Don't forget to floss!"

Charity gave him a shaky thumbs up and quickly dodged through the waiting patients, slipping out the back door and into the car park before anyone had a chance to speak to her.

He didn't ask about the sunglasses, she realised as she walked back to Geoff's car. *How strange.*

Chapter Twenty Two – Lover, Mother, Drinker, Failure

Helen

"So," Helen said, sitting in bed with Connie, a mug of hot chocolate in her hands, "why don't you tell me about Smiling Jack? Geoff mentioned it to me yesterday; he said that some of my autopsy details reminded him of the story."

"Jack's not your culprit, I'm afraid."

"Geoff mentioned that a Walpole finally put him to rest years ago," she said sadly. "I guess it's just not allowed to be that simple, is it?"

"We are cursed to live in a world of infinite complexity," Constance said with a sigh. She frowned slightly as she tried, and failed, to sew together an eyepatch for Cat. "I never was any good with anything much smaller than a knife."

"Want me to do it?" Helen asked, placing her hot chocolate on the night stand. "I used to deal with the living, as well as corpses, and the skills never really leave you."

"Why do you think I started it in front of you?" Connie said slyly as she passed the half-constructed eyepatch to Helen.

"You could've just asked me, Connie."

"You already stitched Cat up last night," she said with mock haughtiness. "To ask your help a second time would be gauche!"

"Third," Helen corrected.

"What?"

"You asked for my help twice last night," Helen reminded her. "You asked me to talk to Geoff; make him see things from our perspective, as it were."

"It didn't work," Connie said with a smile, "so it doesn't count."

I don't think it works that way, Helen thought, deftly stitching the eyepatch together, but she left the words inside her head. Connie sighed heavily again and settled back against the nest of pillows she'd created on her side of the bed.

"I would've gone steady with you, if you'd been of a mind to ask," Connie said unprompted. "Maybe we both could've had different lives; without either the Ministry or the Amberlight Agency."

"Do you regret taking control of the Agency?" Helen asked softly.

"God only knows how bad things would be now if I hadn't," Connie replied. "Still, maybe we should've just jumped on the back of my old Indian and just fucked off into the sunset like you suggested that night.

"Of course, you hadn't met Dennis then, had you?"

"We met at your birthday party the following weekend," Helen said. She smiled at the memory of the young Dennis Walpole; still with a touch of darkness in his hair, and a considerable swagger in his step, but all softened by his unrestrained sense of humour. "I turned down the Ravenblade position because you asked me to, you know.

"You never wanted that life for me, and I never did thank you properly for steering me on to the right path."

"You're welcome, Helen," Connie said, barely audibly. She stared into the middle distance for a moment before speaking. "I only had the twins with Alphonse because I felt like I was running out of time; is that selfish of me?"

"No," Helen said, putting a gentle arm around the Ghost. "If either of us is the selfish one, it's most certainly me; at least you wanted the children you had."

"Den and Lin could've said no," Connie said, but Helen shook her head sadly.

"They did what was expected of them. Harper was right; I did saddle them with children that otherwise would never have existed."

"But the world is kinder with them in it," Connie replied, almost angrily. "They have a positive influence on us, and they'll do better than we ever could, Flash!"

"You've not called me that in almost sixty years," Helen said, blinking back shock.

"Do you know what I thought about when I was teaching Charity to ride?" Connie asked, leaning towards Helen. "What I've thought about every single second since you first set foot in this house?"

"What?" Helen said, putting the finished eyepatch aside.

"That I made a mistake," Connie said tearfully, "and then another, and another, and now I'm old and there's nothing I can do to get that time back!"

"Your life with Geoff and the girls is-"

"It's lovely, yes, but it isn't what I wanted, Flash!" Connie grabbed Helen's shoulder tightly, as if she was fearful that she would suddenly vanish. "I never wanted to get married to anyone, except maybe that intelligent, stupid girl with the flash of white in her otherwise raven hair, but she didn't want me.

"She wanted to *be someone*, and she got what she wanted."

Connie let out a loud sob.

"And I'm happy for you, Helen; I really am." Helen looked at Connie, dumbstruck. "You chose what was right for you and I should accept that, but sometimes I hate you for being so fucking selfish.

"What about me? Huh? You get to be the great Dr Mickelson, constantly pining over Dennis, all whilst I try so hard to forget about you." Connie's tears threatened to overwhelm her. "I hate you so fucking much, Helen, and I never feel so old as I do when you're here."

"Do you want me to-"

"If you so much as even think about offering to leave," Connie sobbed, "I will sit in this bed until I fucking die of grief. You can't just run away when things get uncomfortable, Helen; I know you think it's a kindness, but it's cowardice, plain and simple.

"I've never met anyone as cruel as you, Helen, nor anyone so fucking kind." Connie shook her head angrily and wiped her eyes. "At least Harper has the decency to be evil, through and through."

"She wears it like a badge of honour," Helen muttered, her mouth souring at the thought of the Deputy Director's snide face.

There was a beat of silence between the two women.

I always feel a little drunk when I'm with you, Connie, Helen thought sadly. *I'm not sure what it says about us, but I've a feeling that it's nothing good.*

"There's no guarantee it would've ended well," Helen said after a few minutes of painful quiet.

"There's no proof that it would've ended badly."

"We likely would've died young, Connie." Helen

whispered.

"I think I died a long time ago," Connie replied, her voice flat and expressionless.

"What can I do?" Helen asked, but Constance just shook her head dismissively. "There must be something-"

"We're old, Flash," she said, her voice more lifeless than Helen had ever heard it before. "We're done, my love, and our time is over. There's nothing left for us to do, aside from help our children to do the best that they can.

"It's their time now."

"But-"

"We fucked it, Helen," Connie said, rising from the bed. "There aren't second chances in this world; we missed our moment, and now we get to live with that forever, or at least until it kills us."

She picked up the eyepatch.

"Thanks for doing this, Flash," she whispered. "I'll go give it to Cat now."

Helen watched Connie walk out of the room and, as soon as the door shut behind the Ghost, she let out an explosive sigh. Tears gathered in the corners of her eyes and her lip trembled as she sat in the middle of the otherwise empty bed, surrounded by the ghosts of her achievements.

This is all I have left, she realised. *I'm such a fucking fool.*

An old fool.

She reigned in her tears and got shakily to her feet. She wiped her eyes and decided to head down to Geoff's study to look more into the legend of Smiling Jack.

Yes, work will help, she thought shakily, *but first, I*

need a drink.

Helen was sipping her third glass of Jack Daniel's when her phone rang, cutting through the music she'd put on. She grumbled slightly and answered without even looking at who was calling her.

"Yes?" she said sharply.

"And hello to you, too, Mum," Silas said, clearly affronted. "You're in a good mood."

"There's no need to be sarcastic, Silas." She sighed heavily. "I'm pretty deep in the weeds here, son; can this wait until another time?"

"I guess the social parts can," he said softly, "but I just wanted to let you know that I'm still alive and I'm on my way back from my overseas trip. Oh, I got Noor to look after the ferrets in the end."

"Yes, I know," Helen said. "She called me yesterday."

"Are they alright?" Silas asked, clearly panicked.

"They're fine," Helen replied. "She just needed a favour, that's all."

"And you aren't going to elaborate, are you?" Silas said, disappointed.

"She'll ask if she needs your help." Helen drained her glass, wincing a little as the liquid burned her throat. *I've had worse,* she thought, *but I've also had so much better.* "Is there anything else?"

"Just the one thing," Silas said, pausing for a second before continuing. "Do you have any shares in Cherry Pharmaceuticals?"

"Harper never deigned to give me a slice of that particular pie, and I didn't want to make her richer by buying any, so no." Her brow furrowed in suspicion. "Why?"

"I was going to advise you to sell them, post-haste," Silas said quietly. "In fact, sell anything you have that is either directly owned by Eigenforce International, or any of its subsidiaries. Trust me, Mum, it's the best play right now."

"Did you call me from the other side of the fucking world," she said, the incredulous anger in her voice rising as she spoke, "just to engage in insider trading!?"

"The law requires me to say no," he replied, but she could hear the smile in his voice, which only served to make her even angrier.

"Since when have you ever cared about the fucking law?" Helen snapped.

"I-"

"Thievery, blackmail, fraud, corporate espionage; it's all a fucking game to you, isn't it?" Helen's breath came in short ragged gasps.

"I try to enjoy my work," Silas said through gritted teeth. "You should try it some time; it'll do wonders for your sense of well-being."

"And did you enjoy it when you killed Cooper and Vallance? Were their deaths good for your well-being, you fucking monster?" The words were out of Helen's mouth before she could stop them.

There was a second of stony silence before Silas spoke.

"So that's how it is, huh?" Silas's words were clipped, but the hurt in his voice was plain to hear.

"Silas, I-" Helen began to back pedal, but he cut her off.

"I understand," he said sadly. "You're grieving, and most likely drinking, given your tone, so you're going to say things you don't mean; still, though, you know what a fucking wound that is for me, Mum.

"I've always defended you, even when I probably shouldn't have, and this is what I get from you?"

"I'm sorry, Silas." Her words were so quiet that she wasn't sure he could possibly hear her.

"Just be honest with me, for once," Silas said. "Do you really think I killed those two agents?"

Helen tried to search her heart for the truth, but all she could find was a mire of doubt.

"Your silence is deafening."

"I'm sorry, Silas, but there are so many unanswered questions about that day."

"You're supposed to trust me," he said sadly. "I'm your fucking child, Helen."

"I'm sorry, son, but you've too much of Harper in you."

"And how is the Arch Cunt, herself?" Silas asked, his tone swiftly moving from sorrow to venom. "Did she enjoy your grief at the funeral or was she too busy trying to fuck Lin?"

Helen was speechless.

"I have to go now, Helen," Silas said sharply. "The people who actually care about me need my help. Why don't you go and pay a visit to Harper, hmm?

"She always liked you better when you were drunk."

"Silas-"

"Don't worry, Helen," he hissed, "I'll try not to murder too many people on my way home."

Helen went to respond, but Silas hung up on her.

<u>Chapter Twenty Three</u> – Can I Get a Witness?

Ivy

"I can't believe nobody has seen this thing," Ivy said softly as she strolled around the streets of Long Stratton, trying to catch another psychic glimpse of the man that she suspected was their next victim. Some small unspecified worry niggled at the back of her mind, driving her mad like some sort of mental splinter. "You'd think that a giant black dog would draw more witnesses, but apparently not.

"To be honest with you, Max, I'm a bit stumped on this one."

"I think it's important to ascertain if this beast is actually invisible, or if people just aren't seeing it," Max said, her scarred face reflected in the small mirror that Ivy now carried around with her.

I used to hate looking at my reflection, she thought, *but it's a lot easier now that it isn't really mine any more.*

"Is there are difference," Ivy asked, "aside from semantics, I mean?"

"There's a tremendous difference!" Max looked at her with wide eyes. "True invisibility has only ever been achieved by Ghosts alone, but there are several beasties that take advantage of a kind of proto-invisibility. Others use chameleon-like adaptive camouflage-"

"Squid," Ivy corrected. "Squid use adaptive camouflage, whilst chameleons change colour to reflect emotional state or sexual maturity."

"Is that so?" Max asked, and Ivy gave her a nod. "Well, you learn something every single day. As I was saying, some use a kind of adaptive camouflage, and others can only be seen by their targets; they seem to play on the human urge to overlook things that don't belong, much to their advantage.

"Still, a giant black dog is mundane enough that it would be difficult to ignore."

"Ordinary enough to stick out?" Ivy said, her cane tapping on the floor as she walked.

"Exactly," Max replied. "Do you need the cane today, Ivy?"

"No, but I'd rather have it and not need it, than need it and not have it; it's a long walk home with misbehaving legs." She paused for a moment. "Charity saw our dog, so that must narrow it down, right?"

"Not as much as you might think," Max said sadly. "From what Helen was saying, it seems like she had some sort of recurring nightmare about the dog as a small child; perhaps she was a victim and somehow escaped?"

"That doesn't feel right," Ivy said, frowning. "Don't ask me how I know, but it feels too simple."

"I trust you," Max said. She looked at Ivy, smiling for a moment. "You know, I've worked countless cases over the past centuries, but you are by far the best person to pound the pavement with."

"Who was the previous title holder?" Ivy asked, curious.

"Your brother. He's currently on a boat heading back from the Southern Ocean, and I must say that the weather off the coast of Antarctica is a damn sight better than it is here." Max frowned theatrically as a fat drop of rain struck the silvery surface of the mirror. "I can't say that I care for the constant grey dampness of Britain, truth be told."

"I doubt anyone really does." Ivy let her mind wander a little, casting her psychic net far and wide. She frowned slightly; there was much more paranoia and fear in the air than a few days earlier. "Things are worsening here; more people are *troubled* than before. It's going to take me a while to hone in on our target.

"Why don't you tell me a story? An old case, perhaps, to ease my mind and let the thoughts flow more readily."

"I'd rather not divulge the details of a case; sometimes speaking the name of an ancient evil can wake it from its slumber."

"Very well," Ivy muttered. "Tell me whatever you like."

"Geoff mentioned something about Dwarves over breakfast, and the autopsy report Helen added to the pile made a reference to Windstahl; do you know much about that?" Max asked, and Ivy shook her head. "Well, that seems like a perfect topic for this rainy lunchtime stroll.

"So," Max asked playfully, "are you sitting comfortably?"

Yes, I am, Ivy thought with a smile. She continued to walk through the town, now moving entirely on instinct and extrasensory perception. *Tell me about the dwarves.*

"Just to give you an idea of scale, the Dwarven kingdom used to extend across all of Europe, Asia, and Africa." Max said. "Caverns and tunnels and vast underground buildings were carved into the stone beneath the earth of every single nation spanning half the planet; it was said that you could walk from Kamchatka to Iberia without ever once seeing daylight, going via the tip of Africa if you so desired.

"Their empire was vast, Ivy; so impossibly vast, and it was all a single contiguous city." Max's voice grew quiet with awe. "Not just a city, but *the* City; the biggest metropolitan area on the planet. I won't bore you with the gritty details of their governance, but it is important to the story to know that they were ruled over by a monarch.

"Orbyn, the Under King," Max said, and a touch of venom coloured her voice. "He would later be known as Orbyn the Mad, however, as his rule led to the downfall of his entire civilisation."

"Empires always tumble eventually," Ivy muttered as she grew closer to the Knot in the Tangle that Charity had taken her to before. "What caused this one to fall?"

"Nobody is exactly sure," Max said, almost warily, "but there were scattered reports of infighting, madness, and acts of unspeakable violence between the Dwarves. Some rumours said that their unique skills had caused the rift in their people; they could create items from mere concepts, you see.

"A poem could be forged into a sword, or a promise into a shield." Max sighed sadly. "They were true artists, but such unbridled talent and power can only be wielded for so long before it incurs a terrible price."

Ivy nodded as she entered the area that the woman disappeared in only three nights earlier. She walked towards the bins and squatted down close to the ground, using her cane for support. *There's something here,* she thought.

I can feel it.

"Regardless of what started the slow decline of the Dwarven society, it was completely destroyed by Orbyn; he created something so terrible that it destroyed them all." Max continued as Ivy pulled a planchette from her pocket and turned it over in her fingers a few times. "Some say that it's still down there, miles beneath the earth; a great evil waiting to be unleashed.

"Personally, I hope their entire empire stays buried forever."

"So what's Windstahl?" Ivy asked, ripping open a packet of salt with her teeth. *Takeaways are so very useful.*

"Ancient Dwarven metal, literally forged from the union of wind and steel; there are four different types, depending on the direction of the wind that was used. Weapons forged from Windstahl are some of the oldest and most dangerous in existence."

"Thank you for the history lesson, Max," Ivy said as she sprinkled the salt over the wet ground. "I will have to ask you for some quiet now, please."

Max nodded, and Ivy pocketed the mirror. She kissed the little wooden heart of the planchette and fogged up the glass circle in its centre with her breath, muttering as she did so.

"Show me things unseen," she whispered softly. "Show me that which only I am meant to see."

There was a brief pause as the rain around her seemed to slow down and the condensation on the planchette's window turned to frost. Ivy's heartbeat slowed in her chest as her soul seemed to leave her body for just a moment, but then the frost melted and the rain returned to its normal pace with a dull roar.

Let's hope Teaser was right about this, she thought as she raised the planchette up to her eye and looked through the glass.

What she saw through the window was not only the alley, but the misty shadows of the world beyond.

Whilst Mallory's gift enabled him to see the moment of violence that created the Knot in the Tangle, Teaser had theorised that Ivy's particular skills would allow her to act as a kind of living Spirit Camera; provided she had the right tools to hand, of course.

The special lens in the planchette was taken from Teaser's oldest, and now defunct, camera and she'd applied a special polish to it in the hope that it would be powerful enough to allow Ivy a glimpse into the spirit world.

The eerie sight before her was one of awkward glows, crackling jerks in the outline of stationary objects, and a bizarre kaleidoscope of contrasting colours. It reminded Ivy of some of the old rotoscoped films that Edgar was particularly keen on watching.

He's going to love this, she thought. *It'll be like stepping into a Ralph Bakshi flick.*

Something on the ground before her caught her eye; a footprint, glowing a ghostly pale blue, much like the spirit fire that surrounded the ghosts that Edgar conjured. A closer look revealed that it was a paw print of monstrous size, much like one that a gigantic demon dog would leave in its wake.

"Teaser, you're a fucking genius," Ivy said with a smile. "Well, at least we know that Charity isn't going round the twist, which is no small piece of good news."

She fished around in her raincoat with her free hand and pulled out a lollipop, ripping the wrapper open with her teeth and popping it into her mouth without a second thought. The sugary treat was pleasant on her tongue, and she enjoyed the way it clattered softly against her teeth.

"Well, that's troubling," Max muttered, but she did not hear her words; Ivy was far too engrossed with the footprint to notice the soft grumbling. She opened her other eye, the one not looking through the planchette, and compared the two visions.

"There you are," Ivy said triumphantly, tracing her fingers along the wet asphalt. Where the glowing footprint was in the spirit world, there was an incredibly faint scorch mark on the road in the physical one.

"What have you found?" Max asked eagerly. Ivy looked along the road and realised there were a whole set of scorched paw prints, highlighted by the glistening sheen from the rain. She pocketed the planchette and removed the lollipop from her mouth before speaking.

"The dog has left considerable residue in the spirit world, which suggests that it is absolutely a ghost of some kind. The interesting thing, however, is that it's leaving marks in this world too; there are burns on the road, just there."

"So what are we dealing with?" Max said, and Ivy thought for a moment, thinking through the local lore she'd pored over after making love to Charity the night before.

It doesn't quite make sense, yet, but I think we're getting closer.

"We've been looking at this thing too hard," Ivy said,

with a shake of her head. "This has all the hallmarks of a traditional Black Dog; a Church Grim, if you will. We assumed that it *couldn't* be a Grim because it was taking living people, but everything I've just seen confirms our first, and most obvious, guess; this *is* a Grim.

"It means we've been asking the wrong question all along."

"If this is a Grim, then why *these* people?" Max asked and Ivy nodded.

"The answer doesn't lie in the creature, but the victims." Ivy pulled out her phone and began typing out a quick text to Charity. "We know who our next victim is, and we know what's hunting them.

"All we can do now is learn everything we can about Black Dogs before sunset," Ivy said, hitting send as she asked Geoff and Charity to meet her when they were done with the dentist. "Hopefully, if we focus on how to defeat this thing, we can stop anyone else being taken."

"Then we don't have much time."

"I work better under pressure," Ivy said firmly. "Tell me, Max, have you ever killed a vengeful spirit before?"

"I can't say I have, old girl," she said sadly.

"Well, hopefully today we can change that." Her phone buzzed in her hand, and she quickly read the message. "Time to saddle up, Maxine; they're on their way already."

Chapter Twenty Four – Black Dogs of Legend

Charity

"Where are we headed, Ivy?" Charity asked as the drenched Séance climbed into the back of the idling Volvo.

"Bungay, I think," Ivy said, belting herself in. The lollipop in her mouth clattered against her teeth, making Charity's stomach churn. "What's the matter?"

"The lollipop is a new addition; did you get an injection at the doctor's or something?" she said, trying to cover her discomfort with humour.

"It just helps me focus," Ivy said. "I can get rid of it, if it's making you uncomfortable."

"Please," Charity said, and Ivy wound down the window before tossing the sweet at a bin as they sped past it. Charity blinked in surprise at Ivy's perfect aim. "Damn, Liv, maybe I should start charging for my throwing knife lessons!"

"Consider it a fair exchange for the swordplay I've taught you," Ivy replied cheerfully. "Did you get your tooth fixed?"

"Yeah, in and out, no problems whatsoever," Charity said with a broad smile.

"He didn't even charge her," Geoff said. "He sounds like a lovely, albeit rather odd, fellow."

"Liv, you would not believe how weird this guy was," Charity said, turning to face her lover. "He was a freak, even by dentist standards."

"So, what are we looking for in Bungay?" Geoff

asked.

"I read somewhere that it has a particularly notable Black Dog legend attached to it, so we need to gather as much information as possible. Hopefully I'll be able to pick up a new lead from just being in the right place at the right time."

"I thought that you didn't think this was a Black Shuck, Charity?" Geoff asked, and she nodded.

"I didn't. Black Dogs don't take the living, Ivy." The Ghost stared at her through her sunglasses.

"This one does," Ivy said forcefully, "and it is most definitely a Church Grim; all the signs were there. This one has just switched targets to the living, rather than the runaway dead that they normally go for.

"It's up to us to figure out why."

"But Grim track death!" Charity said, more angrily than she intended to. "If there's nothing dead about you, then a Grim won't attack you."

"And yet that's exactly what's happening, Charity." Ivy clearly wasn't listening to her, and Charity groaned in frustration. She turned back to face the windscreen and stared moodily at the rain-soaked road in front of her.

"People are either alive, or they aren't, Ivy. These people aren't walking corpses that haven't realised that they're dead yet," Charity said as calmly as she could manage. "You also need to be interred in a churchyard before a Grim will come and get you.

"If there's no transgression, then they've no reason to bother you."

"Grave robbers?" Geoff asked, and Charity shook her head.

"I've already looked into it; none of the graves in the area have been disturbed in decades, maybe even centuries. That sort of crime doesn't go unnoticed for long. Even then, a Grim wouldn't come for a grave robber; it's never happened."

"So what do you suggest?" Ivy asked tersely.

I don't know, Charity thought, but she didn't utter the words aloud. They drove along in silence for several minutes as Charity wracked her brains in an attempt to spot what they'd so obviously missed.

"Can they be tricked?" Geoff asked after a while.

"I'm honestly not sure," Charity said after a moment of quiet contemplation. "What exactly were you thinking?"

"I remember reading once that you can throw a police dog off the scent of a body by burying a dead animal a few feet above it," Geoff said. "The handler just thinks that the dog has caught the scent of the animal, and considers the area cleared.

"Is there a way that you can make someone *appear* dead, without them actually having to die?"

"You're a dark horse, Geoff," Ivy said with considerable admiration in her voice. "That's a pretty cunning plan."

"I don't know how you'd do it," Charity said hesitantly, "but I think it could work, at least in theory."

Charity frowned as she mulled over the implications of what Geoff had suggested. With so many disappearances over more than two centuries, it either meant that there was a freakishly high incidence of undead pulling the same trick, or, more likely, that a single entity was behind all of the dog attacks, stretching back many years.

Charity Walpole was not a betting woman by nature, but being a Ministry Agent required a talent for appreciating the odds of a given explanation, and the first option was too much of a long shot for her.

"We're looking for a single, immensely powerful undead creature," she said, after taking a moment to consider any other possibilities. They had all come up short, however, leaving only one final option. "This being has been operating for centuries without being so much as noticed, and now we are digging into the case in far too brazen a manner."

"Meaning?" Ivy asked.

"It must know that we're coming for it," Charity said as a chill ran down her spine. "There's a strong chance that it already knows who we are, and we can expect it to move against us imminently."

"Do we abandon tonight's attempt to protect the victim?" Ivy asked, and Charity shook her head.

"No. We've a duty to save as many as we can, even if it puts us in harm's way; that's our job, after all." She took a deep breath and took a moment to drive the fear from her body. "From this moment until we solve this thing, no-one goes *anywhere* alone. Everyone stays in communication with everyone else, and the separate teams check in at least once an hour.

"Nobody sleeps anywhere but Walpole Manor, which we will turn into a fucking fortress." Her face hardened as the rain intensified, barely kept at bay by the windscreen wipers. "This bastard has the advantage right now, but we will find out who they are, and we will win this.

"None of us are going to die on my watch, understand?"

Ivy and Geoff nodded. Charity was about to continue when she realised that Geoff was smiling.

"This isn't funny, Geoff," she scolded.

"I wasn't smiling about that," he said softly. "I was still thinking about how you'd trick a Black Shuck."

"And?" Ivy asked, a smile twitching the corners of her mouth too.

"And if we can undo the trick," Geoff said, almost gleefully, "then not only will the Shuck be on our side, but it'll lead us right to whatever is behind this."

"Geoff," Charity said, placing a hand on her Uncle's shoulder as they approached the town of Bungay, "you're awfully good at this for a civvie, you know?"

"I like my detective novels," he replied with a grin, "and I love a puzzle."

I hope he's still smiling at the end of this. Charity was nervous, although her Uncle's optimism was pleasantly infectious. *At least it feels like we're getting somewhere.*

We're on alert, you fucker, Charity thought, *so try getting the drop on us now.*

Little did she know just how much danger they were already in.

"I don't like this place already," Charity said as she walked through the graveyard of the church in Bungay. The church itself was crammed into a surprisingly small plot, and a ruin filled part of the space outside, effectively cutting the graveyard in half.

This isn't quite a False Cardinal, Charity thought as she mentally mapped out the graveyard, *but it still feels off.*

The graveyard was hemmed in by streets and small buildings, making it feel isolated and cut off from the rest of the little market town. She saw how it might be an island of calm in a sea of busy clamour to the right person at the right time, but the almost liminal space made Charity feel cornered, like a rat in a trap.

"This isn't it," Ivy muttered. Charity walked over to the Séance, who was crouched down amongst the graves and peering through the little window of her planchette. She looked up as the Ghost approached, shaking her head. "I don't think that this is the right place, Charity."

She stood up with a groan, leaning heavily on her cane.

"Don't overdo it, Liv," Charity said softly. "I want you in one piece when this is all over."

"I'm alright; just achy is all." Ivy gestured to the area she'd been examining. "There was something here, once, and it looks a lot like what we're dealing with now, but it's too old. There should be fresh signs of our Grim here, but this is all historical residue.

"I'm sorry, Charity."

"No need to apologise," Charity said, giving Ivy a quick squeeze. "I didn't think we'd find it here; it's too far away, for a start."

"I'm not sure that distance makes a difference," Geoff said, emerging from the church. "The legend says that the Shuck disappeared here and rematerialised many miles away in Blythburgh, only moments later.

"There are apparently scorch marks on the north door of the church," he said. "Would that be worth checking out?"

Ivy nodded, but Charity shook her head. Ivy looked at her girlfriend, puzzled.

"It couldn't hurt to look."

"You're dead on your feet, Liv," Charity said, "and all the details of the legend are available online. I'm sure you've also got something in one of your books,

Geoff. The important thing is that this isn't *our* Grim."

"So what's the plan?" Ivy asked.

"We go back to Walpole Manor and we get some rest; eat, nap, and gather our strength before sunset. Then, we head out to try and protect our victim." Charity sighed heavily. "This isn't a perfect plan, I know, but I'd much rather try and save someone tonight than lose our only solid lead because we were too busy hitting the fucking books.

"Does that sound fair?"

Both of her companions nodded, and Charity began to feel a little of her old confidence coming back to her.

"What do you think we should take with us?" Ivy asked as they walked back to the car.

"They managed to trap the Shuck in the Blythburgh church," Geoff said softly, "and if memory serves they used an iron cage to do so."

"We'll load up on all the usual weapons," Charity said as she slipped into the front seat. "Salt, iron, white oak, holy water, silver... I don't suppose you've got any powdered Angel feathers, do you, Geoff?"

"Not that I know of," he said with a chuckle, "but I do have an old shotgun that kicks like a beast, if that's any good to you?"

"That will do nicely," Charity said, giving him a broad smile.

"I wish I had my swords with me," Ivy grumbled.

"Yeah, that one's on me, Liv," Charity said sheepishly. "In my defence, though, Prudence is the Seer, not me."

"I'm sure Max has some tricks up her sleeve that I can borrow if it all gets a bit hairy," Ivy said, "but hopefully tonight will just be another one of observation. We could use a little more reconnaissance before we come out swinging."

"Too right," Charity agreed, "but if push comes to shove, we'll be alright. We trounced the Master, so we can absolutely deal with this."

Charity tried to smile at Ivy enthusiastically, but deep in her heart she knew that she was more terrified than she'd ever been before.

At least we know what we're fighting, Charity thought as she tried to muster a little courage. *Although, truth be told, I have no idea how to beat it.*

Chapter Twenty Five – Your Love is a Life Taker

Helen

"Thanks, Annika," Helen said, slurring her words slightly as she hung up the phone before draining another glass of Glenlossie; she'd exhausted the Jack some hours earlier.

Her spiral of drunken self-loathing had not been unproductive, however, and Annika Eastly had been able to send her several post-mortem reports that showed shocking similarities to the body of Peggy Wilbur.

These all look like bog bodies in various states of preservation, she thought hazily, *and they all have the telltale signs of injury from a Windstahl weapon.*

All of the killings had a similar profile; unrelated, senseless murders of people walking alone at night. There was likely a pattern to the dates and locations, but Helen couldn't see it in her current state.

In fact, only one detail had really stuck out in her mind as strange; of all the killings, only one had any kind of missing item of clothing. Amy Wesser, aged twenty, was out for a nighttime jog when she was struck down; her mother said that she had been wearing a blue lizard bracelet when she left, but it was missing from the corpse when Amy's body was recovered. Apparently the bracelet had no monetary value, but it was a sentimental keepsake from a holiday in Lanzarote some years earlier.

The death had shaken her mother badly, but her

father had gone completely mad and hadn't been seen since.

I doubt it's important, Helen thought hazily, *but I suppose I should mention it.*

Before she could do anything else, a text caught her notice; it was one of the Ministry's automated alerts and it raised her eyebrows in shock.

"Thane is on Betony Island?" Helen murmured. "I should tell Charity about that, but first..."

She groaned slightly as she stood up; the floor seemed to move suddenly beneath her feet and she had to grab the table to stabilise herself. She walked unsteadily over to the printer in Geoff's office and switched it on, hoping that it had some kind of Bluetooth connectivity that would allow her to print the files Annika had sent her.

"Bluetooth this and wi-fi that," she muttered angrily. "Whatever happened to fax machines? Reliable things, and they didn't require a fucking app to work! Soon there'll be an app to open a fucking app to check permissions in order to pour myself a drink from a bottle I fucking own."

Helen was aware that she wasn't making much sense, but was far too upset to care. She groaned again and choked back the vomit that threatened to spew from her lips. *I've had too much already,* she thought, her brain muddier than it had ever been before. *I must be close to the danger zone.*

"Am I... am I trying to kill myself?" she asked the empty room, looking at the bottle on the desk with suspicion in her eyes. Helen had never even considered suicide before, but after her disastrous conversations with Constance and Silas she was firmly in uncharted waters.

Instead of stopping, however, she immediately poured another glass of whisky, choking it down in one tearful gulp.

"I suppose I can always walk to the graveyard and be with Den," she muttered, her stomach roiling in protest at the abuse she was putting her body through. Her drinking in the past had always been low level, but constant; a binge like this was entirely new to her, and she did not care for it.

"What does it fucking matter?" she said sadly, slumping to the floor. She scrabbled for her phone, finally snatching it after several failed attempts. Instead of connecting the device to the printer, however, she decided to call Harper.

"What's the matter, Helen?" Harper asked almost immediately as the call connected. "Has something happened?"

"You," Helen said, her voice full of venom, "you made our son into a fucking monster!"

"Are you *drunk*? Jesus, Helen, I know you were having a difficult time, but it's barely mid-afternoon!" Harper tutted disapprovingly. "Let me guess; you tried to get into Connie's bed to get over the loss of your beloved Dennis, but she didn't want to play second fiddle to a corpse?"

The phone trembled in Helen's hand as she fought back the tears.

"Well, darling, that is what happens when you cut your nose off to spite your pox-scarred face, isn't it?"

"What the fuck are you talking about?" Helen growled, her speech slurred and unsteady.

"Do I really have to spell it out for you?" Harper said, trying to convey disdain but her tone was one of gleeful viciousness. "You paired Den and Lin up to keep her from me. You didn't want us together, for whatever cock-eyed reason, so you matched her up with Dennis, and then convinced them to have children.

"Did you really think that Dennis Walpole, the only decent person in our fucked up little quartet, would actually go behind Lin's back to be with you?"

I hoped he would love me more than her, Helen thought, but she couldn't bring herself to admit this to Harper. Instead she just stared into the middle distance as her ex-partner continued to speak.

"You did, didn't you?" She let out a cruel laugh. "Oh, Helen, you're smarter than that! What a stupid fucking mistake to make... Still, it drove you into my arms, which wasn't all bad, was it?"

"I don't know what I ever saw in you!" Helen yelled, far louder than she intended to.

"Misery does love company, Helen, and your actions did make us so *very* miserable. Also, you didn't seem to find the physical component of my company objectionable, if I recall correctly."

In spite of herself, Helen's mouth twitched in a faint smile. Harper's unique gift also meant that sex with her was absolutely unparalleled; no other lover had ever come close to the uplifted ecstasy that Helen had felt with the monster on the other end of the line.

"Of course, I couldn't let what you did go unpunished." Helen could hear the smirk on Harper's face, and her entire body trembled with rage.

"You *did* do it on purpose!"

"That I did, darling; I put that horror in your body deliberately, knowing there was nothing you could do about it."

One of the least understood aspects of Blights was

the fact that medical interventions did not work on them at all. Even common medications did not touch Helen's body, birth control pills included. As such, when she had her brief affair with Harper, there was little she could do to prevent getting pregnant, and when she did, there was nothing she could do that could rid her of her unwanted child.

"Of course, when a Blight recovers from their particular ailment, they're immune to it for the rest of time," Harper said softly, "so it's no wonder that all those attempts to conceive a second child failed."

Helen blinked in shock.

That makes perfect sense, she realised, tearfully. *All the other Blights in history only ever had one child.*

"You... you never worked that one out, did you?" Harper asked, almost laughing with spite as the sobs overtook the drunken Blight. "Goodness, Helen, sometimes you are fucking slow. Still, there's no use crying over spilt milk, as it were.

"You stole Lin away from me, leaving me with only an empty bed for comfort, so I filled the only cradle you'd ever get with a monster; tit for tat." Harper sighed heavily. "Still, now that you know what you've lost, what I've *taken* from you, we're even.

"I don't wish you any ill will, Helen."

"What is wrong with you!?" Helen screamed as she fought the urge to hurl the phone across the room.

"I mean it," Harper said quietly. "I do actually want the best for you, Helen, and I have a gift for you, although it might kill you in the process of setting you free, so ask whatever it was you wanted to know."

Helen looked at the phone in horror. *What else could she possibly do to hurt me?* Instead of following every instinct in her body, which screamed at her to hang up the call, she pressed on with the conversation.

"What did you do to Silas?"

"He was fifteen!" Helen screamed into the phone. "How dare you do that to a *child*!?"

"He had a knife to my throat," Harper replied, "and we both know that he's not above spilling innocent blood when it suits him."

"Why must you keep bringing that up?" Helen asked, shakily. "He... he was acquitted of all charges."

"And even you think that's bullshit, clearly," Harper retorted. "Agent Malarkey mentioned that a scent of peppermint prevailed throughout; is that not Silas's preferred method for blocking out the smell of bloodshed?"

"Yes, but it is also one used by countless other Ministry professionals; me included!" Helen gripped her phone so tightly that she was on the verge of snapping it. "All the evidence was circumstantial, Harper."

"The wounds were consistent with the precision strikes from a practised surgeon, or pathologist, and a prosecting knife was clearly the murder weapon; you know that he's capable of it, Helen, so why do you insist on fighting the truth?"

Because he's my son, she thought tearfully, but she wasn't about to give Harper any more ammunition to use against her.

"Are you still there?" Harper asked after a minute or so of silence.

"I am," Helen said softly. "Don't worry, I didn't black out."

"You never have," Harper responded, and something about her tone suggested that it was a deeply loaded phrase.

"What did you do to him?" Helen asked again, more forcefully this time.

"I uplifted him, as I said earlier."

"No more hiding behind words, Harper," Helen said, her voice icy with rage. "I know that you've built your entire career on being a snake, but we are talking about our child and you will tell the truth, unadorned, or I will make Max public knowledge.

"On that, you have my word."

There was a strangled sound from the other end of the line as her threat finally caught the unflappable Harper Cherry on the back foot. Helen smiled a triumphant grin, and took a moment to savour her minor victory. Harper's next words were exactly what the Blight expected, and they let her know that control of the conversation was hers entirely.

"You wouldn't."

"You wanna fucking bet?" Helen hissed. "What's the matter, Harper? Scared of a little scandal?"

"You'd burn Silas's credibility to hurt me?" Harper asked, but Helen was ready for that one.

"You already did that by not calling Max as a witness to exonerate him." Helen chuckled darkly. "You'd let him swing to save your own skin."

"I would never!" Harper said, but then she took a track that Helen had not foreseen. "You'd throw Ivy under the bus, too, would you?"

Helen paused for a few seconds, but quickly realised her answer. *Forgive me.*

"I would. She's a talented woman, and would recover in time. You, however, would be thrown out of the upper echelons of power for having such a glaring vulnerability for the Ministry's enemies to leverage."

"Which includes you, it seems," Harper muttered angrily. She took a deep breath and her usual constructed demeanour was back in a flash. "You're wrong about me, by the way; I do care about our son."

"Bullshit."

"Yes, he was originally just a weapon to hurt you, but on that night he showed up on my doorstep..." Harper inhaled sharply, almost in reverence of the memory. "Oh, you should've seen him, Helen; he was nothing but pure, unbridled potential. In that moment, I knew that he was my legacy in this world, and that only I could raise him up high enough to touch perfection.

"My darling Silas, striving for the sun, had come to my door to beg for his wings."

"And you turned him into a freak!"

"I set him free!" Harper yelled, the volume of her voice distorting her words. "He wanted wax, but I gave him polished, shining steel; I poured every drop of my power into him and it nearly killed us both.

"He is my magnum opus, Helen."

"He despises you, Harper."

"That..." Harper's voice faltered for a moment. "That's fine. I freed him from the bonds of flesh and blood, so that he could rise above the rest of us, Helen. I thought he would slide into mediocrity, but he's truly exceptional; the very best of our species.

"There's nothing human left in him, and I have never been prouder of something I have created." Harper chuckled softly. "All that chaos with Lamplight, and my expectations were blown out of the water by my own flesh and blood."

"He's a better man than you give him credit for," Helen said, trembling with rage. "He's the most human person I have ever met, and he understands that compassion and gentleness are the true mark of success.

"He is exceptional, Harper, but only because he's nothing like you, in spite of all your best efforts to shape him otherwise." Helen's phone rumbled as message after message arrived, but she ignored it as a cruel smile crossed her lips. "Tell me, *darling,* when did Max abandon you entirely?"

There was a beat of silence before Harper spoke once again.

"As I was saying," Harper said softly, "I have one final gift for you; a truth that you might've missed, or more likely ignored; either way, it's time to wake up and face the sun, Helen."

Helen scoffed, but her smirk faded as Harper went on.

"You're a Blight, dear, and you're immune to the effects of any and all medicines," she said, almost gently, "so I'm impressed that you've convinced everyone that you're an alcoholic."

"I am," Helen said, her heart freezing in her chest. "I'm drunk right now!"

"No, you aren't; you drink to have a convenient excuse that allows you to behave in the manner that you really want to."

The phone trembled in Helen's hand.

"You've always loved being the centre of attention, and who is more worthy of praise than the recovering addict who holds fast against all temptation?" Harper laughed viciously. "I've always known that you were a fraud, my love, and now you have to know that too."

Helen tried to speak, to deny Harper's words, but all she could do was scream incoherently into the phone.

"You're welcome."

Instead of dealing with the truth laid plain before her, Helen hurled the phone at the wall with a guttural cry, destroying it completely, along with her unread messages. She stared wild eyed at the ruined device for a few heartbeats before snatching up the whisky bottle and draining it in a single long gulp.

Anyone else would've vomited immediately, but Helen Mickelson did not; after all, Harper was many things, but a liar was not one of them, especially when the truth could cut more deeply than anything else. Instead of collapsing from alcohol poisoning, she locked the door to the study and crawled underneath the desk, where she remained, silently praying for death.

She's taken everything from me, Helen thought, *even the fucking bottle.*

I have nothing left to live for.

Chapter Twenty Six – Walk the Night

Ivy

"Where's Helen?" Ivy asked as she joined the Walpole family as they gathered in the kitchen of the Big House. "She's not responding to any of my messages."

"She's focussed on research, I suspect," Constance said, but Ivy could feel the lie behind her words. Unbidden, images of empty bottles filled her mind, and she frowned slightly.

"So we do this without her," Charity said, sitting at the head of the table. "It'll be dark soon, and we still need to track down our target. We'll split up to cover more ground."

She looked at the Twins.

"Can you two drive?" Cait shook her head as Cat stared at the table in silence, her eyepatch a stark reminder of the previous day's bout of violence. "Alright; you'll go in the car with Geoff and the heavy equipment.

"Ivy, you'll be riding with Connie."

What?

Charity could clearly see the confusion on her face and gestured for her to speak.

"Don't you want me with you?" Ivy asked, trying her best not to sound hurt.

"I'll move more nimbly without the sidecar, and Connie knows the area better than me; she'll get you to our target faster. Besides, I've already seen the Grim once, so that gives us two opportunities to catch sight of it.

"Is that okay?" Charity asked. "If you don't want to do that, we can ride together."

"No, you're right," Ivy said, swallowing her own feelings for the good of their mission. "This is the best allocation of resources. I'm behind your decisions, every step of the way."

"Thank you." She looked at the twins. "You two will be backup, in the event that anything goes wrong, but if you catch sight of the Grim, I want you to go after it. Don't engage it, though; tracking only.

"I want to know where it's coming from."

Ivy tried not to look at the spectre of Dennis Walpole, who nodded approvingly. The twins did not respond to Charity's words, however, and the Ghost leant forward to stare at them.

"Caitlin, Catarina," she said firmly, "are you with me on this?"

"To whatever end," Cat said immediately, fixing the older Ghost with an intense one-eyed stare. "I apologise for my insubordination earlier; it won't happen again."

"Thank you," Charity said, nodding solemnly. "I feel better knowing that you two are watching my back."

"We always will be," Cait whispered.

They've grown up all of a sudden, Ivy thought, *but maybe not in the healthiest way.*

"I'm still worried about you travelling alone," Ivy said, deciding to voice her fears. "It makes you an immense target."

"I'm counting on it," Charity said with a grin, "and I'm starting to think that Helen's undead horseman might be the bastard behind all this."

"Smiling Jack has been dead for centuries-" Constance began, but Charity cut her off.

"And it could be someone else who knew his secrets," Charity said firmly. "We've wasted too much fucking time already with false certainty, so from this point on, *anything* is a possibility. I want your eyes wide and your minds open, understood?"

Those around the table nodded in agreement.

"As for my riding alone," Charity continued, a touch of her earlier enthusiasm returning, "that's only what it will look like from the outside."

There was a rustle from the collar of her coat as Henbane leant into view, brandishing a needle-thin sword. Charity looked at Ivy and raised her eyebrows.

"Does that make you feel better?"

"A little," Ivy admitted, "but I still feel like we've missed something important. If this horseman comes for you, what are you hoping to achieve?"

"I want to know who he is," Charity said, "and then we go through the usual steps for dispelling a wayward spirit."

"We'll need to find the body first," Geoff said softly, "but I can do that."

"You can?" Cait asked, genuinely surprised.

"I've done it more than once before." His words were dark, and Ivy could feel the spectre of guilt moving through his mind.

"Were you ever part of the Axen Brotherhood?" Ivy asked him, and he nodded sadly.

"For a while, in my youth, until I realised what they were really doing. I've moved in several occult circles since, but I've never forgiven myself for my part in that awful organisation," Geoff whispered.

"I... I never knew that about you," Connie said, taken aback. There was a beat of silence before she continued, a warm smile on her face. "Still, you're allowed to have had a life before me, and you aren't with those monsters any longer.

"You might not forgive yourself, Geoffrey, but I'm happy to absolve you of any external guilt for what you might have done."

"You're the best of them, Connie," Geoff said tearfully. Ivy smiled at the older couple until she realised that Charity was staring directly at her. She turned to face her girlfriend, and gestured for her to speak.

"I have a task for Max," Charity said after a slight pause. "Seeing as we're dealing with ghosts and spirits, we have more need of Edgar than ever before. I'm not entirely sure how it works, but is there any way she can head inside your mind, soul, or whatever, to find him?"

"I can certainly try," Max said, and Ivy nodded on her behalf. "Please tell her that I'm grateful to be trusted with such a task, and I will do my best to not let either of you down."

Ivy relayed her words, and then turned her attention inward as Charity dismissed their meeting and bade them to get some rest before the night's hunt.

Do be careful with Edgar, she said softly. *He's a good man, but he can be a bit... particular. He might take a bit of winning over, but I'm sure he'll come to our aid when he finds out just how dire things are.*

"I hope you're right," Max said, "but the whole time I've been with you, it's just been the two of us, old mum."

Don't call me that, Ivy thought, but a smile still twitched her lips. Ivy wandered towards the makeshift bedroom for a lie down, and her thoughts turned to the mystical sword that Smiling Jack had been said to carry.

Do you really think the secret of stealing life persists? Ivy asked Max.

"No knowledge is ever truly lost," Max said darkly. "It is only ever temporarily misplaced."

I'm not sure if that's comforting, or downright troubling.

"Sometimes a thing can be both," Max whispered as Charity approached. "I shall head inwards, and leave the two of you to get some rest."

Good luck, Ivy thought. *You're going to need it.*

Her words were just thoughts, however; she was alone in her head, once again.

The engine of the bike burbled and grumbled as Connie pulled out away from Walpole Manor. Ivy was still fiddling underneath her helmet, trying to get her earpiece seated correctly; the older woman had provided their team with a set of radio equipment, courtesy of the Amberlight Detective Agency.

"- want to be Ghost One!" Ivy heard Cat say as she finally got the damn thing seated.

"Charity should get to be Ghost One," Cait replied sternly, and the Séance shook her head mirthfully. "You can pick another code name."

"I'm Hillgreen," Charity said, her voice coming through loud and clear. "Black Cat, are you receiving?"

"I've got you, Hillgreen," Ivy said, shuddering slightly at the ease with which Charity defaulted to their Lamplight Designations.

"Brilliant." She sighed heavily. "Everyone call out your designations; let's get this silliness over with before we're in the thick of it."

"Ghost One!" Cat declared.

"Ghost *Prime*," Cait said, not a second later.

"Oh, for fucks' sake," Charity muttered, and Ivy had to stifle a giggle.

"Boss," Connie said authoritatively.

"Nightlight," Henbane confirmed.

I wonder if that was the codename they used on cases with Dennis? Ivy wondered. And then, last but not least, the final member of their group spoke.

"Geoff," Geoff said.

"What a fucking shambles this is," Charity said, stifling a laugh. She then cleared her throat before speaking more clearly. "Okay, instructions incoming; keep the line quiet unless you're giving confirmation of orders.

"Boss, you take Black Cat up the main street and follow her lead."

"Confirmed." Connie revved the bike and set off towards the nearby town. Ivy pulled down her goggles to keep the rushing wind from her eyes, grateful for the break in the rain.

"Geoff, you pitch up in a car park somewhere central. Ghost One, Ghost Prime; I want the two of you to walk the street nearby Geoff's location. At the first sign of trouble, head back to the vehicle and head over to the action."

"Confirmed," all three said in unison.

"I'm gonna head to the sight of the last disappearance," Charity said, "and try to get the attention of our undead bastard. Radio silence until anyone sees anything.

"Over and out."

The three vehicles approached Long Stratton and headed in their separate directions. Ivy settled back in the sidecar and tried to open her mind as wide as she could, searching for the man they'd seen in the pub a few nights earlier.

What struck her immediately was the sheer amount of fear that saturated the psychic airwaves; the entire town was rank with it. She took a deep breath, letting the sea of paranoid terror wash over her.

You are a lighthouse, she thought, *a stationary point in the storm. While ships may be washed away by the tides and swell, you will endure.*

Something clicked in her mind as she mused on the lighthouse allegory; once again, they were going about their search entirely backwards. A smile crept on to Ivy's face as she isolated herself from the fear, cultivating a sense of hope, safety, and protection.

Her eyes quivered in their sockets as she folded the concept in on itself again and again, making it brighter with every passing second. She was convinced that her plan would work, but she understood that it was a double-edged sword; it would allow them to find the Grim's target, but it was likely to draw unwanted attention from the beast's master.

Still, Ivy thought resolutely, *I have to try.*

"I can help you," she whispered into the night air. "Come and find me."

A bright pulse burst out from her, rippling through the psychic fabric that permeated the entire town. Ivy half closed her eyes, and could almost see the wave of light as it flowed through the sea of trouble and fear.

"What the fuck was that?" asked one of the twins, clearly shaken.

"I think that was Black Cat," Charity said proudly, "so clear the channel and let her listen for a response."

I have never felt so powerful.

She let the sound of the motorbike engine fade into the background as she opened her mind fully, waiting for even the smallest reply to her call. Deep in the darkness, somewhere off to her right, a tiny pinprick of light blossomed on the horizon and Ivy immediately focussed her mind on it.

"I'm so afraid," it whispered. "I think I'm going to die."

Gotcha.

"Hillgreen," she said immediately, "I've found him. He's-"

Her voice faltered as another supernatural force appeared on her psychic radar, exploding into being like a dark storm cloud that is heralded by a flash of summer lightning. The power behind the force was incredible, and it made her tremble in her seat.

"Charity," she said, panic driving any thoughts of call signs from her mind, "you need to hurry."

"Then tell me where he is!" Charity yelled in response, and Ivy blasted the location into her girlfriend's mind, not taking a single moment to temper her power in the slightest.

"Hurry, hurry!" Ivy cried out as the darkness sped towards their target with incredible speed. "The Grim, Charity; it's coming!"

Chapter Twenty Seven – For Whom the Dog Howls

Charity

Ivy's mental image of the soon-to-be victim flashed into Charity's mind, almost sending her crashing into a hedge. She blinked away the vision as she wrestled the powerful bike under control. Henbane was saying something in her ear, but her mind was still reeling from the intensity of her lover's mental touch.

"What!?" she yelled, far louder than necessary.

"Ivy said that it's on the way!" Henbane replied. "We've got to go, now!"

"FUCK!" Charity roared as she opened the throttle and the bike thundered down the road towards their target. "Black Cat, where is the Grim?"

"It's on the far side of town," Ivy responded. "It's moving fast, but you should get there first if you punch it!"

"Where did it come from?" Geoff asked.

"What does that matter?" Connie interceded. "Keep the line clear!"

"Everyone, shut up!" Charity yelled as she swerved around a car, barely keeping the bike from skidding out from underneath her. *If I crash at this speed, I am going to die.* "Black- Ivy, answer Geoff!"

"I think it came from Tharston, or somewhere near there," Ivy said, her voice crackling as something interfered with the transmission. "I think it might have come from St Mary's; do you want us to check it out?"

"No!" Charity said sharply. "I want everyone to

form up on my position. Henbane, where the fuck are we?"

"We've just turned on to Hall Lane, heading east."

"The twins are still outside," Geoff said nervously, "should I wait for them?"

"No; you've got all the weapons, and we don't have time to wait for them," Charity said. "Cat, Cait, we'll pick you up when we're done. Please confirm."

"Confirmed," the twins replied in unison.

"Henbane," Charity went on, pausing momentarily as she made a hard right turn, "keep relaying our position to the others and-"

Charity's words were cut short when she saw a flash of gold off to her left.

She slowed the bike enough to glance into a nearby field and saw their ghostly horseman astride a grey-black steed, a shining basket hilted sword in his hand. It was only a passing glimpse, but one detail struck her more than anything else.

He's faded against the night sky, she thought, her eyes widening with horror. *He's invisible.*

"I just saw him!" she cried out, hoping she was still in range of the others. "I saw our horseman! He's a fucking Ghost!"

"We already know he's dead, Charity," Ivy said, clearly missing the nuance in Charity's words.

"Can you identify him?" Connie asked.

"No; not enough time," Charity replied. "He isn't just dead, Ivy; he's a *Ghost*!"

"Oh!" Ivy said softly, and Charity could feel her words sink in, even across the distance between them.

"Are you sure?" Connie said, disbelieving.

"He was invisible!" Charity called out. "He was one of us; that much is certain."

"Do we go after him?" Ivy asked. "We might be able to end this right now."

Charity considered it for a moment and, though the thrill of the hunt was a strong temptation, decided against it.

"No," she said firmly. "We stick with the original plan; head to our victim and cut off the Grim."

"Are you sure?" Connie asked, but Charity did not respond. Instead she slowed the bike and risked one final look back at the Ghost. He was just watching her; something about his pose was taunting her, and it filled her heart with rage.

You killed my fucking father, she thought as Connie's words washed over her.

"God dammit, Charity! Are you still there?"

"Escape, Evade, and Protect," said Freyja Goodweather, a Valkyrie instructor at the Ministry Academy, "is one of the hardest courses you will ever undertake."

Charity stared nervously through her sunglasses, but even though she remained completely motionless as she stood at ease, the Valkyrie seemed to sense her fear. Goodweather approached her, towering over the fifteen year old girl by almost a foot and a half. Charity let her eyes slip out of focus for just a moment, and she could almost see the translucent wings sprouting from Goodweather's back.

"You passed the full roster of Hunter-Killer courses with flying colours, didn't you, Recruit Walpole?"

"Yes, sir," Charity said, and Goodweather scowled at her.

"Don't call me *sir*, Walpole," she said sharply, "I work for a living."

Charity frowned, but did not apologise; she knew the tells that indicated an unstable soldier, and they were adorning Goodweather like a field of red flags. *Play the game,* she reminded herself, *don't act weak, and never, ever cry.*

Project Lamplight had taught her a lot, but how to survive the massive egos of petty military personnel was the most valuable lesson by far.

"You're gonna struggle with EEP, Walpole," Goodweather said, smirking. "Ghosts always do."

"I'm different," Charity muttered, and the Valkyrie raised a sceptical eyebrow. Charity stared back defiantly. "I'll show you; whatever you throw at me, I'll take it down!"

"That's exactly the point, Recruit Walpole; this isn't about how well you can fight." She leant in close, lowering her voice. "This about how well you run, hide, and keep your designated ally safe; not that I'd expect a Lamplight brat to ever keep someone else alive in a crisis. You're destined to fail this, Walpole, so why even try?"

"I said that I was different," Charity said firmly. "Who am I protecting?"

"Well?" Goodweather asked the assembled Recruits. "Who here trusts Walpole to keep them safe?"

Not a single one of her classmates stepped forward to volunteer, and Goodweather looked down at her, a merciless smirk on her face.

"You need to have your allies on side in order to protect them effectively, Recruit; if they don't trust you, then they won't listen to you." She chuckled darkly. "That is the most important lesson I have to teach you, Walpole; Ghosts operate alone, and, as such, they can't lead.

"It's not your fault, of course," Goodweather hissed, loud enough for only Charity to hear, "you're just a defective species."

The Valkyrie straightened up and raised her voice.

"You fell at the first hurdle, Walpole; I consider this an immediate fail."

Charity's stomach churned as her face turned bright red; she'd never failed a course before, and such a public shaming was new to her, so it stung all the more.

"Get out of my sight Walpole," Goodweather said, "and don't come back."

Charity walked slowly out of the room as one of the other recruits called after her.

"Stick to what you're good at, you murderous freak!"

She picked up the pace as other voices joined in the chorus.

"Killing is all you're good for!"

"You'll never save anyone, Hillgreen!"

"Freak!"

No matter how far from the Academy she got, those voices followed her, calling out the truth of what she was.

Killer.

Freak.

Murderer.

Monster.

"Charity, are you sure?" Connie repeated, and she nodded.

Courage, Charity.

"Yes, I'm sure. Form up on me, and don't fucking ask again!"

Nobody else dies tonight.

She revved the bike and took off down the lanes as fast as she dared. She couldn't explain it, but it felt safer to let her intuition guide her around corners and across junctions than it did to actually think about them. She was a creature of habit, though, and had operated on instinct her entire life, so it came naturally to her.

"Ivy, where is it?" she asked, before quickly clarifying. "Just tell me; I don't need another fucking vision slammed into my head."

"It's just turned on to Hall Lane," Ivy replied. "It's already ahead of us, Charity; it's moving so bloody fast!"

It's taking a different path, she thought. *There must be Nifty Ways all over the place.*

"Next time it seems to jump," Charity said into her headset, as calmly as she could manage, "I want you to push as much disorientation and random noise into the aether as possible, okay?"

Let's level the playing field a little, shall we?

Charity swung around a corner just as Ivy unleashed her mind on the psychic airwaves; it still hit her like a freight train, but this time she was ready for it, tucking her mind away from the world for just long enough for the blast to pass.

Henbane, however, groaned and vomited all over her jacket. They lost their grip and would've fallen had Charity not snatched them from the air and awkwardly crammed their tiny body into a pocket.

You can thank me later, she thought as the pixie puked once more.

"Charity," Ivy said, her voice beginning to break up, "Charity, I've lost it. I don't know where it is!"

"You probably knocked it off the path, at least for a

little while," Charity said. "I'll explain later, but good work, Liv."

A bright light shone ahead as Charity rounded the next corner, and she shut her eyes to cut out the glare. Strangely, this did nothing, and she opened them once again as she realised that it was the mental after image of Ivy's initial psychic burst.

Hot damn, she's fucking powerful.

"It's coming!" she heard the terrified man yell as she approached. "It's coming for me tonight; I know it is!"

Charity pulled the bike up beside him with a roar, reaching out for him with a gloved hand.

"Get on!" she yelled, and the man hesitated for a second before moving towards her, but it was already too late.

That heartbeat of indecision cost him his life. The Black Shuck burst from the shadows and leapt at him, snarling as it did so. The nightmarish beast snapped its jaws shut on his arm and began to drag him away, screaming, into the darkness.

"Oh no you don't!" Charity roared, revving the bike before sending it roaring towards both beast and man. "Not now, not ever!"

The Grim stopped to stare at her as the blinding headlight of the bike bore down on it, burning like a luminous Cyclops. Charity reached into her jacket as she barrelled towards the monster, grabbing a packet stuffed with iron filings, natron, saltpetre, and powdered Vedic clay, all burned in holy oil before being dried under the midday sun; it was known by many names, but the most common was Black Salt.

Charity, however, referred to it simply as 'Fuck Off Powder', and it was just as effective against humans, along with being highly explosive. She slammed into the Shuck with the bike, knocking it aside with a crunch of bone and shriek of twisted metal. Charity leapt from the ruined bike, landing between the Shuck and the wounded man.

"You will not touch him again," she growled, and hurled the Black Salt at the injured dog.

The Grim howled in pain as the powder covered it. The spectral beast's flesh burned and boiled wherever the Black Salt made contact.

So you can be harmed, Charity thought with a mad grin as she drew her knives, *and that means you can be killed.*

"Hey, you," Charity hissed behind her towards the prone man, "get up! We need to get out of here!"

He did not respond, and she reached out with her foot to kick him awake, but all she met was empty air. She risked a glance behind her, and all that remained was a bloodstain on the ground; the Grim had taken him already.

"You fucker!" she screamed, rounding on the dog, which was pacing back and forth menacingly a few feet away, growling softly. "You absolute fucking bastard! I was *this* fucking close!"

The dog continued to stare at her, its blood red eyes blazing in the darkness.

"Go on then!" Charity cried out. "Fuck off back to your Churchyard, you monster; there's nothing for you here!"

The dog let out a piercing howl, causing Charity's blood to run cold and her skin to turn to goose flesh as the penny finally dropped.

You have got to be fucking kidding me.

The dog took a single step towards her, and she couldn't help but let out a scream of fear.

"Charity!?" Ivy called, her voice crackling through the headset. "Charity, are you alright?"

"Oh shit," Charity muttered as the red-eyed monster continued to stare her down, ectoplasm dripping from its enormous slavering jaws. She took a hesitant step backwards, dropping the knives as she did so.

"What's wrong?" Ivy said through the headset, but her tone made it clear that she'd already worked out what was happening. Charity swallowed her fear and choked out a reply as the Black Shuck growled at her.

"It's me," she said, her voice cracking. "Ivy, I'm next."

Interlude Two – Playing in the Dark

Paul Duckworth looked at his brother, Daniel, as the sound of roaring motorbikes filled the air along the main street of Long Stratton. The older shook his head angrily and glared through the window.

"I thought we showed that fucking freak who was and wasn't welcome here," Dan muttered, thinking back to the beating they'd delivered to the Walpole woman in the pub. "Clearly they didn't get the fucking message."

"Maybe we should go up to that fancy gaff of theirs," Paul said with a dark chuckle, "and drive them out of town."

"No need for that," Dan replied with a wicked grin. "It's an old place, probably full of clutter and faulty wiring; one spark and the entire estate would go up in flames."

That would show them, he thought as he strolled into his brother's kitchen with the intent of getting another beer from the fridge. *This town has been plagued by freaks for too fucking long.* His smile faded, however, when he realised that Paul's back door was ajar.

"Oi, Paul," he called, "if you aren't careful you're gonna get fucking burgled one of these days!"

"The fuck are you talking about?" Paul replied, grumbling as he joined Dan in the kitchen. He stared at the door in confusion. "I swear I locked that before we sat down... Oh, fuck it, we'd have seen anyone who was in here already."

He reached out to close the door, but it slammed shut before he could touch it.

"What the fuck!?" he said, stepping back sharply.

"Dan did you-"

His words were cut off as something suddenly wrapped tightly around his throat, cutting deep enough into the flesh that Paul began to choke on his own blood. He thrashed at the space in front of him, but his hands met only empty air.

"Paul!" Dan screamed, and leapt forward, only to be stopped with a grunt as something sharp punctured his stomach. He touched his bleeding abdomen and felt, rather than saw, the shape of a wicked knife as it was pulled out of his quivering belly.

Paul dropped to his knees as several stab wounds rapidly appeared on his chest, marked only by a slick, wet sound and the splatter of blood on the kitchen floor. Dan stumbled forward once again, desperate to save his dying brother, only to feel the blade slam into his guts once again.

"What the fuck is happening?" he gasped as the knife struck him again and again, slashing his insides to pieces. "Who's there!?"

"You fucked with the wrong family," whispered a woman from the air beside him. "We look after our own."

"She's right," replied a second voice from behind Paul's dying form. "You attacked our cousin, so now you're getting what's coming to you."

Before he could say anything else, Dan's throat was slashed and he was left on the kitchen floor to die. As his lifeblood spilled out over the cheap linoleum, he wondered who would find the remains of him and his brother.

Ironically enough, the bodies would be reported anonymously a fortnight hence by an opportunistic burglar with a conscience.

In the intervening time, however, nobody would even notice that they were missing. Nobody would ever be arrested for the crime, as the scene was left without a single scrap of evidence; whilst the Walpole twins could be a touch childish at times, they were not stupid.

The Horseman smiled broadly as he twirled his sword through the night air. Oh, what luck he had; for not only had another suitable victim landed in his wicked web, but a Walpole, no less! His smile faltered as the Black Shuck walked past him, growling softly.

It can't see me, he thought, even as his dead heart raced in his rotten chest. *It hasn't been able to see me for centuries, and it's not about to start now.*

He'd been honing his Ghost's gift for his entire life, and now that he was dead it was more useful than ever. Escaping the graveyard had been the simplest part of his plan, but he hadn't expected the Tharston Grim to be so persistent.

"How many people do I need to feed to you, you mangy creature?" he whispered, and the Shuck growled angrily. It clearly knew that something was amiss, but the spirit was easily fooled; the Horseman smirked at the ghostly hound, knowing that he would soon be free of it.

"No longer will you haunt my shadow," he said, "nor shall you dog my footsteps; soon I will be free of you forever."

The Black Shuck growled once again, and Gunpowder whinnied nervously. The horse's fear was unnecessary, however; only creatures interred in the graveyard were at risk from the Grim, and it had been buried in the corner of a shady field instead.

"Easy, Gunpowder," the Horseman said softly. "It isn't here for you, and it won't trouble you much longer. At last, I've been given the key to our permanent escape. Hell, maybe we won't even need Goldthorn's magic any longer."

He sighed as he looked at the wicked sword in his hand. Whilst he hated that a brigand's blade had sustained him for so many years, he was grateful that it existed in the first place; without it, he would still be interred in the ground, buried in an unmarked traitor's grave.

"Our family shunned us," he said to the ghostly horse, "even though we put down the greatest threat this land has ever seen. Betrayed, spurned, and shunned, all for a few stray words; ingrates, the lot of them!"

The Grim barked loudly, and the Horseman laughed.

"Soon, fell creature," he said, a cruel smile creeping on to his face, "you will have a Walpole to fill that grave once again. You can rest at last after centuries of nightly pursuit; all you need to do is hunt her down, and you will have your pound of flesh."

The Grim howled before vanishing into the darkness, and the Horseman turned to face the east, drinking in the beauty of the breaking dawn.

"Admittedly, it won't technically be my flesh," he said with a dark giggle, "but when it's one's own kin, what's the difference?

"Besides, I doubt that stupid hound will care."

He continued to watch from the field, unseen, as a wide eyed Charity Walpole realised just how doomed she was.

"I would apologise, dear child," he said softly, "but your ancestors brought this upon you; your quarrel is ultimately with them, not me. Still, from one Grand Phantom to another, I appreciate your sacrifice.

"Go peacefully to your death with the knowledge that I will enjoy your life more than you ever could."

Charity Walpole felt the hair stand up on the back of her neck, but as she turned to face the rising sun, the field was empty, save for several early birds scavenging worms from the mist covered mud.

Garland Walpole, ghostly horseman and former Grand Phantom, was already gone.

Part Three: The Wolf at the Door

Chapter Twenty Eight – A Brighter Side to Life

Ivy

"This feels like a waste of fucking time, Ivy!" Charity grumbled from the back seat of the car. "We should be out there, hunting this monster!"

Ivy frowned at the slight tremor in her girlfriend's voice. *She's trying so hard to hide her fear,* she thought, *but she can't keep it from me.*

"Our first priority," Geoff said sternly, "is keeping you safe, Charity. The rest of the family can keep up the good work whilst you and Ivy take a moment to breathe. Henbane and Helen are back at the house too, so it's not like we're short on people."

"But-"

"I'm not doing this just for you," Geoff said, sharply enough to startle both women. "I gave my word to Den that I'd keep an eye on you if... *when* he finally went. I'm keeping my promise to a man that was practically a brother to me, Charity.

"The fact that I get peace of mind knowing that my favourite niece is out of danger, well, that's just icing on the cake." Geoff sighed heavily. "Besides, there's a chance that a change of scene will give you a new perspective on this whole mess; no good ever came from staring at a problem until you're blue in the face."

"And none of the recorded disappearances are as far away as Great Yarmouth," Ivy said, placing a reassuring hand on Charity's knee. "I obviously can't say for sure, but maybe the Grim won't be able to come this far away from the churchyard."

"He looked at me like he knew me," Charity whispered. "I couldn't see his face, but he looked right at me."

Charity sighed heavily and put her head in her hands before screaming softly.

"All my life I've been hunting nightmares, monsters, and horrors, but the one that finally does for me is a fucking *dog*!? That's absurd! I hurt it, Ivy; I saw the Black Salt harm it!" Charity reached beneath her glasses to rub the tears from her eyes. "This should be just another fucking hunt, so why am I so frightened?"

Ivy frowned slightly; it was unlike Charity to be so scared of an adversary. *Even when we were dealing with the Hivemother,* Ivy thought, *you were more angry than fearful.* The therapist in her wanted to rationalise her sudden change in emotional state away; the loss of her father, the conflict with her cousin, and the upheaval of grief all provided explanations for the sudden wave of fear her lover felt.

"It's a simple explanation," Ivy muttered, "but it doesn't help us."

"What are you muttering about?" Charity snapped.

"Are you feeling more paranoid than usual, Charity?" Ivy asked, her curiosity piqued by the Ghost's sudden outburst.

"What has that got to do with it?" Charity said evasively, but Ivy could feel the distrust radiating from the woman in the back seat. A small smile crossed the Séance's face as all the pieces clicked into place.

We had it backwards, she thought, shaking her head with a slight chuckle. *Again.*

"What's so fucking funny, huh?" Charity demanded,

kicking the back of Ivy's seat, hard. "What are you fucking plotting now?"

"We got it backwards, Charity," Ivy said, trying to suffuse a sense of calm into her lover. "You don't go mad because the Black Shuck is slowly stalking you; it's a symptom, rather than a logical outcome of being isolated."

"That sounds like splitting hairs," Geoff said quietly.

"I know, but there is a difference," Ivy said as she tried to find the right words. "The psychosis that stems from isolation, fear, and paranoia sets in gradually, and it can be reduced to a certain extent; that's what we initially thought was happening, which is why we thought the victim had more time.

"Instead, it's happened overnight to Charity, and she *knows* that we believe her. Yes, she should be a little scared, but she's actually-"

"Fucking terrified," Charity said, nodding along. "Ivy, you need to ring Helen, as soon as you can."

"Why?"

"This isn't psychosis," the Ghost said. "This is a known quantity, albeit one that very few Ceps ever experience."

"What is it?" Ivy asked, but Geoff answered.

"It's Doom, isn't it?"

"Ceps don't normally feel a sense of impending death," Helen said sharply on the other end of the line. "What we call Doom is a physical manifestation of being hunted; it's a prey response, and very few Ceps are ever in that position."

"I don't care what it's called or where it comes from," Ivy said testily. "I just want to know how to deal with it!"

"I'm getting to that," Helen replied. "Tell me, Dr Livingston, have you ever felt a creeping anticipation that you were certain would end in your demise?"

"I have," Ivy said, thinking back to her first ever encounter with Charity, outside her little Lye Valley home. "It was paralysing; I've never felt that before in my life."

"That is what ordinary folks feel when they're around Ceps for too long," Helen went on, "and when it reaches the level of a chronic debilitating condition, we call it Doom. Charity's body is currently locked into survival mode, but something about the Grim's power pushes her into flight, rather than fight.

"Untreated, this on its own will eventually break her, but even a short exposure will make her easy pickings for such a powerful creature." Helen sighed heavily. "Unfortunately, the fact that she's a Cep is working against her; ordinary people have a kind of inherent resistance to the onset of Doom, but Ceps do not. Ghosts, as misfortune would have it, are particularly susceptible."

"So how do I fix it?" Ivy asked. She glanced at the door to their en suite, but Charity was clearly still in the bath. "I'm still not sure that Geoff leaving us here for a night by the coast was the best thing to do."

"The Grim won't take her tonight," Helen insisted. "It has a pattern, and it will take it a while to hunt her down, if it even can at such a distance."

"So we just twiddle our thumbs until it comes for us?" Ivy snapped.

"You need to make her feel alive," Helen said. "Doom comes from an impending sense of death, so she needs to live as hard as possible in order to keep the symptoms away. Take her out dancing, or to the fair, or fuck her senseless; whatever it takes."

"That's it!?" Ivy remarked, still a little shocked at Helen's suggestions. "That's all I can do?"

"That's all you can do for her *directly*," Helen said. "Now, I'm just getting my computer up and running; when I'm logged in, I'll send you through the documents that my colleague passed on to me; maybe you'll spot a pattern that I missed and we can get a positive ID on our horseman."

"Charity said it was a Ghost," Ivy said, "and Geoff mentioned to her that there were some members of the Walpole family that were excommunicated some years ago; it might be worth talking to him when he gets back.

"I know that Connie and the girls are bound by some ancient Ghost tradition, but I think it will be worth asking them, nonetheless." Ivy thought for a moment. "We've made a lot of mistakes by overlooking the obvious, and we ruled out Smiling Jack without a second thought; what if we were wrong about that?"

"Connie said that a Walpole killed him..." Helen said, but her voice trailed off as the pieces fell into place. "Fuck! I never even considered that Jack's killer could be our horseman."

"Look into it," Ivy said as the bathroom door opened, "and I'll take a look over the files when I get a chance."

"I will do." Helen hesitated before continuing. "On final thing, Ivy; Thaddeus Thane was arrested when he returned from his undercover mission. I don't have any reason as to why, but I was informed that he's being held at Betony Island Prison. I'll try to find out the details for you as soon as I can."

"I... Thank you for telling me." Ivy looked over at

Charity who, clad in her fluffy pink dressing gown, lingered in the bathroom door nervously. "I'll make sure I look after Charity. Happy hunting."

"You too," Helen replied, and the line went dead.

"Any leads?" Charity asked, now chewing absent-mindedly on her fingernails.

Do I tell her? Ivy mused as she thought about Thad. Charity shifted anxiously from foot to foot, and she decided against it. *Later.*

Let's get her back to the land of the living first.

"Tell me, Charity," Ivy said, looking at one of the little brochures that Charity's aunt had sent the two women off with, "have you ever been on a rollercoaster?"

"Can I have another hot dog?" Charity asked, a faint hint of a smile playing around her lips. "I know I've already had three, but I'm still peckish."

"Have whatever you want," Ivy said with a grin, pleased to see a little of Charity's usual self shining through the Doom-driven anxiety that possessed the Ghost. "Today is your day, darling."

"I still can't believe that the Pleasure Beach is open in January!" Charity looked around, and a frown crossed her face. "In fact, we're the only people here."

"About that," Ivy said with a slightly sheepish grin. "Connie called in a favour and got them to open the park with a skeleton crew, just for us. She's also giving all the staff a sizeable tip, which is good of her."

"How sizeable?" Charity asked, raising an eyebrow behind her glasses.

"I thought it impolite to ask," Ivy said diplomatically.

"And if I didn't want to come here?" Charity said,

her hot dog seemingly forgotten.

"Then the owners and staff get a little easy money," Ivy said. "Do you want your hot dog, Charity?"

"Don't try to distract me with food!" Charity retorted testily. "I can't believe she would waste such a lot of money and influence, just to cheer me up..."

"Have you considered that she might not see it as wasteful?" Ivy asked softly. "You're important to her, Charity; to all of us, in fact."

Ivy took Charity's hands in her own.

"We would give anything to get you through this in one piece, darling," Ivy choked back tears as she spoke, "so don't you dare think that you aren't worth it; not for one second. Don't look down on our feelings like that."

"I'm sorry," Charity whispered.

"You don't need to apologise," Ivy said, pulling her into a tight hug. "All you need to do today is enjoy yourself; that's enough for us."

Ivy felt the Ghost's resolve strengthen, and she pulled back from the hug slightly to look at her lover's face. Charity tilted her head, avoiding meeting Ivy's gaze.

"What's the matter?"

"My eyes," Charity whispered, "they feel kinda strange. It's almost as if they're drinking in all the spare light, rather than seeing it."

Ivy frowned as concern swept through her.

"Want me to have a look?" she asked, but Charity shook her head.

"No, I don't think that would be a good idea." She glanced away from Ivy and across the deserted Pleasure Beach. "Can we go on some rides?"

"Of course we can. Where do you want to start?"

She grinned at her. "How about the Ghost Train?"

"A little on the nose, don't you think?" Charity replied, but she couldn't help but match Ivy's smile. "Seeing as we have the entire place to ourselves, I think I just want to ride the rollercoaster over and over, at least twenty times."

"It's your day."

"And then I want to eat all the fair food I can manage before we walk back to guest house," Charity whispered, "and you hold me in your arms until I fall asleep. That, Ivy, is my perfect day."

"Then that's what we'll do." The pair started walking towards the wooden rollercoaster, but something reflected in one of the many shiny surfaces caught Ivy's eye.

How did it go? Did you find Edgar?

"I'm sorry I've been gone so long," Max said sadly, "but try as I might, I just couldn't find him."

You did your best, Ivy thought, looking lovingly at her girlfriend as they climbed the little set of wooden stairs to the rollercoaster. *I only hope Helen and Connie have more luck.*

"Ivy," Charity said softly as they settled into their seats, "can I ask you to do something for me, if the worst should happen?"

"Anything, beloved."

"Thank you," Charity said, smiling as her voice hardened with anger. "If I die before this is over, I want you to hunt that fucker down and use every ounce of your gift to make him wish that he'd had the good sense to stay dead.

"Will you do that for me?"

"That and so much more," Ivy said. "If the time comes, I will unleash horrors upon our horseman, the likes of which he can scarcely dream of."

"I love you, Ivy Livingston."

"And I you, Charity Walpole." The ride suddenly jolted as they got underway. "Now, hold on tight, and don't forget to scream!"

Chapter Twenty Nine – Grim Little Conversations

Helen

"You look like absolute shit," Constance said as Helen began to stir. She moaned in discomfort, turning away from the light. "Of all the times to fall off the fucking wagon, Helen... Well, at least you didn't kill yourself with drink; silver linings, and all."

Harper's final words to her echoed in her mind, and she frowned tightly. *I doubt I could kill myself with booze even if I fucking tried,* she thought, *but I might give it a go anyway.*

"Did you get any further with your research before you blacked out?" Helen opened her eyes tentatively, and saw Connie staring at her, with arms folded and a disapproving frown on her face.

"I did, but..." Helen gestured at the broken phone across the room, "I had a bit of a moment and dropped off the grid."

"Did you get *any* of the messages Charity and Ivy sent you?" Connie asked, and Helen sensed that there was more than disappointment in the ageing Ghost's gaze; there was fear also. "For fucks' sake, Helen, do you have any idea just how fucked we are!?"

"What's happened?" Helen said, her head clearing immediately as she got to her feet. "Tell me everything!"

"We lost another victim to the fucking dog," Connie muttered. "Ivy's convinced that it's a Black Shuck, and that your horseman is the one calling the shots behind the scenes."

"But Grims don't attack the-"

"We've already covered that!" Connie snapped, shoving Helen against the wall angrily. "If you'd have deigned to show up last night, you would already know that this bastard is pulling the wool over the Shuck's eyes. Whatever he's doing, he's getting the damn beast to take innocent, living people in his place."

"To what end?" Helen asked, and Connie slapped her, sending her vision flashing white for a moment.

"To stay alive," Connie roared. "Wake up, you dumb, drunk bitch! How much more of a run-up do you fucking need? Would you like me to draw a picture in fucking crayon-"

Connie's words were cut short as a violent coughing fit overtook her; the harsh barking of her lungs brought tears to her eyes and snot from her nose as Helen glared at her imperiously, her eyes a sickly shade of yellow.

"Jesus Christ, Flash," Connie gasped out, "was that really necessary?"

"Do not hit me again," Helen hissed before releasing her hold on the Ghost. She sighed heavily as Constance collapsed to the the ground, wheezing and in pain. "The Grim has a new victim, and judging by the violence of your reaction, I'm assuming that the beast is coming for one of you."

"Charity," Connie confirmed sadly, and Helen reached down to haul her to her feet. "I'm sorry I hit you, Flash; there's nothing you could've done, even if you were there. It's likely the damage was already done some time ago."

"You think they targeted Charity because she was

looking into Den's death?" Helen asked and Connie nodded, her hand trembling in Helen's. "Well, we better have a chat with her about what we're to do next."

"She's not here, Helen."

"What!?" Helen shook her head in disbelief. "She went back to Oxford, in the middle of all this!?"

"She's gone with Ivy to spend a night at Great Yarmouth," Connie said. "Geoff's driving them up there now."

"Why on earth would she do that?"

"I told her to," Constance said, her anger returning. "That girl has been through enough in the past few days, and one night off isn't going to kill her. Besides, Flash, if you'd have seen her last night, you'd have given her a break too; I've never seen her look like that, even when the Ministry pulled her off that godforsaken island."

"Fear?" Helen asked, her mind already spinning up. "Trepidation, anxiety, possibly transforming into paranoia?"

"Yes," Connie nodded. "What's wrong with her?"

"Doom; I'd bet my fucking career on it." Helen groaned angrily and slapped her forehead with her hand. "We've gone about this so fucking wrong, Connie! Tell me, who has reason to harm Charity?"

"The Walpoles aren't exactly beloved in this area-"

"Just Charity, Connie; this kind of curse has to be placed pretty directly." She frowned and ran her hand through her untidy grey hair. "It'll be someone she's been in contact with in the past few days; maybe there was someone at the funeral..."

"Ivy said that the Shuck originated from the Tharston graveyard, so that makes sense."

"No," Helen said, shaking her head. "If a member of the greater undead crossed into that graveyard during a burial, the Grim would be on them in a second. Hell, even being in the grounds at the break of day would possibly undo the spell that keeps them alive.

"It does at least rule out everyone attending Den's funeral, though." She looked back at Constance. "Who else has she seen?"

"Charity saw the horseman last night," Connie said softly. "She said it was a Ghost."

"Of course!" Helen shook her head in frustration. "How else was it going to hide from the Grim? Gods above, Connie, we're too fucking old for this game."

"Speak for yourself!"

"I need to get my computer up and running," Helen said, heading upstairs to the guest bedroom she was using. "Annie sent me a whole bunch of case files that fit the killing profile of our undead Ghost."

"Do you really think there's *another* Windstahl blade in Norfolk?" Connie asked.

Helen paused at the threshold of her bedroom. *I am so fucking stupid.*

"Helen?" Connie repeated. "Wouldn't that be a bit of a coincidence?"

"It would; almost unbelievably so." She leant on the door frame, suddenly weary and painfully aware of her age. *The old dog's getting too slow to be in the field, it seems.* "Connie; where exactly is Smiling Jack's weapon?"

"Goldthorn is in the family vault, deep underneath the house."

"Is the basket wreathed in golden roses, by any chance?" Helen said, not bothering to look at Constance's response.

"How-" the Ghost began, but Helen cut her off.

"Connie, I need you to be completely honest with me; have you ever actually seen the sword, or just heard about it?"

"It's in a lead-lined chest to keep the lifetaking magic at bay," Connie said, "but I have seen it!"

"The sword, or just the box?" Helen asked, and Connie's pale face flushed with embarrassment. Before she could say another word, however, the house phone rang. Connie was still dumbstruck by her own complacency, so Helen trotted down the stairs and picked up the receiver.

"Walpole residence," she said curtly.

"Helen?"

"Ivy!" Helen said, her voice warming immediately. "Ivy, I need to talk to you!"

"Happy hunting."

"You too," Helen replied, hanging up the phone. She turned to look at Connie, who had ventured down into the vaults to retrieve the box that supposedly held Goldthorn. The Ghost was red faced and panting as she dropped the ancient chest on the hallway floor with a resounding crash.

"That... that thing... weighs a fucking ton," Connie said leaning on the bannister for support. "How... how are the girls?"

"Charity was in the bath," Helen said, "and I've explained to Ivy how she can help alleviate the Doom, albeit only a little. Geoff left them about an hour ago, so he should be home soon."

She looked around the empty entrance hall, confused.

"Connie, where are the twins?" she asked, and the

Ghost matriarch shrugged. "You don't know!?"

"They didn't come home last night, so I assumed they were still out hunting our horseman."

"Ivy had an idea regarding the identity of our horseman," Helen said enigmatically, "but let's open this first, and then I'll tell you."

"It's definitely in there," Constance said, kneeling down to pick the complicated lock on the chest. "I felt it sliding around in there, and it is also fucking heavy as shit."

Windstahl isn't heavy, Helen thought, and mere seconds later her fears were confirmed as Connie pulled out an ancient iron poker from the chest, her face a mask of disbelief and horror.

"What the fuck!?" Connie cried out. "Who could've done this? The house has been in the family for over five hundred years, and only Walpoles know where the vault is! Hell, it took me almost a decade to show it to Geoff!"

"Who put the sword down there?" Helen asked softly.

"My ancestor," Constance said, her anger rising as the poker trembled in her grasp. "The one who killed Smiling Jack."

"What was his name?"

"I don't know," Connie said, her fingers wrapped white-knuckled around the poker's handle. "He betrayed the secrets of the Ghosts to outsiders, so he was cast out; his name was forever lost to us."

"Garland Walpole," said a voice from the bookcase. Helen glanced over and saw Henbane sitting amongst the volumes. "Den asked me to find out for him, along with his resting place; I wondered if he was going to try to honour his memory, in spite of his transgressions.

"I never did find out where he was buried, though."

"Norfolk is a big place," Helen said sadly. "If you had found him, it would put a theory I have to rest."

"You think our undead horseman is Garland?" Connie asked, staring into the middle distance. "Yes, he was a turncoat, but he never *hurt* any of us; Walpoles don't hunt kin, Helen!"

"Then what happened to Cat's eye?" Henbane replied, but the Ghost didn't answer.

She knows, Helen realised. *She knows where he's buried.*

"He hid the sword to keep us safe," Constance muttered, but it was clear that she didn't believe a word she was saying. "Kin looks out for kin, blood for blood; it's always been that way."

Blood for blood, Helen thought, her skin creeping into goose-flesh. *An eye for an eye.*

Kin for kin.

Oh my God.

"Connie, where is your ancestor buried?" Helen asked, putting on her coat and reaching for her shoes.

Constance did not respond, so Helen asked again as she laced up her boots, her words sharper than before.

"For fucks' sake, we do not have time to mess around! Charity's life is at stake! Constance, where is he buried!"

"In an unmarked grave in the Tharston graveyard," Connie replied in a barely audible voice. "Even though he betrayed us, we couldn't let him spend eternity alone. Do you want me to show you?"

"Yes," Helen said, her mind ablaze with ideas, "and bring a shovel."

"Do we really need to disturb his remains?" Connie

asked, clearly uncomfortable at the thought.

"I think we're a bit late for that," Helen said darkly. *Several centuries, in fact.*

Chapter Thirty – A Darker Shade of Black

Charity

"What are you doing in there?" Ivy asked through the bathroom door. "Are you beginning to regret all those hot dogs?"

"I'm just getting something out of my eyes," Charity replied, only half lying. She rubbed at the corner of her left eye and felt a small piece of grit come away on her fingertips. She lowered her voice to a whisper; it wasn't easy to think aloud, but it kept her thoughts away from Ivy.

"Something is happening to me," she muttered. "My gift is... changing; evolving, even. I can risk one more look."

She took a deep breath and lowered her sunglasses as she stared at the mirror.

Her white irises began to quiver and twitch slightly as they drank in the available light in the room, glowing faintly at first, but quickly getting brighter and brighter with each passing heartbeat. Where the glow from a dim lamp would normally have hurt her sensitive vision, the shine from her irises did not.

Still, she replaced her glasses and the glow quickly subsided. She frowned at her darkened reflection; something about her eyes had changed, and she was certain that it had made her far more dangerous than before.

"Accelerants and chemical fuckery," she hissed. "Lamplight, the gift that never stops fucking giving. I thought Ivy said that the Mindlock whatever was supposed to stop this, though?"

Until our deaths, Charity realised, *and if the Black Shuck thinks I'm already dead, then maybe my body does too.*

"Charity, are you sure you're alright?" Ivy asked once again, and the Ghost could feel her girlfriend reach out with her mind. Charity looked at the tiny chip of stone on her fingers once again before tossing it into the bin.

"I'm alright, Liv," she said. "I'm coming out now."

Charity walked out of the bathroom and Ivy gave her a broad smile as she tried to hide her phone behind her back. The Ghost frowned and held out her hand. Ivy's smile faltered and she took a step backwards. Charity opened her mouth, but a distant howl reached her ears before she could utter a single word.

She turned to look out of the window, and the Shuck was there, lurking at the far end of the street. It howled once again, and even the double glazed windows did nothing to filter out the sound; it cut through the building and into the very depths of Charity's soul.

"So it begins," she said, but this time the fear did not take her as firmly as before. The changes that had begun to creep through her body made her feel less like a terrified sheep and more like a cornered predator.

"Charity," Ivy said, standing beside her, "what are you looking at?"

"It's here, Liv," she replied. "It's in the street outside."

Before Ivy could reply, however, Charity snatched the phone from her hands and darted across the room. Her eyes widened as she saw an email from Helen, listing dozens of victim reports along with a shocking piece of news.

"Thane's been arrested!?" She glared at Ivy through her glasses. "How dare you try to hide this from me!?"

"I didn't want to worry you," Ivy said, and Charity could feel the guilt and contrition pouring out of her mind. "I'm sorry; I should've told you earlier."

"Better late than never," Charity said, perching on the edge of the bed. "I suppose you don't know what a Famine is, do you?"

"Max explained it to me," Ivy replied. "She was there when Thad underwent his *change*."

I wonder if she had a hand in it, Charity thought, but she did not voice her opinions. Instead she decided to forward the medical reports to her own phone. The Grim howled in the street once again, but did not draw any closer.

Oh fuck off, you stupid fucking mutt.

"I've sent myself a copy of these," Charity said as she handed the phone back to Ivy. "Two pairs of eyes are better than one, after all, and I've actually seen our horseman. I'm not sure what good we can do from here, though."

"I, uh, I was planning on doing a little bit of remote viewing," Ivy said, almost sheepishly. "Seeing as my gift is amping up and Edgar isn't here to help with the spirit side of things, I thought I could try and build up a mental picture of our killer so I can do my best to locate him.

"Does that sound stupid?"

"No, Liv," Charity said, beaming at her, "that's actually brilliant! You're a natural born investigator, you know!"

"Thank you; that means the world coming from you." Ivy cocked her head to one side. "You seem a bit better, even with the Grim on our doorstep."

"Yeah," Charity said, "I feel it."

"There's something more, isn't there?" Ivy asked, and Charity nodded. "You don't have to tell me about it right now, but if it's important, I'd prefer you told me sooner rather than later."

"Thank you for being so understanding, Liv," Charity said. "I'm not sure I've got enough to actually tell you anything, yet, but when I do, you'll be the first to know.

"So, tell me what you have on our horseman so far."

"Well," Ivy said excitedly, "Helen thought that he might be an ancestor of yours; the one that killed Smiling Jack, to be exact. Unfortunately, he was shunned for reasons unknown, so his identity is lost to us-"

"Garland Walpole," Charity said without looking up from her phone. She continued to speed through the reports as she spoke. "Geoff mentioned his name to me a little while ago. I had my suspicions when I saw the sword last night, but I couldn't be certain.

"Besides, I had other things on my mind." She sighed heavily. "We'd still have to find him though, and..."

Her voice trailed off and she looked closer at her phone, reading the report on the death of a woman named Amy Wesser. One detail had caught her eye; a missing bracelet, blue with a lizard motif.

"What have you found?" Ivy asked.

"Amy Wesser," Charity said. "Can you see if she was killed under a full moon?"

"That shouldn't be too hard to find out; is it important?" Ivy said as she tapped away on her phone.

"It might be," Charity replied, almost too quietly to hear. "I think I've seen this bracelet."

He wasn't confused by the sunglasses, she thought as her blood ran cold in her veins, *and he bent over backwards to meet me.*

"Height of the full moon," Ivy said, confirming Charity's worst fears. "Jesus, Charity; you look pale as death, even for you!"

"I know who he is," Charity whispered. "Our horseman is walking around in the daylight under the name of Nicky Gardener."

"Gardener is a bit on the nose if it is Garland, isn't it?" Ivy said, and Charity nodded. "So where did you see him? Your father's funeral?"

"He was my fucking dentist," Charity growled. "He probably put the curse on me when I saw him; I knew he was a fucking creep."

Ivy stared at her in shock and Charity had to snap at her to get her to focus.

"Ivy!" Charity said sharply, and her girlfriend's gaze finally came back to the real world. "This is not the time to zone out!"

"His practice is abandoned," Ivy said sadly. "It looks like he ducked out as soon as he was finished up with you. We'll have to track him down the old fashioned way, I'm afraid."

"That was fucking quick," Charity said. "You're getting freakishly good at this."

"Wait for my next trick," Ivy said with a smile, and pointed at Charity's phone, which rang in her hand.

"Hello?" she said, answering the call.

"Charity, darling, it's Connie."

"Hi."

"We know who it is!" Connie said breathlessly. "It's-"

"Garland Walpole," Charity said. "We know. We've

also worked out what name he's going under currently, but that was a bust. You need to find his grave and-"

"That's what I called about," Connie said impatiently. "Helen, Henbane, and I are up at the graveyard. Garland's body isn't here, but we've found all the missing bodies, Charity. They were all in his grave, crammed in like sardines.

"I'm sorry sweetheart, but this is a dead end."

Instead of giving into despair, Charity allowed her mind to go blank as she let her instincts take over.

"Connie," she said slowly, "get Geoff to meet us here at ten o'clock tomorrow morning, sharp."

"Do you have a plan?" Charity's aunt asked nervously.

"Not yet," Charity said, "but by the time he gets here, I will do."

"He'll be there. Good luck, sweetheart."

Charity hung up to find Ivy staring at her.

"What?"

"Why not have Geoff come and get us now?" Ivy asked.

"I don't have a plan yet," Charity responded, "and my gut says that we need to be close to here to stand any chance of solving this thing."

"If you're sure."

"I am," Charity said, and then she gave Ivy a broad grin. "Besides, we've already paid for breakfast, and I want my kippers."

"I do love to see a guest enjoying their breakfast!" said Beverly, one of the owners of the guest house the two Ceps were staying in. Seeing as January was a quiet month for Yarmouth, Charity and Ivy were the only guests, so their host had decided to join them for a chat.

"This is splendid, Bev, thank you," Charity said around a mouthful of buttery smoked fish.

"So, um, what's our plan?" Ivy said. The Séance had spent most of the night asleep whilst Charity had been on her phone, poring over the details of Garland's many murders. Ivy shot Bev an uncomfortable look. "If you want to talk about that now, of course."

"Ooh, what are you up to today, ladies?" Beverly asked, leaning forward excitedly.

"Grave robbing," Charity said with a chuckle, playing the whole thing off as a joke. "We're gonna go splashing about in the Broads looking for corpses."

"Why the Broads?" Ivy asked, trying to keep up with the deception. *Come on, Liv, my mind's wide open.*

"I've already got a collection of bog bodies, you see," Charity said with a fish bone-filled smile, "and I think the perfect one to complete my set is out there somewhere; we just need to track it down."

You understand, Liv?

"You are a strange pair," Bev said with a giggle. "Where did the two of you meet?"

"Well," Charity said, "Ivy, here, is a psychic who dug her nose into some rather nasty business concerning vampires so they sent me, an invisible assassin, to kill her. It was love at first fight."

Beverly looked at the Ghost, entirely nonplussed as Ivy stared at her, wide eyed. There was an awkward moment of silence before Charity burst out laughing.

"I'm just fucking with you, Bev," Charity said with a grin. "We met at the Oxford Women's Institute."

"Oh, you jokers!" said their host, laughing along with them.

"Ivy makes the jam, and I do the singing, although I'm more a fan of Queen and 10cc than Jerusalem."

"I hear there are a lot of lesbians in the WI nowadays," Beverly said, and Charity nodded.

"Oh, yeah, there are loads! Did you know that there's a special code, but it's knitted cardigans instead of hankies; lets the others know what you're into, if you catch my drift."

Ivy nearly choked on her bacon as she stifled a laugh.

"Have you got any other plans, aside from grave robbing and splashing about in the broads?" Beverley asked with a chuckle.

"I'm going to meet up with my dentist," Charity said as a wicked smile crept on to her face. "I owe him a little something for the last job he did for me, you see, and I always settle my scores."

Chapter Thirty One – Jenny O' the Fen

Ivy

Nobody can touch me on my mountain.
The flapping of the canvas walls of the tent, all tattered at the edges.
Just follow the path.
The smell of a hot cup of tea in her hands, peppermint and licorice; Kiki's favourite.
Don't stop walking.
The gentle jingle of the bells as they swayed in the wind, their sound almost as bright as the sun.
Take all the time you need.
The chill of the Himalayan air and the serenity of pure isolation.
Learn how to partition yourself.
The coarse hair of the hide blanket, rough underneath her fingertips.
Build a sanctuary in your mind.
"I have never felt so powerful, Max," Ivy said as the two women sat in the Ashram, cups of tea in hand. *We are mirror images of each other,* she thought, and Max nodded.
"Would it help if I was someone else?" Max asked, raising an inquisitive eyebrow.
"Take the form you prefer most of all," Ivy replied, and Max's body immediately shifted. Instead of a woman, he was now a pale man of Ivy's age, covered in a complex web of animalistic tattoos. His pale eyes stared out from beneath his mop of dark hair, and a bundle of knives was arrayed on the floor before him.
The tattoos moved and shifted, bursting with a life

of their own, and Ivy saw shades of herself in him; each inked creature was an Edgar or a Michaela, a division of mind, body, and power. *He still looks like me, though.*

"Is this Silas's body?" she asked, and Max nodded.

"Nothing against your form, but this one is lithe as a cat and as deadly as a coiled viper." Max smiled at Ivy. "Silas doesn't know it yet, but he died the day Harper uplifted him; his body is just a flesh vessel to contain his true essence."

"Which is?"

"A tide of living ink; a billion billion specks of darkness, each one an entire world of possibility." Max smiled at her. "It's a privilege to be bound to the both of you; you're both such powerful beings and you will do great things together.

"Here, let me give you something; a gift, for all the kindness you've shown me."

Max got to his feet and helped Ivy to hers. He reached out and rolled up her left sleeve, revealing her lamplight tattoo. Ivy looked away at the nightmarish reminder of her time on Betony Island, but Max gently turned her head to face the ink.

"Let me show you how to make something beautiful out of a broken dream." He traced his fingers over the stylised stone lantern and the ink twisted and shifted into a swirling nebulous form that boiled beneath her skin with all the potential of a storm cloud. "Look into the whirl and show me what you see."

Ivy looked into the vortex and felt herself falling into the darkness. The wind whistled in her ears as she plummeted through the sky, and yet she felt no fear whatsoever; instead, she let out a wild cry of exultation.

She flung her arms to the side and her fingertips became feathers. Her outstretched limbs formed beautiful wings and she soared through the storm, a being of pure grace and perfection.

This is the purest form of being, Ivy thought. *It's a shame that I can't feel like this all the time.*

"Open your eyes, Ivy." Max's gentle voice brought her back to herself, and she returned to the mountaintop, becoming human once more in the doorway to her Ashram. "Welcome back."

"That was wonderful, thank you," Ivy whispered. She glanced down at her left arm and frowned; her Lamplight tattoo still remained, a indelible scar on her burned flesh. "I had hoped this would be gone."

"Marcel Dupont's work is difficult to unmake," Max said slyly, "but we can turn it to our advantage; borrow some of his power, as it were."

He gestured for Ivy to look at her right wrist, which was still covered by the simple robe that she wore. She carefully rolled up her sleeve and gasped at the beautiful ink that now decorated her damaged skin; standing proud within a whirlwind of cherry blossom was a red-crowned crane.

"Oh, Max," she whispered, "it's beautiful! Thank you!"

"It's more than just art," he said knowingly. "I want you to find a part of your mind, just a tiny fragment, and place it in the crane. Think of it like trying to hold a shopping list or set of directions in your mind. Do you have it?"

"I think so," Ivy said, looking at the crane; she was still awestruck by the artistry of the line work. "What do I do now?"

"Just let it fade into your subconscious, but still hold

it gently, as one holds a wayward moth." Ivy nodded, and he went on. "Now flick your right arm, as if you were imparting flight into the crane, but keep hold of your idea moth."

Ivy did as he said a few times, and felt a strange tugging at her mind when she reached the apex of the movement. She smiled at the bizarreness of the situation, which caught his attention.

"You can feel it, can't you?" he asked, and she nodded. "Then give it an instruction, and when it pulls next time, open your mind and let it take wing."

Locate the body of Garland Walpole, she instructed the crane. *You know how to find him.*

Ivy swung her arm once again, adding in an extra flick of the wrist this time, and an inky black crane erupted from her flesh, taking flight in the skies of her mind. It circled her thrice before soaring off towards the horizon as she stared at it, stunned by the simplicity of it all.

Already the separate part of her mind was feeding her information; the sensations of duality and bilocation came as naturally as breathing to her.

"You're a prodigy," Max said softly. He beamed at her. "The crane is my gift to you, Ivy Livingston. Fly well and often, old mum."

"Does it only work in here?" Ivy asked, and he shook his head.

"No, my dear Dr Livingston," Max replied with a cheeky grin. "This works *everywhere*."

"Thank you!"

"My pleasure, darling," he said, fading slightly. "Now it's time to go back, Ivy; you've work to do."

Ivy opened her eyes as the Volvo hit a slight bump in the road. Charity sat beside her, staring at her exposed right wrist; Ivy smiled when she saw the cherry blossom, along with the space that the crane would occupy when not in flight.

"Where did you go?" Charity asked, and Ivy just winked in response. Before Charity could say anything else, however, there was a stirring in her mind as the crane homed in on its target.

"I've found him," Ivy said suddenly as the information poured into her mind. "I know where to go!"

"Are you sure this is the place?" Geoff asked, and Ivy nodded. She held out her right arm, and the crane swooped back towards her, re-entering the tattoo with a puff of dark particles.

"That's a new trick," Charity said, and Ivy couldn't help but smile at the hint of envy in her girlfriend's voice.

"It's a present from Max," Ivy said softly. She turned to face Geoff. "You'll need to stay here, I'm afraid; this is going to be dangerous, and we might need you to go for help if it all goes to shit."

Geoff nodded as the two women walked into the little nature reserve, beneath the bare limbs of the winter trees. Ivy shivered at the chill and pulled her coat tight around her chest. Charity placed a comforting arm around her and gave her a cheerful smile.

"See, this could be a perfect place for a date, albeit in warmer weather. What makes you think it'll be dangerous?" Charity asked, trying to keep the mood light, but there was tension in her voice.

"If I was keeping my physical form hidden," Ivy said quietly as a pair of birdwatchers passed, "I'd make sure it was somewhere dangerous and well protected from outside interference."

"I know I've said this before, Liv," Charity said with a chuckle, "but you do scare me sometimes."

"Likewise," Ivy replied. She sighed heavily. "I'd feel so much better with my swords and guns."

"You won't have to wait long," Charity said. "When you were asleep last night, I put out the call for additional support; unofficially, of course, but we're still getting reinforcements. If all is well, they should be at the Big House by the time we get back this afternoon."

"Who's coming?" Ivy asked.

"Jess, Teaser, Mallory, and Shy," Charity said with a grin. "In fact, Teaser and Mal were already on their way from Rutland Manor. And before you ask, I told Shy to bring all our weapons from the Folly, so you'll be tooled up to the nines for when we go after Garland and the Grim.

"For now, however, take this."

She pulled out a bone handled knife and handed it to the Séance. Ivy felt the weight and balance before nodding in approval.

"I saw you with these a couple of days ago," Ivy said. "They're fantastic weapons; where did you get them?"

"They were my father's knives," Charity replied. "I found them a few minutes before I met Henbane."

Ivy nodded gently, even as her nose wrinkled; they were getting close to the fen where Garland's corpse was located, if her instincts were correct. The acidic tang of the water stung her nostrils as the reeds rustled in the gentle morning breeze; the woods were dense where they bordered the water, and the dense foliage limited visibility, even in winter.

"The perfect place for an ambush," Charity said. "Listen."

Ivy strained her ears, but aside from the creak of the bare trees and the gentle murmur of moving water, all was silent. *No birds,* she realised. *No mammals; no life at all, it seems.* Her finger reflexively tightened around the weapon in her hand, but Charity shook her head. The Séance took a deep breath, and allowed her body to relax; tension would only work against her in a fight.

Charity dropped into a crouch, dipping her fingers into the mud at the edge of the reed bed, as if testing the texture. Ivy raised an eyebrow, and Charity pointed forward with her muddy fingers, gesturing at the murky water ahead.

It took Ivy's eyes a moment to adjust to the vista of blues, greens, and dark greys, but she soon saw what Charity was pointing at. Several squat, scaly creatures were lurking at the water's edge, their long arms and powerful fingers trembling as they listened for approaching prey.

Neckers, Ivy thought; even without her Ministry training, she'd have recognised the deadly creatures from fairytales and folk stories. *A whole fucking nest of the things.*

Well played, Garland.

"There's too many for a stand-up fight," Charity whispered. "We'll have to ambush them, which is near impossible, unless they're already in a feeding frenzy."

"Damn."

"I fucking hate Nokken," Charity muttered, wiping her muddy hand on her trousers and drawing another knife. "What I wouldn't give for a fucking gun right now."

Her last words were louder than she intended, and the Neckers glanced in their direction, causing the two women to duck out of sight. Slowly, a plan began to form in Ivy's mind.

"Can they see you if you're invisible?" she whispered, and Charity shook her head.

"No, but the splashing will give me away, unless they're already distracted-"

"Good enough for me," Ivy said, and gave Charity a quick kiss, stunning her into silence. "Don't let them drown me."

Before Charity could respond, Ivy burst from their hiding spot and rushed towards the Neckers. They leapt at her, screaming and whooping in their strange underwater tongue, quickly seizing her in their powerful hands. Still, the Séance managed to slash two throats before their combined strength forced her beneath the surface of the fen, foul water covering her face and making it impossible to see.

As the Neckers thrashed and clawed at her, Ivy began to realise that she probably should've explained her plan to Charity before diving into the fray.

She's a smart woman, Ivy thought, *she'll understand what I was thinking.*

Won't she?

Chapter Thirty Two – All For One

Charity

"Fucking hell, Ivy!" Charity hissed as she saw the Nokken wrestle her girlfriend beneath the surface of the water. Even though the telepath had killed two or three of the squat, ugly creatures, there were still an even dozen left to deal with; no mean feat, even for a seasoned killer like Charity Walpole.

She went to dash after Ivy, but something unseen drove a paralysing spear of ice through her heart, pinning her to the spot in terror. A quiet scream began to build in her throat as the seconds passed and Ivy Livingston surely ran low on air.

I can't do this any longer, Charity thought. *I'm too fucking broken.*

Her blade trembled in her hand as she fought the urge to run and hide.

Don't fight it, she thought. *It's a waste to struggle against the tide.*

Go with the flow; make it work for you.

Charity let her terror carry her into the twilight world of invisibility, and she faded from view as the world darkened around her. She removed her sunglasses and slipped them into a pocket as she used the change to spur her into action.

She burst through the reeds and into the water, leaping as far as she could. Her knives met the hearts of two of the Nokken as she landed, killing them instantly. Most of the remaining ten were focussed on Ivy, but at least three had turned to lunge at Charity, and she ducked down, spinning as she did so, slicing open one of the monsters across its distended belly.

The other two reached out with their freakish arms, and she wind-milled the blades, pivoting her feet as she did so, cutting their fingers and causing them to recoil in pain. Her feet started to sink into the foetid slime as she moved, however, costing her precious mobility; soon she would be a sitting duck.

A slight jangle sounded behind her as the hair on the nape of her neck stood on end. Even though she had no reason to do so, she ducked under the water as the Nokken lunged, putting her into an intensely vulnerable position.

Her instincts paid off, however, and a muted roar reached her submerged ears as a shotgun blast ripped through the two attacking monsters. Charity sheathed her blades and reached through the murky water to find Ivy as the weapon fired once again.

The Ghost's fingers closed around Ivy's wrist, and she stood up, pulling the Séance out of the water and shedding her invisibility at the same time. Her skin tightened around her body, growing brittle and painful, like a cocoon of gossamer glass that shattered away from her visible flesh in a wave of almost unbearable agony.

Charity let out a howl of pain as she became visible, and she screwed her eyes closed against the burning glare of the low winter sun. The chill of the water was already sapping her strength, but Ivy's gasp as she pulled in a lungful of air emboldened her, and she quickly slipped on her sunglasses and turned to face the Nokken.

To her surprise, they were cowering at the edge of the water, with some of the smaller creatures backing away into the dense reeds. The strange jangling reached her ears once again, and she turned to face the source of the sound.

Geoff stood at the edge of the water, brandishing a shotgun covered in bells, seashells, small bones, and owl feathers. He glared at the beasts and rattled the weapon once again, and the Nokken howled at the cacophony produced by the assortment of items bound to the firearm.

"Go on!" Geoff roared, his cheeks pink with exertion. "Go on, beasts! Get!"

The last of the Nokken vanished into the undergrowth, and Geoff nodded knowingly at Charity.

"How," she said, taking a shuddering, agonising breath, "did you know that would work?"

"Neckers are ambush predators," Geoff said as he reached out for the women, ready to haul them out of the stinking water as soon as they reached him. "All you need to do is kill a few with a sufficiently loud weapon, and as long as you keep making noise, they'll scatter."

"That's all!?" Charity asked, surprised at the simplicity of Geoff's plan.

"Of course! Don't they teach you anything at the Ministry?" he asked with a grin as he pulled Charity out of the fen. He extended his hand to Ivy, but she slipped back beneath the surface and Charity's heart leapt into her mouth. She moved to help her girlfriend, but Ivy soon emerged once again, with something hideous clutched against her chest.

"Charity," she said breathlessly as she brandished the pickled corpse in her arms, "I've got him!"

The journey back to Walpole Manor was an unpleasant one; both women reeked of decaying vegetation and acidic mud, but that was nothing compared to the unbelievable stink of Garland Walpole's mummified body.

Charity had finally started to dry out when Geoff guided the car on to the narrow country lanes that approached the Manor, but when the Walpole Estate came into view, she let out a shocked gasp. Instead of the gentle hedgerows that lined the boundary of Connie's land, there were wild walls of bracken, interwoven with twisted, gnarled tree limbs.

"How-" Charity began to ask, but then she saw a familiar figure dancing wildly along the borders of the garden, fingers twisting and beckoning the plant life into an impassable barrier that would keep out all but the most determined of intruders.

There's likely more at work than just thorns, Charity thought as Mallory Marsh continued his Dryad's dance, lost to the atavistic flow of power that moved through his barely human body. His clothes were intact, however, and his signature hat was firmly perched atop his head.

"He's gained more control of his power," Ivy muttered. "It's been barely a fortnight, and he's already crafting a protection stave. I honestly thought that he'd never call upon that particular wellspring again."

Marsh's dance slowed as the car approached, and he seemed to return to himself, much like a sleeper waking from a very deep dream. A smile crossed his face when Charity leant out of the window to call out to him.

"Nice moves, Marsh!" she cried out, tears of relief streaming down her face. Charity leapt from the still moving car and gathered the small man up in a damp, smelly hug. "I am so fucking glad to see you!"

"Hiya, Mal," Ivy called, although she remained in the car. "Nice work on the wall."

"Well, we can't have you both being killed by anything as mundane as a dog, can we?" His voice was oddly musical and coloured with the creak of ancient trees, but it was still certainly him. "It's actually been pretty cathartic to use my power again, truth be told.

"Jess and Tea helped me see that my gender is not defined by my blood or body, but by my the contents of my heart."

"And your hat," Charity said, grinning.

"Yes, the hat does play a big part too," Mallory replied with a chuckle. "Everyone else is up at the house; I'll join you when I'm done here."

"Will do. Shake a tail feather, Marsh."

Mallory resumed his dance as Charity climbed back into the car, and Geoff continued up the driveway towards the house. Soon, the lanky form of Teaser Malarkey came into view, and this time Ivy was first out of the vehicle, brandishing the planchette at the Tracer.

Teaser smiled at both women as they walked towards her, but had to choke back a retch when the stench of the Fens reached her highly sensitive nose. She quickly recovered, however, and looked excitedly at the planchette in Ivy's grasp.

"Did it work?" Teaser asked Ivy, who gave her an enthusiastic thumbs up. The Tracer grinned and bounced on her feet excitedly. "Oh, I am *so* fucking *good* at this!"

"Nice work, Tea," Charity said, giving her a congratulatory slap on the back that nearly sent her sprawling. "You're a real asset to this team."

"Oh, one aims to please," Teaser replied as she regained enough balance to stand fully upright again. "How are you doing, Charity?"

"I can't say I'm on top of the world," she admitted, "but I'm all the better for seeing you and Marsh here. Have you met the rest of the family?"

"Yeah; Connie is lovely, and the twins are... a bit intense, but everyone seems to be decent and reliable." She frowned slightly. "Not so excited to see Helen here, but I guess I can't hold her responsible for the actions of her son."

"I think it's best to leave that particular hornet's nest for another time, okay?" Charity said, as much to Ivy as to Teaser.

"Agreed. Jess and Shy are inside the main house with the twins; Commander Holloway has got them polishing all the weapons that we were able to find. Luckily, Shy did managed to bring some of our usual tools, though, so we're not without our favourite toys.

"That includes your swords, too, Ivy." Ivy nodded in thanks and there was a moment of silence as Charity looked at Teaser. The Tracer's face darkened appreciably and she leant in close, lowering her voice as she did so. "More importantly, though, did you hear about Thaddeus?"

"I did," Charity said softly, "and don't worry, Tea; I'm gonna pull every fucking string I have to get him off that fucking island."

"I heard that he's a Famine now," Teaser said nervously. "I didn't even know what that was, at least until Jess told me. Can it really be true, Chaz? Could he really have become something so awful?"

"Maybe, maybe not," Charity said firmly, "but either way, Thane is one of us; we don't leave our own behind. We'll get him out, Tea.

"Famine or not, he's still our Thad."

"Too fucking right," Ivy said. "He's always been there for us, so now it's our turn to show up for him. How's Marsh taking it?"

"You couldn't get a read on him?" Teaser asked the Séance, clearly surprised.

"His head is too full of Dryad stuff," Ivy said with a smile. "I dare not get too close, lest I get lost in it."

"Fair enough," Tea said, nodding. "I've been working with him for years, and even I find the whole woodland enchantment thing a bit overwhelming. Still, I'm glad he's finding an outlet for it; it can't have been easy, keeping it bottled up for so long."

"I know the feeling," Ivy said darkly. "You can't keep power like that hidden away forever; it will force its way out sooner or later."

"Are you going to go inside to say hi to Shy and Jess?" Teaser asked Charity.

"Soon, but I think we should deliver the remains of dear old Uncle Garland to the good Dr Mickelson," Charity said. "I'm sure she'll be able to find out some way to kill him permanently if we give her long enough to pick over his carcass."

"Coroners always give me the creeps," Teaser said with an exaggerated shudder. "Give me formless spirits any day of the week."

"Be careful what you wish for," Ivy said raising her eyebrows playfully. "Do you know where we can find Helen?"

"She's in there," Teaser pointed at one of the outbuildings, "with a *lot* of corpses. I think your Aunt is helping her... examine them."

"Thanks, Tea," Charity said, and went to walk away,

but let out a small cry of surprise as Teaser pulled her into a tight hug.

"We've got you," she said forcefully. "This fucker might be one of the greater undead, but he's up against the Night People."

Teaser released Charity after a few more seconds, letting her walk towards the makeshift morgue once more. As she crossed the lawn, Charity began to feel the first flicker of hope in her heart.

With so many great people beside me, she realised, *I might actually have a chance.*

<u>Chapter Thirty Three</u> – Touched by the Grave

Helen

"Hands," Helen sang softly as she examined the corpses, "touchin' hands. Reachin' out."

"Touching me, touchin' you," Connie continued, grinning at the ageing sawbones. "Sweet-"

The music reached a crescendo as Ivy and Geoff brought in the pickled corpse of Garland Walpole, stopping the singing women in their tracks. Helen pointed to a nearby table and the body was dumped on the creaking wood with all the ceremony and care that a turncoat deserved.

"This is him?" Helen asked, peering through her spectacles at the centuries old skin.

"It is," Geoff said, "and the girls had a hell of a time getting him out of the bog."

"This is *all* of him?" Helen said, frowning.

"All we could find," Ivy said. "Maybe the Neckers ate the rest of him?"

"Neckers?" Connie asked.

"Nokken," Geoff clarified and the Ghost nodded. "So many names for such reprehensible little creatures."

"Nokken do not eat cursed flesh, Livingston." Helen's voice was sharp with worry. "You clearly failed to retrieve some of him; over half of the corpse is missing!"

"You could drain that whole fucking national park," Ivy said angrily, "and you wouldn't find so much as a fucking hair left out there. This is all there is, Helen."

She was about to snap at the younger woman once again, but she kept the urge under wraps; after all, Ivy had been right about almost everything so far. *I need her insight,* Helen realised. *We'll never do this without her.*

Courage, Helen.

"Assuming that this body is protected against all kinds of carrion eaters," Helen said slowly, looking Ivy in the eye, "what do you think is the cause of the damage to the corpse?"

"I'm not a pathologist, Helen," Ivy replied.

"You're not," she said softly, "but you have more of an insight into the mind and motives of this monster than the rest of us, and you've been right on the money with every call you've made. Come on, Dr Livingston; impress me."

Ivy drummed her fingers on the wall of the outbuilding as she thought, softly humming a tune as the wheels of her mind turned over; Helen could feel the deductive reasoning radiating from the psychic therapist, fitting all the pieces together.

"This corpse is partly missing," Ivy mused, "but I don't think it is *damaged,* per se. Look at the edges of the wounds; they're clean cuts with a sharp blade, and they've been made at more than one point in time. Some are fresher than others, even though it's admittedly quite hard to tell, given the state of the body."

"You think it's been dissected?" Connie asked, and Ivy nodded.

"Second point," the Séance went on, "is that the Grim takes both the flesh and spirit of the dead; otherwise, we'd have had corpses aplenty, along with an empty grave. That means that the dog is specifically coming for this body.

"Parts of it are missing, so one could assume that if they were unprotected or unhidden, they would have been in the grave, yet you didn't find anything." Ivy frowned and looked at the little speaker, which was still happily playing Neil Diamond songs. "Can we change the music, please? I can't think clearly to this."

"What would you like?" Helen asked.

"She'll have Nirvana," Charity said from the doorway; she'd come in so quietly that Helen had not even noticed her presence. "Come As You Are, on repeat."

"You know me so well," Ivy said with a smile, and she began to sway slowly to the music, bouncing on the balls of her feet as she did so. Her eyes closed and the dancing became more pronounced.

Helen reached out towards Ivy, to shake her out of her reverie, but Charity shook her head.

"She's feeling out the vibe, Helen," the Ghost said quietly. "Just let her work. She's an artist, not a scientist."

The song began to play for a second time, and Ivy's dancing took her away from the table containing Garland's remains; she moved towards the crushed corpses instead. The smile that was on Ivy's lips broadened as she leant down and put her fingers in the mouth of a dead young man by the name of Tony Shanks.

"What are you doing?" Connie said, clearly disturbed by the actions of the telepath, but Helen's eyes widened as she finally understood Ivy's line of reasoning.

"You think that the missing parts of Garland are in

our collection of grave corpses, don't you?" Helen asked, and Ivy nodded. "How on earth would Garland have the opportunity to do that? You can't just stitch parts of your body into people, and feeding it to them wouldn't stay in their system for long enough."

"I'll let you answer that one," Ivy said, finally opening her eyes to look at Charity.

"Garland is practising as a dentist," Charity said with a sigh. "Specifically, the dentist that I saw a couple of days ago. His current alias is Nicky Gardener, and we've already checked to see if he's still around."

"And?" Connie asked.

"He's gone to ground," Charity said sadly, "but we do now have a tremendous bargaining chip."

"His body." Helen said. She looked at Ivy, who was nodding along to the music. "I think I've figured this out; may I?"

"Be my guest, Helen."

"Garland managed to find away to prolong his life after death," she said, "at least for enough time to escape the graveyard. Obviously, this isn't a permanent solution for him, and he is pursued by the Black Shuck.

"I think he expected this to happen, and had already worked out that he could use his skills as a Ghost, along with some kind of deceptive spell, to hide from the Grim. Unfortunately, this requires pieces of his body, which he has stashed in the Broads for safe keeping..."

Helen paused as the final connection clicked into place.

And there it is, simple as that!

"What have you figured out?" Geoff asked, smiling

softly.

"He needs the corpse to stay intact! Placing it in the fen preserves it, which preserves his false vitality." Helen rubbed her hands together gleefully. "The attacks mentioning Goldthorn have increased in recent years, indicating that the more he takes from the corpse, the less staying power the life-drinking effects of the sword have."

"So why her?" Connie asked, looking at Charity.

"I'm his flesh and blood," Charity replied. "I'll bet that he thinks if he can get the Shuck to take me, it'll think it has him, and he won't need to damage his body any further.

"So, what would happen if we destroyed the body?"

"We don't even need to destroy it," Geoff said. "I can just consecrate it and return it to its grave. Admittedly, I'd still rather burn it first, just to be safe."

There's a plan coming together here, Helen thought giddily.

"If we do that before sunset, we can get the Grim off your back," Connie said excitedly. "Then we can deal with Garland afterwards."

"It's not as simple as that," Charity said. "If we release him from the Grim's hunt, he'll just disappear and use Goldthorn to stay alive forever. If that happens, we'll never catch him."

"This man's name is Simon Wilbur," Ivy said, lingering over the freshest of the corpses in the makeshift morgue. "His mother, Peggy, was the latest victim of Goldthorn."

"What's your point, Ivy?" Helen asked. Ivy pointed to another body, an older man this time.

"This is the father of Amy Wesser, another of Garland's victims. The report mentioned that Amy's father was acting strange around the time of her death, and disappeared shortly afterwards." Ivy looked at Helen. "I don't think he can use Goldthorn unless the Black Shuck is actively hunting someone else, otherwise it will find him."

Geoff chuckled softly from where he stood, and everyone turned to look at him.

"Do share," Ivy said. "I think you might have the final piece of the puzzle."

"When I was studying the occult," Geoff said, "I looked into spells for life transference; whilst there are enough of them to fill a library, they all had one thing in common. If your soul is entangled with another, you can only steal life from that person or, sometimes, their kin.

"I think Goldthorn has such a limitation."

There was silence as the ramifications of what had been said sunk in.

"So, if that's true, then it means that the only person Garland can use Goldthorn on is Charity," Connie said. "At least as long as she's alive."

"I think we can make this work for us," Helen said after a moment of contemplation. "Yes, I think we can end this tonight."

"I'm all ears, Helen," Charity said. "What's the plan?"

"We finish laying the defences around the house," Helen began, sitting around the kitchen table with their entire assembled forces. "We'll have to remove all the pieces of Garland from his victims in order to make the body whole for the consecration and burning to work; unfortunately that includes your tooth, Charity."

"I never much cared for it anyway," the Ghost said, trying to keep the mood light.

"When all the pieces are gathered, Geoff, Connie, and I will head up to the graveyard. We'll wait until sunset before we complete the ritual and return the ashes to Garland's grave. That should allow the Black Shuck to come out one last time."

"Take Jess with you," Charity said. "She's trained in theology and she'll have seen The White Book; if you need to think on your feet, you'll need her."

Jess nodded in approval, and Charity went on.

"I also want the twins in that graveyard with you. We're operating on the theory that aunt or cousin is too distant a link for Garland to take your lives, but if we're wrong I want you in the place he least wants to be."

Cat and Cait agreed, and both placed their right hands over their hearts in a pledge of allegiance to Charity.

Ghosts are a strange breed.

"Please, go on," Ivy said.

"Well, the plan splits here, depending on whether Charity is still bound to Garland." Helen took a deep breath. "Option one, which is our best one, is that the two are no longer entangled. The Shuck will go after Garland, and Ivy can track the beast right to our horseman's door. He won't be able to use Goldthorn without revealing his location, so he'll be vulnerable.

"We hit him with everything we've got, and then the Grim will drag him back into his grave. Hopefully, that should be the end of him."

"And option two?" Geoff asked. "What if Charity is still bound to him?"

"Then Charity holes up here initially to defend

against the Grim. Hopefully we'll be able to either destroy it or disable it, which will allow us to focus on Garland."

"And if we can't?" Charity asked, trembling slightly.

"Then you'll have to run the gauntlet," Ivy said, clearly picking up on Helen's thoughts. "You'll have to race both Garland and the dog to the churchyard. I'll go with you to protect you as best I can, whilst Mal, Tea, Shy, and Henbane head to the church.

"Once you're across the boundary and on hallowed ground, you should be safe from the Shuck. Garland will follow you in, because he needs to kill you to escape." Ivy drummed her fingers on the table. "He's regenerated recently, so he'll be strong, but without the stability of his corpse, every hit we land on him will strip him of his mortality. If we can wear him down enough, he should be nothing but pure spirit by the time day breaks."

"And then he's fucking toast," Charity said, "right?"

"Indeed," Helen said. "If it comes to it, when Garland is in the churchyard we can't let him leave it, and we can't let him kill Charity."

"I'd also rather not die," Teaser said around a mouthful of licorice. "I've got stuff I want to do."

"That sounds like a pretty solid plan, Flash," Connie said, placing a hand on Helen's shoulder. "My only question is how will we know whether Charity and Garland are still bound after we remove her tooth?"

"I'll know," Ivy said firmly.

"Well then," Charity said with a shaky laugh, "let's get this sucker out and see which road we're taking."

"It'll be the hard one," Mallory said, a smile twitching his lips.

"How can you be sure?" Geoff asked.

"It's always the fucking hard one," Charity said with a sigh. "When this is done, we'll tell you about the Nightwalker fungus. Now, how are we going to get the tooth out?"

There was a moment of silence as everyone turned to look at Teaser, who frowned sulkily.

"Oh, for fucks' sake," she muttered, getting to her feet, "I always get the gross jobs."

Charity braced herself for what was about to happen.

"Stay still, Charity," Teaser said, placing one hand on the Ghost's shoulder and drawing the other back into a tight fist. "This is gonna hurt. Sorry."

Chapter Thirty Four – It Comes At Night

Charity

Charity braced herself for the hit, but nothing prepared her for the sensation of having something akin to a wormhole appearing in her mouth for a fraction of an instant. The tooth clattered on to the table as the momentum of Teaser's blow knocked Charity to the ground, nearly sending her sunglasses flying off her face.

"Fuck!" Charity said thickly, her mouth full of blood and tiny fragments of jawbone and gum tissue. "You could've made it a clean snatch, Tea!"

She spat a mouthful of blood on to the tiled kitchen floor as Mallory came to join her. He whispered a few words that sounded something like Welsh, and she felt the wound in her mouth close over.

"I've been doing a bit of research on Druids," he said sheepishly, "and that was the first bit of their knowledge I've put into practice. I hope it didn't hurt too much."

Teaser groaned and Charity glanced over at her. The tall Tracer was cradling her hand, wincing in pain; she'd clearly broken at least one bone, if not more. *For fucks' sake, Tea,* Charity thought as she got to her feet, *someone needs to teach you how to safely throw a punch.*

"Do you have a verdict yet?" Charity asked Ivy, who nodded. "It's the hard way, isn't it?"

"I'm afraid so," Ivy said sadly. "You're still linked, unfortunately."

"Then we run the gauntlet," Charity replied,

suddenly feeling several decades older than she had mere moments ago. "I think the Doom is still on me, too. I can't seem to catch a fucking break."

She sighed heavily and sat down, looking at Teaser as Helen examined the Tracer's hand.

"Some of your bones are mislocated," Helen said, frowning.

"Dislocated, you mean?" Geoff asked, and Helen shook her head.

"You folded your own fucking skeleton?" Mallory asked, shocked. "Jesus, Tea, that's bad, even for you!"

"Fuck off, Mal," Teaser groaned. "It's been a long day and I fucked up."

"Can you fix her?" Charity asked Helen, who shook her head.

"Not in time for tonight. I can break the bones and reset them, but she won't have use of this hand for at least a fortnight." The Blight frowned at the Tracer. "I'm sorry, Teaser, but you aren't gonna be doing any fighting tonight."

"Fucking hell," Teaser said sadly. "I'm sorry, Charity."

"It happens," the Ghost said, her mind already racing. *Improvise, adapt, and overcome.* "Give your gift to Shy; he'll be able to make better use of it fighting Garland."

"Will do," Teaser said, cramming more licorice in her mouth. "What do you want me to do?"

Charity thought for a moment, before settling her gaze on the Pixie that perched on the table. Henbane looked at her, their face both keen and curious.

"You've worked closely with Ghosts forever, right?"

"For at least seventy years," Henbane confirmed. "What are you thinking, Boss?"

Dad said that you always used to call him that, Charity thought with a start, but she put the memory aside for another time. Instead she looked at Teaser, who was still whimpering over her injured limb.

"Do you have the chemicals needed to make flashes for your Spirit Cameras?"

"Yes, but they won't work well as explosives, I'm afraid; all brightness, no force." Teaser looked at Charity's sunglasses for a moment before grinning.

"That's exactly what we need," Charity said, matching the Tracer's smile. "Garland doesn't wear sunglasses, so we can blind the bastard, at least temporarily. Henbane, add a pinch of Pixie fuckery into the chemical mix and make sure that you help Teaser fire off those flashes as quickly as we need them."

"You got it, Boss," Henbane said, and gave Teaser a nod. "Your reputation precedes you, ma'am; it'll be an honour to raise chaos with the famous Agent Malarkey."

"If everyone knows what they're going to do," Charity said, "then they can hop to it. We don't have a lot of time, and nightfall will be on us all too soon."

"What do you want me to do, Charity?" Ivy said, getting to her feet.

"You're with me, Liv," the Ghost said, leading her out of the room. "We'll go over our specific end of the plan in a little while, but first we both need a shower."

And, Charity thought loudly enough for her to hear, *if these are my last few hours, I don't want to spend them with anyone but you.*

"Likewise, my love," Ivy said, slipping her hand into Charity's. "I'll be with you until the end, whatever that may be."

There was a knock on the bathroom door as Ivy towelled Charity's bruised body dry, followed by an awkward cough.

"Who is it?" Ivy called out.

"It's Mallory," he replied. "I, um, I wanted to know what Charity wanted for dinner. Whatever it is, I'll make it."

"We should eat fast, Mal," Charity called out. "We'll just snack on whatever comes to hand; you need to focus on finishing that protection stave."

"It's done, Charity," he said proudly, "and I know that you've been running on empty the past few days. Come on, Walpole, just tell me what you want; I'm not gonna offer to make you a last meal again, you know."

She blinked for a moment, shocked by Mallory's frankness. *Are things really that bad?* The shakes began to take hold once again as she realised that the Doom she'd been inflicted with at the hands of the Grim was still with her, gnawing at her confidence and skill like a beaver with a tree.

Hopefully we can get this done before I come crashing down completely, she thought, and Ivy must've heard it as she took the frightened Ghost tightly in her arms. Her mind was reeling about the seemingly impossible task before them and all thoughts of food were driven from her brain.

"I honestly don't know, Marsh," Charity replied eventually. "I can't really think about that right now. I'm sorry."

"You've been living with her for half a year," Ivy said, "and you're a more perceptive man than most; I'm sure you'll be able to come up with something suitable."

"It's a well stocked kitchen," Mallory replied, "so I'll come up with some options."

Charity heard him walking away and gave Ivy a thankful smile. *She's good enough to run this group, should anything happen to me tonight.* She blinked in surprise when Ivy's face fell.

"Don't think like that," Ivy said firmly. "Your friends and family are with you; we'll get you through to the dawn."

"I hope so," Charity said. "It's still gonna be a hell of a long night, though. Speaking of, how much time do we have until sunset?"

"A couple of hours yet," Ivy said. "Come through to the bedroom; I want to give you something to keep you safe."

Ivy led her through to the dimly lit room and gestured to the katana and wakizashi that lay on the bed. Charity looked at her in confusion, and Ivy nodded. The Ghost picked up the longer weapon with a trembling hand; the perfectly balanced sword seemed to thrum with quiet power.

"Black Jade for destruction," Ivy said before pointing to the wakizashi, "and this one has White Jade for balance. Wield them together, and they will devastate whatever you're up against."

"But Goldthorn is made of Windstahl," Charity said quietly. "Will these even hold up against it?"

"Midori Aoki made them for me, and a Strix told me that they came to me for a purpose; I think they exist to protect you tonight, Charity."

"What if you're wrong?" the Ghost asked, her words muted slightly as she nervously chewed her lower lip. "They could be destroyed entirely!"

"If they break, they break," Ivy said with a sad

smile. "Kiki wouldn't mind, especially if you were the one the doing the breaking. Trust me, I think you'll need these."

"You've only shown me basic drills," Charity said, trying to hand the weapon back, but Ivy refused to take it. "I can't use these, Ivy."

"I'm going to teach you." She placed a hand on Charity's face, instantly transporting the Ghost to a dark forest filled with unseen danger. Charity held both blades in a guard position as thunder rumbled overhead. A strange wailing sound, much like a police siren, cut through the dense trees.

Try as she might, Charity couldn't move.

"This is a memory," Ivy said. "All you need to do is be open and you will learn everything I have to teach you."

The thunder rumbled again as one of the dark shapes dashed from the treeline, and Charity felt her lips speak of their own accord.

"Here comes the rain."

Mallory had prepared an absolute feast; spaghetti with meatballs in a rich tomato sauce, Spanish tortilla, a deeply savoury cottage pie, and several other delightful side dishes. Charity's eyes widened at the table positively creaking with food as the young man beamed at her.

"I thought I'd make a bunch of dishes, and that means you can have a bit of everything."

"Marsh, you're a fucking marvel," Charity said, grinning at him. She placed the swords on the table and pulled her Taylor & Bullock Giantslayer from the holster underneath her left arm. "Would you be able to dish me up some of this whilst I load my Jack, please?

Shy neglected to bring any speed-loaders, so I have to do this the old fashioned way."

"Of course," Mallory said as she took a seat and broke open the under-over revolver.

"You could've asked for them specifically," Shy said, folding into the room and grabbing a forkful of cottage pie in one fluid motion. "Silas wasn't exactly keen to teach me gunplay, you know."

"That's because he prefers to butcher innocent people with his autopsy knives," Teaser said sharply. Her hand was wrapped in compression bandages and covered in a crude attempt at plaster. She held it up to show Charity. "Helen did the best with what we have, but I should probably go to a proper hospital tomorrow."

"That sounds like a plan," Charity said as she slotted the fourth round into the weapon. She reached for a fifth bullet, but something made the hair on the nape of her neck stand on end. She snapped the Jack shut and stuffed it into the holster. She snatched up the swords as she got to her feet, and the first distant howl reached her ears.

"What's wrong?" Ivy asked.

"Dinner will have to wait," Charity said, looking through the kitchen window. "The Grim is coming; everyone get ready!"

"Marsh, Tea, Shy, Henbane; get to the church now! One of you needs to text Jess and tell her to get started..." Ivy's voice faded as she looked through the window, clearly seeing what Charity saw.

The huge, slavering dog had already passed through the protection stave and was stalking up the driveway towards Walpole Manor. *We're not even gonna make it to the bike,* Charity thought. *How the fuck was this plan ever supposed to work?*

There was a clatter as the other four Ministry Agents dashed out of the kitchen, leaving her and Ivy alone to watch the Ghost's doom trot menacingly towards them.

The Black Shuck growled as it approached the house, and Charity's blood ran cold. Suddenly, she realised that this would be the night that it would take her; this was the night of her death.

"Holy shit," she murmured, "this is it. There's nothing we can do."

Her heart was hammering in her chest when she heard the click of unfolding glasses behind her, but she did not turn to look, so transfixed was she by her impending doom. When the faint blue-white glow of spectral fire flared into existence beside her, however, she couldn't help but take a peek.

"You're not dying tonight," said Ivy, but her voice was different; deeper and more clipped than usual. Ghostly flames danced around her hands and behind the lenses of the round dark glasses that she wore. "That's a promise."

It took Charity a few seconds to realise who she was looking at, but when she recognised him, she couldn't help but cry out his name in relief.

"Edgar!"

Chapter Thirty Five – Running the Gauntlet

Edgar

"Stay inside the house," Edgar said firmly as he walked towards the front door. "Once I've got the attention of the Grave Hound, break cover and get to the shed. When you're ready, rev the engine and I'll try and deal with the beast."

"Can you sense Garland?" Charity asked nervously, and he shook his head.

"He's adept at hiding from ghostly observers, but Max and Ivy are working on it." He stopped and glanced over his shoulder at her. "I'm sorry it's been so long since we've spoken, Charity; I was grieving."

"I understand."

"I'm sorry about your father," he said, looking at the spirit of Dennis Walpole as he stood behind the Ghost. "Know that he is with us tonight, and let that give you strength."

Charity nodded tearfully as Edgar turned away and strode down the corridor, crossing the entrance hall and shutting the door firmly behind him. He walked out into the cold darkness, his breath fogging in the air before him.

The Black Shuck barely noticed his presence; it was far too focussed on Charity Walpole and her spiritual entanglement with Garland. Edgar stared at it for a moment, taking his time to drink in the appearance of the Grave Hound.

It was a colossal beast, clearly bred for fighting, but

the spirit world had exaggerated its features to almost grotesque proportions. The ectoplasm that foamed around its oversized jaws glistened in a pearlescent manner than made him think uncomfortably of freshly spilt semen.

Its fur was matted with clods of earth and patched with slicks of dried blood that shone like maroon oil. The eyes glowed red, burning like hot coals, but the light was cold, like the warning signal on a train track that, if ignored, would lead to a fatal crash.

Everything about the creature was optimised to inspire dread, fear, and disgust, but none of these emotions even touched Edgar; he had long since learned to close his heart to the worst that the world had to offer, and Kiki's death had hardened the fabric of his soul into impenetrable armour.

"You've been a bad dog," he said firmly, his words resonating with spectral power. The Grave Hound's stride faltered, and it looked at him askance, clearly shocked that a mortal being dared to address it. "You might be a monster, but you're still just an animal, and I am a human.

"You will bend to my will, dog."

Edgar smiled quietly as the Grim turned to face him, snarling and padding back and forth as it tried to break his nerve. Instead of running, however, he crouched down and traced his fingers through the wet grass, never once looking away from the beast before him.

It howled and he felt the waves of terror emanating from it, but they broke on his indifference like the ocean on a granite headland. The Black Shuck might be the Grave Hound of Tharston, but he was Edgar Wainwright, Keeper of the Dead, and he knew it.

"Well, dog," he said as he straightened up, smiling

even wider as he saw the rotted remains of a collar around the monster's neck, "we can do this the easy way, or we can do this the hard way. Regardless, you will not be harming anyone I care about tonight.

"So, which is it going to be?"

He saw Charity slip from the house and dash into the shed that contained the motorcycle they would use to escape to the churchyard. Off in the distance, at the edge of the protection stave, he was dimly aware of Garland and his ghostly steed as they waited for Charity to leave the safety of the Manor.

At least it kept one of them out.

The dog growled and snapped at him as he looked away, so he rounded on the monster and roared out a single command, waves of spectral flame flooding across the lawn as he did so.

"SIT!"

The Grave Hound whimpered for a moment, taking a terrified step backwards before settling back on its trembling haunches; it had clearly never encountered such a creature before, let alone a Séance who spent his time striding along the boundary between life and death.

Edgar smiled as he walked towards the beast, and he ran a hand over its filthy coat and rotten collar. The bluish ghostly fire blazed over the surface of the Black Shuck, turning its fur a brilliant white and restoring the Hound to its former glory; gone was the matted filth, replaced by a coat that blazed like the sun and swayed like sea grass in the spring tide.

"Armand," Edgar said, reading from the renewed collar. Speaking the Grave Hound's name aloud solidified their bond, and the Séance realised that he would always be able to call on the dog in times of peril. He smiled, scratching the immense beast behind the ears. "Good boy, Armand."

Time seemed to fade away as man and dog slowly circled each other, lost in their dance of endless undeath and ghostly understanding. Edgar did not realise it, but minutes flowed into hours, and soon the night sky began to lighten in the east, signalling that the end was near.

The motorcycle revved in the shed and Edgar snapped back to reality; he knew the time had come. He straightened up and turned his gaze inward for a moment.

"Are you ready?" he asked Ivy and Max, who nodded.

Charity burst from the shed, tearing towards him on the motorcycle, the swords tucked between the bike and sidecar. She yelled for him to get in, just as he handed over control of their shared body to Ivy and projected his spirit into Armand.

Walk with me.

Edgar, now in the form of the pale Grave Hound, ran alongside the motorbike as it tore down the driveway towards the main gates of the Walpole Estate. He felt, rather than saw, a form lingering out on the road and he shared this information with Ivy.

Charity eased up on the throttle as Edgar charged ahead, phasing through the solid wrought iron of the gates without issue. His spectral sight did not allow him to see Garland, for the Ghost was still too powerful for that, but he could see the undead horse that stood beneath him.

He lunged at the grey-black stallion, snarling and slavering as he did so, snapping angrily at the horse's throat. Gunpowder whinnied and reared, almost throwing his rider, just as Charity and Ivy slammed through the gates on the motorcycle, tearing down the lane towards the church.

Garland got the beast under control and gave chase, galloping hard after the two women. The horse was possessed with the Ghost's will, giving it the devil's speed, and Edgar was hard-pressed to keep up. Both hooves and paws pounded the asphalt, running at a near impossible pace, as they gained on the the bike as it screeched around a corner.

"Edgar, slow him down!" Ivy cried out, her voice echoing in their shared mind.

Time to be a very bad dog, Edgar thought with a canine smile, and he snared one of the horse's front legs in his mouth, ripping at the undead flesh as he poured every drop of the Hound's terror into the beast of burden. Even though Gunpowder could feel no pain, the Doom set in and he reared once again, forcing Garland to yell in frustration as he fought to get his steed under control.

He flickered for a moment, then his invisibility faded with a glimmer like dawn light on early morning fog. Edgar grinned and leapt at the man, trying to take his left leg from the stirrup. Garland responded by slashing at the Hound with Goldthorn, but Edgar was expecting such an attack and ducked underneath the horse, ripping into its belly with his long, ghostly teeth.

The force of his attack sent Gunpowder into a frenzy and Garland was finally thrown from the saddle as the undead horse bolted, continuing down the road towards the two women. Edgar snapped and snarled at Garland as he rolled around on the ground, trying to get to his feet, harrying him until Edgar was positioned to chase him towards the church.

Kill the horse, he thought, just as Gunpowder seemed to regain his senses and headed towards Garland once again. The Ghost sprinted away from the Hound and leapt nimbly into the saddle, charging after the motorcycle once again.

He slowed to a canter after a few seconds, however, as he realised that he had lost sight of them. Edgar hugged the ground as he crept up behind both horse and rider, dimming his ghostly light to aid his stealthy approach.

Just give the word, he thought, *and I'll send them running towards you.*

Garland frowned and pulled back on the horse's reins as he realised how close they were to the church; the tower was a black shadow against the lightening sky. Still, the need to consume a life pushed him on, and Edgar could smell the faint tang of incense and holy oil on the air.

Garland and Edgar both felt the consecration of the horseman's remains at the same moment. The Ghost cried out in fear and terror, just as a rush of wild, trembling exultation spread through Edgar's mind.

The birds were singing in the bare trees and the last of the stars were fading in the sky; they had held out until the twilight, destroyed the remains, and now the pressure was on Garland to either flee or fight.

Both would be his end, but if he decided to stand and fight he at least had a whisker of a chance to perpetuate his undead existence; all rested on slaying Charity Walpole, however. Ed saw the fear cross Garland's face, but there was confidence there too.

He knows he can beat her, he realised, *and if he*

does, we'll have set him free.
This is it.

The shared mind that bound him and Ivy together stirred slightly, and he knew that the time had come for their final strike; dawn was less than fifteen minutes away. Garland held Goldthorn aloft as Edgar let out an unearthly terrifying howl, driving Gunpowder over the edge of reason and headlong into insanity.

The beast bolted up the road, mad with fear, and Charity Walpole stepped out of the shadows, swords in hand. Garland took an unsteady swing at her, but she easily ducked the clumsy blow, striking as she did so.

She cut Gunpowder out from under him, catapulting the rider into the road. He quickly recovered, however, even as his horse collapsed into ash behind him. He snarled and swung the cursed blade at Charity, but she batted it away with the katana and slashed at him with Ivy'a wakizashi.

Garland stepped backwards, but Edgar howled again as he approached, driving the horseless horseman back into Charity's onslaught. He brought his sword down hard, and the Ghost caught it with both of hers, locking the Walpoles together for a moment. The Kitsune swords began thrum, however, and promptly shattered under the force of the Windstahl blade.

The force of the blast was enough to knock both Ghosts off balance, but Charity recovered quickly, dropping the sword hilts and turning her momentum into a vicious roundhouse kick that sent Garland staggering backwards. She turned on her heel, drawing her Jack and firing it as she did so; a double tap to the chest, followed by a swift shot through the space between Garland's nose and upper lip. He stumbled, completely unbalanced and stunned by the perfectly executed Mozambique Drill, which gave Charity a chance to sprint for the churchyard gate.

Garland drew his own pistol, a single shot flintlock, and fired at her. She fired her last shot at the same time, moving entirely on instinct; there was a small shower of sparks as bullet met ball, knocking Garland's shot clean out of the air. Charity tossed away the pistol and drew her knives as she crashed through the church gate.

Garland glanced anxiously at the sky; night was fading fast. Still, the need for a sustaining life drew him after Charity, and he followed her into the churchyard.

Two shapes emerged from the shadows of the lane; Ivy and Max had been waiting for Garland to enter the hallowed ground before they came out of hiding. Max nodded at Edgar who formed up beside them, ready to charge into the fray when they were needed.

The birds continued to sing the dawn chorus, and the end drew nearer with every note.

"Everyone ready?" Ivy asked softly, and both Max and Edgar nodded. "Good. Let's finish this fucker, once and for all!"

Chapter Thirty Six – The Night People

Charity

"Come on, Garland," Charity growled as she twirled a blade in each hand. "Come and take the life that you desperately want; the only life that can keep you alive!"

All I have to do is keep him in the churchyard until daybreak, Charity thought as the undead Ghost strode through the little wooden gate. *Remember, every blow strips the stolen mortality from him.*

"You killed Gunpowder," he yelled, his fingers white-knuckled around the hilt of his sword. "He has been with me for centuries, and you killed him, you worthless fucking cunt!"

"That," she said, pointing at the bracelet with a bone-handled knife, "does not belong to you."

"Then come and get it, bitch!" he goaded, dropping into a guarded stance, entirely too close to the gate for Charity's liking. The two stared at each other for a moment, waiting for the other to make a move, but Garland's need was greater and he rushed towards Charity, bringing the lethal sword around faster than she thought possible.

She dropped to the ground as the blade whisked through the air where her head had been mere moments ago. *He's so fucking quick,* she realised as she narrowly rolled away from a downward stab that would've skewered her to the ground. *He's too fast for me.*

I don't think I can do this alone.

Charity got to her feet just as Garland thrust towards

her. She parried the attack with her off-hand blade, which broke as she barely deflected a killing blow.

"There's no escape from your fate!" Garland roared, moving to strike again.

Instead of hitting her, however, he was knocked off balance as Cat crashed into him, appearing seemingly out of nowhere. Cait leapt out of the pre-dawn gloom and whipped a glinting wire through the air, which wrapped around Garland's neck. Cat pulled out a vicious looking blade and drove it into Garland's back, again and again.

The twins pulled him to the ground, garotting and stabbing the undead highwayman as they went. Before Charity could wrestle the Windstahl blade away from him, however, he flashed the weapon through the air, severing the wire that held him down.

Charity saw his eyes glance towards the eastern horizon and widen in horror as he realised their plan. He pushed the twins aside and rushed towards the church gate, aiming to fight another day. As he neared it, however, a blinding flash sent him staggering to one side.

Teaser Malarkey dropped the specially formulated camera flash, and Henbane handed her another in case she was needed once again. Garland howled in agony and tried to bring the sword to bear on both woman and pixie, but his arm was suddenly ensnared in a twist of vicious bracken as Mallory wove a Dryad spell around him.

Garland screamed and strained against the vegetation, abandoning the wicked sword in order to escape. The air before him trembled in a kaleidoscopic whirl as he took a single step forwards, and Shy Turner unfolded and drove the bayonet of an antique rifle into Garland's chest, forcing him back.

There was a deafening volley of shots as Jess, Helen, Geoff, and Connie opened fire with their guns, ripping through Garland's stolen flesh. Blow after blow landed on him, and soon he was reduced to a skinless monstrosity.

This... this is actually working!

There was a blood-curdling howl as the Black Shuck, now a brilliant white and blazing with Edgar's ethereal fire, tore into the churchyard and dragged Garland to the ground, savaging him as he did so. Ivy and Max, indistinguishable in the eerie twilight, were not far behind. Ivy had snatched up the handles of her shattered blades, and slashed Garland with the jagged remnants.

Max deftly kicked the Windstahl sword out of Garland's reach as his now-skeletal hand groped for it, following the move up with a sharp, bone-snapping stomp that shattered Garland's sword arm.

Charity leant down, driving her dagger into Garland's heart as she ripped the bracelet off his remaining wrist. He cried out, but still fought against the Shuck that held him tight. Charity snatched up the sword and prepared to deliver a killing blow.

"Don't," said a voice to her side, as a pale man took the weapon from her stunned hand. "If you hit him with that, you'll die."

"Dad?" Charity murmured, and Dennis nodded, his spectral form tightening his grip on the ancient weapon.

"It's me, darling, and I need to finish what I started. You can't kill a ghost like him," he said as he drove the blade through Garland, all the way up to the golden hilt, "but I can."

Garland's skeletal face turned towards the eastern sky as he let out a final, ear-splitting scream. Dennis stared triumphantly at the monster as the first ray of sunlight touched its bleached, bony form, and it crumbled into dust.

The spectral fire around the Black Shuck faded, and it let out a final, mournful howl before vanishing into the morning light. Charity blinked in shock and disbelief as she stared, open-mouthed and stunned, at her father.

The rest of the Night People looked on, equally dumbfounded by the man's sudden appearance; all, that is, except Ivy, who simply had a knowing look on her face. Dennis caught her eye, and she nodded gratefully at him.

"You did it," Charity said breathlessly, finally finding her words as the sun continued to creep over the horizon. "You got the bastard that killed you!"

Dennis Walpole smiled at her sadly and shook his head.

"But you did!" Charity said, almost hysterical now. "Garland murdered you!"

"It was just an accident, sweetheart," Dennis said softly as he took her into his arms. "Sometimes people just die, Charity, and there's no reason for it."

"Everything you left for me," Charity murmured, thinking of the papers in her father's study, "it was all just dumb luck?"

"Luck's got nothing to do with it," Dennis said, beaming at her. "My daughter was on the case, and there's nothing she can't do; I'm so proud of you, Charity."

"I'm proud to be your daughter," Charity said softly, and she felt Dennis's form begin to fade in her arms.

"Do you have to go?"

"My purpose here is done, so I have to move on," Dennis said.

"To solve the case?" Charity asked tearfully.

"To keep you safe." Dennis's form was beginning to disappear in the morning light now, and he removed his glasses to look at Charity with his pale eyes one last time. "I love you, Charity, and I was so lucky to have you as a daughter."

"I love you too, Dad." Charity's lip trembled as Dennis slowly vanished into the daylight. She managed to croak out her final question in the nick of time. "Daddy, I don't want to kill any more, but I'm not sure what else I'm good for; what should I do?"

"Do what you've always been best at, love," he said quietly, his words only for her ears. "Keep saving people."

And then, with a gentle stirring of the morning breeze through the churchyard, he was gone.

The birds were still singing when the ragtag group staggered, exhausted and battle-weary, into the kitchen of Walpole Manor. Charity slumped into a chair at the head of the table, dropping Goldthorn on the wooden surface with a loud clatter.

"Welcome to the rest of your life, Charity," Geoff said with a smile as he leant against the counter. "You faced down death itself and defeated it; not many can claim that accolade."

"I had help," Charity said with a smile. She grimaced as her stomach growled hungrily. "I mean it, folks; if it hadn't been for you, he would've killed me."

"He almost made it," Connie said with a stunned smile. "That was the closest call I've ever fucking seen."

"We've had closer," Mallory said through a mouthful of cold cottage pie. "Does anyone want anything to eat?"

"Fuck yes," Charity said. "I am so hungry that I could eat a horse."

She paused for a moment as Ivy snickered.

"Not *that* horse, though," she clarified. "One of those young, plump Icelandic ones, though... oh, fuck, that would be the best thing ever."

"What was your closer call?" Cat asked as Mallory placed the entire cottage pie in front of Charity, who proceeded to dig in with her bare, filthy hands.

"Mal got turned into a vampire at one point," Charity said, her mouth full of savoury meat and potato. "And then there were these witches who nearly got Jess to hang herself-"

"And made you stab Ivy," Jess said, cutting in. "That one's still a bit too fresh to joke about."

Ivy looked at Helen, raising an eyebrow.

"Were you there for the Night of the Rat?" she asked, and Helen shook her head.

"No; I arrived the morning after. I'm sure Max can tell you all about it, though; Silas was right in the thick of it, as was Shy."

"Who's Max?" Teaser asked, wincing slightly as Shy returned her gift to her. Charity paused her eating as she debated how to answer, giving an opportunity for Henbane to snatch the pie away from her. "You know what, I don't need to know right now; let's leave it for another time."

"I'll have a chat to you about it soon." Ivy placed a hand on Teaser's shoulder and gave her an affectionate squeeze. "You'll have your answers, that much I can promise you."

"Isn't it nice when we all eat as a family?" Mallory said, slurping up cold spaghetti directly from the pan.

"I'm not particularly hungry," Shy said, "but I will put the kettle on."

There were cries of delight and gratitude as the young Cep set about making close to a dozen cups of tea. Charity looked at the sword on the table, before reaching into her pocket and pulling out the blue lizard bracelet.

"This cracked the whole fucking case," she said, looking at it sadly. She handed it to Helen. "Make sure Mrs Wesser gets that, will you? She deserves to have something to remember Amy by."

"I will do." Helen sighed. "When we're done here, I'll give Annie a call; hopefully she can send all the bodies back to where they belong in a way that squares the books and doesn't draw too much attention.

"These people deserve a proper send-off, and their loved ones definitely will appreciate the closure."

"That they will," Charity said, staring at the sword. *He saved me. Even after all the differences we had, he still fucking saved me.*

Why?

"Because he was your dad," Geoff said. Charity stared at him, surprised. "I don't need to be a mind reader to know what's going through your head, darling. I know it hurts now, but you'll start to feel better soon.

"You did right by him, and that's all a parent can really hope for."

"Are you going to stay for a few days?" Constance asked Charity, and she shook her head.

"I need to get back to Oxford," she replied. "I want to walk the streets, watch the river, and drink in the history; even now it feels like I've been away too long. What are you going to do with the sword?"

"We could destroy it," Cait said, but Helen shook her head.

"It's Windstahl," she said, smiling gratefully as she accepted a cup of tea from Shy, "so it won't break easily. Besides, that thing is a relic; it could be thousands of years old. I'd offer to take it on behalf of the Ministry, but I dread to think what hands it will wind up in."

"Bury it with Dad," Charity said quietly. "Then we'll know where it is, if we should ever need it."

There were murmurs of assent around the table. Henbane strolled over to Geoff and perched beside him.

"I think I'll stick around here, if nobody minds," they said. "It'll be good to have some familiar company, at least for a while."

"You're welcome here," Connie said, before looking around the kitchen. "You all are."

"Would one of you mind taking me to the hospital to get my hand looked at?" Teaser asked, and Geoff offered to take her once he'd had some sleep.

"I'll go with you, Tea," Mallory said. "Who knows what trouble we'll get into on the way?"

Teaser groaned as Mallory laughed.

"I can take you back to London, Jess," Helen offered.

"Much appreciated. I'm not particularly busy, if you want to get some sleep first."

"Oh, I certainly will," Helen said. She looked at Charity and Ivy. "I assume the two of you will be travelling with Shy."

Charity nodded, hoping that the young man wouldn't need to linger too long before they got underway. He seemed to read her expression and informed her that they could get going as soon as the two women were ready.

In less than an hour they were all packed up, and the tearful goodbyes and empty promises of visits were exchanged at the threshold of Walpole Manor. Charity helped Ivy to the gaudily painted vehicle; the effort of the night's conflict was taking a serious toll on her. Once the Séance was safely seated, the Ghost went around to the passenger side door.

"I always hated this part of the world," Charity said as she climbed into Shy's van. A small smile crept on to her face as he started the engine, and then they were underway. "Finally, we can leave all this madness behind us.

"Let's go home."

Epilogue – We Only See Each Other at Funerals

"So that's it?" Teaser asked, frowning at Ivy.

"That's it," she confirmed. "At least, that's all Max knows, I'm afraid. I know you've no love for Silas Cherry, but Max insists that he didn't kill your partners, and I'm inclined to believe her."

"Well, let's just say that I'm unconvinced," Teaser replied. "But, as a favour to you, I won't kill him on sight."

"Much appreciated," Ivy said, just as there was a knock on her door. "Do you mind if I-"

"Go ahead," Teaser said, and promptly folded to somewhere else in the Folly. Ivy chuckled and called out for her mystery caller to come in.

"Hey, Liv," Charity said, brandishing an envelope. "You've got a letter from Gaunt & Barlow; it looks like they're a legal firm."

"At last!" Ivy said. She took the letter and opened it, a grin crossing her face as she found a cheque inside. "It's the insurance payout for my house!"

"The one *we* destroyed?" Charity asked, her tone clearly implying that Ivy had, at the very least, bent the truth a little to get her claim paid.

"The one that exploded in a *tragic accident*," Ivy corrected playfully.

"How much is it for?" Charity asked, trying to get a peek, but Ivy kept it from her.

"Enough to buy a new house on the outskirts of the city," Ivy said with a smile, "with a garage for a couple of motorbikes, if you wanted to come with me."

"Leave the Folly?" Charity asked. "Are you sure?"

"Charity, darling, I'm tired of living at work. Whilst I love the communal atmosphere, you keep saying that we need to get some new recruits into the Oxford Office; we could turn my floor into a series of rooms for our new Rooks."

"I... I'm not sure about this," Charity said nervously. "I've never lived in a place like that before, Ivy. It would be a bit of an adjustment."

"You wouldn't be alone," Ivy said with a smile. "Far from it, in fact! Still, you don't have to decide now; we've all the time in the world."

"Do you really mean it?" Charity asked, a glimmer of hope on her face.

"I do. I want to make a home with you, Charity Walpole; one that is ours, not one that belongs to the Ministry." Ivy ran her fingers down Charity's face. "I want us to have a life together."

There was a heartbeat of silence before Charity broke out in a wide grin.

"Fuck it, let's do it!" she said excitedly. "I do have one request, though."

"Go for it," Ivy said, running her hands through Charity's hair.

"Could I maybe have space for *three* motorbikes, instead of two?"

Ivy couldn't help but burst out laughing as she pulled her partner into a fierce hug.

This is going to be fantastic, she thought. *Finally, my life is coming back together.*

Charity walked the streets of North Oxford, giddy with joy; she would be moving in with Ivy Livingston, and she would finally have a real home! She had a spring in her step and a grin on her face as she strolled aimlessly through the leafy avenues and quiet side streets.

She was so happy, in fact, that she did not hear the footsteps racing up behind her. In fact, when she was slammed into the side of a house by an unseen assailant, she was taken entirely by surprise. Her sunglasses clattered to the ground and she screwed her eyes shut against the glare of the street lights.

"Give me your fucking purse!" yelled the man who held her, and he spun her around to face him. "Give me your phone and your fucking money, or I'll kill you."

Charity had come out unarmed, and was still too stunned to strike back against the stranger. Instead she acted entirely on instinct, opening her eyes wide to stare at her assailant. She could barely make him out, but as her eyes drank in the light her irises began to glow brighter than before.

"What the fuck?" the man said, releasing her and taking a step backwards as her eyes suddenly flared, releasing their stored power. The man gasped in pain and tried to cover his own eyes, but his hands would never reach them.

His skin turned grey and pockmarked as the power coursed through him, and a crunchy crackling sound filled the air as his flesh calcified and turned to stone. His look of abject horror was forever locked in place on his petrified face, even as his frozen hands tried in vain to protect his vulnerable eyes.

I did that!? Charity thought as she scrabbled to pick up her glasses from the floor. In all her time with the Ministry, she had never heard of anyone or anything that could turn people to stone, but now that power lurked within her.

Her hands trembled as she walked away, slipping into invisibility reflexively as she fled the scene of the crime. *I didn't mean to kill him,* she thought wildly as she broke into a run, sprinting in the direction of the Folly. *I didn't even know I could.*

I have to tell Maxine about this, she thought frantically. *She'll know what to do.*

Helen sat on a bench in the garden of her little Richmond home, listening to the birds singing softly in the trees above. The plants were beginning to wake up after their long winter hibernation, and it always brought her tremendous joy first thing in the morning.

I wonder what today will bring, she mused as she sipped her cup of tea.

"I thought I'd find you out here," said a familiar voice. She looked down as a black cat settled next to her on the bench. "You know, I've been waiting for a few days to speak to you, but you're clearly a very busy person."

"Are you spying on me?" Helen asked with a smile.

"No," Silas replied as an inky black crow cawed conspicuously in the tree at the end of the garden.

"I went to spend a couple of days with Constance and Geoff," she said. "I'm getting old, Silas, and I want to enjoy whatever time with my friends that I have left. Heaven knows, I've wasted enough of it."

"And?" Silas said, peering at her with his yellow feline eyes.

Helen sighed. *He has a point.*

"I'm sorry for calling you a murderer." She frowned slightly. "I spoke out of anger and frustration, although not at you. I know that you didn't hurt anyone, and I really am sorry."

"Apology accepted," Silas said matter-of-factly. "Max did a lot of legwork to get me to this point, you know."

"Have you met your sister yet?" The little cat shook his head. "Are you going to?"

"Perhaps," he replied enigmatically. "We've both got a lot on, and I'm trying to steer clear of Ministry business for a while."

"In your own time," Helen said. The two sat in silence for a while, but soon Silas's tail began to flick as he eyed the sparrows on the bird feeder hungrily.

"Speaking of not being a murderer," Silas began, leaning forwards, but Helen clapped her hands, sending the sparrows flying into the air. "Hey!"

"If you eat any of my birds, I'll put you in a bag and throw you in the Thames," she said with a grin.

"That's better," Silas said with a smile. "I was worried we were getting too deep into the whole mother-son thing. So, tell me about your supernatural outbreak."

"How about I come down to the Cupid Office and tell you there?"

"Do you have time for that?" Silas asked.

"No," Helen replied, "which makes it all the more important that I take the time to do it."

Edgar paced around the cosy living room, hesitant about setting to work on his task. He had decided to clear the remainder of Michaela's clutter and leftover belongings from their shared mind to make room for Max, but it was easier said than done.

He'd already managed a few of the communal

rooms, but now he stood in the living room of their first home; Michaela's favourite place. Above the sideboard hung a stern self-portrait of the late Michaela Inglewood, which was as good a place to start as any.

"Maybe this will be easier without you staring at me the entire time," Ed said as he reached out to remove the painting from the wall. His fingers had barely touched the wood when someone in the room spoke.

"Leave that up," the voice whispered behind him, almost too softly to be heard. Still, Edgar whirled around, peering over his round sunglasses as his eyes searched the room. He could see nothing, however, and was about to resume his task when he spied his mug of hot chocolate on the little table.

It was still there, steaming and full, but another cup, covered in a hideous floral pattern, stood next to it. Even from across the room, he could see the dregs of recently consumed hot chocolate sitting in the bottom of the cup. A smile crept on to his lips, and he decided to leave the picture in place.

"It's good to have you back, Kiki," he whispered.

Life at the Folly returned to its usual pace of training and casual investigations as the year rolled by, bringing birthdays and parties and the gentle rains of spring. Mallory seemed to come alive with the blossom on the trees, and Teaser's photography turned from spirits to the sun as the Solar Maximum approached its incredible apex.

The Night People gathered in the darkness just outside the small village of Tackley as the Aurora Borealis coloured the sky with pinks, greens, and reds, drawing whoops and cheers from all present. Teaser photographed the impossibly beautiful display all night as Mallory tried to capture the celestial spectacle in oils, but he eventually gave up and spent his time simply staring at the wondrous sight above him.

Shy had travelled to visit his sister for the event, but Ivy and Charity strolled out into a field to lie in the grass and stare at the sky. Charity removed her glasses, affording her an unparalleled view, whilst Ivy was careful not to look directly at her lover, lest she fall victim to her newly petrifying gaze.

The things we do for love, Ivy thought.

Summer soon came, albeit with no word from Thaddeus. Mallory had long given up hope of seeing him again, and had taken the time to memorialise him in the garret of the Folly, even as the seven story tower was occupied by a number of new recruits.

Little did he know that events hundreds of miles away would set the ball rolling for him to be reunited with his lover once again, albeit under strange and stressful circumstances.

The sea lapped lazily at the beaches of the south Devon coast, almost as if it, too, had grown sluggish in the early summer heat. The cloudless sky, full of twinkling stars, promised no relief in the form of shade or rain, but the seaside town of Torquay was bustling with people enjoying the warmth of the short summer night.

One person, however, stalked alone on the promenade, several bottles deep as they tried to drown their sorrows. The other walkers gave her a wide berth as she staggered unpredictably towards the edge of the sea wall.

"I can't believe it," Mindy Darling sobbed, leaning

on the pale blue railing. "I'm only twenty three! I'm supposed to have my whole fucking life ahead of me!"

Mindy had never been a fan of going to the doctors, but after an especially troublesome fortnight of upset stomachs and dashing to the bathroom, she had finally relented. The investigations had taken a little over three months, and the results had been devastating.

The bowel cancer eating at her insides was inoperable, and there was little that chemotherapy or radiation treatment could do to help her; besides, if she was going to die young, Mindy wanted to enjoy every second of it, rather than spend it housebound and hairless.

Still, the inevitability of her death was hitting her hard, so she'd decided to hit the bottle even harder. Young and poor, Mindy could not afford to even rent her own flat, let alone live out her final months in the manner that she wished.

"No," she said bitterly, "I'm doomed to die in this seaside shithole."

"I'm sorry you're having a difficult time, Ms Darling," said a rich voice beside her.

Mindy turned to look, but all she could see was the empty night sky. She frowned a little, then stepped back with a start as a swathe of starry blackness moved, revealing a person beside her, seemingly clad in the twinkling heavens.

"How... What are you?" she said, certain that the cancer had suddenly spread to her brain, denying her even her sanity in the autumn days of her life.

"I'm a friend," the starry stranger said. "I noticed that you're having a tough time, so I thought I'd offer to help you."

"What could you possibly do?" Mindy scoffed.

"In a word, anything," the man said; Mindy was certain of his gender, for no woman she'd ever met had sounded like the stranger before her. "So, Ms Darling, what can I do for you?"

"I..." She hesitated as some part of her felt the seriousness in his voice. Mindy considered asking for a cure for her illness, but she'd made her peace with death; instead she still mourned all the things she would never get to do. "I've never seen a whale in real life, up close. Could... Could you make that happen?"

"I could," the man said, a smile in his voice now, "if you really wanted me to."

"I do!" Mindy said, dropping her bottle to reach out for the man, desperate to show her keenness for his offer.

"Tell me, Ms Darling, what would you give to make this happen?" he asked, but his tone said that he knew what her answer would be.

"Anything!" Mindy cried. "I'd give absolutely anything!"

"That, Ms Darling," he said with a sly chuckle, "is exactly what I wanted to hear."

There was a sudden breeze, and the starry man was gone, leaving Mindy Darling with a deep sense of unease. The warm night seemed suddenly cold, and she wrapped her arms tightly around her chest as a single thought wormed its way into her mind.

I've just made a terrible mistake.

Witness even more strange happenings as they unfold in...

THE ILLUMINATED MAN

Acknowledgments

This series began life (at least in writing) on the train home from my father's funeral. It was a difficult time for me and I have held on to that stress until now, and I am grateful for the medium of fiction for granting me a place to vent the pain and grief I felt on that day. I also wanted to tell a story about a scary dog and an evil dentist, which is certainly a weird way to process my emotions, but it definitely worked!

I actually did some boots on the ground research with Syd for this book, spending two days in and around Norfolk. I would like to especially thank Arthur and Debbie of the Cleasewood Guest House, in Great Yarmouth, the various staff members who made our day enjoyable at Yarmouth Pleasure Beach, and the nice fella who locks up the church in Tharston; you all helped our research trip (and anniversary holiday) to be the best possible experience.
I would like to extend a special mention to the old lady wearing the England Flag themed Punisher t-shirt during the England-Serbia game. I did not speak to you, but please know that you fascinate me and I speak of you often. I would love to hear your story.

There are others to thank, of course, because such a book cannot be written in isolation.

Firstly and most importantly, I would like to thank my partner, Syd, for the love, support, and the tremendous help proofreading/editing of this story. She has listened to me talk about this for months, and has given me both inspiration and encouragement in spades. I love you, darling, and I am so lucky to have you in my life.

Likewise, I would like to thank my metamor, Ben Wright. Thank you for all the support and discussion that has helped this book become the nightmare that it finally grew into.

I would like to thank you both for inviting me into your life and your (now our) home; I feel loved, wanted, and cared for, which I am grateful for beyond measure.

I would also like to thank our guinea pigs, both for their reassuring presence and constant source of amusement. There will continue to be references to you scattered throughout my writing.

A big thank you goes out to my best friend, Dr Georgia Lynott. You are a source of light in my life and always a joy to spend time with. I hope you will enjoy this book, and the series as a whole.

I cannot write a horror novel without thanking my parents, Steve and Samantha Farrell, my grandparents, Frank and Lorraine Keeley, and other members of my family; you have all played a crucial part developing my absolute love of horror. From late night films to tatty paperbacks read in the car on long journeys; it all has culminated in this book, and all those that follow it. Thank you.

I would like to extend my thanks to my childhood friends, James Bullock and Colum Taylor, for all their support and all the horror films we watched together over the years.

Once again, I would like to thank my therapist, Zayna Brookhouse, for her help in turning my fear and grief into something constructive that I could share with you all.

I'd like to thank all the musicians, artists, writers, and cinematographers that have contributed to the horror genre. I write to music, so your help was invaluable in the creation of this work.

A special thank you goes out to Pekka Saukko and Bernard Knight, who have produced a fantastic resource in the form of Knight's Forensic Pathology (Third Edition). This book has drawn a lot from your work, especially Helen's chapters.

Of course, I'm sure that I have missed people off of this list; it is not exhaustive, after all! So, to all the other Parrots out there who helped to make this work a reality, I thank you.

And, last but not least, you, dear reader, for choosing to read this book.

Thank you.

About the Author

Eleanor Fitzgerald is a polyamorous non-binary trans woman living in and around Oxford. Eleanor uses any and all pronouns, and is neurodivergent and disabled. Eleanor is hard of hearing, and completely deaf on one side.

They have a fascination for all things weird and wonderful, and have thoroughly enjoyed writing this work for you. Rest assured, it will not be the last!

Eleanor also paints (physically and digitally), and created the artwork for this book's cover illustration. This was one of their first all-digital covers, and there are many more to come! Their particular style is impressionism, which they love immensely.

If you have any questions or comments, they can be reached at the following email address:

eleanorfitzgeraldwriting@gmail.com

Printed in Great Britain
by Amazon